O'NESS
FALKIRK COUNCIL LIBRARIES
30124 02222959 7
19 JUL 2014
18 NOV 2015
D0493069

YOURS, FAITHFULLY

Also by Sheila O'Flanagan

Suddenly Single
Far From Over
My Favourite Goodbye
He's Got to Go
Isobel's Wedding
Caroline's Sister
Too Good To Be True
Dreaming of a Stranger
Destinations
Anyone But Him
How Will I Know?
Connections

YOURS, FAITHFULLY

Sheila O'Flanagan

First published in 2006 by HEADLINE REVIEW
An imprint of HEADLINE BOOK PUBLISHING

1

Cataloguing in Publication Data is available from the British Library

Hardback 0 7553 0754 2 (ISBN-10)
Hardback 978 0 7553 0754 8 (ISBN-13)
Trade paperback 0 7553 0757 7 (ISBN-10)
Trade paperback 978 0 7553 0757 9 (ISBN-13)

Typeset in Galliard by Palimpsest Book Production Limited,
Polmont, Stirlingshire

Printed and bound in Great Britain by
Clays Ltd, St Ives plc

HEADLINE BOOK PUBLISHING
A division of Hodder Headline
338 Euston Road
London NW1 3BH

www.reviewbooks.co.uk
www.hodderheadline.com

Thanks as always, for their support and encouragement, go to:

Carole Blake, my agent and friend
Marion Donaldson, my (very) patient editor
Team Headline in so many different locations and in many different guises – all of you have been wonderful, I'm lucky to work with you
My family, fantastic in every way
All of my friends in Ireland and overseas, and in particular everyone from Raheny Badminton Club, who never let me forget about other equally important things (like match practice . . .)
Colm, *un gran abrazo*

Extra special thanks on this occasion to Damian Hogan of An Garda Síochána who was so very helpful when it came to researching this book, and to Detective Garda Donna McGowan who gave up so much of her time to talk me through some of the more technical aspects of the story. Obviously any procedural mistakes are very much mine and not theirs!

A very big thank you to all of you who take time to email me and let me know what you think of my books, and to everyone I've met at book signings and on my various travels – it's been a real pleasure to hear from you and to meet you. You can get in touch and see pictures from various events on my website www.sheilaoflanagan.net

Chapter 1

Iona Brannock wasn't pregnant.

She supposed she shouldn't be surprised. It had been rather optimistic to assume that her first serious attempt at conceiving a baby would be an unqualified success. It wasn't as though women could simply get pregnant on demand, after all. But Iona was an optimistic person. And what did surprise her was the sense of bitter disappointment which now engulfed her and how unexpectedly let down she felt by her own body. She'd been so sure of herself. So sure of both of them.

The thing was, she told herself pensively, all of those other times over the past four years when they'd come together beneath the sheets and cried out in mutual passion had been about themselves and the pleasure that they were giving to each other. Now it was different. Making love this last month had been a unique experience because there had been a new purpose to it, and the thrill of their nights together had intensified as a result. Iona hadn't thought it possible that she could love Frank any more passionately than she already did. Or that their sex life could have been any more fulfilling. But she'd been wrong. Trying to make a baby with him was the most intense and passionate experience of her life.

They'd talked about it first, of course. There'd been a long and involved discussion about the whole idea of bringing another life into the world. Frank had been certain that it was the right thing to do. It was Iona who'd had the serious doubts. She simply wasn't certain that she was mature enough to be responsible for another life. The enormity of the task was terrifying, she whispered, as they lay side by side in the big bed together. And then Frank had kissed her and told her that it was precisely because she was scared that she would be a great mother and that he could think of nothing that would bind them together more closely than having a baby. It would make them a real family, he said. And he wanted to be part of a family with her. There was no need for her to be scared. Besides, wasn't she already great at everything she did? Wasn't she fantastic at her job in the house rental agency, dealing with demented tenants and equally demented landlords? Wouldn't a baby be simple in comparison?

She'd smiled then. Anyhow, he added, he'd be with her every step of the way.

'Promise?' She'd been touched by the sincerity of his words.

'Promise,' he replied.

And so they'd made love with the hope of having a baby and it had been the most wonderful of all their nights together. But now, Iona had to admit, wonderful and all though that night and the other baby-making nights that followed might have been, they was still just more nights of great sex because she wasn't pregnant after all. The sudden pain in the small of her back and the crucifying cramping of her stomach confirmed it.

It seemed daft now that she'd consulted her feng shui book and set up a children area in their house, despite Frank's amused scepticism. But as she'd pointed out, there was no harm in harnessing whatever power there might be around the home (hadn't leaving the toilet lid down worked its magic as a way of stopping money leaking out of the house? He'd landed a major contract the day he'd moved in, which proved it really.) and so she'd placed a few photos of her niece, Charlotte, aged six, and nephew, Gavin, aged four, on the plain oak sideboard at the south end of the living room; then she'd added a home-enhancer crystal bowl on the wall shelf nearby. By the time she'd finished upgrading the energy of the home she'd felt certain that getting pregnant would be an enjoyable formality given all the effort she was making.

She debated for a moment or two about whether to phone Frank now and tell him the discouraging news about the baby but she decided against it. It wasn't the sort of conversation she wanted to have with him first thing in the morning and she was pretty sure it wasn't the kind of conversation he wanted at that hour either. But she was glad that he was coming home that night so that they could hold each other tight and reassure each other that maybe the next time they'd be successful.

Iona had never told Frank that it had taken her own mother five years to get pregnant. She didn't tell him of the many despairing visits that Flora Brannock had made to the doctor to find out whether everything was all right and her mother's subsequent slavish adherence to a range of different diets, lifestyle regimes and goodness knows what else to help things along. Because in the end it hadn't mattered – Flora eventually succeeded with Iona's older sister, Lauren; then a couple of years later Iona; and finally Craig. There hadn't been a production problem really just a delay in getting started, as she'd told her daughters when giving them her practical facts-of-life discussion as soon as they'd asked the inevitable 'where did I come from?' question.

Iona twisted the thin gold wedding band on her finger. She wouldn't have the same problems as her mother, she knew she wouldn't. Charlotte and Gavin were Lauren's children and Lauren hadn't experienced any delay in conceiving. So there was no big issue here just because Iona hadn't got pregnant at the first attempt.

But still, she thought, as she broke the seal on a box of Tampax, it would have been nice to have the whole thing sorted. She wasn't good at waiting. She knew that. Flora had always called her the impatient daughter. Lauren was the serene one – nothing ever upset or perturbed her and she seemed to float through life without any stress whatsoever. Iona, on the other hand, was always anxious for things to happen, cut up with frustration when she was told that she was too young or too small or just plain not allowed to do something she desperately wanted. Iona had been the one to make the forbidden climb on to the roof of the garden shed, and the one to rip her leg on the thorns of the rose bush as she'd jumped off it. Iona had been the one, aged six, to try riding a two-wheeled bicycle on her own without any supervision whatsoever, and the one who'd managed to wobble a few yards down the road before crashing into the wall of the Delaneys' house, splitting open her lip, banging her nose and knocking out her two front teeth. As a teenager, she'd been the one who'd stayed out past the accepted coming-home time, sneaking in through the bathroom window for three nights in a row before getting caught because Flora had moved the cactus plant on the windowsill and Iona had sent it clattering on to the tiled floor with her foot. At twenty, she'd been the first to move out of the family home, wanting a place of her own while Lauren was still content to live with their parents.

Craig, the youngest, was simply 'the son'. He was tall and broad with deep soulful eyes which made him look particularly sensitive and meant that the impressionable girls on the estate where they lived fancied him like crazy and hung around outside their house to get a glimpse of him. Iona grinned to herself as she thought of her younger brother, now working as a telephone engineer in China and probably still breaking hearts. Their father had been a new-man sort of bloke long before it became fashionable for men to do the washing-up and show their emotions in public and she had no doubt that David Brannock loved both his daughters dearly and expected great things of them; but when Craig had been born there was a whole thing about 'the son' that hadn't been around for 'the girls'.

Iona didn't care. She knew that her parents loved them all equally. The son-and-heir thing – well, it might be old-fashioned, but a part of her understood it. Even though, as she'd pointed out to her father, she'd kept the family name after her marriage so that everyone still knew her as Iona Brannock. And the agreement with Frank was that their daughters would carry her surname, while their sons would carry his. It would all work out fine, she knew. All she had to do was get round to having the children.

She finished in the bathroom and walked into the tiny bedroom. This was something that would have to change when all the lovemaking finally paid off. Right now, she and Frank lived in a two-up two-down artisan house near the old Iveagh Markets building in the Liberties district of Dublin. It was a great house in a great location because it was so convenient for the city centre and meant that if she didn't need the car during the day to drive to rental showings she could walk to work; but it wasn't very big, especially since one of the bedrooms was used as an office. Frank had his own company, DynaLite. He arranged the installation of complex lighting systems in hotels and nightclubs and customised lighting shows for special occasions. It was extremely successful for a venture that operated from their back bedroom and from a serviced office on the south side of the city, although that was because Frank was totally committed to the company, travelling throughout the country every week to meet his clients and sometimes having to stay away for days on end to get a particular project completed on time.

Iona, whose job at the rental agency allowed her to work from home sometimes, also used the bedroom as an office, though not as much as Frank did. It was there that they stored all of their work-related stuff; there where they kept the computer and printer and fax; and there where one or the other of them retired to when they absolutely didn't want to be disturbed. That didn't happen very often. With Frank spending so much time away from home, they liked to be together as much as possible when he returned.

But using the bedroom as an office meant that they essentially lived in a one-bedroomed house. Iona felt a bit guilty about her assertion that they'd have to move once they started a family, since she knew that years ago enormous families were reared in the two-up two-down houses, but times had changed since the 1930s and 40s. And besides, their house had been bought from some lunatic interior designer who had done a fantastic job on it but who had styled everything with a single male occupant in mind. Iona was perfectly certain that the trendy glass staircase and angular units would be a death-trap for a toddler even though they fitted perfectly with her personal Zen ideas.

She smoothed the skirt of her blue hound's-tooth Zara suit over her hips. Last night, when she'd been two days late and begun to allow the hope of pregnancy to grow in her mind despite herself, she'd thought about maternity clothes and wondered where she'd be able to buy stylish clothes that would take her through the nine months. She knew that there were plenty of maternity boutiques around the city because she remembered Lauren enthusing about them when she'd been expecting Gavin. But she couldn't remember the name of a single one. She'd stood in front of the mirror with a pillow stuffed beneath her pale pink T-shirt and contemplated her potential change in figure. It would be radical, she thought, because she was (as her father so often pointed out) a mere slip of a girl – exactly five feet and one inch tall (that inch was very important to her), with short ink-black hair which she sometimes wore in gelled spikes but more often allowed to settle into a gamine crop framing her heart-shaped face. Her eyes were blackberry-blue and her lips, even without lipstick, a pouting rosebud red. Her nose was small and neat, though a tiny bump (a legacy of the crash into the Delaneys' wall) robbed it of any cuteness it might otherwise have had. Iona's looks were exotic rather than beautiful, but then she'd never much cared for beautiful over interesting. Anyway, there was no point in her caring, since Lauren was the one who'd been handed the beauty genes, with her clear, smooth skin, violet eyes and burnished copper hair which fell in soft waves around her perfectly proportioned face. Lauren's nose was perfect too. Iona knew that her sister had obviously been handed the leftover height genes as well, because Lauren was a willowy five-six with an enviable figure which had looked fantastic even when she was pregnant. Iona rather thought that she herself would just look dumpy when it finally happened for her.

It doesn't matter, she told herself now as she shoved her mobile into her bag, checked her appearance in the mirror once more and picked up her house keys. Nothing has changed yet. Everything is still exactly the same.

The rental agency had its offices in Dame Street, close to the imposing (though, thought Iona, incredibly ugly) Central Bank building with its smooth piazza, fountain and bronze sculpture facing on to the street. The office was also near Trinity College, a building which Iona much preferred and where she often went during sunny lunchtimes to eat a sandwich on the grassy lawns. Today, despite the promise of clear blue skies and a warm breeze from the south, there would be no lunching on the lawns of Trinity or anywhere else. Her agenda was full – administration in the office in the morning and then back home to collect her lime-green Volkswagen Beetle so that she could drive to the six different apartments she was showing that afternoon and evening.

Her stomach was cramping again as she sat at her white wood desk and logged on to her computer. She hated this time of the month. She hated the bloated feeling that always engulfed her, the nagging pain in the small of her back and those damn cramps which racked her for the first day or two. She opened her desk drawer and took out a couple of gel capsules. When you're in labour, she reminded herself as she swallowed them down, the pain will be worse. Much, much worse! She shivered a little. She was definitely ready to be pregnant now, but she was scared of the physical aspect as well as everything else. Although she was absolutely and utterly determined to do everything as naturally as possible, she worried that the intensity of the pain might stop her. It was extraordinary, she mused, that with all the evolutionary things that had gone on over the past few millennia, humans hadn't yet come up with a better way of having babies. Hens had it cushy, she thought. An egg was a much better shape for the birth process – no inconvenient arms and legs which might present themselves at the wrong moment.

'Morning, Iona!' Ruth Dawson, who looked after rentals on the north side of the city, greeted her. 'How's it going?' She saw the packet of evening primrose oil and starflower capsules on Iona's desk and grimaced sympathetically.

'I'll be fine,' said Iona, 'though I wish I hadn't agreed to so many viewings this afternoon.'

'Take some Feminax,' suggested Ruth. 'I have—'

'Thanks but no thanks.' Iona smiled at her. 'These work fine for me.' She winced.

The other girl opened a desk drawer and took out an assortment of aspirin, paracetemol and ibuprofen which she spread out on the desk in front of her.

'Sure?'

Iona looked at the display and shook her head again. 'You should have shares in Glaxo,' she said disparagingly. 'I'll give you the name of my yoga guru; much, much better for you than all that.'

Ruth snorted and then picked up her ringing telephone.

'Rental Remedies,' she said. 'Ruth speaking. How can I help you?'

It was after ten before Iona finally rang Frank. He'd been meeting clients in the south-west of the country all week but he was due back in Dublin later that evening. Iona wanted to check on his timetable. She knew, because they had an on-line calendar which each of them updated every evening, that he'd had a meeting at nine this morning but she reckoned he should be finished by now. Frank never needed much time to make a sale. He was born to it, homing in immediately on the issue that most affected his potential customer and managing to make that customer feel as though he personally cared very deeply about any problem they might have. As he truly did, he told Iona. After all, his customers were the ones who paid the bills! And besides, most of them were very nice people. Iona usually chuckled at that – Frank always saw the good in everyone. He insisted in giving them all the benefit of the doubt. It was one of the things she loved about him.

He answered her call almost immediately and she smiled involuntarily at the sound of his voice. Frank had a very, very sexy voice. It was Pierce Brosnan, Richard Burton and Sean Connery all rolled into one. As, indeed, was Frank himself. Iona had been somewhat stunned at the fact that she'd managed to snare a man who was sexier than Colin Firth in a wet shirt.

'Hi, sweetheart,' he said.

'Morning, lover-boy.'

'How's things?'

'Oh, grand.'

'You're not pregnant.'

'How did you know that?' Iona thought she'd managed to keep her tone sufficiently neutral.

'I have my ways,' said Frank, who was adept at reading her voice. 'Don't worry, darling. It'll happen.'

'I'm not worried,' said Iona. 'I know it will. And we'll have a great time making it happen.'

'That's my girl,' said Frank. 'I do love you, you know.'

'You can say those things 'cos you're in the car on your own,' said Iona.

'And you can't because there are people listening in?'

'Exactly. But I do too.'

'You think they can't guess what we're talking about?'

Iona glanced at the desk opposite her. Ruth's dark head was bent over a printed spreadsheet and she appeared to be absorbed in her work, the tip of her pink tongue sticking out between her teeth while she ticked off numbers on the page in front of her. As Iona watched her in silence, Ruth glanced up and gave her a brief smile.

'Oh, you're right as always!'

Frank laughed. 'I know you girls, that's all.'

'What time will you be home?' asked Iona.

'I'll leave as early as I can but it's still a four-hour drive,' said Frank. 'So it'll be after six before I get in, seven if the traffic is bad. What about you?'

'I'm showing apartments until seven myself,' said Iona apologetically. 'I couldn't manage to schedule it better.'

'Don't worry,' Frank told her. 'Give me a call when you've done the last, and if I'm first home I'll order in some pizza.' He chuckled. 'And no saying that a green-leaf salad would be better for you. You need comfort food tonight, sweetheart.'

'You're a pet, you know that.'

'Of course I do. Weren't you lucky the day you met me?'

'OK, OK, you're pushing me to the limits here.'

'And I was lucky the day I met you,' added Frank.

'Charmer,' she said. But she was smiling as she replaced the receiver.

By two o'clock that afternoon Iona was in her car and heading for the first showing, a very luxurious apartment in the suburban town of Dun Laoghaire. The potential tenant had been seconded to a financial services company in the city from its head office in Barcelona, and Iona had already shown him apartments in the docklands area. But Enrique Martinez wanted somewhere further from his place of work and so she'd decided to wow him with an expensive sea-view apartment in the upmarket suburb. I'd rent it myself if I could afford it, thought Iona, as she took the lift to the top floor. It's absolutely gorgeous. Though it's a single person's apartment despite the space, and I – well, I have to start thinking in terms of semi-detached houses with enclosed back gardens. She opened the door and looked in – the apartment was twice the size of her red-brick house and, thanks to its big windows and careful layout, twice as bright and airy too.

A tap at the door signalled that the client had arrived. As with the previous times she'd met him, he was dressed in a carefully tailored suit and the double cuffs on his shirt were held closed by gold cufflinks. His black hair was sprinkled sparingly with grey, his face was square and he wore small but fashionable glasses on his nose. He wasn't as old as he looked, Iona reckoned. But he was choosy and proving to be a difficult client to satisfy.

Her mobile rang just as she was extolling the virtues of the decked balcony and the impressive sea view over the harbour where small boats bobbed merrily at their moorings in the blue-green water.

'A bit delayed,' Frank told her. 'Sorry, sweetheart. I'm only leaving my last meeting now so I might get caught up in some evening traffic. But with luck I should still be home by seven thirty.'

'It'll probably be eight before I make it,' she said. 'My seven o'clock is on the Shelbourne Road. That's my last, though, so you go ahead and order the pizza. Extra cheese for me, please.'

'You got it. And I'll text you when I get in,' promised Frank. 'Maybe later we'll have another shot at the baby-making?'

'Um . . .'

'Ah. Of course.' Frank's voice softened. 'Would you like me just to rub your shoulders instead?'

'You promise the nicest things.' She giggled. Then a noise made her glance up and she saw her businessman standing in the doorway between the lounge and the master bedroom. 'Gotta go,' she said quickly. 'See you later.' She smiled brightly at her client. 'So, Señor Martinez,' she said. 'What do you think? Have we got it right this time?'

By the time she'd finished the Shelbourne Road viewing at seven thirty, she was tired and frazzled and her cramps were worse than ever. All she wanted to do was to get home and put her feet up on the comfortable leather sofa which took up far too much of their tiny living room and gorge herself on takeaway pizza with extra cheese. And garlic bread, if Frank thought about it. He could massage her aching feet afterwards, she thought hopefully.

She took her mobile out of her bag and frowned. He hadn't called or sent a text. Which probably meant that he'd set out even later than he'd hoped and was now stuck in Dublin's notorious rush-hour traffic. (The rush hour starting at about four o'clock in the afternoon these days and not really finishing until nearly eight!) She rang his number but was diverted to his voice-mail.

'I'm on my way back now,' she said as she got into her car. 'If I get home before you I'll order the pizza. But I hope you do. Get some garlicker too, will you? I want to come home to the heady aroma of takeaway cooking. Oh, and Frank – 'cos I couldn't say it earlier I will now. I love you!'

She ended the call and slid her phone into its stand. Then she started the car and headed for home.

Chapter 2

Sally Harper looked at the test in horrified amazement. She closed her eyes, counted to ten, then opened them and looked at the test again. The pink line was as clear as anything. She was, unbelievably, but beyond a shadow of a doubt, pregnant.

She put the test equipment back into its box and shoved the lot into the waste-bin in the cluttered en-suite bathroom. At least Jenna wouldn't see it there and ask awkward questions. Not that Jenna asked her questions at all these days, or even spoke to her on a regular basis if she could help it, but better to be safe than sorry. Christ, she thought as she sat on the edge of the bath, better safe than sorry! Pity I wasn't thinking on those lines a few weeks ago.

She hadn't seriously thought that she was pregnant, though. She'd bought the test more to eliminate it from consideration than anything else. She hadn't wanted to go to Dr Dowling's surgery and go through the whole palaver of an unnecessary test – because how the hell could she be pregnant at this time in her life? She was forty-one years old, for heaven's sake! It was supposed to be hard to get pregnant at forty-one. The home test was meant to be a formality, not a confirmation of something that she'd wanted and wanted for years but which hadn't happened since Jenna's birth.

She felt the sudden heave in her stomach and launched herself at the toilet bowl, retching into it uncontrollably. When the vomiting stopped, she sat, shakily, on the edge of the bath again and wiped her face with a damp cloth. This can't be happening to me, she thought in panic, it really can't. I don't want to be pregnant now. It's not at all convenient. It's not at all what I want for my life. I've gone past all that. And, she gritted her teeth, I've just lost over a stone on that damn South Beach diet. She snorted. What a waste of time that was! All that good carb, bad carb stuff. Being ruthless with herself so that she was having to cook different meals for Frank and Jenna, neither of whom had a spare ounce of fat on them anyway. And for what? So that she'd end up pregnant and looking for maternity clothes again. How fair was that?

What the hell would her husband have to say? As far as he was concerned they'd started and finished their family with Jenna, and although it had been a deep disappointment to them not to have more children (because both had been only children themselves and had wanted a bigger family for Jenna's sake), they'd accepted it in the end. They'd built their entire lives around the fact that their daughter was and always would be an only child. They believed that the Harper family was just the three of them. Frank, Sally and Jenna. She didn't know if there was room for someone else now. She certainly couldn't imagine Frank thinking there'd be time for someone else. Their lives were no longer based on nappies and night feeds and brightly coloured plastic toys. They'd moved on from that – even if moving on meant not understanding the teenage girl that their daughter had become !

He'll be gobsmacked, thought Sally, as she fought with another bout of nausea. Utterly gobsmacked. Nearly seventeen years after Jenna had been born, she knew that she was gobsmacked herself.

And what in God's name was Jenna herself going to say? Sally presumed that her currently rebellious and truculent daughter, who'd once thought that the sun, moon and stars shone out of her parents' behinds, would now think it was disgusting that they were having sex at all; but that the act had resulted in Sally getting pregnant at forty-one – well, Jenna's reaction to that just didn't bear thinking about. Everything Sally did was wrong and embarrassing these days. Getting pregnant would probably now move quickly to the top of the list ahead of her old-fashioned hairstyle and Frank's penchant for trying to sing along to Top Ten hits. Those would definitely be outdone by Jenna's embarrassing mother having embarrassing sex with her embarrassing father and the embarrassing result being plainly obvious for all to see.

Sally's empty stomach heaved again. She didn't remember being this sick before. Maybe it was worse when you were older. She didn't know. As far as she could remember (despite a difficult labour) she'd sailed through her actual pregnancy with Jenna, although maybe the length of time since then had played tricks with her memory. But now . . . there could be all sorts of complications, couldn't there? After all, forty-one was old for a pregnant woman. She knew that. As far as the obstetricians were concerned, she might as well show up with a bus pass and pension book. They'd have to take special care of her, do additional checks on both her and the baby. And then, when the time came, she'd be in a room or a ward with young mothers, hopeful mothers, women who were nothing more than children themselves. Like she'd been, sort of, with Jenna.

And after that – leaving aside the whole pregnancy thing – what about her life? She'd begun to feel she was reclaiming it lately, what with losing the weight and Jenna growing up and being more independent and (despite the silences, shrugs and current practice of dressing in nothing but black) being a fairly responsible sort of daughter even if they had indulged her too much because of her only-child status. In the last few months Sally and Frank had been able to go out together a lot more, trusting (more or less) Jenna to be OK by herself. They'd even taken a weekend break in Galway together, leaving her at home in the company of her best friend, Samantha, with a list of instructions a mile long. Sally had been quite determined not to call to check up on her, but when she'd finally cracked on the Saturday night and phoned the house at ten o'clock, Jenna had told her that she and Sam were watching a video and would Sally and Frank please not worry. (It had been the most sociable conversation she'd had with her daughter in months!) And when they got home the following evening Sally was pleasantly surprised to find that the house hadn't been trashed and that Jenna hadn't held any parties or engaged in any antisocial activities and had, in fact, bought fresh milk and a selection of pastries for when they got home. Her next-door neighbour, Philly, told her the following day that everything had been thankfully normal and that she was lucky to have a daughter like Jenna.

Jenna was a basically good girl, thought Sally, as she washed her face and patted it dry. If dressing in black and monosyllabic communication was as bad as it got, she'd consider herself lucky!

The nausea eased and she dotted tinted moisturiser on to her face. She stared at her reflection in the bathroom mirror. When the new baby reached Jenna's age, she'd be fifty-eight. If she sometimes felt exhausted by her teenage daughter now, what the hell would it be like when she was fifty-eight and dealing with adolescent tantrums? As it was, she couldn't even begin to think what having to go through the whole routine of changing nappies, sterilising bottles and mixing feeds interspersed with minimal sleep all over again would be like. And as for Frank – well, he liked his full eight hours! He'd been utterly useless with Jenna at night. Great during the day – a loving and devoted father who'd taken her on long walks to the park and shamelessly indulged her whenever he thought that Sally wasn't paying attention – but when it came to the night-time stints, Frank had been and would be a write-off.

The new baby would be due in December. Sally didn't want to appear gloomy and negative about the whole thing when the reality was that it was a complete miracle really . . . but December! The month when you got up in the dark and came home from work in the dark; the month with the shortest day in the whole year. Jenna had been a summer baby and that had helped because the days had been long and the nights hadn't been as all-enveloping as winter nights. She'd coped in the summer when she was a mere twenty-four years old, full of energy, and happy and excited about her first child.

She smoothed some more moisturiser on to her face. I don't look forty-one, she told herself hopefully. People could mistake me for a woman in her mid-thirties. Maybe. She pulled at the edges of her face to tighten the skin around her eyes. Damn wrinkle lift cream – a horrendous price and it didn't make the slightest bit of difference! Her eyes, a luminous blue-green, had always been her best feature. They still were, despite the tiny network of wrinkles. Until now Sally had always thought that the fine lines gave her face character. But now she was afraid that they simply gave away her age.

She ran her fingers through her thick mane of hair. Her hair was also a good feature, she reminded herself, despite the fact that Jenna didn't like its length. Mature women didn't let their hair grow past their shoulders, she often told Sally. And then putting it into a plait was naff beyond belief. Sally hadn't plaited it yet this morning and it gleamed in the morning light, strands of auburn and gold naturally highlighting the overall chestnut colour. And hardly any grey! That pleased her. Now that some of her friends were spending an absolute fortune getting their roots done every month, Sally appreciated even more the fact that she'd managed to escape, so far at any rate, that most telltale sign of ageing.

But there was no doubt that she'd be grey at fifty-eight. She stopped twisting her hair around her fingers and let it flop on to her back. She wanted to think that she could be happy about this pregnancy, but she wasn't sure that she could.

She'd be happy if Frank was happy. At least she thought she would. If he turned out to be supportive and understanding, and if he decided that the whole thing was an absolute miracle – well, then she'd be able to see it that way too. But if he (as she had when she'd looked at the thin pink line) saw this baby as an intrusion into the rest of their lives together, she simply didn't know how she'd cope.

Sally exhaled slowly and walked out of the bathroom. This *was* absolutely a miracle, she reminded herself. It really was. How could she be so upset about a miracle?

She slid her white blouse over her shoulders and then pulled on her black pencil skirt. Not that she'd be able to wear the pencil skirt for very much longer. But right now it still fitted. So that looking at herself sideways in the mirror she wouldn't have known that she was pregnant at all. She could even pretend, at least for another few hours, that she wasn't. She tried to block it out of her mind as she began teasing her hair into a plait, but it was impossible.

With her hair finally done, she went into Jenna's room, picking her way through the discarded trousers and tops and shoes, and shook her daughter by the shoulder. Jenna moaned and burrowed deeper beneath the heavy-duty duvet. (She wouldn't allow Sally to change it for a lighter-weight one until later in the summer, even though now, just after Easter, the weather had begun to improve and the nights were getting warmer.)

'Come on, Jen,' said Sally impatiently. 'We haven't got all day.'

'Don't feel well,' muttered Jenna.

'Get up.' Sally's voice was sharper than she'd intended and Jenna poked her face over the duvet.

'We don't have time for messing about,' said Sally. 'I have to talk to a couple of members of staff before school starts.'

'Yeah, well, I don't.' Jenna hated the fact that her mother was the vice-principal at the Holy Spirit School just outside Bray where she herself was a pupil. It was utterly loathsome having a parent on the teaching staff. It made the pupils suspect you and the teachers demand more of you. And the fact that Sally was the vice-principal made things even worse, because Jenna knew the teachers were afraid that she might report back on them if they didn't keep good control of the class. Not that Jenna ever would. It wasn't like she actually cared or anything.

There should be a rule about it, she thought. Of course Sally had asked her about it before she'd taken the job the previous year. The rationale that her mother used was that Jenna only had a couple more years to go and then she'd be off to college so it wouldn't matter. But this opportunity for Sally to leave the school in Sutton where she currently worked (and which was an hour's commute on the Dart) to be so much closer to home, was too good to pass by. She'd asked but she wasn't really asking, just telling, so in the end Jenna hadn't felt any option other than to say that it was all right with her even though her heart sank into her boots at the thought.

'Honestly, Mum, I'm a bit queasy this morning,' she said now as she brushed her dark hair out of her eyes. (She'd inherited Frank's brown eyes instead of Sally's wonderful blue-green ones but her hair was as thick and lustrous as Sally's own.)

'Well, I wasn't feeling the best myself either,' retorted Sally, 'but I'm up and about and I expect you to be out of that bed and downstairs in the next fifteen minutes. Come on, it's Friday. You can sleep late tomorrow.'

Jenna looked at Sally in disgust. That was another thing about her mother. She just didn't believe in illness. Queasiness, nausea, unexpected aches and pains – she had no time for any of it. Jenna didn't think that Sally had ever had a headache in her life. Which meant she had very little sympathy with people who did. When Jenna had been studying for her Junior Cert and had complained of headaches, Sally had simply bought her a better table lamp to use and told her to stop slouching.

She pushed the duvet off the bed and swung her legs reluctantly over the side. At least Dad would be back home today. Sally was always more relaxed when Frank was around, less determined to be in control of things and have everything running like clockwork. Frank made her laugh, allowed her to forget that she had to go to the supermarket or wash the kitchen floor or do the hundreds of mundane, boring, housewifely things that she always wanted to do when he was away on one of his customer service trips.

That was why her parents had a good marriage, thought Jenna, as she stumbled into the bathroom. Frank was light-hearted and easy-going. Sally was a bit of a control freak. But they balanced each other out pretty well. Though, in all honesty, she preferred her father's more relaxed attitude to life. After all, he was a successful businessman. They were comfortably, if not extravagantly, well off. It just went to show that you didn't have to account for every second of every day . . .

'Jen, hurry up!' Her mother's voice, tight and anxious, wafted up the stairs.

'All right, all right!' And what the hell was eating her this morning? thought Jenna irritably as she picked up her hated uniform skirt of bottle-green from the back of the soft grey tub chair in the corner of her room and pulled it up over her hips.

The sooner Dad gets back and brings a bit of laughter into the house again the better, she muttered grimly. I can't bear it when he's away. I really can't.

Chapter 3

Siobhán Farrell was sitting on the end of the bed and thinking about sex. She hadn't had any since her fiancé, Eddie, had headed off on his business trip to Boston five weeks ago. But he'd be home soon and she had plans for an orgy of hedonistic lovemaking to make up for lost time. Bedtime fun with Eddie was one of the most pleasurable things in her life (and it would be a long time, she told herself, before they messed it all up by having kids). She looked at her watch. Right now he was somewhere in the skies on his way back to her. She'd been busy over the past few weeks and sometimes it had suited her that Eddie wasn't around. But she was surprised at how much she'd actually missed him.

She picked up the silver-framed photo of him which she kept on the untidy dressing table. She'd had it done over a year earlier and had brought it with her when she'd moved into his apartment in Blackrock six months ago. Eddie had been amused when she put it on the dressing table, telling her that she hardly needed the photo when she had him, but she'd pointed out that there were many times when she woke up and he wasn't there, and it was nice to see his ugly mug first thing.

It wasn't an ugly mug, of course. Eddie McIntyre was a handsome man with a strong face and a smile which, she once told him, reminded her of Elvis Presley. At which Eddie had snorted and pointed out that he had fair hair and grey eyes and so didn't look anything like The King. Siobhán had grinned at him and said that it was still an Elvis smile and that since her mother had been an Elvis fan and had brought her up to be an Elvis fan too, the least that he could do was accept this as the biggest compliment she could possibly offer him. And Eddie had conceded that it was always nice to get compliments and that he'd have to work on swivelling his hips a bit more. So she told him to stop slacking and get back to the gym, which would surely help his hip-swivelling abilities.

Siobhán and Eddie had met in the gym. The day they'd first spoken she'd been working on the rowing machine, her carrot-red hair pinned up on her head and a thin sheen of perspiration glistening on her face as she attacked the machine, trying to better her time. She'd noticed Eddie around the place before, an attractive man in his T-shirt and shorts without being one of those overmuscled types. She'd seen him pounding the treadmill and lifting weights but she hadn't noticed him standing behind her as she rowed intently, focused only on the job in hand. And then he'd asked her if she wasn't actually trying to propel the damn machine out of the building, a question which had broken her concentration and caused her to slow down for a moment.

She'd looked up at him, a curl of damp hair falling over her forehead and her grey top darkened by sweat, then picked up the pace again.

'You waiting for this machine?' she asked.

'God, no,' he replied. 'You've beaten it into submission already. It wouldn't be fit for someone else tonight.'

She glanced at the timer. Five minutes of her workout left.

'Was there something else you wanted?' She looked at him enquiringly.

'Nothing major,' he told her.

She rowed even more intensely.

'Do you ever stop?' he asked.

'In four minutes thirty seconds,' she replied. 'So if there's something you want to say to me, how about you leave it till then?'

He sat on one of the aerobic steps beside the rowing machine and waited until she'd finished. She picked up her towel and ran it through her crop of curls.

'Well?' she asked.

'Jeez, woman, I'm not sure how good an idea this is now,' he said. 'You're scaring me.'

'Why?'

'Well . . .' He looked despairingly at her. 'I'm trying to hit on you, for heaven's sake. Didn't you guess?'

Siobhán stopped towelling her hair and stared at him.

'Is it a crime?' He laughed uneasily under the steady gaze of her clear blue eyes.

She chuckled. 'Actually, no. That one isn't.'

'Whew.' He smiled in mock-relief. 'So – well – how about it?' He held out his hand. 'Eddie McIntyre.'

'Siobhán Farrell,' she replied cheerfully, completely unaware that she was about to fall in love with him.

The sound of a car horn outside the apartment block brought her attention back to the present. She opened the chest of drawers and rummaged through her underwear, wishing that she hadn't, once again, ruined a perfectly good bra and knickers by throwing them in the wash with Eddie's black socks. Her underwear set had been snow white. Now it had joined the rest of the legion of blue-grey garments. Oh well, she thought, nobody to see it today anyway. She took a plain white blouse from the wardrobe and slid it on and completed her outfit by selecting charcoal-grey trousers and a grey jacket from the mound of clothes piled up on the big armchair in the corner of the room.

Then she picked up her brush and tugged it through her wiry locks, pulling them back from her face and securing them with a soft velvet scrunchie and a couple of barrettes. On her time off she allowed her hair to run riot around her face but she always tied it back at work. She looked at herself in the mirror and narrowed her eyes. Efficient, she thought. In control. The kind of woman who knew how to use her Smith & Wesson .38. Eddie had been taken aback on their first date together when she told him that she was a detective garda. He'd blinked a couple of times and had stared at her with a look which told her that he thought (like her other boyfriends before him) that she was taking the piss. And then (also like other boyfriends before him) when he realised that she wasn't, his expression had changed to one of nervous humour.

'Yes, I could cuff you and make you do whatever I wanted,' she told him, 'but I'm not that kind of girl. And I don't care if you've once jumped a red light or exceeded the speed limit or if don't separate your recyclable stuff from your normal rubbish.'

'I've never dated a policewoman before,' he said.

'If it's too much for you, you don't have to date me again,' she responded. 'We do say that the only people who should marry cops are bankers, civil servants and other cops.' And then she blushed because she hadn't actually intended to use the M word on their first date.

'I think it's kind of cool,' he said. 'I'm just trying to get used to the idea of telling people that my girlfriend is a detective. Have you ever done a murder?'

'Well, I haven't personally murdered anyone.' Her blue eyes twinkled. 'But from time to time I've thought of stabbing my partner.'

'Investigated one,' he amended.

'Yes.'

The rest of the date was spent with Siobhán telling Eddie what it was like to find a dead body. Not exactly what most people would recommend as a topic for a first date, she thought, as they walked hand-in-hand through the city streets later. But his initial ghoulish interest had actually turned into a more general curiosity and suddenly he was asking her if she'd like to come out with him again and she was saying yes.

He had been the one to persuade her to live with him. She'd tried to explain that she worked crazy hours and that when she was deeply involved in a case she could become dreadfully antisocial and that there were times in her life when basically she wouldn't be interested in what he was doing at all, but he said he didn't mind. He told her that he loved her and that he didn't want to live without her. And he'd asked her to marry him. It was her first marriage proposal. Most of her relationships hadn't even got close. She was surprised at how excited she was about it. And how flattered. He'd asked her. He'd actually said, 'Will you marry me,' just like in the books and the movies. (Not that she actually read many books or watched many movies where the outcome was people getting married. Siobhán liked crime fiction and action thrillers and preferred a shootout to a soppy ending any day.)

She loved him but she wasn't ready to marry him. Not yet. It was hard enough being a female on the force (even if things had improved over the past few years); she wasn't ready to take on the baggage of being a married woman too. Her career was important to her. Besides, Eddie's career was just as important to him and she simply didn't see the need for them to get married yet. Eddie worked in investments. Siobhán had no idea what that really meant, other than the fact that he actually enjoyed listening to business bulletins and read the *Financial Times* every day. He talked about things that went so far over her head as to be completely meaningless, but the flip side of the boring stuff was that he made a great deal more money than most of the guys she'd ever known before (and significantly more than her, despite the fact, as she sometimes told him, that she was the one keeping the streets safe for him and his BMW), and he spent a lot of it on her. He'd brought her to Paris for Valentine's Day – a trip which had caused her to suffer more than her fair share of ribbing in Bray garda station, from where she worked. Eddie travelled a lot for business reasons too – a few weeks before the Boston trip he'd spent a week in New York – but that suited her. She liked being with him. She also liked the times when they were apart. Which was why she was happy to be engaged to him but wasn't quite ready to marry him yet. The wedding was planned for a year from now. Which gave her plenty of time to work on her career before people started treating her like a married woman and asking her when she was going to have kids. That was absolutely not on their agenda.

But now, she thought, as she hurried out of the apartment and jabbed the call button for the lift, she was looking forward to being back together with Eddie again. Being single had its attractions, but being part of a couple was even nicer.

At their cruising altitude of 37,000 feet, Eddie McIntyre was watching an in-flight movie. At least, the movie was showing on the personal screen in front of him, but he wasn't really taking any interest in it. He was thinking about the five weeks he'd spent away from Siobhán. Businesswise it had been great. New clients, new money, new investments. A resounding success. The firm would be delighted. He'd e-mailed them and spoken to them already, of course, so they knew just how successful it had been. But it was always great to walk into the office as a conquering hero.

He shivered involuntarily. He didn't feel like a conquering hero. Not now. He wiped away the beads of sweat which had suddenly broken out on his forehead. Things seemed great whenever he thought about going into the office. But whenever he thought about seeing Siobhán, a black cloud seemed to envelop him.

He got up and went to the toilet. The harsh light made his face seem pale, even though he'd acquired a decent tan over the last few weeks. But otherwise he didn't look any different. It was weird, thought Eddie, that you could look exactly the same and yet feel completely changed. He couldn't help thinking that Siobhán would know straight away. As though by looking at him she would guess that the fabric of their lives might have been changed for ever. And yet why should she? She might be a detective, he told himself, but she wasn't a bloody clairvoyant.

He splashed water on to his face and made his way back to his seat. The steward walked by and asked him if he'd like something to drink. Eddie ordered a whiskey. He hardly ever drank whiskey, but somehow it seemed the right drink for him now. When the steward returned and handed it to him, Eddie knocked it back in three swift gulps. He didn't really feel any better afterwards, but at least it might help him to get some sleep. And that would stop the torrent of thoughts running through his head.

Frank Harper wasn't thinking about how he looked. He wasn't really thinking about anything very much. Perhaps, if forced to say something about his thoughts, it would be that he liked driving. He always had. He liked the feeling of being cocooned in his car, cut off from everything around him while still being an observer of life as he passed it by. He particularly liked it on a day like today when the sun was shining from a china-blue sky dotted with white puffball clouds, and when the countryside was bursting with spring-green meadows and unfurling leaves on the trees.

In the car, cruising along the highways and byways, he could listen to radio phone-ins or country and western music with no one to criticise his choice or ask to switch over to some damn classical station or to self-important twaddle on Radio 4 (not that reception for Radio 4 was anything much in the car anyway – and once you drove any distance outside Dublin it was impossible to get).

The other thing he liked about being in the car was driving through the different towns on his various journeys, towns with interesting names like Birdhill or Oilgate which resonated with past history; or whose Irish names had been anglicised so that people forgot that Killduff actually meant 'black church' and Kenmare meant 'the head of the sea'.

He liked observing the changes too: the improvement of the roads (in some areas at least); new paint jobs on the rectangular houses that lined the main streets; whole new housing developments springing up in places that had once been considered rural but were now being touted as within commuting distance of the nearest city.

He knew that some people disliked the urbanisation of the countryside and he supposed that at some point he'd dislike it too; but it was a sign of the better times that Ireland had gone through in the second half of the 1990s, a time that had given him the opportunity to move his life on, to make a bit of money and to become a different person.

Frank thought about change a lot when he was driving. Mostly he thought about how easier communication had made the country smaller and people always accessible. Nowhere was really isolated any more. Owning a mobile phone meant that you could be contacted on the side of a mountain or in the middle of a lake even if there was nobody for miles around. Nowhere was safe from the people who wanted to get hold of you. That thought had once scared him. But now it didn't bother him at all.

He glanced down at the three mobile phones in the seat pocket of his car. A red one. A blue one. A yellow one. Honest to God, he muttered under his breath. Three damn phones. Sometimes I wonder if I'm off my head completely. At least the three of them were silent right now and he wasn't expecting them to ring.

He looked at the clock on the dash. After five and the traffic was building up, even in the smaller towns. He frowned. He'd messed it up this week, got everything arse over tit so that his whole schedule had been thrown into disarray. He'd made promises that he wouldn't be able to keep and he still hadn't figured out the best way around them. But he would. He always did no matter how complicated things got. That was why he did so well in business; he would invariably come up with a solution for even the most demanding of clients. He'd manage something today too for himself. Only he hadn't quite decided what yet. But he wouldn't push it. It was all about confidence and not letting yourself get rattled, and Frank never allowed himself to get rattled any more. He'd almost been rattled when the letter had come and he'd looked at it with astonishment and complete surprise, but then he'd managed to deal with that too. He'd copied it, as he always did with important stuff, then put the original away and resolved not to think about it but let a decision simply float into his mind instead of thrashing through all the options. He knew he'd do the right thing in the end. He was confident about that.

He whistled tunelessly and allowed a huge oil tanker to overtake him. Bloody fool, thought Frank. Exceeding the speed limit and passing him on a poor stretch of road. And for what? He'd worked out himself, long since, that belting along didn't make a whole heap of difference to the journey in the end. Maybe got you to your destination five or ten minutes earlier than a steady fifty-five or sixty. But you got there stressed out and tense, whereas if you travelled more slowly and in a more relaxed manner the journey didn't become a battle. Yet most people didn't realise that. Most people were sucked into the whole rushing around sort of thing as he'd once been. He was glad to have left that part of his life behind him.

He flexed his shoulders. There was no doubt that these days his life in many ways was actually busier and more stressful than it used to be. But it was all about compartmentalising things, not letting them get the better of you. Finding ways to unwind and people to unwind with. Developing the sort of lifestyle that allowed you to get the most out of everything. The trouble with so many people in the world, Frank thought as he slowed down to go through the next small town (which had once been nothing more than a pinprick on the map but now boasted a huge shopping centre and discount designer outlet, as well as an irritating set of traffic lights), was that they forgot that they only had one life to live and they forgot to extract every moment of pleasure from it that they could. And, in the end, they ended up missing out on the big things because they spent far too much time fussing over the little things.

It had taken him a while to work that out. But once he had, well, everything had just slotted into place for him and he hadn't looked back.

A sudden bump and a pull at the steering made him swear out loud. A puncture. As if he didn't have enough to deal with today! Frank felt his hard-won stress-free mood rapidly recede as he coasted to a stop on the grassy verge. Not the best place to get a puncture, he thought, as he took the large red warning triangle out of the boot and walked back a hundred metres or so to put it on the road. But then that's the way things go sometimes. He took off his jacket and slung it on to the back seat of the Honda. Then he took the jack out of the boot and began to raise the car.

Actually (and he knew that people would think he was crazy if he admitted this), he didn't normally mind changing a tyre. It didn't happen that often, of course, but when it did it reminded him of the mechanical nature of the car. These days they were so damn comfortable that sometimes he forgot the whole magic of petrol and ignition and axles turning wheels. Getting a puncture brought it all back to basics. And he kind of enjoyed rolling up his shirtsleeves and getting a bit grubby from time to time.

He whistled as he worked, even as his mind wrestled with the timing problem that getting back so late to Dublin would bring. He made his decision, and when he'd finished the work and put all of the equipment back in the boot, he picked up the bright red mobile and pressed the speed-dial.

'It's me,' he said to the voice-mail message. 'I'm sorry. I really am. I'm running much later than I thought. I might end up staying here tonight and get back to Dublin tomorrow. I'm really sorry. Give me a shout later.'

He got into the car and put the phone back in the door pocket. Then he frowned. It was covered in oil. He looked at his hands and grimaced. He hadn't noticed the stain on the edge of his palm. He took a tissue from the box on the passenger seat and wiped it. But he was still grimy. He'd end up getting oil all over the steering wheel at this rate.

He knew that there were a couple of pubs side by side a few miles along the road. He'd drive to them and wash up in one of the men's rooms. Since he'd made the phone call, the last vestiges of pressure had disappeared. He placed two tissues on the steering wheel to protect it as he drove. And now people really will think I'm crazy, he thought in amusement. Maybe that I've got some kind of cleanliness complex, that I'm afraid of germs or something. Howard Hughes, that's me! He grinned to himself as the pubs came into view at the crest of the hill on the turn of the road. The first was undergoing some kind of renovation. Its front was swathed in scaffolding and green tarpaulin which flapped gently in the wind.

He pulled in to the gravelled car park of the second pub (though car park was probably too grand a word for what was just a bit of space in front of the building with three other cars already parked there) and switched off the engine. He slid the blue phone into his jacket pocket and the others into his briefcase, which he took with him. He'd once had his car broken into in a pub car park and he didn't leave things to chance any more. He walked into the pub, narrowing his eyes to adjust to the gloom inside. The publican was behind the bar, polishing pint glasses, while another customer – an elderly farmer with a tweed cap pulled down over his brow – sat at the dark wood counter sipping a pint of Guinness. Two younger men – businessmen, thought Frank, passing trade like himself – sat in a corner with a sheaf of papers in front of them.

'Just a mineral water,' he said as he put his case on the bar.

The barman nodded at the new arrival and took a bottle of Ballygowan from the fridge beneath the bar.

'I'll use your facilities first.' Frank didn't want to get oil all over the glass too. He gestured towards the briefcase. 'This OK here?'

The barman nodded again and Frank walked through the pub to the gents'. He wondered why it was that the toilets in so many Irish pubs were so utterly awful. The blue wall tiles were coated in grease and there was black fungus on the grouting. The single urinal was detaching itself from the wall and was caked with limescale. And the sink, the only item that he actually wanted to use, was cracked, the tap dripping incessantly.

Oh well, he thought philosophically as he turned the tap on full. It won't kill me.

He began whistling again.

Chapter 4

Sally was both relieved and annoyed that her husband had called to say that he probably wouldn't be home. She was annoyed because he'd been away all of the previous week and three days of the week before. It seemed to her that over the past few years his work had taken him away more and more often, and the semi-detached nature of their marriage was beginning to irritate her. It hadn't at first – she'd liked the fact that the two of them were independent people who didn't need to be joined at the hip to be happy. She'd enjoyed going on weekend breaks without him and him going away without her too. Their reunions were always passionate and welcome, and last year, for their eighteenth wedding anniversary, she'd bought him a plaque in the shape of a heart inscribed with 'Absence makes the heart grow fonder', which she'd told him to put up in his office.

Of course when they first married his absences had been much shorter. But that had changed in the last few years, mainly because the business had grown so much and he had to be away a lot more frequently. It was something that she was going to have to talk to him about. Especially now that she was pregnant again. That, though, was one of the reasons she was relieved he wasn't coming home tonight. She hadn't quite come to terms with the whole idea herself yet and she wasn't ready to talk to him about it. Only she knew that the moment he walked in the door she would have to blurt it out. She was aching with the need to tell someone and that someone had to be him.

'Jenna!' she called up the stairs. 'Are you ready to eat now?'

'Not hungry,' came the reply.

Sally sighed deeply. Another thing to worry about. Jenna was forever telling her that she wasn't hungry or requesting a simple salad for a meal which she then pushed around her plate and only ate a small portion of. Whenever Sally broached the subject of eating properly, Jenna looked wearily at her and told her that she wasn't anorexic or even bulimic but that she was simply going through a not very hungry phase.

'But darling,' Sally would say in her most coaxing tone, 'you need nutrients. You're a growing girl and you're working hard at school.' (Though the second part of her sentence was only half true, because Jenna's grades had slipped over the past few months. The worst part of being a teacher in the same school was knowing how her daughter's behaviour had changed and having the other teachers discuss it with her in detail.)

It didn't matter how much Sally wheedled, Jenna ate what she wanted when she wanted. And then, just to keep her off balance, Sally thought, she would sometimes tuck into an enormous dinner and smile at her like the Jenna of old and ask for more.

I wish I knew what was going through her mind these days, Sally thought. Everyone thinks that because I teach I should know. But I bloody well don't!

Jenna lay on her single bed and gazed up at the ceiling. A tiny crack snaked its way across it from one side of the room to the other. The crack had been there for as long as she could remember. When she'd been very small and noticed it first, she'd rushed downstairs to tell her parents that the house was falling down. She'd burst into the living room to find Sally buttoning up her blouse and her father looking flustered. It was only years afterwards that she realised that the sound of her four-year-old footsteps clattering down the stairs had alerted her parents to the imminent interruption of their lovemaking. She'd shivered when she thought about it – her mum and dad having sex together. It revolted her. She didn't know quite why it revolted her when the idea of making love, to Gerry Cullinan, a guy she'd met at the local sports centre, was so appealing. Last week, in the shadow of the high wall behind her house, Gerry had kissed her in a way she hadn't ever been kissed before. And as his hands had slid down her back, cupping her buttocks and drawing her ever closer to him, she'd held him fiercely too, wanting to merge her body with his until they were one person. One of Gerry's hands had then moved upwards and under her Nike T-shirt, until it covered her left breast. At that moment Jenna thought she would faint with the pleasure of it.

'I don't have anything,' Gerry had whispered. 'I'm sorry.'

Jenna had been shocked. Both at the fact that he'd thought she was ready to have sex with him and the fact that he was being responsible about it.

'Neither do I,' she'd whispered back as though this was a perfectly normal conversation.

Gerry had pulled away from her then. 'Next time,' he said.

Jenna had fallen in love with him a little more. After all, most of the time adults talked about teenage boys it was to say that they had all the self-control of a lit firework. But here was Gerry Cullinan, not making love to her because he didn't want to get her pregnant. He was the most wonderful bloke she'd ever met. She'd pulled him towards her and kissed him again, and she knew that if he hadn't pulled away, she wouldn't have stopped him.

She was going to go into Dublin and buy condoms. She couldn't buy them here, in Bray, because someone would be bound to find out. The town was big but not big enough to keep really important things secret. Even if she went to the chemist at the far end, where the pharmacist didn't know her or her mother or father, she'd be bound to bump into someone there who did. It was the way of things. But if she went into the city to buy them she'd be OK. She could nip into Boots and throw them into a wire basket along with a new mascara and some lippy and nobody would take a blind bit of notice.

And then, when she met Gerry at the party tomorrow night as they'd arranged, she'd be able to let him know that she was sorted, that she had something and that they didn't have to stop with kisses and his touch on her breast.

Remembering it again brought back all of the pleasurable feelings. She moaned softly to herself and closed her eyes.

Sally sat at the huge wooden table and poked at the pork chop on her plate. She wasn't really hungry. She'd only cooked it because she'd taken the chops out of the freezer that morning, thinking that they could have a nice family meal once Frank got home. Whenever Frank was in the house Jenna seemed marginally more prepared to eat with them, as though making an effort for her father's sake. Sally pushed the chop to one side and scooped some savoury rice on to her fork. She lifted it as far as her lips and then replaced it, untasted, on the plate. Maybe it was just as well Jenna had shut herself away in her bedroom. If she'd been watching Sally playing aimlessly with her food she'd have considered it justification for her own lack of appetite these days.

Although Sally had been relieved when he left the message earlier, she now felt miserable at the thought of another night without Frank. She wanted the warmth of his arms around her, the closeness of his lips on hers and the sheer joy of making love to him, regardless of the fact that she was pregnant. She stared unseeingly at her plate. It had been Frank's skill as a kisser that had entranced her when she'd first met him at an all-night party in a run-down flat in Ranelagh twenty years ago. Sally had known the girl who rented the flat; Frank had come with a group of friends. They'd met as they both tried to grab the last can of Heineken from the fridge.

'I think you'll find that's mine,' Frank had told her.

'I brought ten,' Sally informed him. 'I haven't had more than six. So it's definitely mine.'

They'd stared at each other, both aware of an electricity that crackled between them as his brown eyes held her blue-green ones, and then he laughed.

'How about payment?' he suggested.

'Excuse me?'

'Well, I let you have the beer in return for payment.'

'And that might be?'

'This.' He leaned forward and kissed her.

It was astonishing, thought Sally now, how much the memory of that kiss still had the power to move her. Of course he'd kissed her hundreds of times since then, and every time had been utterly marvellous, but that first kiss had been so unexpected and so wonderful. Sometimes, when she was mad at him for not coming home or having to work over holidays or travel abroad to meetings and miss important family events . . . well, if she remembered the kiss she couldn't help but forgive him.

Remembering the kiss would make her remember the first time they made love too. A week later, after he'd asked her out and taken her to the cinema (she couldn't for the life of her remember what it was they'd gone to see, as they'd spent the entire two hours in an orgy of kissing), they'd gone back to his flat, small and not very appealing with its underlying smell of damp, and she'd felt her excitement at being with him wane in such uninspiring surroundings. Then he'd kissed her again and begun undoing the buttons on her rather prim blouse, and he'd done it so slowly and erotically (and so unlike the other guys she'd gone out with before who were usually all fingers and thumbs in their haste to get down to business) that she'd almost come there and then simply standing in front of him. They'd made love on the padded quilt of his bed and Sally had fallen head over heels in love with the man who was the most sensitive lover she'd ever had. And was ever likely to have, she thought later. She'd wondered, as she went home afterwards, whether you could make a lifetime commitment on the basis of out-of-this-world sex. She felt, somewhat regretfully, that there was probably more to it than that. And then Frank sent her flowers (the only man in her life ever to have sent her flowers) and she knew that there was more to him than being good in bed.

He was a wonderful husband. Other female friends would often joke (enviously) that he was too good to be true. That nobody could be as understanding of a woman's needs as Frank. And not just her physical needs, her emotional needs too. He remembered birthdays. He remembered significant moments in their lives. He knew when she was bothered by something and knew to leave her to her own devices until she'd sorted herself out. He supported her teaching career, pushing her harder than maybe she would have pushed herself so that she finally got the position of deputy principal (although he told her that she really deserved to be the head). And if the flip side of that was that he had to be away more and more because of his business, well, Sally could put up with that. Most of the time.

It was definitely better that he wasn't here tonight, she told herself, as she got up from the table and scraped her uneaten dinner into the bin. Her thoughts were all over the place. Her feelings were equally haphazard. She needed time to be alone.

But part of her didn't want to be.

Iona arrived home at a quarter to eight. The house was in darkness with no sign of Frank. She felt a spurt of anger at the fact that he'd been delayed still further and hadn't bothered to call her. She took her phone from her bag and checked it. No missed calls. No messages. No texts.

She drew the curtains in the tiny living room as she dialled the pizza delivery and placed an order. She asked for their Cajun special with extra cheese on the basis that this was her favourite although not one Frank particularly liked. But she was punishing him for being so late. Childish, she thought, as she hung up. But she didn't care. Besides, the takeaway pizza and garlic bread (even though she was really looking forward to it) was a big concession on her part. Always conscious of eating well, she'd been even more choosy in the last few weeks, wanting to get herself into peak condition for getting pregnant. So she'd been loading up on green-leaf veggies and folic acid and cutting out junk food completely.

She massaged her stomach. The worst of the cramps had eased now but she still felt bloated and uncomfortable. She went up to the bathroom and began to run a bath, decanting a few drops of ylang ylang oil into the warm water. The resulting scent was restful and soothing. She went into the bedroom and took off her work clothes. The pizza place had said it would be forty minutes before they could make the delivery. She'd be out of the bath by then, although surely Frank would be home within five or ten anyway. It wasn't like him to be late and not to let her know. She pushed the sliver of worry to the back of her mind. He'd call. He always did. But she picked up her mobile and rang him anyway. All she got was his voice-mail. She left a message saying that he'd better hurry, that the pizza was on its way, and then she went back to the bathroom.

She slid into the silky softness of the bath and closed her eyes, allowing her breathing to slow down and become steadier. A few minutes later, feeling much calmer, she opened her eyes and began massaging her tired legs with the tips of her fingers. She slid lower into the water, feeling the tensions of the day dissolve away from her and the bloatedness of her stomach finally ease as she drifted between wakefulness and sleep. Frank laughed at her ability to sleep in the bath and she knew that he worried (very slightly) that she might slide beneath the water and drown. She always told him that it was impossible in their shortened bathtub, even for someone of five feet and one inch.

There was a ring at the door. Her eyes snapped open again. Bloody pizza people were early for once, she thought. And Frank still hadn't come home. Well, he could just reheat his half in the microwave and he'd have to lump it that it never tasted the same afterwards!

She wrapped her towelling robe around her and padded down the stairs. Unless it was Frank himself, she thought hopefully, having forgotten his keys or something. As she opened the door she realised that she was being particularly stupid. He wouldn't be able to drive the car without keys. And besides, she'd know in advance if it was Frank. She always believed that she was intuitive like that. There were many times when she'd be thinking about him, her mobile would ring and it would be him. It wasn't just Frank either. When Lauren had come down with a debilitating virus, Iona had phoned her the very day she'd been diagnosed, even though they hadn't spoken in weeks. And the day Craig had received the letter from the engineering contractors about the Chinese job, she'd phoned him too, just knowing that something had happened. Iona put her intuition down to the fact that she was in tune with her body. The knowledge comforted her, made her feel as though there was nothing that could ever happen without her being aware of it first.

The pizza delivery girl stood on the doorstep. The warm, tomato-laden aroma wafting from the huge flat box made Iona's mouth water and she realised that she hadn't eaten since her mixed nut salad at lunchtime. She took the box from the girl and tipped her a euro. She set it down in the kitchen, nipped upstairs to give her hair a brisk rub with a towel, thankful that its shortness meant that it dried quickly, and then came down again to attack the food.

She switched on the TV and realised that they were showing *Erin Brockovich*, which was one of her favourite movies. She hacked a slice from the pizza, curled up on the sofa, and indulged herself while she waited for Frank to come home.

Long before the movie ended she began to worry again. She tried Frank's mobile once more but her call was still being diverted to his mailbox. She left another message, this time telling him that she was probably worrying unnecessarily but asking him to give her a shout and let her know where he was. She tried not to think of the fact that he might have had an accident – Frank was one of the safest drivers she knew. Maddeningly safe, in fact; she often got impatient with him. But although he wasn't the kind of man to do something stupid on the road, other people were. Some lunatic, maybe overtaking on a bad bend, could have smashed into him. Iona swallowed hard and looked at the congealing half of the pizza she'd left for him. She closed her eyes and visualised him driving along the motorway from Cork to Dublin. She couldn't see any problems. She just couldn't understand why he hadn't called.

The movie was failing to keep her attention. Her eyes darted around the room and came to rest on the wedding photo – apart from the recent additions of the photos of her niece and nephew, it was the only photograph on display in the room. Both she and Frank preferred paintings to photos (and especially disliked photographs of themselves), but they agreed that the wedding photo was the one exception. They were standing on the white sands of a Barbados beach, she in her long white dress, an arrangement of colourful flowers in her dark hair, he in a white tux and red bow tie which she'd told him at the time was a bit over the top but which actually looked great against the stunning blues of the sea and sky behind them. They were laughing and toasting each other with champagne. Iona smiled at the memory. It truly had been the happiest day of her life, and it hadn't mattered to her that none of her family was there because being alone together had made the experience somehow more intensely personal.

Four years ago, she thought, and it truly does only seem like yesterday!

She picked up her mobile and called Frank again. She could feel the worry escalate as she listened to him asking her to leave a message.

'Frank,' she said, and she had to struggle to keep the anxiety out of her voice, 'where the hell are you? Call me. I know it's stupid but I'm worried.'

Somehow saying out loud that she was worried seemed to lessen it somewhat, as though by admitting it she could see for herself how silly it was to be concerned. She pressed the end button and stared at the TV screen. *Erin Brockovich* had finished.

Chapter 5

It was early evening when the call came in to the garda station in Ardallen, just as Garda Tim Shanahan finally finished the crossword in the *Herald*. It had been a quiet day in Ardallen, a country town about an hour's drive from Dublin, but Tim wasn't feeling in the slightest bit guilty about having some down-time – they were all still shattered after the two-day jazz festival that had taken place at the GAA sports park the previous week. It was the minor public order offences that were so time-consuming, he thought. All those people getting drunk and pissing in the streets and having rows with each other. A big case would be a damn sight more exciting, even though they really didn't have the manpower for big cases in Ardallen.

'Ardallen garda station. How can I help?' Tim liked sounding pleasant on the phone even though he knew that many of his colleagues still answered it abruptly, as though its ring had disturbed them from far more important business.

'Jesus, Tim, come quick,' said an excitable voice. 'There's been a massive great landslide at Kavanagh's pub and the side of it is buried under rock.'

'Who's that?' he asked, although he was fairly sure that it was Margaret Hobson, who lived on the hillside opposite the pub.

'For crying out loud, Tim, it's me. Mags. I was going to call 999 but I thought it'd be quicker to call you myself. But you'd better come quick 'cos it's a hell of a mess.'

'Right, Margaret,' he said. 'We're on our way.'

He called for his colleague, Ronan Tierney, to join him, The two of them jumped into the marked car outside the station and sped to Kavanagh's pub. As they drove, Tim called the ambulance service – if things were as bad as Margaret suggested (and he trusted her, she was a sensible woman despite her excitable voice), then they'd need them.

Kavanagh's was a well-known pub in the area, although it amused Tim that it was right next door to the much more upmarket Ardallen House, which was currently undergoing its third remodelling in almost as many years. This one was far more radical than any other, since it was to allow for a nightclub on the premises, a fact which wearied Tim because the location of the pubs, five miles outside the town, already caused problems with customers who drove there and then realised that after a few pints they shouldn't really drive back. Having a pub with a nightclub attached would make things even worse. Years ago it wouldn't have mattered that much, but there was now a zero-tolerance policy in Ardallen regarding drink-driving which had made Tim and the rest of the guards both heroes and villains in equal measure.

'Holy Mother of God.' Tim swung the car to a stop outside the pub and looked at it in stunned amazement. Margaret Hobson hadn't been joking. The entire side of the pub was nothing but a mound of rubble and the place was a complete disaster area.

'Let's get some traffic control going,' Tim told Ronan. 'The ambulances will be here soon and we don't want rubbernecking onlookers in the way. And you'd better call for back-up too.'

He scanned the scene as Ronan got to work. He recognised Noel Kavanagh, the owner of the pub, who was sitting on the single wooden table outside the front of the premises, a red blanket around his shoulders. He was unnaturally pale although that could also have been because he was streaked with dust. An elderly man who Tim knew to be Bennie Harrison was sitting beside him. Margaret Hobson was with them, offering them tea out of an old-fashioned thermos flask. Two other men, both in torn and dusty white shirts spattered with blood, were also being comforted. As he watched, a couple of ambulances arrived and the paramedics got working on the injured men.

'Christ.' Ronan Tierney rejoined him. 'What the hell happened?'

'God only knows,' said Tim. He looked around as the sound of sirens indicated the arrival of the reinforcements. 'Get one of the lads to follow the ambulances, Ronan. See how everyone's doing.' He scratched his head. 'I'll have a word with Noel and see what he has to say before they haul him off. We need to know if anyone is trapped inside.'

'D' you think it was deliberate?' Ronan's voice was a mixture of hope and horror.

'Deliberate?'

'Like a terrorist attack or something.'

Trim looked at his young colleague. 'Ah now, get a grip,' he said. 'I have a feeling that terrorists have bigger targets in mind than Kavanagh's pub.'

'Well, a gangland thing then,' suggested Ronan.

'Jesus Christ, Tierney, what sort of stuff are you reading these days?' demanded Tim.

'Well, I hope there weren't too many people inside,' said Ronan, tacitly accepting that Ardallen probably wasn't a gangland or terrorist target.

'Noel says that some bloke came in just before it happened,' said Margaret Hobson, who'd trotted over to them. 'Besides Bennie and those two other guys he was the only person there. He ordered a sparkling water and went to the gents'. The gents' was at the side there. Where the wall fell down.'

'Jesus.' Now Tim could see exactly what had happened. Somehow, in the renovating of Ardallen House, which was higher on the hill than Kavanagh's, the wall at the side of the pub had collapsed and fallen directly on to the other building, burying half of it. And effectively burying whoever was in the gents' toilet at the time.

'We haven't found him yet,' said a fireman.

'Not local?' said Ronan.

'Doesn't sound like it, but you never know,' Tim remarked. 'I'd better talk to Noel.'

As he walked over to the wooden table there was a shout from the paramedics still at the scene. Others hurried over to join them. Then a wheeled stretcher was brought over. Tim watched as a body was lifted out of the rubble and a drip inserted into what seemed to him to be a lifeless arm.

With a blare of klaxons the last ambulance departed, followed by a squad car, and Tim set about taking statements from a still shocked Noel Kavanagh and a considerably more garrulous Bennie Harrison.

Neither of them was particularly helpful. Their statements were very similar. They'd been sitting in the pub, minding their own business, when they'd heard a muffled thud and the next thing they knew they were being buried in rubble and dust. They'd fled out of the main door, terrified of being trapped inside, although the collapse of the wall had mainly confined itself to one side of the building. They didn't know anything about the man who'd ordered the Ballygowan, although Noel thought that he'd spoken with a Dublin accent.

'The two other men,' Tim said to Noel. 'Did you know them?'

He nodded gingerly. 'They meet here once a month or so. I don't know much about them – one of them is a rep from somewhere in the north of the country. The other's from Waterford. I can't remember their names.'

'OK, Noel,' said Tim. He turned to Ronan and waved in the direction of the car park. 'Do a check on the cars, find out who they're registered to.'

He poked his head nervously through the entrance to the pub. The place was covered in bricks and dust. He could see a tan briefcase on the counter in front of him and he picked his way cautiously through the rubble to get it.

'What the hell do you think you're doing!'

He whirled around at the voice. A fireman looked at him in anger. 'This building isn't secure.'

Tim grabbed the briefcase and stepped outside again. 'Just checking,' he said.

'Don't be such a goddamn fool,' said the fireman. 'Christ almighty, we don't want another fatality.'

Tim looked at him. 'The guy you pulled out? Is he dead?'

The fireman shrugged. 'I don't give much for his chances, let's put it like that.'

'Bloody hell,' said Tim.

His attention was caught by the sudden arrival of more cars and vans. The media, he thought sourly. All with questions that he couldn't answer yet, all after the human angle to the story as well as looking for someone to blame. He recognised Joely McGuirk, a reporter from the local newspaper, as well as Pat Dolan, a photographer. Tim knew that more media wouldn't be far behind.

'Make sure they stay behind the tape,' he warned Ronan. 'Tell them I'll talk to them in a minute.'

Tim felt as though he was on the set of a movie. Yet the destruction around him was real. The men carried off in ambulances to the nearest hospital were real. The shock of Noel Kavanagh and Bennie Harrison was real. It was just hard to believe it.

He opened the briefcase he'd retrieved from the pub, while Ronan dealt with the media hacks. The papers inside were mainly brochures and A4 notepads with scrawled diagrams and notes. There were also two mobile phones in the case. He picked up the red one and scrolled through the address book. There was one number under 'Home'. It was a Dublin area number, although Tim wasn't immediately sure what part of the city it was from.

'Any luck on tracing the cars?' he asked Ronan.

'They're coming back to me,' he said.

'Find out about this number too,' Tim told him, handing him the mobile.

He picked up the yellow one and began scrolling through that too. As far as he could see the numbers on this were all business ones. One phone for personal calls, one for business calls, he decided. Fair enough.

More and more onlookers arrived at the scene, and finally the television cameras. Tim had been interviewed by RTÉ and Sky News once before, although that was when an international pop star and her fiancé had married in Ardallen Castle on the outskirts of the town. It was meant to have been in complete secrecy but the news had been leaked to just about everyone who wanted to know. Tim had laughed and joked with the reporters then, telling them that there was nothing he could say, feeling a little like a media star himself.

But this was different. He told the reporters that the incident was obviously very serious and distressing and that at this point he had no further information. As soon as he had, he told them, he'd let them know.

'We've got ID on the cars,' said Ronan, 'and the two guys who were taken away. I've spoken to our lads at the hospital. The injured blokes are being kept in overnight for shock but actually they're not that badly hurt. They've called their families themselves.'

'And the other guy?' asked Tim.

Ronan made a face. 'They're stabilising him but they think they'll have to transfer him to Dublin. They don't have facilities for him at the county hospital. Looks like a head injury.'

Tim rubbed the back of his neck. He hated hearing about head injuries. He looked at his colleague, who shrugged helplessly and then answered his phone as it rang.

'The third guy,' he said, 'him with the head injuries – the phone number and the car reg match. Frank Harper, River Valley Estate, Bray. The name also matches the business cards which were in the glove compartment of his car – we managed to open it a few minutes ago.'

Tim nodded. Now he recognised the area phone number. Bray, of course, wasn't strictly in Dublin. It was in Wicklow, about a forty-minute drive from the city.

'There are a couple of photos in the phone's memory,' added Ronan. 'A woman and a girl. Could be family.'

'We'd better get to the house and see what's what,' Tim said. 'At least, we'll get Bray to do it. These are always horrible situations.'

'He's not dead yet,' said Ronan.

'If he's got a serious head injury . . .' Tim didn't bother finishing the sentence.

'Maybe it's not that bad,' said Ronan optimistically as Tim called the station in Bray.

Chapter 6

The sound of the phone ringing broke Siobhán Farrell's concentration. The evening shift at the station was a good time to deal with paperwork without being interrupted every five minutes, and she'd been sitting at her desk reviewing the money-laundering file for the past hour. The case was almost ready to go to the Director of Public Prosecutions and Siobhán wanted to be sure that she'd dotted every I and crossed every T and that it was as complete as it was possible to be. The most frustrating part of police work was seeing a case not followed through because of mistakes which would have it thrown out of court. She'd once had a case dismissed on a technicality – she'd called a company Havisham Holdings instead of Haversham Holdings – and she'd never forgotten it.

'Hello,' she said abruptly, annoyed at the interruption. Tim Shanahan winced. That was the kind of phone-answering he didn't go in for. Women were even worse than the men these days in being abrupt and rude, he thought. He introduced himself and explained about the Ardallen incident.

'How awful.' He could hear the genuine sympathy in the woman's voice and he warmed to her a little. 'And you think that one of the victims is from our district?' Tim read out his name and Siobhán nodded. 'I know the area.'

'We need someone to go and check out the house,' said Tim. 'Break the news.'

'How grim is it?' asked Siobhán.

'It doesn't sound good to me,' he said. 'I asked whether his wife should come here or wait for them to send him to Dublin. They said come here, he won't be stable enough to be moved for a while yet.'

'OK,' said Siobhán. 'I'll go around to the house right away.'

'Thanks,' said Tim. He gave her all the information he could. 'Sorry to land this one on you.'

'It's better than having to tell them that he's dead,' said Siobhán matter-of-factly. 'I've had to do that before and I just hate it. At least this way there's still a bit of hope.'

'He looked fairly beat-up when they took him out of the rubble,' said Tim. 'I don't know whether he'll make it.'

'Hope all the same,' Siobhán said.

She hung up on Tim and waved at the uniformed garda who was walking past her door.

'Cathal, the very man, I need you to come with me,' she told him. 'We might have to break some difficult news.'

Cathal Rothery sighed. He was always chosen when there was bad news to be broken. He had a choirboy face and a very sympathetic manner which put people at their ease. 'Fill me in,' he said as they walked out towards the car.

Iona was extremely worried. He'd said that he'd be home around seven thirty and it was now ten o'clock. Three more frantic messages to his mobile had remained unanswered. She couldn't think of a single explanation for this that didn't involve Frank in some kind of accident, because she couldn't believe that he was deliberately ignoring her calls. They hadn't had a row; when she'd last spoken to him everything had seemed perfectly normal. He'd talked about ordering in the pizza, for heaven's sake!

She looked at the remnants of the Cajun with extra cheese, as well as the half-baguette of garlic bread, now cold and unappetising. She closed the pizza box and brought it into the kitchen.

She'd turned on the news earlier to see if there had been anything about accidents on the road from Cork but there had been nothing. Now she went into the office to check breaking news on the internet, just in case. She sat nervously at her computer screen, the metallic taste of fear in her mouth as she logged on and looked at her Irish news service.

There were a number of accident reports but none on the Cork to Dublin road, which was the route that Frank would have taken. Iona stared at the screen with its myriad pop-up ads and colourful exhortations to buy a new phone or sign up for something free and she felt the worry knot inside her stomach and make her cramps even worse.

Maybe, though, he hadn't had an accident. Maybe he'd been taken ill and had been brought to hospital. Appendicitis, perhaps. Or one of his migraines. That could be it, she supposed, feeling the knot unravel slightly. If he'd started feeling a migraine coming on he might have pulled over to the side of the road to wait until it had eased. But deep down she knew that she was only clutching at straws. Unless something was actually preventing him from calling her, Frank would have phoned by now. He always called when unexpected things cropped up, because in his business they often did and they always delayed him.

She went downstairs again and stacked her used crockery into the dishwasher, trying to keep a lid on her mounting fears. She put the uneaten slices of pizza on a plate and covered them with clingfilm, but she threw the unappetising-looking garlic bread in the bin. Then she went into the living room and looked out of the front window. The street, a narrow cul-de-sac, was practically deserted. Parked cars stood outside their owners' homes but none were being driven along the road. A couple walked hand in hand past the house, not noticing her eyes peeping through the slatted blinds.

There's a perfectly good explanation, she thought as she looked at her watch again. And I'm getting worked up over nothing. Frank is always going on at me about getting into a state about things. It's probably worse because of the time of the month. She rubbed her stomach which, since her bath, had settled into a dull ache. I'm hormonal at the moment. I'm not seeing things straight.

She frowned suddenly and ran upstairs again. She flung open the door of the double wardrobe. There were two suits missing, the one Frank had been wearing the day he'd left and a second which he always brought when he travelled in case he needed to change. Six shirts had gone from the top drawer of his dresser, as well as socks and a few ties. Nothing abnormal about that. He hadn't suddenly deserted her, hatched some plot about running off with a fancy woman from Cork!

Iona laughed shortly at her own silliness. Frank would never leave her. He loved her. She loved him. From the first moment she'd met him she'd known he was someone that she could love. She'd sensed it straight away.

Their meeting had been totally accidental. She was having a snatched lunch in a crowded city-centre bar, looking through leasing agreements as she ate her spicy chicken wrap and not taking any notice of the people milling around her. So she hadn't spotted Frank standing near the tiny circular table where she was sitting until he cleared his throat a couple of times and said, 'Excuse me.' She'd been taken aback by his good looks, his strong face, dark wiry hair and warm brown eyes. She could never quite explain it afterwards, how it was that she'd been instantly physically attracted by a man she didn't know, so that almost as soon as she'd looked at him she was wondering what he would be like in bed. She'd felt the colour rush into her normally pale cheeks.

'Anyone sitting here?' he asked. 'Would you mind?' He nodded at the vacant seat beside her.

'No, of course not,' she said, sweeping the leasing agreements into her briefcase.

'I'm sorry for interrupting you.' He put his overflowing ham and cheese baguette and a pint of sparkling water on the table in front of her. 'It's jam-packed in here today, isn't it?'

She nodded.

'Never usually so full,' he said as he hung his jacket on the back of the chair.

'I wouldn't know,' she said. 'I've never been here before.'

'I think it's the current in-place,' he told her. 'Apparently Bono or Daniel O'Donnell or someone comes here a lot.'

She giggled at the idea of the two very different singers and personalities enjoying the same pub.

'Or maybe I'm just making that up.' He grinned at her and his brown eyes twinkled.

Iona hadn't been able to go back to the single leasing agreement which she'd left on the table. She'd talked to Frank right through her lunchtime until she realised, with a squeak of dismay, that she would be late for her appointment.

'Shame,' said Frank. 'I was enjoying our conversation. Never mind, maybe I'll see you again sometime.'

She'd looked at him for a moment and then blurted out, 'Tomorrow night? I'm going to a terribly boring work dinner thing and I'm supposed to have someone to go with, only . . . well . . . I've split up with my boyfriend and I don't have someone I can call on . . . What d'you think?' She'd been horrified the moment the words were out of her mouth. For a start, she'd never asked a bloke on a date before. Secondly, it was probably the world's worst date. And thirdly, she didn't know exactly how old he was but it seemed to her that he was certainly older than her usual boyfriends. What the hell was she doing?

He'd considered it for a moment and she'd felt a wave of mortification swamp her. A complete stranger, she mentally hissed to herself, are you out of your mind! And then he'd said yes, why not, and it had been as though the sun had come out from behind the clouds.

She remembered every detail of the following evening together. He'd been formal and distant with her at the dinner itself but afterwards he told her that he'd make sure she got home safely and, sitting beside him in the taxi, she'd felt hot waves of passion gripping her. She couldn't understand it. He was just a bloke. And he seemed perfectly unaffected by her. She couldn't believe he didn't sense that she was imagining ripping his clothes off and making love to him right there and then on the back seat of the cab!

When they got to her house she asked him, as diffidently as she could, whether he'd like to come in for a coffee. She ignored the muffled guffaw of laughter from the cab driver and prayed that Frank would say yes. He hesitated, but in the end he agreed.

They never got around to the coffee. In fact they'd barely got inside the door when she turned to him and he kissed her and she felt herself grow weak with longing for him. And she'd led him upstairs, into her carefully feng shui-ed bedroom, where he'd made love to her like she'd never been made love to before. She'd known then that she was in love with him. She'd know then that she'd always be in love with him. She'd known then that one day she'd marry him.

Knowing that she'd marry him was one thing; making it happen hadn't been quite so straightforward. After a couple of dates Frank told her that he wasn't the marrying type.

'I didn't think I was either,' she told him one night after they'd made love twice, and the second time had been even more wonderful than the first. 'But it's different with you.' She realised what she'd said and felt a wave of embarrassment rush over her. That sentence had been a virtual proposal, she thought. And if anything could freak out a non-marrying man more than a virtual proposal she didn't know what it might be.

But he'd laughed and said that it felt a bit different with her too, that he'd never felt so totally caught up in someone else's life before.

'Maybe it's because you're a little older than me,' she continued with more confidence (she'd discovered that Frank was exactly ten years older), 'but you seem to know what it is I want, even before I do. You're good with women, Frank. I can't understand how you've escaped unscathed before now!'

He'd chuckled then and said something about the luck of the draw.

Once the subject of marriage had been brought up, Iona found that she kept going back to it. She tried not to; she didn't want to force Frank into anything and besides, getting married hadn't been something that was particularly high on her agenda before then. But she didn't want him to get away. He was perfect husband material.

Getting married in Barbados had been his idea. It would be different and special. And it wouldn't matter, he told her, that being an only child whose parents had died he didn't have any family to share the day with, and that hers didn't like him; they could have an idyllic wedding in an idyllic location.

'My family does like you,' she protested. 'Well, of course my parents haven't met you, but quite honestly Mum and Dad aren't the sort of people who interfere in our lives. They're happy once we're happy.'

'Your sister and her husband aren't very keen.'

'Oh, Lauren!' Iona dismissed her with a shrug. 'She thinks every man should be like Myles, boring old fart that he is. Anyway, she hardly knows you really.'

It didn't bother Iona that she'd been going out with Frank for nearly six months and that he'd only met Lauren twice, her brother Craig once and her parents not at all. He hadn't met Flora and David because they had retired to their tumbledown (but now renovated) finca near Javea, on the east coast of Spain, almost as soon as Craig left college.

And so they'd decided on the Barbadian wedding, which had been every bit as wonderful as Frank had promised her. A few weeks later they'd flown to Spain, where Flora and David had met them, and stayed at the finca for a couple of nights before heading on to spend a few days in Barcelona.

'I like him,' Flora had told her daughter as they sat on the veranda overlooking the orange grove (wearing jumpers because it was February and the evenings were cold). 'I'm delighted you've found someone you want to be with, even if he's a bit old.'

'Mum! He's not that much older than me.'

'More experienced, though.'

'I guess he's lived a bit.'

'You're right.' Flora hugged her. 'And you're happy, that's the main thing.'

Iona hugged her mother back. She liked the fact that personal happiness was at the top of her mother's list. But then it always had been. It was through Flora that Iona had developed her interest in feng shui and yoga and generally trying to keep a good balance between her body and her mind. She knew that she'd never be quite as into it all as her mother, who (Iona thought) could actually be quite dippy about New Age stuff from time to time; but she'd always been glad that Flora counted happiness as more important than money or careers or material goods. When the other girls at school had been worrying about exam results and college and what their parents would say if they didn't get the right number of points for the courses they wanted to do, Iona had felt happy and secure in the knowledge that Flora wouldn't consider it a disaster even if she flunked everything.

But she hadn't. She'd always been quite academic and had had a knack of doing well in exams even when she hadn't studied as much as she might have. A good technique, one of the teachers had once told her, and Iona had agreed. Also, she had a good short-term memory and was brilliant at last-minute revision.

Her academic success, plus the fact that she was good at games, meant that she didn't score quite so highly on the dating front. In fact Iona had only gone out with two boys during her entire time at school and she hadn't actually liked either of them. Even afterwards, when she'd started work and expanded her social life dramatically, she still wasn't very successful with men. She was good with them as work colleagues and good with them over a pint or watching football or rugby in the pub, but not good with them as a girlfriend.

Until she met Frank. And he changed everything.

Now she looked at her watch again. There was something badly wrong and it wasn't just her freaking out over something stupid. She had to face facts. He should be home by now and he hadn't called, either because he didn't want to or because he wasn't able to. And regardless of the reason for his silence, it had to be bad news for her.

She took a deep breath, picked up the phone and dialled her sister's number.

'Hello?'

She grimaced. Her brother-in-law, Myles Leary, had picked it up. Iona was never really sure why it was that she and Myles didn't get on, but the fact was that they'd never hit it off. And Myles didn't like Frank either – she'd heard him once refer to him as a smarmy git.

'Hi, Myles,' she said as lightly as she could. 'Is Lauren around?'

'She's out,' replied Myles. 'It's her line-dancing night tonight.'

'Oh.'

'Will I tell her you called?'

'I – yes – yes . . . well, listen, Myles . . .' She couldn't believe she was going to confide in her brother-in-law, but now that she was talking to someone she felt as though she had to share her worry. 'It's probably nothing, but Frank is late home and I can't contact him. I'm a bit concerned.'

She was sure that she heard a knowing snort at the other end of the line.

'He's probably stopped off somewhere for a quick pint and switched off his phone,' said Myles.

'Maybe that's the sort of thing you do,' retorted Iona, 'but Frank isn't like that.'

'All men are like that given half the chance,' said Myles drily. 'It's not that late, Iona. Don't panic.'

'It's after ten,' she said. 'And he was due home by seven or eight.'

'Where was he?'

She explained about the business trip and about checking the news to see if there had been any accidents on the Cork–Dublin road.

'And there haven't, so there's no need to worry. Look, something probably happened to delay or distract him and for some reason he can't call you. There's no reason to get hysterical over it.'

'I'm not hysterical,' she said. 'Just anxious.'

'I'll talk to Lauren when she gets home,' said Myles. 'Let me know if he shows up before then.'

'OK.' She replaced the receiver feeling, as she always did after talking to Myles, somehow silly and foolish. She didn't care what he thought, though. Frank would have phoned her. He always phoned her. That was the way their lives together worked. And now, because he hadn't, she was scared that for the first time in their relationship it wasn't working. And she didn't want it not to work.

Chapter 7

Sally had almost finished unloading the dishwasher when the doorbell rang. She swore softly under her breath and put the last of the crockery on the kitchen table. She knew it was probably one of Jenna's friends looking for her to come out, but that meant the usual battle about how late Jenna could stay out and where she could go and who she was going to be with. Tonight, still anxious and worried about her unexpected pregnancy, Sally didn't have the energy to argue with her daughter. It wasn't that she was a particularly strict parent. On weekend nights, like tonight, she allowed Jenna to stay out until 12.30 a.m. But she still insisted on knowing who she was with and where she was going, and Jenna often either didn't want to or couldn't give her the information. Jenna's view was that it didn't make any difference as long she was home on time, and she was always home on time – even, she'd add, on weekdays, when a ridiculous 10 p.m. curfew was in place, a time which nobody else had to stick to. Sometimes Sally wavered over the curfew but she never gave in. All the same, it's so hard to get the balance right, she thought despairingly. How the hell do other mothers manage it?

She listened as Jenna thumped down the stairs and opened the door. She waited for a call of 'Going out, back later,' which would signal the start of the great 'Where are you going?' debate, but instead there was a low murmuring of voices and then the kitchen door was pushed open. Jenna walked in, followed by a tall, serious-faced woman dressed in a neat fawn suit, her frizzy red hair clipped back from her head, accompanied by a very young-looking male garda. Sally looked from them to Jenna anxiously. Despite her best efforts, had her daughter got into trouble of some sort to bring the police to her door? God, she thought, Frank will totally freak out if Jenna has got into trouble with the police.

'Hi, Mrs Harper.' The woman smiled at her but Sally could see that it was a professional smile. 'My name is Detective Sergeant Siobhán Farrell. I'm with Bray garda station. This is my colleague, Cathal.'

'Yes?' Sally looked at them, her anxiety level increasing.

'We've had a call from our colleagues in Ardallen,' said Siobhán. 'There's been an incident there where—'

'We don't know anyone in Ardallen,' Sally interrupted her. 'Whatever it's about, I think you have the wrong people.'

'. . . where part of a building collapsed causing some injury,' continued Siobhán evenly. 'At the moment there are no fatalities but we do have a serious injury and we're trying to establish the identity of the person concerned.'

Sally saw a sudden flash of sympathy in the other woman's eyes as she read out a car registration. 'It's registered to a Mr Frank Harper, of this address,' said Siobhán. 'We think it's possible that your husband was injured in the incident. He's in the local hospital closest to Ardallen and we think you should probably go to see him.'

'But . . . but . . .' Sally looked at her in bewilderment. 'Frank is away at the moment. He's in the south-west. Cork and Kerry. He's not coming back until tomorrow. There's no reason for him to be in Ardallen. That's only an hour or so away.'

'Maybe he changed his mind,' said Siobhán. 'The local gardai checked out his mobile phone. Again, it was registered to this address. And the home phone number in the mobile's address book matched this phone number.'

'Mum?' Jenna, who'd been standing beside the kitchen table, suddenly slumped on to a chair.

'Are you all right?' asked Cathal Rothery. 'Would you like a drink of water?'

Without waiting for her to answer, he walked to the sink, took the single glass that was on the drainer, filled it and handed it to her. Jenna sipped it even though she felt sick.

'Are you telling me . . .' Sally was still finding it hard to put her thoughts into words, 'that my husband is hurt? He can't be! He's wouldn't have any reason to be in an unstable building. He's a businessman. He installs commercial lighting equipment and displays. Well, he doesn't usually install them himself, he has people to do that. He organises it. He sells the systems. But if he occasionally has to visit a site he always wears a safety helmet. He's very safety-conscious. So he can't be hurt.'

'I don't have the full details,' said Siobhán. 'But it appears that he stopped at a pub and it was while he was there that the building beside it collapsed. He was trapped under the rubble.'

'But . . . but Frank doesn't drink and drive!' cried Sally. 'I've been married to him for eighteen years and he's never once touched alcohol if he was getting behind the wheel of the car. And there's no way he'd stop somewhere like Ardallen for a drink – he'd come home first, definitely. But he wasn't meant to be home tonight. He told me he was staying in Cork!'

'Like Siobhán says, maybe he changed his plans.' Cathal's voice was soft. 'Perhaps he was going to surprise you by being home early. He could have stopped for any number of reasons.'

'Well . . . yes . . . maybe . . . but . . .' Sally's thoughts were whirling around her head but she couldn't seem to get them into any order. 'But he just doesn't *do* that. He's very organised. And he *called* me to say that he wasn't coming home. He only made that decision this afternoon. So he wouldn't have changed his mind.'

'Why don't you ring his phone, Mum?' said Jenna anxiously. 'I bet he'll answer it.'

'My colleagues have his phone,' said Cathal quickly. 'I really think that the best thing for you to do, Mrs Harper, is to get to Ardallen tonight. Is there anyone who can drive you?'

'I . . . I don't know.' Sally gripped the edge of the dishwasher. Her breath was coming quickly and she felt faint.

Cathal pulled out a chair and helped her to sit down.

'A family member, perhaps?' suggested Siobhán. 'A brother or sister close by?'

'Mum doesn't have any brothers or sisters,' said Jenna. 'We're it.'

'Perhaps your dad has someone?'

'No.' Jenna looked at them blankly. 'That's the whole thing. It's just us. Me and Mum and Dad.'

'We can arrange for you to get to the hospital,' said Siobhán quickly. 'Don't worry about it.'

'Maybe Denise could bring me . . .' Sally could hear herself speaking but the words sounded like they were coming from somebody else. She shot an anxious look at Siobhán. 'She works with me. And she's a friend.

Only she'd have to come from Sutton and it's a long way away, right across town and . . . 'Her head snapped up and she looked straight into Siobhán's blue eyes. 'How bad is it? How urgent? How critical?'

'Well, we think it would be a good idea for you to get to the hospital,' said Siobhán. 'I don't have a lot of information right now, Mrs Harper, but he was quite seriously injured.'

'Might he die?' Jenna's words came out as a gasp.

'It would be best if we went now,' said Cathal. 'I can drive you.' He glanced at Siobhán, who nodded.

'I'll get my jacket,' said Sally blankly.

'Whatever you need,' said Cathal.

The two garda exchanged looks as Jenna and Sally went to get their coats.

'Sometimes I hate this job,' said Siobhán.

Cathal nodded. They waited in silence until Jenna and Sally returned.

'I'm going to swing back past the station to let Siobhán out,' said Cathal as they walked out to the car, 'but then I'll drive you straight there – OK, Mrs Harper?'

Sally nodded. She got into the back seat, Jenna clambering in after her. As the car pulled away from the house she noticed the twitching curtain at Noeleen Sharp's house directly across the road. Neighbourhood Watch had its advantages and disadvantages. Sally knew that there would be talk on the road about her and Jenna getting into a garda car, people speculating on what Noeleen might tell them. Not that it really mattered. What mattered was that Frank was all right.

She felt Jenna's hand slide across the back seat and grasp her own as the blue light on the top of the car began to flash. She squeezed it in return, looking quickly towards her daughter, who was actually facing the other direction, peering out of the window as they sped down the road to the garda station. They stopped briefly to let Siobhán out. She smiled at them and wished them good luck. Then the car sped away again.

They were on the N11 now, hurtling along the road towards Arklow and Ardallen. He would have come this way if he was coming home, thought Sally. But why would he be on his way home tonight when he'd told her that he wouldn't be leaving Cork until the morning? It didn't make sense to her. Frank was always such an organised person, there was no way he'd suddenly change his mind about coming home. And never to surprise her. She wasn't a woman who particularly liked surprises and he knew better than to say one thing and do another. So he couldn't really be the person who'd been caught under the rubble of the collapsed building. He was probably in Cork, just like he was supposed to be, and the whole thing was a terrible mix-up.

The car sped over a dip in the road and her stomach somersaulted. She swallowed quickly, choking back the nausea. She'd felt OK since her bout of morning sickness earlier, but the sudden sinking feeling now reminded her of the unexpected pregnancy, which already seemed a distant, unlikely event. I'm not really pregnant, she thought. And Frank's not really hurt. And this is, really, a big, big mistake.

She squeezed Jenna's hand again as the car turned in to the hospital and stopped directly in front of the main door.

Cathal Rothery killed the engine, got out and opened the door for Sally, who, now that they were here, felt quite unable to get out of the car herself. She took Cathal's extended hand and then turned to help Jenna out. They all went up the steps together.

'Mrs Harper and her daughter,' said Cathal to the receptionist. 'The man who was brought in earlier. Building accident.'

'Oh yes!'

The sudden flash of sympathy in the woman's eyes was unmistakable. Sally moistened her lips with the tip of her tongue. It wasn't Frank. It just wasn't.

The receptionist spoke into a mike and a couple of minutes later a young doctor arrived. He smiled at them but, like Siobhán Farrell's smile earlier, it was professional.

'Your husband is stable,' he told Sally. 'He has a number of injuries – ribs, shoulder and legs as well as cuts and contusions. And he suffered a blow to the head.'

'It's not my husband.' Sally was quite definite. 'Frank's away. It can't be him. He's not injured and there's nothing wrong with him.'

'Shall we go down?' The doctor indicated the corridor.

Sally and Jenna, accompanied by Cathal, followed him. He stopped outside the window of a small room. Mother and daughter looked at the bruised and battered figure in the bed, surrounded by drips and tubes, a nurse sitting beside him.

'Oh, Mum,' said Jenna, and fainted.

* * *

Iona had switched off the television and was staring at the blank screen when the phone rang. She jumped on it before seeing the caller ID and her voice was breathless and anxious.

'Hello?'

'It's me.'

'Oh.' The anticipation left her as she recognised her sister's voice.

'Is he home yet?'

'No.'

'Are you still worried?'

'Of course I'm still worried!' snapped Iona. 'It's nearly eleven. He wouldn't do this to me, Lauren, you know he wouldn't. He'd call if something had happened.'

'And you've called him?'

'Give me a break!' Iona could feel her anxiety level rising. 'Yes, I bloody called him. I've called him loads of times but I keep getting his bloody message-minder.'

'Look, if something had happened to him you'd have heard by now,' said Lauren comfortingly. 'That's the thing about life these days. Communication is instant. They'd have found out who you were and called you.'

'Not if he was kidnapped,' said Iona.

'Kidnapped?'

'Well, why not?' she said, articulating her most recent thoughts about the situation. 'He's a successful businessman, more or less. Maybe there's something weird—'

'Get a grip, Iona,' said Lauren. She paused for a moment. 'Is he into anything dodgy? You know, businesswise?'

'No!' cried Iona. 'He isn't. Nothing. He's just an ordinary bloke.'

'So why would anyone kidnap him?'

'I don't know!' But, Iona told herself, Frank being kidnapped made a whole heap more sense to her than Frank leaving her of his own accord.

'Do you want me to come round?' asked Lauren.

Iona wiped at her eyes. There was nothing Lauren could do. But she didn't want to be on her own.

'Yes,' she said eventually.

'OK I'll be there in twenty minutes. But if the fucker comes home, ring me on my mobile. I don't want to arrive just as you two are having the biggest bust-up of your married life.'

'Sure,' said Iona wearily.

'I hope you do have to ring me,' said Lauren gently. 'And I bet there's some perfectly rational explanation.'

'I bet,' said Iona, even though she couldn't think what it could possibly be.

She paced around the tiny living room, willing him to come home, squeezing her eyes tightly closed and visualising his car pulling up in front of the house. But when she finally did hear an engine she knew that it wasn't Frank's car. The sound of the door as it closed wasn't the familiar thunk she was used to either. The doorbell rang.

'Hi,' said Lauren.

'Hello.'

'So, no sign of him?'

Iona shook her head. Lauren walked into the house and took off her short fake-fur jacket, draping it over the back of the black leather sofa.

'Would you like some tea?' asked Iona.

'I'll make it.'

'No,' Iona told her sister. 'I have to do something. You sit down. Maybe by the time I've brewed it up he'll be back.' She walked rapidly into the kitchen.

Where are you? she muttered under her breath. Where in God's name are you, and what the hell are you doing and why are you putting me through this?

When she came back into the living room with the tea she saw that Lauren had switched on the TV but had left the sound mute.

'I was looking for the late news,' said Lauren. 'But I think we missed it.'

'I checked the internet again,' Iona said. 'There was nothing new on it.'

'Have you rung hospitals?'

Iona looked at her unhappily. 'I tried. But they wanted to know when he'd been admitted. I said I didn't know, that I thought he might have been in an accident. They told me to call the police, that they couldn't give out information to me.'

'And did you?'

Iona shook her head. 'I was afraid.'

'Maybe you should.'

'Where should I call?'

'What's your local station?'

Iona shrugged. 'I'm not sure. Kevin Street, I think.'

Lauren picked up the telephone directory and looked up the number. 'Will I?'

Iona took a deep breath. 'I suppose you'd better.'

Kevin Street was a busy station, but Garda Keith Carew answered the phone quickly.

'Missing person?' he said. 'How long has he been missing?'

'Well, just tonight,' said Lauren. 'But he's a really punctual person normally and he's not answering his phone. It's totally out of character for him and so we were wondering if he might have been in an accident.'

'Do you have a car reg?' asked Keith.

'What's the reg?' Lauren turned to Iona, who told her. She repeated it to Keith, who tapped the details into the computer. Rather surprisingly, because the system was cumbersome and overloaded, information flashed up almost immediately. He frowned.

'Would you repeat that?'

Lauren repeated the registration.

'And the missing person's name is?'

'Frank Harper,' said Lauren.

'Am I speaking to Mrs Harper?'

'No,' said Lauren. 'I'm her sister, Lauren Brannock.'

'And her address is?'

Lauren felt herself grow tense as she reeled off Iona's address. She'd expected the guard to dismiss her but he seemed to be taking her seriously. And now she was beginning to feel a knot of worry on her sister's behalf.

Keith continued to check the information he'd received as Lauren held the line. There was a Frank Harper listed as an accident victim, although in this case due to a building collapse. But he'd been identified through his mobile phone and a car registration. The car was registered to an address in Bray. Yet the number was exactly the same.

'I'm going to make some enquiries,' he told Lauren. 'I'll get back to you. You're at the address in the Liberties now?'

'Yes,' she said.

'I'll be back to you as soon as possible,' said Keith.

He hung up and stared at the computer screen for a couple of seconds. Normally he wouldn't have bothered with Lauren's enquiry straight away. Frank Harper hadn't been missing for long enough, and in his experience most blokes who didn't come home on time had simply gone on the piss with their mates and were afraid to call to say where they were in case they got an earful from their wives. They preferred to roll home out of their tree with drink and suffer the consequences then, rather than have their night's drinking ruined by an ear-bashing. But there was something odd about this. He tapped his teeth with his pen for a couple of seconds. Then he picked up the phone.

'Well?' demanded Iona.

'He's checking it out. He's going to get back to us.'

'But there wasn't anything he knew about?'

Lauren shook her head. 'He's making enquiries.'

Iona swallowed hard. 'That sounds terribly official. I don't need it to be official. I just want to know what's happened to him.

Lauren said nothing.

'Something must have happened. Something terrible. He'd never leave me worrying like this—' Suddenly Iona burst into a fit of crying while Lauren put her arms around her and hugged her as tightly as she could.

At the hospital, Jenna and Sally were drinking the hot, sweet tea provided by the staff after Jenna's faint. A nurse sat in the small room with them.

'Is he going to die?' Jenna looked up at her mother. 'Is Dad going to die?'

Sally glanced at the nurse and looked into her daughter's eyes. 'I don't know,' she said.

'You didn't think it would be him,' said Jenna accusingly. 'You were sure.'

'It shouldn't be him,' Sally said tightly. 'He shouldn't be here.' She picked at the waxed cup of tea. 'He said he was late and he had another meeting and he wouldn't be home till tomorrow. So he shouldn't have been on the Ardallen road.'

'Maybe he finished early after all and decided to come home.' A sob caught in Jenna's throat. 'He didn't want to be away from us and so he rushed back anyway.'

Sally said nothing. She'd thought the same, wondered whether Frank had guessed at her irritation over all the days and nights he spent away from them, wondered whether that had made him decide to come home unexpectedly, wondering if it was all her fault.

The young doctor came back into the room.

'We're moving your husband now, Mrs Harper,' he said. 'An ambulance will take him to Dublin. They'll be better able to look after him at one of the major hospitals.'

Sally nodded. 'Can both of us go with him?'

'I don't know,' said the doctor. 'I'll ask the ambulance crew.'

'Why don't you and Jenna wait in reception, Sally?' suggested the nurse.

Sally nodded again. She wasn't used to doing what people told her all the time. But right now she didn't seem to have any choice.

Chapter 8

Siobhán hadn't exactly forgotten about Sally and Jenna Harper when she went back to Bray but she had immersed herself in work again, completing the money-laundering file and opening another, so that when she answered the phone to Keith Carew from Kevin Street garda station she wasn't thinking about car registrations and building collapses, but about her imminent court appearance with regard to a domestic abuse case. She hated going to court and was always afraid that she would sound uncertain about her evidence simply because she was nervous about speaking in public. So when the phone rang she was going through her notes again in order to get everything exactly right. Now, though, she listened with increasing concern as Kevin talked, and the court case was instantly pushed to the back of her mind.

'So, let me get this straight,' she said when he'd finished. 'There's a woman on the phone saying that she's Iona Harper's sister and that Iona's husband is missing. And the car reg matches that of the Frank Harper in the Ardallen incident. Only *that* Frank Harper has already been identified by Sally Harper. I know this because I was at Sally Harper's house earlier and one of my guys drove Mrs Harper and her daughter to the hospital.'

'Yeah, well . . .' Kevin sighed. 'This other woman seemed very definite about it.'

'Two Mrs Harpers?' Siobhán sounded sceptical. 'Don't you think that's just plain crazy?'

'Hell, Siobhán, you know that in this job everything's crazy,' said Kevin. 'God knows what the true situation is, but the current bottom line appears to be that we have a seriously injured man and two women who seem to be connected to him. One is definitely his wife. The other . . .'

She sighed. 'Let me call the Ardallen guys.'

'Great,' said Kevin. 'Then let us know what to do.'

Siobhán hung up and then spoke to Tim Shanahan, who had, theoretically at least, finished his shift. He whistled when she told him the situation.

'My guys are at the hospital with the Harpers now,' he told her. 'I'll contact them, see what's going on. Then I'll get back to you.'

Siobhán hung up again. So much of police work was waiting for people to come back to you. And so much of it was not really liking what they told you when they did.

Tim called her back within ten minutes.

'We have a problem,' he said. 'The Harpers are on their way to Dublin with Frank. They left without his stuff, though. Including a mobile phone.'

'You've already double-checked his identity from his mobile phone,' said Siobhán.

'A different mobile phone,' said Tim grimly. 'This one was in his pocket and, amazingly, wasn't damaged. When we switched it on, we found it had a different home number, even though it's also registered to Mr Frank Harper. It's the number of the other woman claiming to be Mrs Harper.'

'You've got to be kidding me.'

'Nope,' said Tim. 'We've got one injured man with, apparently, two wives.'

'Holy shit,' said Siobhán.

'He's from Bray,' Tim said. 'It's probably your case.'

'I don't want a mess like this,' protested Siobhán. 'I'm really busy.' Tim said nothing and eventually she groaned softly. 'Oh, all right. I'll go and see the second Mrs Harper. But I can't see this being anything but a flippin' disaster for everyone.'

'Me neither.' Tim's words were heartfelt. And he was very glad that the issue of the injured man's wives was out of his hands.

It took Siobhán nearly forty-five minutes to reach Iona's tiny house in the Liberties. She stood outside the door for a moment, gathering her thoughts. This Mrs Harper might just be calling herself by the man's name, she reminded herself, and might not be married at all. Or maybe that was the situation with the first Mrs Harper. After all, they had no idea who was who exactly. But no matter what the tangled relationship might turn out to be, the immediate issue was that the man Iona Harper was living with was still the man who'd been seriously injured in the Ardallen building collapse, and that she was going to have to break the news to her. She sighed deeply and rang the bell.

The door opened. An attractive woman with auburn hair cascading around her shoulders, and dark, soulful eyes answered the door.

'Mrs Harper?' asked Siobhán, wishing that she didn't always feel so inadequate when faced with really beautiful women.

Lauren shook her head. 'That's my sister, Iona. I'm Lauren Brannock. My sister is Iona Brannock but she's married to Frank Harper.'

'I'm Detective Sergeant Siobhán Farrell from Bray garda station,' Siobhán told her. 'I'm here about your sister's call regarding a missing person.'

'I called you,' said Lauren. 'At least, I called Kevin Street. Why the hell have they sent someone all the way from Bray? That seems incredibly inefficient when they're only round the corner! My sister is inside.'

'Can I come in?'

Lauren hesitated. 'Is everything all right?'

'Can I come in?' repeated Siobhán.

Lauren stood back and motioned her into the room. Iona looked up as she entered. Her huge dark eyes were now ringed with red and her normally pale, smooth cheeks were roughened by rubbing with a tissue.

'Mrs Harper?' said Siobhán.

She nodded. 'But I call myself by my own name.' She repeated what Lauren had told her. 'Iona Brannock.'

Siobhán nodded. She wished Cathal Rothery was with her for support. She took a deep breath and began to speak. 'You reported your husband missing earlier,' she said. 'And you feared he might have been in an accident. You gave my colleagues the registration of his car and we've checked it out.'

Iona suddenly felt light-headed. She knew by the tone of the other woman's voice that they'd found something out. And she knew it wasn't good.

'The thing is, Iona,' said Siobhán, 'we had a report of a man injured in a building collapse today.'

Iona nodded. 'Ardallen. It was on the internet. It talked about someone being injured but that absolutely couldn't have been Frank. He had no reason to be in Ardallen. It's not on his route home.'

'Maybe not,' said Siobhán. 'When this man was taken to hospital to be treated he was actually identified by someone else. They identified him as a Mr Frank Harper.'

'It can't be my Frank,' protested Iona. 'He wouldn't even know anyone in Ardallen. That's near Bray, isn't it? We don't have any friends in Bray.'

'Since then, though,' continued Siobhán, 'and because we saw a few anomalies on the system, we've looked at this a little bit more closely. He was identified by his wife, Mrs Sally Harper. The car registration that Mrs Harper agreed was theirs is the same one you gave my colleague tonight. It also seems that Mr Harper had a mobile phone with him that has your number as his home number.'

Iona stared at her uncomprehendingly. 'So what are you telling me?'

'Well, Mrs Harper – Ms Brannock – it looks awfully like you and another woman are both talking about the same man.'

This time it was Lauren who spoke. 'But that doesn't make sense,' she protested. 'Frank and Iona are married. They've been married for the last four years.'

'And from what we found out earlier,' said Siobhán evenly, 'the other woman who calls herself Mrs Harper has been married to him for eighteen years.'

This time it was Iona who fainted.

When she came to, she was lying on the sofa. Lauren was beside her while Siobhán Farrell stood motionless behind them.

'I feel sick,' said Iona.

'Have a sip.' Lauren held a tumbler of water to her sister's lips. Iona sipped it cautiously then began to sit up.

'Don't,' said Lauren. 'Wait for a minute or two. You've had a shock.'

Iona tried to pin down the flurry of thoughts that were chasing around in her head. She tried to focus on the fact that Frank – her Frank, no matter what anyone else was trying to imply – was seriously injured. She should be with him. He'd want her there. She struggled to sit up again.

'I need to get to the hospital,' she told Lauren. Her sister looked uncomfortably at Siobhán, who shrugged helplessly. 'Look, I know you all think there's something weird going on here. So do I. But the point is, I need to see Frank. If he's hurt, I need to be there.'

'The thing is, Iona,' said Siobhán gently, 'the other woman is there at the moment.'

'I don't give a toss whether she's there or not!' snapped Iona. 'She's made some kind of mistake. She's obviously a complete crackpot. I want to go and I want to go now.'

'We can't stop you, of course,' said Siobhán.

'Of course you can't.' Iona got unsteadily to her feet. 'Lauren, you'll drive me, won't you?'

'Sure.'

'We'll have to get in touch with you again, Ms Brannock,' said Siobhán. 'To sort this situation out.'

'I'll sort it out when I get to the hospital.' Iona's voice was getting stronger and grimmer by the second. 'I'll fix this woman, whoever she is. I'm going to get dressed.' She walked out of the room and up the stairs.

Lauren looked uneasily at Siobhán. 'What's the story really?' she asked urgently.

'We're honestly not sure,' Siobhán replied. 'This other woman says she's married to Frank Harper. Your sister says so too. Both of them can't be right. Maybe it's a case of two different men and it's just a horrendous mix-up. It could be one of life's extraordinary coincidences.' But Siobhán's expression indicated that she clearly didn't believe in coincidences.

'None of this makes sense,' Lauren told her. 'Iona and Frank were married in a perfectly legal ceremony. I've seen the video! There was a pastor and witnesses and everything. It was lovely!'

'There's no point in everyone getting into a state until we work out the exact situation,' said Siobhán comfortingly. 'Best thing is to get your sister to the hospital . . . but try and keep her out of the way of the other Mrs Harper.'

'Easier said than done, don't you think?' muttered Lauren as Iona came back into the room.

Lauren rang Myles as they drove to the hospital, merely telling him that it looked like Frank had been injured in an accident and they were off to see what the story was. Meanwhile Iona sat silently in the car, staring unseeingly out through the windscreen.

The drive seemed to take for ever and at the same time be over in an instant. Iona's heart was hammering in her chest as they walked into the hospital and spoke to the man behind the reception desk.

'Oh yes,' he said as he consulted the screen in front of him. 'Mr Harper is in surgery at the moment. You can wait . . .' He hesitated. 'Actually, I need to speak to the sister in charge of that area.'

'Why?' demanded Iona. 'I need to see him right now.'

'You can't see him immediately,' said the receptionist. 'As I said, he's in surgery.'

'Well, where's that other woman?' asked Iona. 'The one pretending to be me? Seems to me I don't see anyone else hanging round here waiting. Have you let her in to see him? You know she's crazy, don't you? You know you shouldn't let her anywhere near him?'

'Io, please,' said Lauren. 'Let him call whoever's in charge.'

Iona glared at Lauren and then shrugged. But while the receptionist dialled a number, she suddenly ran away from the desk and bounded up a nearby flight of stairs.

'Oh, shit!' Lauren looked after Iona's fleeing figure. 'Io – come back!' She glanced at the receptionist, who looked flabbergasted by the turn of events. 'Shit,' said Lauren again. She took off her high-heeled shoes and ran after her sister. There was no sign of her on the first floor. Then she heard Iona's voice shouting Frank's name over and over.

She chased after the sound even as doors were opened and nurses appeared in the corridors. She ran up and down stairs so that she lost track completely of where she was. Finally she caught up with Iona, who was being restrained by a security guard. She'd found the waiting area. And the other Mrs Harper.

Lauren's first thought was that Sally Harper looked old. Much, much older than Iona, although that might have been because the other woman was unnaturally pale, with dark smudges beneath her eyes. Her chestnut and gold hair was escaping from an ageing plait and her entire body seemed to be collapsing in on itself. A much younger girl stood beside Sally, quite obviously her daughter. She too was deathly white.

'This is the woman who identified Frank!' cried Iona. 'She's obviously completely off her head!'

Sally looked at Iona in total bewilderment.

'I've no idea who you are or what you're talking about,' she said, her voice shaking. 'I'm here because my husband was involved in a major accident and—'

'*Your* husband!' Iona interupted her. '*Your* husband! You stupid, stupid woman, you've got it all wrong – you're talking about *my* husband.'

Sally shook her head.

'Don't you think I wish that I was?' she said tautly. 'Someone's made a terrible mix-up here and I'm sorry that you're in the middle of it, but I know my own husband . . .' Her voice broke, 'even in the state he's in now.'

'You're on the wrong end of the mix-up,' Iona told her. 'I know that because the police came and told me that Frank was involved in an accident and he was brought here and—'

'Frank?' Sally stared at her.

'My husband,' said Iona.

'It's a mix-up with names,' said Sally. 'It has to be. And like I said, I'm sorry that you're here and your husband has been in an accident, but I know it's my Frank because I've seen him.'

Iona clenched and unclenched her fists in frustration.

'You're wrong,' she said. 'I don't know why you're so insistent, but you're wrong.'

'My mum knows my dad,' said Jenna anxiously. 'And so do I. And I don't know why you're here talking rubbish while he . . .' She swallowed frantically. 'You're a horrible, horrible woman to do this.'

Iona glanced swiftly at the teenage girl and took a deep breath before turning back to Sally.

'You think I want to be here?' she demanded. 'I was at home waiting for him but he didn't show up and he's been in an accident and I know, I just know it's him.'

'But you haven't actually seen him yet,' said Jenna tightly. She held on to her mother's arm. 'We have. I don't know who you are, but you've some nerve coming here and upsetting me and my mum when my dad is so sick.'

'I'll tell you who I am,' said Iona heatedly. 'I'm Iona Harper. I'm married to Frank Harper. And I'm here to see him.'

The two women and the young girl stared wordlessly at each other.

They were still staring at each other when a doctor arrived and introduced himself as John Carroll.

'I believe there's a certain amount of confusion about Mr Harper's identity,' he said.

'No there isn't,' snapped both Iona and Sally at the same time.

'I'm afraid there is.' Dr Carroll looked at them sternly. 'But screaming and shouting in my hospital won't help matters. You're distressing yourselves and my patients as well as my staff.'

The rage and shock suddenly left Iona's body. She swayed slightly and the doctor took her by the arm.

'Sit down,' he said gently.

Iona sank into a seat and started to shake.

'I can't breathe,' she said suddenly. 'I can't . . . I can't . . .'

A nurse who was standing nearby disappeared for a moment and returned with a white paper bag which she handed to Iona.

'Breathe into this,' she said. 'Take your time. You're fine. You are really.'

Lauren watched anxiously as Iona put the bag over her nose and mouth. Sally and Jenna watched too.

'Attention-seeker,' muttered Jenna.

Sally squeezed her daughter's arm.

'Dad wouldn't have anything to do with someone like her,' whispered Jenna. 'You know how he is about people getting dramatic about things. He hates it.'

'I know,' said Sally. She pulled her coat more tightly around her.

'She's lying,' Jenna said aloud.

'I wish I was.' Iona lifted her head from the paper bag and looked at Sally and Jenna.

'You haven't even seen him yet.' Sally repeated Jenna's words of earlier. 'You've come in here and created a great big fuss and scared me and my daughter, who, I have to remind you, is just a teenager – and you haven't even seen him.'

'Nobody can see him right now,' said the doctor. 'He's in surgery and likely to be there for some time yet.'

'When he comes out . . . can I see him then?' asked Iona.

'Of course,' said the doctor.

Sally felt herself grow tense. She didn't want this other woman sitting in the hospital at the same time as her, waiting for news of Frank. She had no right to be here, intruding on their worry and their grief. And Jenna was right. Frank wouldn't be interested in a drama queen like her. He liked his women to be calm and measured, like her. With a bit of spark in the bedroom, of course. But not this public hysteria, this over-the-top sobbing and breathlessness.

'You don't have to look at me like that,' said Iona.

'Like what?'

'Something the cat dragged in,' Iona told her. 'You have no right to sit there and look down on me.'

'I'm trying not to look at you at all.'

Sally closed her eyes. Despite her certainty that Frank wouldn't be interested in Iona, the fact was that the woman was here. And, thought Sally as she peeped through her lashes, she wasn't an unattractive woman either. Not pretty, of course, but she could see why some men might find her worth the effort. What she couldn't see was the possibility of any relationship between her and Frank. But what if there was? Obviously she couldn't possibly be telling the truth about being married to him, but maybe there was something . . . There couldn't be, though. There just couldn't be. Frank was a faithful man. She knew that.

'I realise this is distressing for everyone.' Hearing Lauren's voice made Sally open her eyes properly again. 'And I do understand how you feel, Mrs Harper—'

'*I'm* Mrs Harper,' said Iona. 'You know that, Lauren.'

Jenna reached out and opened her mother's handbag.

'Yeah, well, what's this then?' she demanded as she produced Sally's driver's licence and handed it to Iona.

She blinked at it a number of times as she read the description of Sally Harper. Then she opened her own bag and took out her licence, which she handed to Sally.

'Iona Brannock is what this says.' Sally refolded it and put it in its plastic cover. 'It means nothing.'

'That's my maiden name.'

'Still don't see anything to do with Harper on it.' Jenna sounded triumphant.

'My sister *did* marry a man called Frank Harper,' said Lauren. 'I know you think that she's wrong about the man here tonight, but she's telling you the truth about that.'

'Look,' Sally told her, 'the police came and told me about the accident.

I drove to the hospital with them before they transferred Frank here. I recognised my own husband, for heaven's sake.' She turned to Iona. 'I'm really sorry if you've been misled, but I can honestly tell you that the man in surgery is Frank Harper and he's my husband. And you should be relieved because it's my husband who's in there on life support, and wherever the hell yours is he's better off than that! Frank is seriously, seriously injured and I have to stand here and listen to your drivel when I should be giving him my support . . .' Her voice broke and she rubbed her eyes with the back of her hand.

'And I'd give anything for you to be right!' cried Iona. 'But if it's not my Frank, then how come he has a mobile phone with my number on it and how come I gave the police the registration of the car he was driving? And how come I'm here at all?'

'Are you his . . . mistress?' Sally could feel herself growing light-headed again. 'Are you having an affair with him? Is that it?'

'Don't be so bloody silly!' cried Iona. 'D'you really think I'd come haring out here if I was having an affair with him? I'm not. I'm married to him. I married him four years ago in Barbados and it was the happiest day of our lives.'

'This isn't getting us anywhere.'

John Carroll was tired. He really didn't want to have to cope with this scene but he had no alternative. 'I'm told that Mr Harper will be out of surgery in about half an hour or so. At that point I will take you' – he turned to Iona – 'to see him. You won't be able to go into the room but you can see him through a window.'

'Why?' demanded Sally. 'I've already seen him. It's my Frank.'

'Please, Mrs Harper,' said John evenly. 'There's clearly some kind of mix-up here. Don't you think the best thing is to sort it out rather than have everyone getting more and more uptight about things?'

'There's no mix-up except in this woman's head,' said Sally firmly. 'But if it makes you happy, Jenna and I will wait and find out exactly what her problem is. Because she has the problem, not us.'

'No I fucking don't,' snapped Iona.

'Please,' said John. 'Can't you just be calm until we sort everything out? Believe me, the hospital wants things clarified just as much as you do. Can I get you all some tea, perhaps?'

'I'd love a cup of tea,' said Lauren feelingly.

When the tea arrived, laced with sugar, Iona wrapped her hands around one of the waxed cups and sipped the scalding, too-sweet liquid. It burned the roof of her mouth and the tip of her tongue, but she didn't care. She stared unseeingly in front of her as she tried to figure out what the hell was going on. How was it that only this morning the worst thing that could have happened in her life was that she wasn't pregnant? And now, less than twenty-four hours later, everything had been turned upside down. Frank hadn't come home like he'd promised. A man was in surgery, seriously injured, and all the indications pointed to it being her husband, her Frank. She didn't want it to be him, but everything so far made her believe that it was. Everything, of course, except for the fact that she was now sitting in a waiting room with another woman who was also claiming to be his wife.

Iona sipped her tea again and peeped over the top of the cup at Sally and Jenna. Not only was there a woman claiming to be his wife, but there was also the glowering girl who claimed to be his daughter. Iona simply couldn't believe that Frank had a daughter. He'd talked so movingly and lovingly about wanting a child of his own with her that it was difficult to accept that he was a father already. She simply couldn't see how he'd kept that from her. And it had been Frank, not Iona, who'd really wanted the baby. At least he'd been the one to suggest it, even though she'd then come to agree with him that the time was right. He'd talked about his need for a family, but why did he need a family with her if he already had one? Why had he made her feel that what would happen between them would be unique and wonderful when it couldn't be? Right now, Iona couldn't figure whether she was more upset about the daughter than the wife.

She'd never even suspected that there might be another woman in Frank's life. How could there be when he was so busy and when their own lives together had been so full of happiness and togetherness? And what was it about them that kept him with them? The woman was nothing to write home about, with her lank hair and tired eyes. The girl . . . Iona swallowed hard as she looked at the girl. The problem was that, although she was clearly Sally's daughter, she also looked like Frank. Until now Iona had tried to push that thought to the back of her mind, but there couldn't really be any doubt. Admittedly her hair was a dark shade of auburn, while Frank's was dark brown sprinkled with grey. But her brown eyes were Frank's eyes, not just in their colour but in the way they looked out at the world. Almost fearless, but with a hint of hidden depths. Iona had been beguiled by Frank's saturnine good looks and brown eyes. She could see that same attractiveness in Jenna.

But how? she wondered. How could it all be? Why would Frank have married her when he had this family already? Was the marriage unhappy? In which case, why hadn't he divorced Sally? And, even worse, why had he been so keen to start a family with her when Jenna was living proof that he'd been down that road before?

Her head was beginning to spin. She couldn't get a firm grasp of the conflicting thoughts and emotions whirling through her mind. She felt as though she was going crazy.

It was nearly forty minutes later before the surgeon came to tell them that Frank was now in the recovery room.

'Will he be all right?' Jenna asked anxiously.

'It's hard to say at this point.' Sean McManus kept his voice deliberately neutral. 'He had a lot of injuries and we were concerned about his head—'

'Is he brain-damaged?' asked Sally, rigid with fear.

'Like I said, it's difficult to assess at this point. But we've done everything we possibly can.'

'Brain-damaged.' The words left Iona's mouth in a whisper. 'He can't be. Not Frank.'

Sally and Jenna hugged each other. Lauren put her arm around Iona's shoulders.

'Would you like to come along?' John Carroll turned to Iona, who nodded wordlessly. She stumbled as she stood up and Lauren put her arm around her again.

'I don't want it to be him,' whispered Iona in anguish as they walked along the corridor. 'I want it to be that other woman's husband. I want to be the one who's made the mistake.'

Lauren and the doctors exchanged glances over the top of Iona's head. This is not good, thought Lauren, not good at all.

They stopped in front of a window. Iona moved close and looked through. The figure in the bed was swathed in bandages and surrounded by tubes and wires. But it was undoubtedly Frank. Her Frank. She felt a tear slide slowly down her cheek.

'It's him,' she whispered raggedly. She pressed her hands against the window. 'Oh Frank.'

Lauren looked at Dr Carroll. 'What's the prognosis?' she asked.

'Currently Mr Harper is in a coma,' he replied. 'Until he comes out of it we really have no idea of the extent of the damage.'

'But there is damage?' Lauren asked the question while Iona continued to stare at Frank. 'To his brain? To his head?'

'It may be minor,' replied the doctor, 'but we have no way of knowing at this point.' He shrugged noncommittally. 'There's some swelling to the brain which obviously we need to go down as quickly as possible. Mr Harper may be left with nothing more than a severe headache. But we simply can't be certain.'

Lauren rubbed the bridge of her nose. She looked at Iona, who was crying softly.

'Best thing is to go home,' said Dr Carroll. 'Get some rest. Call us in the morning.'

'What if . . . what if something happens during the night?' Lauren asked anxiously, at the same time thinking that it was already closer to morning than night.

'Right now Mr Harper is stable and on life support. Of course we'd contact you immediately if anything changes, but that's unlikely at the moment.'

'What about the other woman?'

The doctor looked uncomfortable. 'We'll have to contact her too. It's a most unusual situation.'

'Yes,' said Lauren. 'It is.' She put her arm around Iona's shoulder. 'Come on, sis,' she said. 'Let's go.'

'I can't go.' Iona turned her tear-stained face towards her. 'I can't leave him like this.'

'You need some rest,' said Lauren. 'Come home with me, get some sleep and we'll come back in the morning.'

'What about her?' demanded Iona. 'Is she going home too?'

'We've made the same recommendations,' said the doctor.

'But people stay, don't they?' demanded Iona. 'You give them places to sleep.'

'We don't have anywhere for you to stay,' he told her. 'Either of you. I really do recommend you go home and get some rest. I doubt there's any likelihood of Mr Harper regaining consciousness for at least another twelve hours. So you're not doing yourself any favours by staying here. You need rest, you really do.'

'He's right, Io,' said Lauren. 'We'll come back tomorrow.'

Iona's shoulders sagged. 'All right,' she said dully. 'If that's what you think.'

Lauren sighed with relief. Dr Carroll led them away from Frank's room but in a different direction to that from which they'd come. Before they left the hospital he repeated the promise to contact them if there was any change.

'Make sure she gets some rest.' He handed Lauren a tiny envelope. 'Valium,' he said. 'Try and get her to take it.'

Lauren nodded and ushered Iona along the corridor and out of the hospital. A faint promise of dawn was lightening the eastern sky as they drove out of the grounds.

'It's all a horrible mistake,' said Iona. 'That woman didn't know what she was talking about. Stupid fat cow.'

'I know,' said Lauren comfortingly. 'We'll get it sorted. Don't worry.'

'I can't help worrying.' Iona leaned her head against the passenger window. 'He's my husband and he's in a coma and another woman thinks she's married to him. Of course I can't bloody well help worrying.'

Chapter 9

Sally and Jenna got a taxi from the hospital to Bray. They too had been told that it would be a good idea to go home and get some sleep and that they would be contacted immediately if there was any change in Frank's condition.

Sally hadn't wanted to leave. When John Carroll had come back to her in the waiting area and told her that Iona had identified Frank as being her husband, her first thought had been to rush to the recovery room and shake Frank awake to find out what the hell was going on. She still couldn't believe it was true. And yet as Iona had walked away to see Frank, she'd been overcome with a deep sense of dread that it was true, that Iona wasn't the complete flake that Sally wanted to believe she was.

The doctor had brought more tea even more liberally sugared and she and Jenna had drunk it in silence. Sally was worried about Jenna, who hadn't said a word since John Carroll had confirmed Iona's identification of Frank, but she couldn't think of a single comforting thing to say to her. What was the point in the usual assurances that everything would be all right when clearly everything was all wrong? What could she say to Jenna that would in any way help matters? So she sat and sipped the tea and worried about what the hell she was going to do now.

Jenna, too, found it impossible to focus on the reality of the situation. All she kept thinking about was that Frank was her father and she loved him and he'd always been the one on her side in an argument and that she'd thought she'd known him but that she obviously hadn't known him at all. And she simply couldn't accept that the dark-haired woman (who looked light-years younger than her mother and was so completely different to her in just about every way) and the father that she loved were in some way connected. Not in some way, she kept telling herself. They're supposed to be married. Which means he lives with her too. And sleeps with her. At this point Jenna gagged and suddenly the nurse who'd been hovering around the waiting area was beside her with the same sort of paper bag she'd given Iona earlier and holding it up to her mouth.

Jenna made a conscious effort not to be sick. She didn't want them to think that she was so upset by everything that she would throw up. And she didn't want to worry Sally any more than her mother was worried already.

It was after the gagging incident that both the nurse and John Carroll suggested that Sally and Jenna go home and get some rest.

By the time they were deposited outside their neat semi-detached house, morning had almost arrived. The birds were already singing in the sycamore trees that lined the road and, as they got out of the taxi, Sally could hear the shrill of Steve and Philly McCormack's alarm clock going off next door.

Jenna hadn't spoken on the way back from the hospital. In fact she'd slept for some of the journey back, her head lolling from side to side with the movement of the taxi. Now, in the kitchen, she looked wearily at Sally.

'That woman is wrong,' she said. 'Isn't she?'

'Of course she is,' said Sally as robustly as she could.

'Her driving licence . . . she has nothing to prove that she knows Dad at all. So why is she saying that stuff?' Jenna could feel her voice rise with anxiety. 'She can't really be married to him. She can't! Why would she do this when Dad is . . . is . . .' Suddenly she began to cry, short sobs at first and then an almost uncontrollable spasm of tears.

Sally put her arms around her.

'Sssh,' she whispered softly. 'We'll fix things, Jen. Don't worry.'

'But . . . but how can we fix things?' Jenna raised her tear-streaked face to her mother. 'He looked so awful, Mum. So helpless. And all those monitors and tubes coming out of him . . . and her screaming and shouting and everything.'

'I know, I know.' Sally felt a fraud trying to comfort Jenna when she was so scared herself. 'She's got it all wrong. We both know that. So it's just a question of sorting things out. And as for the tubes and stuff – well, that's what it's like when people are in intensive care. You know that, honey. It looks really scary but the doctors are wonderful and, well, in a few days, please God, he'll be back to himself.'

'But he's hurt his head.'

Sally swallowed hard. 'Yes. But your dad is a really strong person. He'll fight. He'll get better.'

Jenna sniffed.

'Come on,' said Sally. 'Let's get you to bed.'

Jenna nodded wearily. Both of them went upstairs. Sally stayed in her daughter's room until she was satisfied that Jenna had really fallen asleep. Then she went into her own bedroom and sat on the edge of the bed, feeling as though she was in some crazy parallel universe. Suddenly she felt the newly familiar heave in her stomach. She propelled herself off the bed and into the bathroom. The sound of the dawn chorus echoed through the windows as she was sick into the sink.

She put her hand into her pocket and took out the small plastic packet containing the Valium tablets the doctor had given her. Somehow she didn't think pregnant women should take Valium, even though a part of her would have loved to swallow the tablets and drift into oblivion. And she really wanted to take Panadol for her pounding head too. Reluctantly, and despite knowing that she really wasn't supposed to dispose of tablets in this way, she threw the Valium down the toilet and flushed it.

She tiptoed out of her room and across the hallway. Frank's home office was in the tiny spare bedroom. She opened the door gently.

The office was as neat as always. A self-assembly desk, pushed against the wall, was the main item of furniture. A four-shelf bookstand filled with technical manuals and blue plastic ring-binders took up a second wall. Beside that was a chrome stand with a number of wire baskets which contained a variety of lighting equipment.

Sally sat at the desk. Frank's closed laptop computer was neatly placed in the middle of it. She hadn't noticed the fact that he'd left without it, although he didn't always take it with him. She opened it and pressed the power button. While it whirred and clicked into action she opened the drawers in the pedestal beneath the desk. The top drawer contained pens and markers as well as a stapler and sellotape. The second was filled with stationery. The third contained a number of folders. Sally took them out and spread them on the desk in front of her. She thought there might be a clue in the folders, an explanation for what had happened tonight. She wasn't sure what sort of explanation there could be, but she wanted to find one. However, the folders merely contained letters to clients and maintenance contracts for installations he'd done. There was nothing at all that said anything about a girl called Iona who thought that Frank was her husband.

The computer was password-protected. Sally looked at the log-in screen in front of her. She had no idea of Frank's password. She typed in his name and, when it rejected that, tried her own name, followed by Jenna's, then the names of the various pets they'd had over the years: their dog, Dimwit; their rabbit, Connie; Romulus and Remus, the pair of hamsters which Jenna had brought home from school because someone had to look after them during the holidays and which had freaked Frank out. Each time the screen beeped at her and asked her to try again.

She tried a selection of birthdays and anniversaries. But none of those were the password either. She stared at the screen helplessly. Then, tentatively, she typed in the name Iona.

She was more relieved than she'd imagined when it beeped at her again. She wasn't sure how she would have reacted if Iona had been the password. She closed the computer again and leaned her head on the desk. And although she hadn't believed that she could, she fell asleep.

With the help of the Valium (which she'd at first refused to take but which Lauren had later tricked her into swallowing by telling her it was one of her herbal remedies), Iona, too, was asleep. In fact she'd fallen asleep almost as soon as she'd lain down on the double bed in Lauren's guest bedroom. Lauren had stayed with her, sitting on the edge of the bed, until she was certain that her sister really was out for the count. Then she walked as silently as she could into her own room.

Myles turned to her as she got into bed.

'What the hell is going on?' he asked.

Lauren was so tired she found it difficult to talk. She knew, as she related the night's events to Myles, that it all sounded impossibly far-fetched. Listening to her own words made it sound even more outlandish. But it was fact nevertheless.

'Jesus Christ,' murmured Myles when she'd finished. 'I always knew that bloke was bad news.'

There wasn't much Lauren could say. It had been a bone of contention between Iona and herself that Myles had never taken to Frank.

'He was too smarmy by half,' said Myles, as he pulled Lauren closer to him. 'Always smiling, always going on about how much he loved her. Ratbag.'

'Well, we don't know the full story yet.' Lauren yawned. 'Maybe there's a reasonable explanation.'

Myles snorted. 'If you think that, you're even softer in the head than Iona.'

'Oh Myles, I just feel so sorry for her,' whispered Lauren. 'I mean, it's bad enough that your husband is in a coma, but that there's someone else who thinks she has as much right to be there . . . oh, and there's a daughter too.'

'Bloody hell.'

'About sixteen or seventeen.'

'It's a mess, isn't it?'

Lauren nodded. 'And I've no idea how it can be sorted out.'

Siobhán arrived home much earlier than either Iona or Sally, but it was still late by the time she eased into the parking space beneath the apartment block and took the lift up to the fourth floor. It was at times like this she was glad Eddie was away – he was a light sleeper and hated being woken up when she arrived home at all hours. She slipped out of her shoes and walked in her stockinged feet into the kitchen, where she put on the kettle and shook a cappuccino mix into a large mug. It didn't matter that there was caffeine in it. She reckoned she was too tired from the events of the evening even for caffeine to keep her awake. As she waited for the kettle to boil, her eyes scanned the apartment.

She hadn't noticed until now, but in the weeks of Eddie's absence it had become a tip. Not a filthy tip, she told herself as she looked at the piles of magazines and newspapers scattered around the room and the collection of bottles on the worktop which she hadn't bothered to take to the bottle-bank; but a messy, untidy tip. Eddie would freak out at the sight of it. He was a neat and meticulous person and she knew that he only barely tolerated her habit of stepping out of her working clothes when she came home and simply throwing them carelessly over the back of the chair beside the bed. Eddie always hung up his suits and folded his shirts and generally left the place as he found it. (Although, she acknowledged, maybe if she spent vast amounts of money on designer gear like he did instead of simply rummaging through the rails at Top Shop looking for bargains, she'd be a bit more careful about hanging things up too!) As she eyed the burnt-down candles dotted around the apartment (she'd had a pampering evening a couple of weeks ago and had turned the place into a grotto of flickering lights to help with the ambience) and the wine glasses which she'd also not bothered to clear away, Siobhán wondered how on earth Eddie put up with a slut like her instead of finding a domestic goddess instead.

Maybe it was a case of opposites attracting, she thought, as she mixed her cappuccino. All the same, she'd better do a bit of a tidy-up before he got home. No sense in bringing him back to earth with such a resounding thud! She'd do it in the morning, though, before she picked him up from the airport. She didn't have the energy to do it now.

She finished her coffee and then got ready for bed. She slid between the cotton sheets and closed her eyes. But whether it was because of the coffee after all, or whether she was simply too tired, sleep just wouldn't come. She found herself thinking about the Harper case again. It had the potential, Siobhán thought, to become very messy indeed. One marriage of eighteen years, she reflected again. Another apparent marriage of four years. Could it be, she wondered, that Frank Harper had met this younger girl and – instead of acting like most men going through a mid-life crisis and having an affair with her – decided to marry her instead?

When she'd got back to the station she'd looked up the law relating to bigamy. The bottom line was that if Frank Harper had knowingly married Iona Brannock while he was still married to Sally, then he was a bigamist. Since both of the Harper wives seemed to think that they were legally married to Frank, she knew that her job would be to see whether the first marriage was valid, and whether the second ceremony was carried out in an accepted way. And whether anyone at the second ceremony knew about the first marriage – in which case they'd have aided and abetted in the crime.

She knew that she had to check Frank's background too. Maybe he was a serial bigamist. Perhaps Iona and Sally were only two in a whole harem of wives. Though God knew, thought Siobhán, it must be hard enough to carry on a double life, let alone a whole network of lives. But if Frank travelled overseas, for example, there was always the chance that he might have married someone outside the country too. Maybe there had been other weddings in Barbados! Siobhán wondered fleetingly what the likelihood was of her superintendent allowing her to go to the Caribbean to take a few statements. Slim, she thought. But it'd be a nice change from having to interview suspects in the dull rooms of the garda station! Actually Frank was the person she really needed to interview, but of course he was currently in a coma and there was no immediate sign of him coming out of it. So no chance of asking him whether Iona and Sally were the only two Mrs Harpers around.

But what did it matter if the poor bugger died? Siobhán had already wondered about the usefulness of conducting the enquiry if the suspect had little or no life expectancy, and then realised that there would probably be all sorts of legal and financial issues to be sorted out whether Frank Harper died or not. So she had to investigate it. It would be up to the Director of Public Prosecutions to decide whether the matter went any further. Their brief would be to see what harm had been caused, and what public interest would be served by prosecuting him. Her job was to present them with the facts. She had to find out the truth of the matter even if she didn't really want to get involved, and even if it would prove to be painful to the two women concerned.

She shook her head and pummelled the pillow into a more comfortable shape. Why did people do crazy things like this? she wondered. Wasn't life complicated enough without making it even worse? I'm glad I have a nice, uncomplicated relationship, she told herself. One which might one day end in marriage. But thankfully not yet. She put her arm around Eddie's pillow and dragged it towards her. Then she fell instantly asleep.

The ringing of the phone jolted Sally into immediate wakefulness. She winced as she lifted her head from the desk and reached for the receiver. It was the hospital, to say that Frank's condition was unchanged and that the doctor looking after his case would meet her at midday. She looked blearily at the wall clock. It was nine o'clock.

She went into the bathroom and stood under a lukewarm shower, rotating her neck from side to side under the jets to try to ease the tension in her shoulders. When she came out and went downstairs, she found Jenna sitting at the kitchen table again.

'He's dead, isn't he? That's what they were phoning to tell us.'

'Of course not,' said Sally. 'We're to go in at twelve and they'll talk to us then.'

'What about her?' asked Jenna. 'The madwoman? What's she doing?'

'I've absolutely no idea,' replied Sally. 'And I couldn't care less.'

Jenna's mobile phone beeped and Sally looked at her questioningly.

'It's Gerry,' she said.

'Gerry?'

'You met him, Mum,' said Jenna. 'He's my boyfriend.'

'Oh. Right.' Sally remembered a tall, gangly bloke who'd called around to the house one evening and who'd blushed red as he asked for Jenna. She hadn't realised (always assuming that she was thinking about the right guy!) that he was Jenna's boyfriend. I'm not taking enough interest in her, she told herself. I need to know more about what she's up to.

She watched as Jenna sent a text message to Gerry.

'What are you telling him?'

'That I can't go to the party tonight because my dad's had an accident.'

The phone beeped again. Jenna read the message and her eyes welled up with tears. She pushed her chair back from the table.

'I'm going upstairs,' she said, and left Sally sitting on her own.

Lauren took the call from the hospital while Iona was still sleeping. They gave her the same information about Frank and suggested that Iona come in at one to discuss the case.

'And what about the other woman?' demanded Lauren.

'Sally Harper is coming in at twelve.' The administrator sighed. 'It's a most unusual situation.'

'Well she'd better be gone before my sister arrives,' Lauren warned them. 'She's very emotional right now.'

'I do understand that,' said the woman at the other end of the phone. 'We are aware of the sensitivities involved.'

'Good,' said Lauren. 'Because I don't think you were last night. Iona felt that you weren't taking her seriously.'

'Believe me,' said the woman at the other end of the line, 'we're taking the entire situation very seriously indeed.'

When she woke Iona – a difficult task, as the Valium had clearly knocked her out completely – her sister's first question was why Sally was going in first.

'I don't know,' said Lauren.

'They're making her out to be more important than me. But she isn't. I'm his wife and I'm entitled to be there first.'

'Io – please.' Lauren looked at her sister despairingly. 'Someone has to be first.'

'But why her? Why not me? Because they think it's more likely she's his wife. Well, they only have her word for that. She can say all she likes about having married Frank but it's just not right.'

'She obviously does know Frank.'

'Maybe she went out with him before. Maybe she did have his baby.' Iona gulped. 'I can accept that even if I don't like it. But who's to say that she's actually married to him? We only have her word for that. And she could easily be a pathological liar.'

'Maybe she thinks the same about you.'

Iona stared at Lauren in a silence which crackled with anger and tension.

'Thanks very much for that!' she said furiously. 'You know I'm not lying. But you're prepared to believe that shit she was coming out with last night. You think that she's married to him even though you were the one who saw me and Frank off at the airport. You've seen our wedding photos!'

'Oh, look, Io . . .' Lauren caught her sister by the hands. 'I don't believe anything. I'm just saying that . . . well . . . for people who don't know . . . maybe they think it's more likely she's his wife.'

'That's just great.' Iona's voice was laden with disgust. 'You're giving her the benefit of the doubt. Why? Just 'cos she's older and looks like a hag? You think that's a more likely person for Frank to marry than me? Come on, Lauren, you know Frank! You know what he's like. D'you seriously think he'd want that dowdy old dear with the narky kid more than me? Honestly?'

'No. No, of course not.'

'Good.' Iona got out of the bed and then caught her breath in a jagged cry. She pressed her fingers to her stomach.

'Are you all right?' asked Lauren anxiously.

'Yeah. I'm fine. It's just . . .' She shrugged. 'D'you have any Tampax?'

Lauren nodded. She went out of the room and returned with a box of Super. 'These OK?'

'Thanks.' Suddenly a tear rolled down Iona's cheek and plopped on to the box.

'Come on, honey.' Lauren put her arm around her sister. 'Everything will be all right.'

'But what if it's not?' Iona turned her tear-filled blackberry eyes towards her. 'What if . . . what if he dies, Lauren?' She swallowed hard. 'We were trying for a baby. We'd finally decided . . . I'd finally decided that I could cope with the whole motherhood thing. And if he dies – then there'll never be a baby.'

Lauren squeezed her sister's shoulders very hard. 'He'll be fine,' she said fiercely. 'You know he will. And you'll have your baby.'

Sally and Jenna parked in the multistorey car park. They walked in silence to the hospital, each wrapped up in her own thoughts. They remained silent even when they were directed up to a waiting room on the ICU floor. The room made an effort to be cheerful, with brightly coloured upholstered chairs arranged around a small table stacked with magazines, and a hot-drinks vending machine in the corner. Sally selected tea for herself and hot chocolate for Jenna. They sat and waited for the doctor to arrive. When he did, it was a different man from the one they'd spoken to the previous evening. He introduced himself as David Bream and then sat down beside them. He told them that Frank was still in a coma although there had been some generalised responses. Which meant that his body was reactive but it was inconsistent and not specific. At this point Frank was still unaware of his surroundings. But, said the doctor, the trauma hadn't been as bad as they'd first feared. They'd managed to reduce the pressure on his brain and to surgically repair damaged blood vessels. There had been a blow to his occipital lobe which would probably impair his vision or perhaps his recognition of visual objects at first. It was hard to tell until he regained consciousness.

'Is he brain-damaged?' Sally had let the jargon flow over her and now asked the question tentatively.

'I can't say,' replied the doctor. 'However, we're hopeful that we will be able to move him off life support soon and with a bit of luck he'll wake up.'

Sally nodded. 'A coma's not really the same as him just being asleep, is it?'

'I'm afraid not. We need him to come out of it, Mrs Harper,' said the doctor.

'Can you guess when that will happen?' asked Jenna.

'Not really.' He smiled gently at her. 'You know, it's not like in the movies when someone opens their eyes and suddenly gets better. Sometimes patients can open and close their eyes but still not respond to their surroundings. It can take a while. The brain is a sensitive organ. But the human body is amazing too.'

'Can we see him?' Sally got up.

They followed David Bream to the window of the ICU room. As far as they could see, nothing had changed from the previous night. Frank was still hooked up to a vast array of instruments and still looked waxy and unlike himself.

'Has she been here yet?' asked Sally.

'I'm sorry?'

'The madwoman from last night? The one who lied about him?'

'Not yet,' said David uncomfortably.

'Whatever she's saying, it's not true.' Sally stared through the window at Frank. 'He's my husband. I love him. And I'll be the one to make him better.'

Iona was shaking as she sat in the waiting room. It was a different room from the previous night, at the far end of the corridor. A row of orange plastic chairs lined the wall. A small TV, mounted on a bracket, was showing Sky News. There were a few ancient magazines on a table in the centre of the room; otherwise it was empty. No other families were waiting for news of loved ones.

David Bream pushed the door open.

'Iona?' He looked uncertainly between the two women in front of him.

'I'm Iona.' Her dark eyes looked intently at him.

'Do you want to come with me?'

As Sally and Jenna had done a little earlier, Iona and Lauren stopped by the glass window. Iona burst into loud sobs as she looked at Frank while Lauren held her tightly.

David went through the same explanations as he'd given Sally and Jenna. As he talked, Iona wiped her eyes.

'Has he made any responses at all?' she asked.

David was surprised at the suddenly more businesslike tone of her voice.

'Some. But he's not aware of his surroundings.'

'How d'you know?' demanded Iona. 'What about all those people you read about who seem to be totally out of it and then they say that they could hear everything that was going on, and they remember people saying things about them. I don't want Frank to hear anything bad said when he's there. I don't want people walking into his room and muttering that he's never going to wake up.'

'Nobody will do that,' said David.

'I want to spend time with him and talk to him and let him know that people love him,' said Iona.

'Her favourite TV programme is *ER*,' said Lauren apologetically.

'Don't be so facile,' snapped Iona. 'I've had time to think about this, and I know I've been crying and upset and everything but it doesn't mean I'm completely hopeless. I want to stay with him 24/7 if I have to.'

'Well, Iona, that's all really positive,' said David Bream. 'Of course there are other people who want to visit him too . . .'

'Who?' demanded Iona. 'He has no family. His parents are dead. He doesn't have brothers and sisters.'

'Indeed. But as you know—'

'If you're talking about that other woman, she has no right to be here.'

David exchanged uncomfortable looks with Lauren.

'I've thought about that too,' said Iona relentlessly. 'If he was, at some point, married to her it makes no difference. For the last four years he's been married to me. So I'm the most important person in his life. If that woman wants to see him, she has to ask me first.'

'I'm really not so sure that—'

'I'm sorry, but that's the way it is,' said Iona.

'And I'm sorry, but we're going to have to work something out,' said David firmly.

Iona looked angrily at him. 'Don't you understand?' she cried. 'Other patients have people with them all the time, helping them. Because of this . . . this . . . nonsense . . . Frank doesn't have anyone. He needs me.'

'He needs support,' agreed David. 'He doesn't need dissent.'

'So what did she say to you?' asked Iona. 'That she wanted to be here all the time too?'

'To be honest with you,' said David, 'I'm not sure either of you being around will be very helpful at this point. If Mr Harper is aware of what's going on, he could be extremely anxious. We want to keep him calm.'

'So what are you saying? That I can't be here?' Iona's voice was filled with fury. 'I'm telling you, I'm his wife, and you're trying to keep me away from him. You've no right to do that.'

'I'm saying that you and Mrs Harper—'

'Can't you get it into your thick skulls that *I'm* Mrs Harper!' cried Iona.

'You and the other Mrs Harper,' amended David. 'Well, neither of you should be here if it upsets him.'

'You can't seriously think that he's better off on his own?'

'I don't know enough about the situation,' said David. 'But I think you need to discuss it with her and come to an arrangement.'

'You've got to be kidding me.'

'I said the same to her.'

'And what did she say?'

'More or less the same as you. But really and truly, until you come to some kind of arrangement you're doing more harm than good.'

'How dare you?' hissed Iona. 'How dare you imply that I'm doing harm to Frank by being here?'

David Bream sighed deeply. He'd been in situations where there were family feuds before, where sisters or brothers who hadn't spoken to each other for years suddenly turned up at a parent's bedside and then fought over who should care for them. And he'd been in situations where a patient's lover had shown up, wanting to see him or her after the family (including wife or husband) had left. But he'd never had two women both claiming to be married to a man turn up in ICU before. And he really didn't feel equipped to handle it.

'Is she still here?' asked Iona.

David nodded. 'She travelled from Bray. It's a long way.'

Iona exhaled slowly. 'I'll be back at six o'clock this evening. Make sure she's gone by then.'

She pressed her face against the glass once more.

'I love you, Frank,' she whispered. 'I really do. I won't let you down. And we will have our baby.'

Chapter 10

Siobhán made a determined effort to tidy up the apartment the following morning. She gathered up all the papers and magazines and put them into the big box which they kept in the store cupboard for paper recycling. She put all the bottles (she hadn't realised she'd lashed into quite so many bottles of wine over the last few weeks on her own!) into their other recycling box. She gathered up the empty pizza cartons and Chinese takeaway bags from the previous few weeks and tied them up in a black refuse sack, thinking that as well as having drunk too much wine she'd certainly eaten far too much takeaway food. But, she told herself hopefully, the wine would help with the fat content of the food. So maybe her diet had been perfectly balanced after all!

When she'd finished tidying stuff away, she rushed around the apartment with a duster and a tin of Mr Sheen, shook out the cushions, and finally gave the rugs a quick going-over with the Hoover. When she'd finished, she eyed her handiwork critically. There was still a pile of ironing heaped up on the bed in the spare room waiting for attention. Ironing was something she often didn't mind doing because it helped her to think, but she'd been too busy over the last few weeks to bother with it. Oh well, she thought, out of sight and all that sort of thing. Overall, the apartment was a lot tidier. Although certainly not as tidy as when Eddie was around. It was a bit disconcerting to suddenly realise that he was the one who kept the whole domestic side of their lives running smoothly.

It's not my fault, she told herself as she stood in front of the mirror and massaged tinted moisturiser into her naturally pale cheeks. I don't do domesticity. It was never really an option for me. She thought briefly of her upbringing as a middle child among five brothers who had all inherited the usual male genes of complete aversion to housework. Her mother had fought a losing battle against the tide of male paraphernalia around the house and had eventually told Siobhán that it was what was deep down, not appearances, that counted. Siobhán agreed with her mother, but she also realised that sometimes appearances did count. And she certainly didn't want Eddie coming home to an apartment which looked as though it had been part of a stakeout operation.

In fact, she thought, a proper girlfriend would have made the place warm and welcoming and romantic so that he'd realise just how much he'd missed her. God, but she was useless with the soppy stuff. She stood indecisively in front of the mirror. She should do something, she thought, to mark his return. Most women would do something, surely?

She slicked some lipstick on to her lips and grabbed her jacket from the back of the bedroom door, vowing that she'd hang it up properly when they got home. Then she rushed out of the apartment and across the road to the convenience store where she bought three bunches of flowers and a couple of scented candles (she was really overdoing the whole candle thing these days, she thought, but what the hell!). Then she nipped into the adjoining off-licence and bought a bottle of champagne. She raced back to the apartment, shoved the flowers into their beautiful Louise Kennedy vases (a gift to Eddie from a grateful client), placed the candles in the bedroom and put the champagne in the fridge.

Now I'm a proper thoughtful girlfriend, she told herself as she hurried down the stairs and into the car.

Frank Harper could hear the nurse in the ICU unit talking. He knew that she was a real person and that he wasn't living some sort of dream, but what he didn't know was exactly where he was and why he was here. And he couldn't quite pin down what she was saying either. He knew that, in some way, he was the object of her concern, because her voice was gentle whenever she was near him. He just didn't know why she was worried about him. He felt perfectly all right. Tired, of course. And not quite ready to open his eyes yet because really that would take far too much effort. In a lot of ways he was very content with how things were.

Marion. That was her name. He remembered now. Marion was looking after him, which was kind of ironic of course because he was the one who was supposed to be looking after Marion. She was his girlfriend, after all. But obviously something had happened and now he was in bed and Marion was concerned about him.

Had he drunk too much at the party? Was he suffering from alcoholic poisoning? She'd said that to him last night. Drink any more of those vodka shots and you'll end up with liver failure. But she'd laughed. She hadn't really meant it. And he'd told her that he was drinking them because . . . because . . . The thought was somewhere just out of reach and he struggled to capture it. Yes. He remembered now. He was drinking because it was her going-away party. She was leaving him. Abandoning him for America with her Morrison visa and her hopes of a new life with brighter prospects. He hadn't wanted her to go. He'd told her he loved her. She'd laughed at him then and retorted that she knew perfectly well that it was all about sex and nothing really to do with love. Hadn't Johnny Doherty told her that both himself and Frank pursued nurses because they had a reputation for being up for anything?

Frank had responded with shock in his voice. He'd said that he loved her for herself and not just for sex, even though sex with her was wonderful. He couldn't bear the thought of her abandoning him.

Only now she was here. She hadn't gone. Frank was finding it difficult to concentrate. If she was in the room with him now, she couldn't have boarded the Aer Lingus flight to New York departing this morning, 12 April 1986.

He needed to wake up. It was easy to lie here with his eyes closed and think about Marion and how his life might turn out now that she was still here, but it would be better to snap out of his drunken stupor and get back into things again. Only he didn't really feel like it. His head hurt. His body hurt too. Better leave it for a while.

Terri Cooper, the nurse in charge of the ICU unit, heard her patient sigh. She looked at him. His eyes were open but they were staring blankly at the ceiling. As she watched, he closed them again.

He was still in a coma.

The traffic in Dublin was, as always, appalling. Siobhán sat in her car and fumed, wishing that she could stick her blue light on the roof. But she was driving her own car, and besides, even in a police car she wouldn't be allowed to use the light to clear a route from Blackrock to the airport just so's she could be on time to meet her fiancé from the plane. Pity, she thought. It'd be a nice perk to the job. Despite the delays, however, she arrived five minutes before Eddie emerged into the arrivals hall.

She squealed with delight at seeing him and rushed towards him, flinging her arms around him and hugging him tightly to her. He hugged her too, so tightly that she couldn't even move.

'OK, OK,' she said eventually. 'You'd better let me come up for air.' She wriggled out of his hold and then kissed him on the lips. He moved away from her and she looked at him in astonishment.

'Sorry,' he said. 'I'm . . . you know . . . in public.'

Her eyes opened wide. Kissing in public had never been an issue before. At least, she didn't think so. They didn't do it very much, Eddie was a very private person, but still . . . She clamped down on the feeling of hurt which she felt.

'But it's wonderful to see you,' he told her, and she didn't doubt the sincerity in his voice. He put his arms around her and hugged her close to him again. 'I really, really missed you.'

Her hurt feelings evaporated and she leaned her head against his shoulder.

'I missed you too,' she said.

He yawned widely. 'I'm so sorry. Jet lag. I know I should sleep on the plane but I can't.'

'Never mind,' she told him as they walked back to the car park and retrieved the car. 'You can sleep for hours when we get home. I'm going to drop in to the station early this evening. I have loads to do.'

'New case?'

She told him about the potential bigamy situation. 'I need to do some background checks,' she said. 'Find out about this Harper bloke. For all we know he could have dozens of women stashed away.'

'You think so?' he asked as she edged out of the parking space.

She made a face. 'Hard to know. Depends on his motive, I guess.' She chuckled. 'Most guys I know struggle with one wife, let alone two.'

Eddie nodded, then opened the glove compartment and slid a CD into the deck.

'You don't mind if I chill for a while?'

Siobhán shook her head as the voice of Aretha Franklin filled the car.

Eddie fell asleep fifteen minutes into the journey and she had to wake him when they eventually arrived back at the apartment building. He yawned widely, then got out of the car and took his case from the boot.

'You're lucky you came home at the weekend,' said Siobhán as they made their way to their apartment. 'At least you don't have to be alert for the morning.'

'I have to go through some of my paperwork,' he told her. 'Get everything in order for next week.'

'No problem.'

She unlocked the apartment door and he followed her inside. He dumped his case in the bedroom, then walked back out into the living room again. He looked around critically before picking up a used tea-light which Siobhán had overlooked in the great clean-up.

'I thought the place would be trashed,' he told her.

'Why?'

'I didn't think you'd manage to keep it so tidy. And I'm impressed by the flowers.'

She grinned. 'OK, I have to admit it wasn't like this all the time. But I did my best.'

'I think we should get professional cleaners in,' said Eddie.

'It's not that bad!'

'On a regular basis,' he told her. 'So that you don't have to bother with it.'

'It's impossible to get a reasonably priced cleaner,' she told him. 'And really this place isn't that big. I'll make more of an effort next time.' She opened the fridge and took out the bottle of champagne. 'Come on, honey. I do feel that the domestic goddess scenario means that I should be a goddess in the bedroom too.' She opened the bedroom door again. 'Grab some glasses for the bubbly and see what you've been missing the last five weeks!'

By the time Eddie followed her inside, she was already pulling off her jeans and sliding into bed. He undressed more slowly, as always hanging his clothes carefully in the wardrobe before getting in beside her. She put her arms around him and pulled him towards her.

'I've so, so missed you,' she whispered. 'I didn't realise how much you mattered to me until you'd gone.'

He put his arms around her too and held her close. She slid her hand down his side and between his legs.

'You know what,' he mumbled into her flame-red hair, 'I'm just totally knackered right now. I can't think straight. And my body is wrecked.'

She moved away from him and looked at him in puzzlement.

'You don't want to?'

'Of course I want to,' he responded. 'I'm just really, really tired.'

'Oh. Well, come on, let's have the champagne anyway.'

He looked at her apologetically. 'I appreciate it, I really do. But maybe later? Right now would you mind awfully if I went to sleep?'

'No. No, that's fine.' Her voice was hesitant. 'I thought . . . but you're right. You've been awake all night.'

'Stay with me,' he said. 'I like to know you're close to me.'

'Sure.'

They lay side by side for a few minute and then Eddie's breathing became slower and steadier. Siobhán raised herself on to one elbow and looked at him. He was sound asleep. She eased herself out of the bed and took the bottle of champagne back to the fridge, then made herself a cup of tea instead.

It was mid-afternoon when Siobhán pulled up outside the neat semi-detached house in Bray. She got out of her unmarked car, noticing in the daylight that the front lawn was neatly trimmed and the flowerbeds carefully tended. The windows sparkled and the paintwork on the hall door had recently been redone.

She got out of her car and walked up the cobbled driveway.

A middle-aged woman answered the door. She raised her eyebrows in silent query, but Siobhán simply gave her name and said that she was here to see Sally.

'Sally's resting. I don't think she needs to see anyone right now.'

Siobhán walked past the woman and into the living room. Sally was sitting on the long settee, her legs drawn up under her. Her face was pale, with blue-black shadows under her eyes.

'I told her you were resting . . .' Sally's neighbour, who had called in to see her and taken it on herself to fuss over her, had followed Siobhán into the room.

'It's OK,' said Sally. 'This is the garda who told me about Frank's accident.'

'And I'd like to talk to Mrs Harper on her own for a while,' said Siobhán firmly. 'So if you could leave us to ourselves . . .'

The neighbour reluctantly picked up her bag from a chair. 'Well, you know where to find me if you need me.' She nodded to both women and let herself out of the house.

'How are you?' Siobhán asked gently.

Sally hesitated before answering. 'I don't know,' she replied eventually. 'I was at the hospital this morning. Frank is still in a coma. That other woman was there.'

'How's your daughter?'

'She's gone out,' said Sally. 'I think that's a good thing. Her boyfriend called around for her and I told them to go for a walk.' Sally nibbled at her thumbnail. 'Why are you here?' she asked.

'Well, Sally, we need to investigate the whole situation between you and Iona and Frank.'

'There is no situation,' said Sally. 'I'm his wife. Everyone knows that.'

'Do you have a marriage certificate?' asked Siobhán. 'And Frank's birth certificate too, perhaps?'

'Of course I do.' Sally uncurled her legs and got up from the settee. She went out of the room. While she was alone, Siobhán walked around it. It was a big L-shaped room with an olive-green settee and armchairs at one end and a walnut dining table and chairs in the short end of the L. The furniture was old-fashioned, darker than Siobhán herself preferred, but of a good quality. There were framed prints on the walls and one portrait photograph of Frank, Sally and Jenna. Siobhán guessed that Jenna had been around ten or twelve when the photo had been taken – her wide beaming smile revealed train-track braces on her teeth. There were two other photographs in the room, both in silver frames. One was of Jenna as a baby, a wide smile on her chubby face; the other was of Frank and Sally on their wedding day. It was an outdoor photograph taken in a garden setting, with spectacular views over Dublin Bay.

'The Deerpark Hotel in Howth,' said Sally as she came back into the room.

Siobhán replaced the photograph on the sideboard.

'It was a beautiful day,' continued Sally. 'Cloudless blue sky and very warm. I was too hot in my dress really.'

Siobhán looked at the photograph again. Sally's dress was very traditional, with a square neck and puffed sleeves. Her hair had been teased into a myriad of curls on the top of her head and her veil was secured by a glittering tiara.

'It looks naff now,' said Sally, 'but it was the height of fashion then.'

Siobhán grinned at her. 'I know what you mean. You think you're getting something timeless but years later you wonder what in God's name you were thinking. That's a nice dress, though.'

'Are you married?' asked Sally.

Siobhán said nothing. Instead she walked back towards Sally and held her hand out to take the certificates from her. She had no intention of discussing her personal life with Sally Harper.

'I brought you our wedding album to look at too,' said Sally. 'Not that there were a lot of people there; Frank and I are both only children.'

'Best man and bridesmaid?' asked Siobhán as she looked at the glossy photos.

'A friend of Frank's,' said Sally. 'Johnny Doherty. He's living in the States now. Or maybe Canada, I'm not sure which. And the bridesmaid is a girl I was in college with. Denise. We're still good friends – work together, actually. She lives on the other side of the city, though.'

'How many people were there?' Siobhán continued to look at the photographs. She stopped turning the pages and looked at one of them more closely. 'Parents, of course.'

'Mine,' said Sally. 'And Frank's dad. His mum left them when he was a kid.'

Siobhán continued to look at the photograph.

'They're all dead now,' said Sally starkly, which made Siobhán look up at her. 'Well, you can see that my folks were getting on a bit. My mum was . . . old . . .' She stumbled on the words and Siobhán put an arm around her.

'Sit down,' she said. 'D'you want me to get you a drink of something?'

'No.' Sally shook her head. 'No, it's fine. What I was going to say was that my mum was quite old when she had me. She was forty-five. She'd lost three other children.'

'Oh.'

'I mean, it's not old, of course,' said Sally. 'But old for a baby.' She struggled to keep herself under control and kept her hand on her own stomach while Siobhán watched her carefully.

'Anyway, she'd never been in the best of health, so it wasn't unexpected. My dad died two years after her, of a broken heart I always thought.'

'I'm sorry.'

Sally moistened her lips with her tongue. 'It was a long time ago now,' she said more easily. 'And it wasn't as though it was entirely unexpected.'

'And what about Frank's father?'

'Oh, rude health for years,' said Sally. 'Then had a heart attack and died sitting in front of the telly.'

'Is the family from Dublin?' asked Siobhán.

'Oh, gosh, no. Frank was born and raised in Sligo,' replied Sally. 'He's still a country man at heart. He used to stay with his dad once a month until Mr Harper's heart attack.' She shrugged. 'I went a few times too, but to be honest with you, I wasn't interested in driving for a couple of hours to a dark old house that needed repairing. I never really got on with the old man and I don't think he liked me very much either. I know it sounds crazy, but Frank's dad really wanted him to marry a Sligo girl and settle back there. I think he was afraid that I'd be flighty, like his own wife.

'He tried to trace her, I think, but gave up on it. All we know is that she headed to London when Frank was two or three. He doesn't talk about it much any more. I don't know whether she's still alive and neither does Frank. She was from Dublin too, and so as far as old Mr H. was concerned we're a bunch of Jezebels! I don't blame her for heading off, though – he was a grumpy old man and not very nice, to be honest with you. I don't think he actually liked women very much. Frank himself did go out with a Sligo girl for a while but she went off to the States or something.' Sally looked at Siobhán ruefully. 'You know how it was, everyone headed out of Ireland twenty-odd years ago!

'I didn't want to live in Sligo after Frank and I got married but Mr Harper took it as a bit of a slight. Said that I thought I was too good for them. Complete nonsense. As far as I was concerned, Sligo in the 1980s – probably the whole north-west in the 1980s – was a dump.' She laughed faintly. 'I always feel terrible when I say that. As though he can hear me. But the thing was, I had a good teaching job in Dublin and I didn't want to move anywhere else. In the end, though, Mr Harper left the house to Frank. He renovated it and he rents it out. He goes up to Sligo once a month to check things out. The current tenants are a local family with a child, so I know that there isn't something awful going on there.'

'And how would you say your relationship with Frank is?' asked Siobhán.

A tear slid down Sally's cheek. 'Good,' she said eventually. 'We have a good relationship.'

'No trial separations or anything like that?'

Sally looked at her angrily, her eyes still bright with tears. 'I've just said we have a good relationship,' she snapped. 'Of course not.'

'And yet there's a girl who claims to be married to him,' said Siobhán gently. 'Why would she say that, d'you think?'

Sally grabbed a tissue from the box on the coffee table in front of the settee. 'I've no idea. She's obviously deranged.'

'What I thought was that perhaps she's in some kind of relationship with him,' suggested Siobhán, 'and likes to say that they're married. Is it possible, do you think, that there is something between them only you didn't know about it?'

Sally rolled the tissue into a ball and said nothing. She stared at the blank TV screen in the corner of the room. Siobhán watched her silently.

'What does any of it matter?' asked Sally eventually. 'Frank can only be married to one person and that's me.'

Siobhán remained silent.

'There was a period,' said Sally edgily, 'when things weren't great between us. About five years ago.' She pulled at the tissue, shredding it between her fingers and finally dropping it into the wastepaper basket beside her. 'The company where he worked was bought out. Frank was offered a job with the new crowd, a good job, but he didn't want it. He said he didn't like their ethos. I told him I didn't care about their ethos; the point was they were actually offering him an increase in salary. But Frank just wasn't interested. He said he wanted to go out on his own.'

Sally pulled another tissue from the box and blew her nose.

'I was really worried about it. He didn't have a lot of money to back it up so I couldn't see how we were going to cope. He said we'd manage by increasing the rent on the Sligo house, selling the one we were living in and moving out here. We were near the city, you see, where prices had gone through the roof, whereas it was much cheaper here. But I didn't really want to move. I was working on the north side of town, in Sutton, so it was much further away. Frank said that I could get the train across every day and it'd be much quicker than driving even though it was further.'

She threw the second tissue into the wastepaper bin too.

'I suppose I'm a terrible stick-in-the-mud sort of person. I hate being in debt. I hate not knowing where the money is coming from. I thought Frank felt the same way but he didn't really. He was so excited about the new business and he didn't seem to mind working all the hours God sent. I suppose that during that time, what with moving here and him working and all that sort of stuff . . . well . . . there could have been a point where he . . .'

She broke off and sighed. 'But I don't see where he would've got the time, to be honest. He really was working like crazy. And, you know, in the end we resolved it all. He loves me and I always knew that.'

Siobhán nodded. 'How is he?'

'No change,' said Sally. 'We're going in to see him later.' She sniffed. 'It's all so unreal. He's in a coma. He might never wake up. And instead of being able to concentrate on him and what I can do for him and how he is and all that sort of stuff . . . all I'm thinking of is why on earth that girl thinks that . . . It's not possible, you know. Absolutely not. There was never a chance of Frank and me getting a divorce. Never. We went through a rough patch but so does everyone and it was never so bad that we even for a second contemplated divorce.'

'I'll be visiting her,' said Siobhán. 'I'll keep you in touch with whatever's going on.'

Sally's smile was weak. 'Thanks.'

'Can I ask you something else?'

'Go ahead.'

'Well, what about Christmas and holidays?'

'Christmas is a busy time for him,' said Sally defensively. 'He sometimes has to stay over if a hotel's doing a spectacular display. He gets well paid for it, though. To be honest, I've never really minded. Once your children are grown up the whole thing sort of loses its appeal . . .' Her voice trailed off and she rested her hand on her stomach while she stared unseeingly at the far wall of the room.

'Are you all right, Sally?' asked Siobhán after a moment or two.

Sally blinked. 'Yes. Yes. Sure.'

'I'll be getting on then,' said Siobhán. 'As soon as I have any more information I'll contact you. In the mean time, are you sure you don't want me to ask your neighbour to call in again?'

'God, no,' said Sally with feeling. 'I want to be on my own for a while.'

'OK.' Siobhán got up. 'Look after yourself.'

'I will,' said Sally as she let her out.

Chapter 11

It took Siobhán a little longer than she'd expected to drive the thirty kilometres from Bray to Dublin and she was afraid that Iona would already have left the house. She'd earlier called Lauren, who'd said that Iona had gone home to change before going to the hospital that evening. Siobhán hadn't wanted to insist on Iona waiting for her, but she did want to talk to her.

The green VW was still parked outside. Siobhán drew up behind it and got out of her car. The area where Iona lived was very different to Sally's. The houses here were much older and smaller and faced directly on to the street. Previously the home of working-class families struggling to make ends meet, the Liberties of Dublin had become a sought-after district for young urban professionals. Siobhán liked the higgledy-piggledy streets and the wildly different colours of the houses, though she supposed that for modern families it might all be a little too cramped.

She rang the bell to Iona's house and heard the muffled sounds of her coming down the stairs.

'Hi,' she said when Iona opened the door. 'How are you?'

Iona shrugged. Siobhán saw that, like Sally, she was very pale. In her case the dark shadows under her eyes seemed even more pronounced. But there was a defiant gleam in her dark eyes.

'What d'you want?' she asked rudely. 'I'm getting ready to go out.'

'I know that,' said Siobhán. 'I'll only take up a few minutes of your time.'

Iona looked at her disbelievingly.

'We do need to clarify a few things,' said Siobhán. 'The sooner we sort it all out the better.'

'There's nothing to sort out.' But Iona opened the door wider and allowed Siobhán into the house.

'I know that's what you think,' said Siobhán, 'yet obviously there's a situation here, Iona. And it's in everyone's interest to resolve it.'

'You believe her, don't you?' Iona's glance in Siobhán's direction was contemptuous. 'Mrs Suburban Lifestyle Dream. You think she's really his wife.'

'I don't think anything,' answered Siobhán calmly. 'I just want to know the truth.'

'Oh, quit talking like a TV cop,' snapped Iona. 'You don't care what the truth is. You just need to close a file that you shouldn't have opened in the first place. It's none of your damn business.'

'Unfortunately it is my business at the moment,' said Siobhán. 'And you're right, I want to resolve it and move on.'

'I don't believe in the state poking its nose into people's private lives,' said Iona rudely. 'You should be out catching real criminals, not getting involved in a personal matter.'

Siobhán sighed. She couldn't begin to count the number of times that members of the public had told her to go off and catch real criminals. But police work was more than that. At least that was how she looked at it. Maybe, she thought, she was just a fool.

'What I was wondering,' she said as she sat down on one of Iona's cream leather armchairs, 'was whether you had a marriage certificate.'

'Of course I do,' said Iona. 'I'm not unhinged. I didn't make the whole thing up, you know. Frank and I are legally married.' She stomped out of the room and up the stairs.

As she had in Sally's house, Siobhán took the opportunity to look around the room. Not that there was much to see. Unlike the warmth of the house in Bray, with its jumble of photos and ornaments, Iona's place was much more modern and minimalist. Siobhán recognised the feng shui bowl on the sideboard, but she was surprised to see two framed photographs of children there too. She wouldn't have thought of Iona as the maternal type. The only other photograph was one of Frank and Iona on their wedding day in Barbados.

'Here.' Iona came downstairs again and thrust the piece of paper into Siobhán's hand. 'Marriage certificate. Barbados. Iona Brannock and Frank Harper.'

Siobhán studied the certificate. 'And who were these witnesses?' she asked.

'Oh, just a couple we met while we were there,' said Iona. 'They were both from England. We didn't keep in touch, though. I think they run a nursing home in Yorkshire. Nice couple, but you know how it is on holiday. You meet people and they're friends for a fortnight but that's it.'

'Any of your family there?' asked Siobhán casually. She thought the department would probably send her to Yorkshire if she needed. Not as glamorous as Barbados, though!

Iona shook her head. 'It's not like it was spur of the moment or anything, but we just wanted to do it on our own. Besides, Lauren had only given birth to Gavin a few weeks earlier so she wasn't really interested in travelling. My folks are retired and they live in Spain.'

Siobhán sighed. Sometimes she hated her job. No matter what, there always came a time when she had to tell people things they didn't want to hear. And those people in turn always hated her for it.

'I was with Sally earlier,' she said. 'She has a marriage certificate too.'

Iona's eyes darkened even further. 'It's all nonsense,' she said.

'I don't see how it can be.' Siobhán kept her voice soft and even. 'It seems possible to me that Frank and Sally did get married.'

'Well they must be divorced.' This time Iona's eyes glittered with tears. 'I'm telling you, he loves me. We have a good life together. How could he possibly be married to someone else?' She blinked a few times and looked angrily at Siobhán. 'I mean, you're suggesting that he's living some sort of double life. That's just not realistic! I'd know about it if he was.'

'Did he ever stay away for long periods?' asked Siobhán. 'Or have to head off unexpectedly for a while?'

Iona said nothing.

'I know it seems impossible,' continued Siobhán, 'but we have to eliminate the impossible to work out what the exact situation is.'

'Why do you care?' burst out Iona. 'What does it matter?'

'Well, there are a whole heap of things that matter,' Siobhán told her. 'In terms of your rights and entitlements as a married woman. In terms of why – if he married you when he was married to Sally – well, why he did it, what he hoped to gain by it—'

'He had nothing to gain!' Iona cried. 'It's not like I'm rolling in money or anything.' She covered her face with her hands.

Siobhán watched her, wishing once again that she hadn't got involved in this case but had stuck with the money-laundering instead. Meanwhile she hoped fervently that there weren't any more Mrs Harpers waiting to emerge from the woodwork. A sudden image flashed across her mind of a dozen more Sallys and Ionas claiming to be the one and only Mrs Frank Harper.

'We were trying for a baby,' whispered Iona finally. 'He wanted a baby. More than me at first. And so we were trying for one.' The tears trickled through her fingers and rolled across her wrists and down her arms. 'Why would he want a baby if he already had a daughter?'

'Oh, Iona, I don't know.' Siobhán got up from the armchair and sat on the sofa beside Iona. She put her arm around her shoulders and hugged her tightly.

'He has to stay away a lot.' Iona spoke through her hands. 'He has a business of his own. He works from the house and from an office in Stillorgan. It's one of those serviced offices, you know, a lot of people use them. But the work means he has to travel a lot, and so . . . yes, there are times when he's not here.'

'What about . . . what about holiday times, like Christmas or New Year?' asked Siobhán.

'Our first Christmas we went to Salzburg,' said Iona dreamily. 'It was absolutely wonderful. It snowed and everything was totally Christmas-cardy. We went skating at an ice-rink wearing turn-of-the-century clothes. Frank's a good skater but I kept falling over. I was covered in bruises! And last year we went to Tenerife. It was so cold and gloomy here, if you remember, and I really wanted some sun. Frank doesn't particularly like the sun. He likes being outdoors but he prefers a bit of cloud, even though he tans quite easily. But he agreed to Tenerife for me. We had Christmas lunch by the pool and then the hotel did a big dinner . . .' Her voice trailed off and she sniffed again.

'And the other Christmases?' asked Siobhán.

'Well, it's his work, you see,' said Iona. 'Light shows and that sort of thing. He has to be away sometimes because he might be looking after a particular display . . . Christmas and New Year are busy times.'

'And the summer?'

Iona shrugged. 'We never take two-week holidays; usually just a week at the beginning and a week at the end as well as lots of long weekends. Frank doesn't like being away from the office for more than that. We were planning to go to Italy in May and maybe Prague in September.'

'Did he ever stay away from you for more than a week at a time?'

'Of course,' said Iona. 'There's the annual industry conference – that's nearly a fortnight. And other events from time to time too.'

'And where is the annual conference held?'

'It depends,' replied Iona. 'Last year it was in Malta.'

She rubbed her eyes and looked at Siobhán.

'Are you trying to tell me that he wasn't at a conference? That he was with her instead?' Her voice rose. 'Is that it?'

'Look, Iona, I know this is really stressful for you. You love Frank and he's badly injured and in hospital, so everything else is just a distraction to you. But the point is . . . well, it does seem very likely that he was still married to Sally when he married you.'

'But why!' wailed Iona. She got up and stood in front of the feng shui bowl. 'Why would he do that? He didn't have to get involved with me. Nobody forced him . . .' Her voice trailed away again as she thought of the number of times she'd mentioned marriage to Frank. How, in the end, she was the one who'd practically proposed to him. But she hadn't made him say yes! If he hadn't been able to marry her, then why on earth had he done it?

Iona looked at the wedding photograph again. It just wasn't possible, she told herself for the hundredth time. How could he have taken her to Barbados and married her knowing Sally and Jenna were at home? And how could he have told her, only the other day, that he was looking forward to the time when their baby arrived and they'd be a real family. He wanted so much to be part of a family.

'I don't know why,' said Siobhán in answer to Iona's question. 'I really don't. To be honest, it's not something that I've ever encountered before. We have had cases of bigamy, but they were nearly all related to immigration issues. I've never come across a situation where a man has apparently married two women just for the hell of it.'

'It wasn't just for the hell of it!' cried Iona. 'It was because he loved me.'

Siobhán said nothing. Iona sat down on the sofa again and rested her head on her knees.

'I've got nothing.' Eventually Iona raised her dark eyes towards Siobhán. 'If this is true . . . if he married me . . . and he wasn't entitled to marry me . . . then I've got nothing.'

Siobhán stayed silent.

'I mean – if she's his official wife, then she's the one they'll talk to about his treatment,' continued Iona miserably. 'They won't want to know me. She'll be the one to take all the decisions. And that's not fair!'

'Maybe you'll be able to come to some kind of agreement,' suggested Siobhán.

'Agreement! You're joking!' Iona looked at her angrily. 'You saw how she reacted. She thinks – if anything – I might be his bit on the side. But I'm not. It was never like that. I'm the one who brings him to the dentist because he's so scared of needles and stuff. I'm the one who found a decent physio for the shoulder injury he got lugging boxes around the place. I help him with updating his business records. What kind of input does she have into all that? Nothing as far as I can see. But everyone will take her side because she's the legal wife. If she was all that great, then why did he come to me?'

'I can't answer those questions for you,' said Siobhán. 'You'll have to deal with it yourself. I guess what I have to find out is if there was any particular reason he decided to go through with this marriage.'

'I told you. He loves me.'

'As I said, what would he hope to get out of it? I'm sorry I have to ask you this, Iona. I really am. But – is your family well off? Would you expect to come into an inheritance?'

Iona stared at Siobhán in disbelief. She was quite unable to speak.

'A lot of times it does all come down to money,' said Siobhán apologetically.

'I already told you I'm not rich!' cried Iona eventually. 'I – for heaven's sake, look at where we live! Sure it's my house – I bought it before I met Frank. It's cute and convenient but it's hardly the home of a millionaire! As for an inheritance – that's a joke. My parents are totally unmaterialistic. They live in a small farmhouse in Spain and they're practically self-sufficient. Dad has a pension and they have some olive groves which bring in a little money, but it's certainly not a vast business empire.'

She got up from the sofa and went into the kitchen, reappearing a few moments later with a bottle of green-gold oil.

'This is from the finca,' she said, holding it out to Siobhán. 'They sell it in the local market and sometimes to tourists.'

'Is the finca worth much?' Siobhán unscrewed the top and sniffed at the oil. It was rich and aromatic, with a slight hint of lemon.

'No it bloody isn't,' said Iona. 'Well, I suppose property prices have gone up a bit, but it's nothing spectacular.'

'Do they have a house here?' asked Siobhán.

Iona nodded. 'In Templeogue. It's a very, very ordinary 1970s house which is currently rented out. The rent isn't anything spectacular but it's a steady income. Mum and Dad decided not to sell it because they wanted to have something to fall back on. Not that they'd come home, of course, just that they could sell it for extra funds. But the rental seems to be enough to keep them happy.' She looked at Siobhán curiously. 'Why does this matter?'

Siobhán said nothing.

'You don't think . . . you don't think that Frank was planning to kill me or something, do you?' Iona's voice was laden with bewildered scorn. 'I mean, this is real life, not some stupid made-for-TV play.'

'We have to think of everything, no matter how silly it may seem,' said Siobhán.

'Yeah, well, if Frank was thinking of knocking me over the head and making off with anything, he should've done it a couple of years ago,' said Iona. 'When I met him first he was struggling with financing for his company. But he managed to put it all in place. And he didn't need the off-chance that I'd pop my clogs and leave him a third share in a suburban house to keep him going. You're just being ludicrous.'

Siobhán shrugged. 'I still have to ask.'

'Have you asked her?' demanded Iona. 'Have you asked her why he married her and then decided to marry someone else? Have you?'

'I've spoken to Sally, yes,' said Siobhán.

'And I suppose she's full of it now.' Iona bit her lip to keep it from trembling. 'I suppose she thinks that everything's fine and that she's the one in charge.'

'Everything isn't fine, of course it isn't,' said Siobhán. 'Regardless of the legal situation, you've had a relationship with Frank and you think of yourself as his wife. That can't be easy for her either, you know.'

'I don't give a shit about her,' snapped Iona, 'and she doesn't give a shit about me.'

'But you both love Frank.'

Iona sighed. The fire had suddenly gone out of her eyes.

'I don't know,' she said softly. 'I love someone. But if Frank isn't the person I thought . . . then how can he be the man I love?'

Chapter 12

Frank was incredibly tired. His arms and legs were too heavy to lift and he simply didn't have the energy to make the effort. He felt bad about this because he knew that he should at least try. But he didn't want to. He knew, too, that . . . that . . . He struggled to remember her name and at last it came to him. Sally! Sally Campion. Sally would be furious with him. She hated it when he got himself into this kind of state, too drunk to move. It didn't happen very often these days, of course, but it did happen. And then her blue-green eyes would harden and her lips would thin and she would leave him to his misery, also leaving him in no doubt that he would have to spend time earning back her forgiveness.

He didn't mind that really. He loved Sally. As he lay there he thought about how much he loved her and how good she was for him. He remembered meeting her at a party and having some make-believe quarrel over a can of beer, and he remembered kissing her.

It had been a bit obvious, kissing her like that, but she hadn't objected. And it had been a surprisingly good kiss. He'd kissed a lot of women since Marion but none of them had kissed him back in the same way as Sally. And afterwards she'd smiled at him so that he couldn't help but imagine her naked, her copper tresses falling tantalisingly across her porcelain-skinned body. He'd seen lots of women naked after Marion too. But this woman was different. He didn't know why. But he did know that he wanted to sleep with her and he didn't want to let her go.

Remembering made his head hurt. When he'd been going out with Marion she used to look after him if he'd gone on a bender. She'd been sympathetic. She'd put something cool on his forehead and make him drink a concoction that she said all the nurses swore by. It didn't always make him feel better but at least it was something.

Sally wasn't like that. Sally was impatient with illness and didn't like it when he got drunk. And because of that, and because he loved her, he didn't drink so much any more. Hardly ever, actually. Which was why he was surprised to realise he had such a hangover now. Where had he been to get so wasted? Had he been out with Sally? But surely he wouldn't have gone out with her and got drunk. When he went out with Sally they did cultural things. They went to concerts – not gigs in the park type of concerts, real grown-up concerts in theatres where the men wore suits and the women dressed up; they went to the theatre, they went to art galleries. And he liked doing these things with her. Of course he also liked it when they went to the latest action movie or for a basket of chicken and chips in their favourite pub. But Sally added something to his life. An extra dimension. And he liked it.

He liked her. He loved her. And he didn't want her to be angry with him. The thing to do, he thought, as he tried to ignore the pounding in his head, the thing to do was to marry her. Because he wouldn't find anyone better. Marion had been his first love. And maybe he should have tried to hang on to Marion, because they'd been good together. Actually, yes, he should have tried to hang on to Marion, because they'd been more than good together. They'd been fantastic. Sally was good in bed, but not as good as Marion. None of them had been as good as her.

He sighed. Marion wasn't coming back, though. She'd sent him a letter telling him about her great job in the States and how she'd never come back to boring old Ireland. She didn't even say that she missed him. He should have made her miss him, should have treated her better so that she wouldn't leave him.

But Sally would actually be better for him because she didn't indulge him like Marion. And she was good in bed too – not as intuitive as Marion had been, but good all the same. Nurses and teachers, of course. Everyone knew they were good in the sack!

He'd let the nurse go. He needed to hang on to the teacher. He *would* hang on to her. As soon as he felt half-human again he was going to bring her out for the most expensive meal he could possibly afford and he was going to ask her to marry him.

Jenna looked at her watch and then slid out of Gerry Cullinan's arms.

'I have to get home,' she told him. 'We're going to the hospital again in half an hour.'

'And will that other woman be there?' Gerry was stunned by the idea of Jenna's father having another wife. He'd listened in amazed silence as she'd blurted out the story of Iona arriving at the hospital, claiming to be married to Frank. He'd been as sympathetic as possible, even though there was a part of him that was quite taken with the idea of a bloke having an unknown extra wife, a small part of him that was saying, 'Fair play to you, Frank.' Because he knew that the idea of a second woman and the reality were two different things.

'I don't know whether she'll be there or not.' Jenna's voice was taut in response to his question. 'She's a nutter, you know. Real dramatic. Stomping her feet and being rude to everyone. But she's not married to my dad. I know she's not.'

Gerry looked at Jenna sympathetically. 'I know it's shit for you,' he said. 'If there's anything I can do to help . . .'

'Thanks.' Jenna rested her head on his shoulder for a couple of seconds and then lifted it again. 'But right now I don't think there's anything anyone can do. Unless you happen to own a helicopter? It's such a long way to the hospital.'

'Can't they move him closer to Bray?' asked Gerry.

'I don't think so.' Jenna sighed. 'Maybe when he comes out of intensive care. I hate it there.' She shuddered. 'All screens and tubes and equipment. He looks like some kind of robot. And I hate the hospital smell too. It makes me feel sick.'

'It probably won't be for long,' said Gerry comfortingly.

'From what the doctors are saying, it could be for ever.' Jenna choked back a sob. 'Nobody seems to know when he might come out of it. And you hear about it, don't you? People who've been in comas for years and who just don't wake up.'

'He'll not be in a coma for years,' said Gerry.

'How d'you know?' demanded Jenna. 'If they don't know, you don't know.'

He said nothing as she walked down the road ahead of him, her back ramrod straight, anger crackling around her. Eventually he called her name and she stopped. She turned to him as he caught up with her and he could see that her eyes were bright with tears.

'I'm sorry,' he said. 'I was trying to be helpful. But I suppose it isn't helpful when you're right and I don't have a clue.' He put his arm around her again and pulled her close to him. She looked up at him.

'It's OK,' she said. 'I guess I'm just . . . well, a bit strung out.'

'Understandable.' His cheek was close to hers.

'You've been great,' she said softly.

'I care about you,' he told her.

'Thanks.'

She was the one who kissed him. They moved into the shadow of the large sycamore tree at the corner of the road. Jenna slid her hands under Gerry's black leather jacket and hugged him close to her. She loved him. She really did. He was so great about everything, so understanding . . . Abruptly she pulled out of his arms again.

'I really have to go,' she said reluctantly. 'I don't want to be late.'

'I know.'

'But I don't want to go.'

'I know.'

'I love you,' she said.

'My parents are away next weekend.'

She looked into his eyes. 'Call me.'

'Of course,' he said.

They walked the rest of the way to her house in silence.

'Hope everything's OK,' he told her.

'Yeah. I hope so too.'

She put her key into the door and unlocked it. She knew that she was later than she'd promised and that her mother would probably be annoyed with her, but she didn't care.

'I'm home,' she called as she walked into the living room.

There was no sign of Sally. Jenna felt a spasm of fear and her heart began to race as she looked around the empty room. Then she heard the flush of the toilet upstairs and the sound of running water in the sink.

'I'm sorry I'm late,' she said as she climbed the stairs and poked her head around her mother's bedroom door. She stopped. Sally looked dreadful. Her long hair was damp and her face was pale. 'Are you all right?'

'Upset stomach,' said Sally.

Jenna felt the spasm of fear again. 'There's nothing wrong with you, is there?' Her voice was suddenly childlike.

'Of course not,' said Sally. She ran her fingers through her hair. 'Obviously I'm upset and worried about your dad, and that probably has something to do with it.'

'You can't get sick too,' said Jenna anxiously.

'I won't,' Sally assured her. The colour was already coming back into her cheeks. 'I'm fine, pet, honestly.'

Jenna looked at her uncertainly.

'Really I am,' said Sally. 'And you're not too late because Denise got stuck in traffic so she won't be here for another few minutes. I'm just going to change into something a bit more suitable for going out. How about you?'

'I'm all right,' said Jenna.

'Fine. Well, I'll see you downstairs.'

'Are we going to have to do this every day?' asked Jenna.

'What?'

'Go to the hospital all the time? What about school? What about your job?'

'We'll work something out,' said Sally. 'It'll be different when we get the car back, which should be any day now.'

'But you can't spend all day, every day in the hospital.' Jenna looked worried. 'Neither can I.'

'I'll take some time off,' said Sally. 'You can too.'

'I'll miss out on stuff,' said Jenna anxiously. 'I'll fall behind.'

'I can help you,' said Sally.

'Not with Irish,' said Jenna. 'You're hopeless at Irish.'

'Look, honey, please don't worry. We'll sort it out. Anyway, there's plenty of evening visiting hours so we can go after school.'

'I won't have time to do my homework.'

'You don't have to come every day,' said Sally. 'Dad'll understand.'

'Yeah. Seems to me it's us that have to do a lot of understanding,' said Jenna. 'I mean, Dad . . . well . . . you know. That woman.' Jenna swallowed hard. 'How could he, Mum? How could he?'

'That's something we have to sort out too,' agreed Sally. 'But there's no point in us getting into a state about it now, is there?'

'Well it's all wrong!'

'I know.'

'She's there and what – what if they have a kid too?'

Sally looked at Jenna in shock. She'd never even considered it.

'I don't think that's likely,' she said eventually.

'Yeah, well, Dad having another wife stashed away wasn't exactly likely either, was it?'

'Jen, please.' Sally sighed. 'I know it's difficult, but we can't keep going on and on about it.'

'We can't ignore it either. We can't pretend that he hasn't lied to us. That he isn't a complete bastard and that I hate him.' Jenna looked accusingly at her mother, then walked out of the room.

Sally sat on the bed and pressed her fingers to her temples. Her head was pounding and she desperately wanted some paracetamol. It was the headache that was making her feel ill, she told herself, although she knew that part of her nausea was due to Jenna's question about whether Frank and Iona had a child. Another thing to worry about. And the gardai were involved too. Since Siobhán Farrell's visit Sally hadn't been able to rid her mind of the fact that her relationship was now part of some kind of police investigation! Siobhán had been polite and sympathetic but Sally had felt humiliated having to show her a marriage certificate and photographs of her wedding. And she couldn't help wondering about that other woman too. Sally knew that Siobhán was going to see Iona as well. Would she have a marriage certificate and wedding photos to show her? And if so, how had it all happened?

Sally desperately wanted to stop thinking about it. She wanted to concentrate on Frank's accident, not on Frank's other wife. Mistress. Whatever. She kept telling herself that she was Frank's legal wife, but that wasn't much comfort when Iona had identified him as her husband too. So who would be in charge of his treatment? What if everything went terribly wrong for Frank and there was a question of turning off life support? What if this woman wanted to kill him but she didn't? Sally knew that she would never switch off Frank's life support. She felt herself grow hot at the idea. And tonight. She'd phoned the hospital about coming tonight and John Carroll had told her that Iona wasn't going to be there in the evening, but how could he be sure about that? As far as Sally could see, the woman was demented enough to show up whenever she liked. And the thing was . . . she pressed her fingers to her temples again . . . the thing was that if she really believed that she was married to Frank, then why shouldn't she?

But how could she believe it now? After all, Siobhán would have told her that Sally was Frank's lawful wife, so Iona would know that her position was completely untenable. In which case she should be staying at home. Sally felt the pressure in her head build up again as her anger at Frank grew. How could he have done this? How could he have betrayed her like this? She'd felt herself grow hot and cold with embarrassment as Siobhán Farrell had quizzed her about her marriage, asking her about the likelihood of Frank having somebody else. She'd never, not for one second, imagined that there'd been another woman. Even during that bad time when things had been so strained between them, she'd believed that Frank still loved her. She'd never supposed that the nights he spent away were nights spent with another woman and not, as he'd told her, dealing with his subcontractors or having client meetings at far-flung places in the country.

And the other woman! That was what was so awful about it. If there'd been someone on the side, or occasional lapses, well, maybe she could have dealt with it. But his relationship with Iona was obviously different. He must at least have thought he was in love with her to have gone through a marriage ceremony with her! What in God's name had he been thinking at the time? And what in God's name did it mean now, both for Sally's past and for her future?

'Denise is here!' Jenna's voice wafted up the stairs and galvanised Sally into action. She changed into a pair of stretchy jeans and a freshly ironed T-shirt, then pulled on a lightweight jumper over it. Although the temperature outside was cold, she knew that the hospital was uncomfortably warm.

Denise and Jenna were in the kitchen. When she saw her friend, Sally felt like crying all over again. She'd known Denise for years; they'd trained together and worked together and they'd only ever had one argument. That had been about Frank. Denise had never really liked him, even though she'd eventually admitted to Sally that she'd been wrong. Only maybe she hadn't after all.

Denise hugged her and Sally kept her head on the other woman's shoulder. She hadn't told Denise the whole story, although she knew she would have to tell her at some point, so Denise didn't yet know about Iona Brannock. All she knew was that Frank had been critically injured.

'Come on, come on,' she murmured comfortingly to Sally. 'Every thing will be fine. Frank's a hard nut. He'll get over this.'

Maybe he will, Sally thought as she got her emotions under control again; but will I?

* * *

The apartment was empty when Siobhán finally got home. There was a note from Eddie to say that he'd gone for a walk to clear his head and that he'd be home shortly. But there was no time on the note and so Siobhán had no idea how long he'd been gone. She made a face at the empty room. She'd hoped that he'd have been rested by now and that they might have indulged in the champagne and sex which they hadn't got round to earlier. She picked up the phone and dialled his mobile number but was diverted to his mail-box.

'I'm home,' she said. 'And waiting for you!' She stood indecisively in the living room for a moment and then decided that she would continue with her earlier flurry of domesticity. She made herself a cup of coffee first and then set up the ironing board (almost, as always, losing the tips of her fingers as she opened it out) and plugged in the iron. Then she gathered up the mound of clothes that needed ironing.

Even though she did find it restful, she was also aware of the fact that she was fairly hopeless at ironing, managing to put razor-sharp creases into things that shouldn't have creases in them at all. Actually Eddie often brought his shirts in to work because there was a pick-up and return laundry service there, but of course there was no such thing in Bray garda station, and even if there was, Siobhán couldn't justify the expense to herself. That was the thing about living with Eddie. He could afford so much more than her. Like earlier, when he'd talked about the cleaning service. She never thought of herself as the kind of person who could afford cleaners. Still, it was a nice thought! But the money issue rankled a little. Siobhán wanted to be an equal partner in their relationship, but financially she never would be. And she found that difficult to accept. She'd read before that money was one of the biggest problems that people had in their marriages and she could see why. Money was one of life's biggest problems, full stop. The pursuit of money was why most crimes were committed after all.

Thinking of crimes made her thoughts turn to the potential bigamy case again. If money was the motivation for most crimes, then money was probably the motivation behind this one too. And yet . . . having talked to both Sally and Iona, Siobhán wasn't so sure.

Frank's relationship with Iona had obviously commenced while he was going through a difficult patch in his marriage to Sally. The two women were like chalk and cheese – intriguing in itself, because experience told Siobhán that people usually formed subsequent relationships with people who were very similar to those in previous ones. Maybe Frank had wanted something very different to the cosy domestic set-up he seemed to have with Sally. But then why would he actually set up a second home with Iona? And heavens above, she thought as she accidentally ironed a crease across the back of her favourite white blouse, how on earth had he managed to keep his two lives separate for so long? At least if he'd been simply having an affair with Iona he would have been at home at Christmas or other holiday times. And yet he'd seemed to work it all very well. His job gave him a perfect excuse to be away, even over the holidays, and neither Sally nor Iona seemed to be too worried about his absences. She would've thought that they'd be suspicious of him not being there, but of course why would they? After all, she herself had been at work last Christmas – although Eddie had been really annoyed about it, complaining that he'd be stuck in the apartment on his own for the whole day, which surely wasn't the spirit of the season, was it?

Her next step would be to investigate Frank Harper's background. She'd go to Sligo and do a bit of digging there, check out the house (Christ, she hoped there wouldn't be a third Harper wife holed up there) and find out a little more about the Harper family. She'd also check to ensure that Sally and Frank hadn't actually divorced despite Sally's firm statement that it wasn't ever on the cards. Sally and Jenna seemed genuine enough, but heaven only knew what was really going on. Siobhán was prepared to believe anything about anybody. Once you joined the police, your views of human nature changed for ever.

She'd just finished the ironing when Eddie walked in the door. She smiled at him and told him that he could fold up the finger-snapping ironing board while she put away the clothes.

'I brought back some chicken wings and dips from the deli down the road,' Eddie told her. 'Thought you might fancy something to eat.'

'Only you.' She grinned at him. 'But that can wait, I guess. You're actually quite right, I'm starving. I didn't have any lunch, just a coffee and a KitKat when I got home.'

'I'll get some plates,' said Eddie.

Five minutes later they were sharing the chicken wings in front of the TV.

'So tell me about Boston,' said Siobhán as she nibbled at a wing. 'Was it good fun?'

'Hardly fun,' Eddie told her. 'I was working.'

'Yeah, yeah.' She grinned at him.

'No, truly,' he said. 'It was all about securitising debt so that—'

'Zzzz.' Siobhán yawned exaggeratedly. 'Don't know. Don't need to know.'

'Revel in your ignorance,' said Eddie.

'I will,' she said. 'Actually I nearly got there myself a few years ago.'

'Did you?'

'Well, sort of. It was a drugs thing. The gang had an operation near here but they were getting stuff from the States. But those lucky bastards in the drugs squad went instead.'

'Poor you.'

'Ah well. Next time maybe. Or there's always the Caribbean.'

'Huh?'

'The bigamy case? Remember? The second wedding was in Barbados. I could so go for an investigative trip there.' She took another wing. 'But the furthest I'm really likely to get is Sligo, which is where the bloke is from.'

'Brave man,' said Eddie. 'Two wives.'

'Ah, but neither of them as hot stuff as me.' Siobhán snuggled up to him. 'Hope you had a good sleep earlier, because you're going to have things done to you tonight that you've never had done to you before.' She slid her palm beneath his shirt.

He caught her wrist with his hand. 'Not now.'

She looked at him. 'I wasn't going to do it now. But . . . I thought . . . Is something wrong?'

'I'm sorry,' he said. 'It's long flights. They just . . . they take it out of me.'

'But you've been asleep for hours.'

'I know. I know. Later. I'll be fine later.'

'OK.' She kissed him on the cheek. But she was frowning as she got up and cleared the debris from the chicken wings away.

Chapter 13

Iona didn't know what to do next. The thinking part of her brain told her that she needed to get some legal advice on her situation (as well as some information about Frank's business – she was worried about his clients and what might happen to them), yet all she could really think about was that Frank was still critically injured and that somehow she wasn't the most important person in his life or the only person who had an interest in his recovery. And since the hospital – having spoken to Siobhán Farrell – had accepted that Sally was Frank's lawful wife, they'd made it clear to her that Sally was the one who had to be consulted about his treatment.

The accident would have been bad enough by itself, but now it was as though a whole chunk of her existence had been suddenly ripped away and there was nothing she could do to replace it. Everything she'd believed about herself and about Frank had been based on a web of lies and deceit. She was angrier than she'd ever been in her life; but it was impossible to maintain the level of fury that she felt while at the same time worrying herself sick about the fact that he was still in a coma.

After her meeting (or interview, as she supposed Siobhán Farrell would call it) with the detective, she'd simply curled up on the sofa and cried. Lauren had called around later to see how she was and Iona was completely incapable of talking to her. Lauren had begged her to take another Valium but Iona had refused and had then had a complete fit of hysterics when she realised that Lauren had given her one the night before. Her older sister had suggested that she spend the night at her house again, but she'd refused to do that too. She wanted to stay in her own place with her own things around her where people couldn't fool her into taking prescription drugs against her will. Anyway, it was bad enough that everything else had been taken away from her without uprooting herself and spending another night at Myles and Lauren's. Besides, the kids would be up and about and she knew she wouldn't be able to cope with them right now.

She was aware that Lauren was worried about her but she couldn't help that. She promised her sister that she wouldn't do anything stupid like overdosing on valerian or slashing her wrists (Lauren had an occasional tendency to imagine the worst), but the fact that she said these things at all seemed to worry her sister all the more. In the end Lauren had insisted in staying the night at Iona's, sleeping on the sofa because of the fact that the spare bedroom had been given over to office space.

Now, at six o'clock on Sunday morning, Iona had woken properly from her fragmented sleep. She pulled a heavy Aran jumper over her blue cotton pyjamas and stuck her feet into her enormous green fluffy slippers before making her way into the office. She was looking for anything that would give her a clue as to why Frank had done what he'd done.

If he'd done what he'd done. Deep down she wanted to believe that it was still all some terrible, terrible mistake.

She didn't find anything in the office. In fact, she thought, as she looked through the files, there was remarkably little information even about Frank's business. And nothing on the desktop computer. She knew that he mainly used a laptop for business, which she assumed he'd taken with him, but she'd always thought that he kept a few files and folders on the desktop too. Yet when she went in to look at them she found that they were simply template letters or links to folders on the laptop, with nothing in them.

What would happen with his business? she wondered again. Who would deal with his clients? Where was his business phone? Maybe people were already calling, looking for him. He often got calls at the weekends even though he rarely did installation and maintenance work himself. He contracted all that out. But Iona suddenly realised that she didn't have a clue who any of those people were. With Frank now lying in hospital, the business which he'd so carefully built up could go down the tubes. He wouldn't want that to happen. She knew he wouldn't. But how could she stop it? Maybe his solicitor could do something – always provided he knew about the business. She sighed. She would find out who Frank's legal people were and contact them first thing in the morning. That, at least, would be something worthwhile to do.

Meantime she opened her internet browser and typed the word

'bigamy' into it. There was nothing especially helpful there; most of the sites seemed to deal with marriages of convenience that turned out to be bigamous. As far as the cyber-community was concerned, people didn't get married over and over again just for the fun of it. Of course they didn't. What normal person did?

Swallowing hard, she typed 'coma' into the search engine. *A profound state of unconsciousness*, she read, *where a person is alive but unable to move or to respond to his environment.* The scariest thing, she thought, as she clicked her way through the pages, was that people knew so little about it all. Most comas rarely lasted longer than a month but there was nothing definite about it. And, of course, people could lose their thinking functions and be in a vegetative state for years.

Her hands were shaking. She couldn't begin to think of Frank being in a coma for years. She leaned her head against the screen and began to cry again. And she didn't know whether she was crying with worry or self-pity or anger.

'Are you all right?' Lauren's voice at the doorway made her sit up straight again. She grabbed a tissue from the box on her desk and wiped her eyes.

'I suppose I will be,' she said. 'But right now – not really.' She swallowed hard. 'It's just that nothing about us was true!' she choked. 'He lied to me every single day about every single thing. I mean – a wife! A daughter! A whole other life and I hadn't a clue! How stupid could I be?'

'Look, honey, nobody could possibly imagine that their husband had a second wife,' said Lauren. 'Maybe that they're having an affair or that they're having problems at work or something, but how on earth could you have guessed?'

'The thing is, I feel like it should all be a mistake,' cried Iona. 'I trusted him completely.' This time she wiped her eyes on the extra-long sleeve of the Aran jumper. 'I could've understood if he'd been married before and didn't tell me. I'd have been hurt but I could have dealt with it. Sometimes it's hard to tell people things. But that he was still married! And living with her at the same time as living with me! I can't believe it. Everyone will look at me and think that I'm the world's biggest eejit and they'll be dead right.'

'No they won't,' comforted Lauren. 'They'll think that he's a slick bastard.'

'But he isn't!' wailed Iona. 'That's the whole point. He was lovely to me. Always.'

Lauren rubbed her sister's shoulders.

'I know Myles hates him,' mumbled Iona. 'I suppose he's basking in the knowledge that everything he ever thought about him has turned out to be right.'

'No he's not,' said Lauren. 'He's horrified, of course. Maybe he did think that Frank was a bit too good to be true. But he never wanted you to be hurt.'

'What am I going to tell Mum and Dad?' continued Iona. 'They loved him. At least . . .' She hesitated. 'I know Mum said that the important thing was that he made me happy. I can't help wondering whether she suspected.'

'Of course she didn't!' Lauren paused in her shoulder massage.

'Well, not suspected,' admitted Iona. 'How could she? But she did comment on him being a bit older and . . . well, maybe she didn't really like him that much after all. Only you know Mum, she wouldn't have said anything.'

'I called her,' admitted Lauren.

Iona pulled away from her sister. 'Why did you do that?' she cried. 'It wasn't up to you.'

'Io, honey, she was going to have to find out sooner or later,' said Lauren. 'But I told her to leave it a bit before contacting you; give you time to get to grips with everything.'

Iona clenched her jaw and shook her head in despair. 'You see, that's just what I hate. People talking about me. Feeling sorry for me. Wondering when they should phone me.' She swallowed hard. 'How could I have been such a bloody fool? Being married already is obviously why he insisted on having the wedding in Barbados. I thought he was being romantic but he manipulated me. I'm a moron.'

'It's not your fault,' said Lauren. 'How were you to know?'

'I should've guessed.' Iona turned around on the swivel chair and faced her sister. 'You know, I felt like a total idiot in front of that policewoman. I could see that she thought I was a complete simpleton. She asked me what happened about Christmas and holidays and of course I said what Frank had told me – that sometimes he had to stay over at venues because they might need his expertise. And that we didn't go for long holidays. And that he did sometimes go to conferences without me. And all the time she was making notes and I bet they were saying how gullible I was to believe a word he told me.'

'But we do believe people when they tell us things,' said Lauren. 'Why should you have doubted him?'

'Why? Maybe because normal people don't spend Christmas in a hotel away from their families claiming that they have to stage-manage a lighting spectacular. Maybe normal people bring their wives to conferences and stuff – in fact he probably did bring his damn wife to the conferences; it just wasn't me.' Iona rubbed the back of her neck. 'D'you have any headache tablets? I feel as though my head is going to explode.'

'Sure,' said Lauren, thinking that Iona must be feeling really awful to ask for paracetamol. 'In my bag. Come on downstairs and you can have them.'

Iona hit the sleep button on the computer. She hated taking paracetamol or ibuprofen. But right now she needed something stronger than what nature had to offer.

Sally still felt embarrassed walking into the hospital. She couldn't help feeling that all the doctors and nurses knew exactly who she was and what had happened, even though she told herself over and over again that they had better things to talk about than the woman whose husband had married someone else and never said a thing. There was no point in her pretending otherwise as far as Frank's second marriage was concerned. Iona's reaction had been heartfelt. And Siobhán Farrell had contacted her again to tell her about Iona's Caribbean wedding and the marriage certificate that didn't really count.

Sally didn't know how she would have reacted if she'd found out about this when Frank was fit and healthy. She would have definitely been equally shocked. She told herself that she'd probably have thrown him out of the house, although that was a difficult thing to be sure about given that she was pregnant with his child.

She touched her stomach unconsciously. Frank didn't deserve a second child. Not with her. Not with anyone. He wasn't a fit person to be a father and it didn't matter how wonderful and loving he'd been towards her, or even how good he'd been with Jenna, he was a deceiving bastard and he didn't have the right to be with either of them.

And yet, as she sat alone in the room with him, listening to the sounds of the machines gently hissing and whirring, and the rhythmic beat of the heart monitor, she knew that she couldn't simply abandon him. Besides, if she did that, maybe Iona would take over.

Sally rubbed the back of her neck. She didn't want Iona taking over even though she was finding it hard to forgive Frank herself. Though the younger woman mightn't want to have anything to do with him either, now that she'd discovered that she too had been duped. She hadn't turned up at the hospital again and Siobhán had said that as far as she could see, Iona had accepted the fact that her marriage wasn't legal.

Poor girl. Bad enough as she felt herself, Sally thought it would be even worse to discover that she hadn't been married at all. So although she hated Iona for taking Frank away from her, she also felt sorry for the younger woman because her life with him had been based on a lie.

She studied the man in the bed. Already Frank was beginning to look like a different person, his handsome face pale and expressionless, the tubes and machines almost a part of him. Despite his still attractive features, Sally couldn't see in him the person who'd almost literally swept her off her feet, who'd charmed her in an instant, who'd helped her discover that her body was an almost unlimited playground of desire. Frank looked old in the bed. Dependent. He'd never been dependent on her before. He'd always been the one to take charge of things. She hated seeing him like this and she knew he'd hate to think of her sitting with him, watching and waiting.

What would happen if he didn't come out of the coma? Everyone in the hospital was trying to be positive, despite their concerns. Sally wanted to be positive too. She couldn't believe that he wouldn't open his eyes in a day or two and look around and ask where the hell he was and what the hell he was doing here.

Would he expect to see her? Or would he think that Iona was the one who should be beside him? She swallowed hard. How would she feel if he opened his eyes and asked for Iona?

'Hi, Mrs Harper.' The nurse who'd been there on the first night was on duty again. Sally glanced at her name tag to remind herself of who she was.

'I just need to do a few bits and pieces for him,' Terri Cooper said. 'You can stay if you want, or wait outside.'

Sally got up. She needed a break anyway. She walked down the corridor and got herself a coffee from the dispenser. Jenna hadn't come with her on this visit. She'd asked, in a worried tone, whether it would be all right not to come because the hospital gave her the creeps. Sally had nodded in agreement. She didn't want Jenna to feel that her whole life had to revolve around hospital visits. Besides, the place gave her the creeps too.

'Finished now.' Terri smiled brightly at Sally, who finished the tepid coffee and crumpled the plastic cup in her hand.

'Will he get better?' Sally knew that the nurse wouldn't be able to give her an answer, but she couldn't help asking anyway.

'You'd be surprised at how many people get better,' said Terri. 'Though I have to be honest with you and say that it takes time for them to get back to normal. It's a huge trauma.'

Sally nodded.

'We're all keeping our fingers crossed for him,' Terri said. 'He's a very attractive man, isn't he?'

'He's more attractive when he's awake,' said Sally wryly.

Terri grinned. 'But you can see it in him all the same.'

'Seems more than me did.'

Terri looked at her cautiously. She'd been trying to be cheerful with the sad-faced woman, but of course in this case saying that her husband was attractive might have been like waving the proverbial red rag at a bull.

'It's an awkward situation,' agreed Terri.

'This morning the doctor told me to talk to him,' Sally said. 'And so I read him the papers. But what if it's not me he needs to hear? What if it's her?'

Terri shrugged uncomfortably. 'I'd say any familiar voice would be a help,' she said.

'Maybe I should just get my daughter to do it,' said Sally. 'At least we know that he loves her.' Her eyes opened wide. 'Is there another one?'

'Pardon?'

'Child? Does that woman have a child? She didn't say and I didn't ask, but . . .'

'I don't know,' said Terri.

'Oh fuck him!' cried Sally suddenly, startling Terri. 'Fuck him, fuck him, fuck him!' She threw the crumpled coffee cup across the corridor.

'How could he do this to me and to Jenna? How could he do it to Iona either? I thought I loved him but he's nothing but a bastard!'

'You don't really mean that, Sally,' said Terri gently. 'You're overwrought.'

'I'm not,' snapped Sally. 'I'm just – I'm just . . .' The fight went out of her and she swayed on her feet. Terri put her arm around her and guided her to a chair.

'Sit down,' she said. 'It's been a huge strain on you and anyone would be upset.'

'A strain for everyone except Frank,' she said bitterly. 'He's lying there with everyone fussing around him but we're left to cope with the mess. I don't know what to do about his work – I've never had anything to do with it. I'm not sure what I'm supposed to do myself about my own job. I don't know what to do about Jenna and school . . . He's left us with all these problems and I just can't bloody cope!'

'Sit there and I'll get you something,' said Terri. 'Isn't there anyone with you today?'

'I got a taxi,' said Sally. 'The AA are bringing our car back tomorrow. That's another thing to worry about. I have to deal with everything. All he has to do is lie there!'

Terri gestured to Susan Carpenter, another nurse, who was walking down the corridor, and whispered into her ear. Susan returned a few moments later with a small pill and a cup of water.

'Come on, Sally,' said Terri. 'You'll feel better after this.'

'I can't take those tablets.'

'Of course you can,' said Terri. 'It'll help you to relax, and you need to relax right now.'

'You don't understand.' Sally looked at both of the nurses and closed her eyes in despair. When she opened them again they were both watching her anxiously. 'I can't take the damn tablets because on the day he was in the accident I discovered I was pregnant.' Her laugh was short and croaky. 'As if I didn't have enough to be dealing with, huh?'

Terri and Susan exchanged shocked glances. Then Susan walked away with the water and the pill and Terri put her arm around Sally's shoulders again.

Chapter 14

Iona wasn't sure how to go about finding Frank's lawyer, but in the end it was Myles who said he'd check it out for her. Lauren had told him of Iona's concerns about Frank's company and Myles said that he would use his legal and accountancy contacts to find out what he could. Iona wanted to thank him but she was finding it difficult to talk to Myles, who she was sure would only tell her that he'd told her so and that Frank was the complete shit he'd always thought him to be.

'Myles isn't like that,' said Lauren, when Iona finally admitted this to her sister. 'I don't understand why you've always been so horrible to him.'

Iona heard the sudden break in her sister's voice and she looked at her in surprise. 'I'm not horrible to him,' she said.

'You are,' said Lauren. 'Even before you met Frank. You always went on and on about Myles being a boring accountant.'

Iona flushed. What Lauren had said was true. She did think accountants were boring.

'I'm sorry,' she said. 'I didn't mean that he was boring. Only that it was a boring profession.'

'You know, you've a bit of a cheek thinking that when Frank works in lighting and you work in a damn letting agency,' said Lauren.

Iona looked contrite. 'I know. Though I always wanted to do something more exciting than house-letting,' she said.

'Well maybe Myles wanted to do something more exciting than accounting,' said Lauren. 'Only he's got a wife and family to provide for and it's a damn good job.'

'Just as well I wasn't planning on Frank providing for me,' said Iona shakily. 'Just as well I wasn't pregnant after all.'

'Oh, hell, Io . . .' Lauren looked at her sympathetically. 'I'm sorry.'

'I don't know where to go from here,' said Iona. 'I'm not married to him. I really don't have any say in what's going on. I want to go to the hospital but . . .'

'Maybe you can come to some arrangement with Sally.'

'I don't want to come to an arrangement with her,' said Iona fiercely. 'As though she can give me permission to go and see the man I've been sleeping with for the last four years. As though she's somehow in control.'

'She *is* in control, it seems,' said Lauren. 'You have to decide what you're going to do. Did you talk to your solicitor this morning?'

Iona nodded. 'He said they could try to prosecute me if they thought I was part of some crazy plan,' she said. 'Not that I even thought of that, which is just as well or I . . .' She shook her head tiredly. 'He's going to contact Frank's solicitor, once we find out who he is. He wants to try to establish some rights based on the fact that I thought I was married. To be honest, though, I don't see the point. I know the situation. I can't be part of it all, Lauren. Not while she's the real wife and I'm nothing. I'm not going in to see him again.'

'But you need to think about this a bit more,' said Lauren. 'After all, what if he dies?'

'I don't want to think about him dying,' said Iona.

'But you're entitled to something, surely?'

'Like what?'

'Well . . .' She shrugged. 'There's the house in Sligo, isn't there? And if his company was profitable you should have a slice of that. After all, you supported him with it, didn't you?'

'I helped out from time to time,' said Iona. 'That was just doing letters and stuff for him.'

'All the same . . .'

'I can't!' Iona thumped her fist on the table. 'Lauren, if he dies there's just me. But for them – well, it's Sally and her daughter. They're entitled to more.' She exhaled sharply. 'I don't want to think about him dying. I want to think about him getting better.'

'And that'll create even more problems.'

'Maybe,' said Iona. 'But I'd rather them than anything else.'

Later that day Siobhán phoned both Sally and Iona and asked them to make witness statements about their relationship with Frank. At first neither of them was very happy about the idea, but, each concerned about what the other might say, they finally agreed. Siobhán told them that it was an easy process and that she'd call out to their houses if that was what they wanted. But somewhat to her surprise they both said they'd come into the station instead. She'd been taken aback when they'd both suggested Thursday and in the interests of peace and sanity had asked if Sally could come a day earlier.

So on Wednesday afternoon Sally found herself sitting in the bright reception area of Bray garda station while she waited for Siobhán Farrell to take her to an interview room. Even though they'd lived in Bray for the past five years Sally had never been in the station before, although she'd often driven by it on her way to the town centre. It was big and modern and as unlike her preconception of a garda station as it was possible to be. She thought, as she gazed at the pastel-painted walls and watched the young garda behind the reception desk deal with a telephone query, that it was relatively welcoming and certainly not as threatening as she'd expected. But she was overcome by a sense of unreality at the idea that she, Sally Harper, was here as a witness to a crime and that that crime was that her husband had married someone else. If she'd ever had to come up with a reason for visiting a garda station, that wouldn't have even appeared on the list. She sat on the wooden seat and stared at the blue sky through the angular glass roof while she tried to slow down the rapid beating of her heart. She was nervous about the interview and uncertain what Siobhán would want to know.

When the detective walked into the reception area to greet her, Sally couldn't help feeling that the other woman was much more serious and formal than she'd been previously, even though she smiled warmly at Sally and thanked her for coming.

'D'you want to follow me?' she asked.

Sally grabbed her bag and walked after the detective, who showed her into a small interview room and told her to take a seat. Sally noticed that there was a video camera over the door of the room which was pointed in her direction. She swallowed nervously as she tugged on the arms of the black leather chair to bring it nearer to the table. It didn't budge. She pulled it again.

'It's heavy,' said Siobhán. 'We normally have suspects in here and we don't want them to be able to lift up the chair and throw it at us.'

Sally swallowed nervously again at the thought of the other people who might have sat in that chair, and Siobhán smiled reassuringly at her.

'You're not a suspect in anything, Sally,' she said. 'You're just here to help us sort things out.'

Sally's eyes flickered towards the camera.

'We're not recording anything either,' Siobhán told her. 'Don't worry.' She stood up and popped a button on the video console. 'There you go, there's nothing in there.'

'OK.' Sally swallowed hard.

'D'you want me to get you a drink?' asked Siobhán. 'Water? Or tea, maybe?'

Sally shook her head. Now that she was here, she just wanted to get on with it.

'Right-o,' said Siobhán. 'Let's get started.'

She went over much of the ground she'd already covered, although she asked the questions in a different way. Sally found it a surreal experience as she gave her answers honestly but with an increasing feeling that the detective must surely take her for a complete fool. All the same, she was utterly unable to take in the fact that as far as the legal system was concerned, Frank was actually a criminal. A lying, philandering shit maybe, she'd thought that morning as she sat on the edge of the toilet following her regular bout of morning sickness, but not a criminal. Here, though, in the station, everything seemed much more serious than it had done until now.

She wiped a bead of sweat from her forehead and then looked anxiously at Siobhán. What if the detective thought she was sweating because she was involved somehow in a scam of Frank's? What if she thought it was some elaborate hoax that the two of them had perpetrated.

'Are you going to charge him?' she asked.

Siobhán looked at her noncommittally. 'It's not up to me. It's the Director of Public Prosecutions who decides, and to tell you the truth, Sally, I've no idea what he'll think. I guess it depends on whether he believes the public interest would be served in charging him.'

'And would it?'

'It depends on how things eventually pan out,' said Siobhán. 'I mean, what did Frank stand to gain by marrying Iona?'

'Great sex?' Sally looked at Siobhán wryly.

The other girl blanched. 'I'm sorry?'

'I've no bloody idea what he had to gain,' said Sally. 'But Frank wasn't . . . isn't good at sex outside a relationship. He told me before that he didn't like one-night stands. Of course this is different, I know, but . . .' She chewed the inside of her lip. 'Frank is good at sex.'

Siobhán tried to hide her unease. She didn't want to hear about the Harpers' sex life – especially not how good it might have been. But Sally was suddenly talking about how she and Frank had met and how there was an instant attraction between them; how, in fact, they'd hardly been able to keep their hands off each other. And that there was something more to it than that – Frank was a vibrant person who made a woman feel good about herself. Sally knew that she blossomed in his company because her self-confidence grew when she was with him. So maybe it was the same with Iona. She looked at Siobhán questioningly.

'That's the thing.' Siobhán had regained her composure. 'Mostly there's a more tangible benefit than, well, just sex. There's plenty of that available without having to get married! Usually in these cases people are trying to gain nationality. Or sometimes it's financial. But I can't see a financial reason here.'

'Maybe she's incredibly rich,' suggested Sally morosely. 'Maybe there were money problems I didn't know about. Maybe he felt that by marrying her . . .' Her voice trailed off. She didn't like where her thoughts were taking her.

'It doesn't really seem like it,' said Siobhán. 'Although obviously we're checking out that angle.' She looked apologetically at Sally. 'We're also looking into Frank's company, to see if there were money problems. And – I know this is hard for you, Sally, I really do – but under the circumstances, I'd like to take Frank's fingerprints.'

Sally's expression was shocked. 'Why?'

'I need to check to see if he's been in trouble before,' said Siobhán.

'For crying out loud!' Sally looked at her in exasperation. 'He's an ordinary bloke. Of course he hasn't been in any trouble. Except maybe a few unpaid parking fines. Or perhaps you got him on camera breaking the speed limit or something. Only he doesn't. He's a careful driver. He's a law-abiding man.'

'I do understand that,' said Siobhán. 'But it would help in the investigation.'

Sally sighed deeply. She liked Siobhán, who, she thought, had been kind and understanding and very non-judgemental about the situation. But she wished that the other woman wouldn't talk about Frank as though he was a criminal. He wasn't. He was her husband.

'If you really need to do this, then go ahead,' she said tiredly. 'But you know, Sally, I truly loved him. I know, I absolutely know, that he wasn't involved in anything dodgy and you're wasting your time if you think that. His solicitor has been in touch about the company. Frank has critical illness cover, which kicks in for me. Frank's accountant is contacting the clients and arranging for them to be looked after. I gave him Frank's mobile. There's absolutely nothing dodgy going on. And you probably think that I'm crazy saying this, but I do know my husband. He's an honest man. Obviously I don't understand why he did all this. How the hell can I? But I understand some of it.'

'Jeez, Sally, nobody understands everything to do with men,' said Siobhán with feeling. 'If we did we'd all be a lot bloody happier.'

Sally raised an eyebrow. Siobhán's words had been heartfelt.

'Are you married?' She repeated the question which Siobhán hadn't answered when she'd been at Sally's house.

Siobhán shook her head.

'Anyone special?'

She thought of Eddie. He was special.

'I'm engaged,' she told Sally.

'Do you live with him?' asked Sally.

Siobhán considered before answering. By talking about her own life, even a little, she hoped she might reassure Sally that she wasn't her enemy. She nodded.

'I never lived with Frank before we got married,' said Sally. 'I slept with him, of course, but in those days people didn't live together much. There wasn't plenty of it around without having to get married. In fact getting married was probably the only way to have a regular sex life!'

Siobhán looked at her sympathetically.

'Will you have a family some day? Or are you one of those really dedicated career women? Are you looking to be the chief superintendent or something?'

'Oh, I'll never make chief super,' said Siobhán. 'I'm probably very lucky to be where I am at all.'

'Rubbish. I bet you're great at your job.' Sally glanced around the spartan room. 'Is it horribly male-dominated?'

'It's not as bad as it used to be,' admitted Siobhán. 'And of course crime has changed too over the past few years. There's more technological stuff going on. And domestic crimes . . . well, I know it's a cliché, but women are often good in those situations.'

'I suppose me and Iona are a domestic crime,' said Sally.

Siobhán smiled at her. 'I'm not really sure how we'll categorise this.'

'I don't want them to prosecute him,' said Sally urgently. 'I know he's done an awful thing and I hate him for it, but . . .'

'I just prepare the file,' said Siobhán. She shifted in her seat. 'And with him being so ill, it's difficult to say . . . How is he doing now?'

Sally sighed deeply. 'Still in a coma,' she said. 'The longer he stays that way the more worrying it gets. I've taken this week off work so that I can spend as much time as possible at the hospital with him, but I can't stay out indefinitely.'

'And your daughter?'

'Jenna went back to school today. It wasn't doing her any good being at home, moping around. At least this way she's kept busy.'

'You're being really brave about everything,' said Siobhán.

'Not really,' Sally said. 'I cry a lot.'

'I don't blame you,' said Siobhán. She closed her files. 'Come on,' she said. 'Why don't we go for a coffee?'

Sally looked at her uncertainly. 'Coffee? Are you allowed to go and have coffee with the wife of a criminal?'

'You'd be surprised at the kind of people I sometimes have coffee with.' Siobhán grinned and Sally couldn't help smiling too.

Although there was a kitchen and coffee area in the station, Siobhán thought it would be better to take Sally outside. It was about half a mile to the town centre. Siobhán decided to drive. She could justify spending some time in having coffee with Sally, she thought, but not in strolling to and from the town, even though the day was warm and sunny and a gentle walk would have been very pleasant. She parked in the Herbert Street car park, then led the way to a small bright café where she ordered a frothy cappuccino for herself and a skinny latte for Sally. They sat in a window seat and looked out at the bustling street.

'What other sort of crimes do you investigate?' asked Sally as she tipped brown sugar into her coffee.

'All sorts.' Siobhán talked about the petty crimes that made up so much of the daily workload of the station, as well as some of the more difficult cases, while Sally half listened and half watched the people walking by.

She liked Siobhán. She felt as though it were somehow disloyal to Frank to like the person who wanted to brand him a criminal, but she couldn't help it. Siobhán was an easy person to talk to, and because at the moment she was one of the few people to know about Frank's other wife, Sally felt more comfortable with her than anyone else. She hadn't told anyone – still not even Denise – about Iona. She simply couldn't. Everyone was being so kind and thoughtful and worrying so much about him, she didn't have to heart to tell them that he was a two-timing git. And the worst of it all was that she still hadn't really accepted that he was a two-timing git herself. Every time she thought about his marriage to Iona, it seemed unreal to her.

She realised that Siobhán had finally stopped talking about the Bray garda station caseload and was staring absent-mindedly into her coffee mug.

'Siobhán?' Sally looked at her enquiringly. 'Is everything OK?'

'Sure, sure,' she said quickly. 'It's fine.' She looked at her watch. 'Listen, I'm sorry but I have to get back. I have a meeting in a few minutes.'

'Of course.' Sally nodded. 'I didn't mean to keep you out for so long.'

'That's OK,' said Siobhán. 'I enjoyed it.'

'So did I.' Sally surprised herself by her comment. How could she have enjoyed sitting talking to the policewoman? But she had. 'When are you going to take Frank's fingerprints?' she asked as she gathered up her things.

'I'm not sure,' said Siobhán. 'Depends on when I get time.'

'Yeah, well it's not as though he's going anywhere,' said Sally wryly.

'I do hope he comes out of the coma soon,' said Siobhán.

'D'you know what? I'm not so sure about that any more.'

Sally pushed back her chair and walked out on to the street.

Iona had been dreading her visit to the police station. It was years since she'd been to Bray. Even though the seaside town wasn't really that far away, she didn't know anyone in the locality and never had any reason to go there. As a child, though, she'd often come with her family during the summer and, as she drove into the town now, fragmented memories of walking along the seashore resurfaced in her mind.

She parked in the visitors' area of the station, getting the last available space, and hurried into the building. The garda in charge looked at her with interest as she asked to see Detective Siobhán Farrell. Iona felt herself blush as she spoke. She supposed that everyone in the police station knew about the situation, and now that she thought about it, they were probably all thinking what a fool she was. But the garda didn't make any comment about her foolishness and merely told her to sit down and wait while he contacted Detective Farrell.

Iona perched on a wooden seat and rubbed the back of her neck. The headache that had started on the day of Frank's accident still hadn't gone. Sometimes it was more noticeable than others, but it continued to pound away at the back of her head and she didn't know when it might ever lift.

Five minutes later Siobhán walked into the waiting area and asked Iona to follow her. She led her to the room where the previous day she'd sat and taken Sally's statement, and now went through exactly the same procedure with Iona, although she soon realised that the younger woman was much more businesslike about the whole thing than Sally had been. Iona seemed to have recovered more quickly, even though Siobhán could see that she had huge dark circles under her eyes.

'Obviously I don't know whether the DPP will actually prosecute this case,' Siobhán told her, pre-empting the question that Sally had already asked. 'Given Frank's current health it seems unlikely. On the other hand, it is a criminal offence.'

Iona nodded wordlessly.

'I'm really sorry,' Siobhán told her. 'I know this must be difficult for you.'

'Oh for heaven's sake!' Iona looked at her despairingly. 'It's more than bloody difficult. It's impossible!'

'Unfortunately—'

'I didn't mean that literally,' Iona interrupted. 'Of course it's possible in the sense that he obviously did it! It's just . . . it's just an impossible situation to be in.'

'I understand that too,' said Siobhán.

'Yeah, well, I can't see that there are many people who could,' retorted Iona. 'I'm sure your experience of the wives of criminals is that they might be shocked that their husbands have raided a bank or something. Not that their husbands turn out not to be husbands at all.'

Siobhán grimaced.

'You know what the problem is?' said Iona. 'I can't tell anyone what's happened. That's the problem.'

'What d'you mean?'

'I'm off work right now and I've told them I have a bug, that I'll be back soon. I can't tell them that Frank's been in an accident because they'll want to send him flowers, and what's the point in that? And I don't know how to tell them that he's not and never was my husband! They'll think I'm barmy. Tell you the truth, *I* think I'm barmy! I didn't even guess.'

'I'm sure they'll understand,' said Siobhán.

'Oh, get a grip, woman.' Iona looked impatient. 'Of course they won't.'

'Well, I'm sure they'll sympathise,' amended Siobhán.

'I don't want sympathy,' said Iona fiercely. 'I want certainty. I want to know when he'll get better and I want to know why he did it, but nobody can answer either of those questions for me and it's driving me crazy.'

Siobhán nodded. 'I do understand, honestly. Come on, let's get a coffee. I know a good place in Bray.'

The café was crowded but they got the last remaining table.

'I don't know what I'm supposed to do,' said Iona as she added sugar to her latte (Siobhán had been slightly taken aback that Iona ordered the same coffee as Sally). 'I mean – if we had been married and I found out about someone else I could divorce him. But as it stands . . . well, as it stands it's just like he's suddenly out of my life. I can't go to the hospital and I don't have any say in his treatment.'

'Really?'

'I suppose I could insist,' said Iona. 'My solicitor wants me to try. But honestly, Siobhán, what's the point? He was married to Sally for eighteen years! I've only known him for five.' She took a sip of the coffee. 'And besides, they have a daughter to consider. How would she feel to see me there?'

Siobhán looked at her sympathetically. 'I can see that it's hard.'

'Part of me wants to be there and part of me doesn't ever want to see him again,' said Iona. She massaged the back of her neck. The headache had started to pound more ferociously again.

'You know, I'm sure Sally would come to some arrangement with you,' said Siobhán.

'You're joking!' Iona snorted. 'We nearly came to blows at the hospital, you know. I can't remember exactly what we said to each other but I'm pretty sure none of it was pleasant.'

'Tempers have cooled a little since then,' Siobhán told her. 'And Sally is as gutted about everything as you. Don't forget he was cheating on her too. So she's angry about that.'

Iona shrugged. 'I guess so.'

'I might be wrong,' said Siobhán, 'but it can't do any harm to call her and see if you can work something out.'

'I'm not sure if I want to,' admitted Iona. 'There's a part of me that feels he can just rot away in hospital for all I care.'

'It's up to you.'

'I'll think about it,' said Iona. She stared into space for a moment. 'You know, ever since we talked before, I keep asking myself over and over again what he had to gain by marrying me.'

Siobhán looked at her with interest. 'I wonder about that myself,' admitted Siobhán.

'He could have told me that he was married and that his home life was shit and . . . well . . . I probably would've believed him. Maybe I would have been one of those really good mistresses who provide sex and a haven for the poor stressed-out married man.' She shrugged.

Siobhán said nothing.

'But then I wondered whether it was simply that he wanted me for himself.'

Siobhán raised an eyebrow.

'He's very possessive. And we were great in bed together. Maybe he didn't want to think of me with anyone else.'

Siobhán gulped. Her efforts to be warm and sympathetic to the two women were rewarding her with far too much insight into their sex lives!

'There's just something about him.' Iona sighed. 'He's good with women.'

'So it seems.' Siobhán couldn't keep the wryness out of her voice.

'Look, I know you probably think that Sally and I are both bonkers,' snapped Iona, 'but you've got to understand what it was like. Frank – well, he's special. I might be mad at him – more than mad at him now, I guess – but I can't . . . I can't really hate him. I want to, but I don't. He gave me such a great time . . .' Her voice trailed off. She finished her coffee and looked ruefully at Siobhán. 'I suppose I'd better get going. I'm sorry if I've ranted on a bit.'

'That's OK,' said Siobhán. 'It helps to talk.'

'I'm sure you've better things to do than listen to me,' said Iona.

'There's always something to do,' said Siobhán. 'But if you need to talk to me about it any time, you're more than welcome to call.'

'I asked him to marry me,' said Iona abruptly. 'I practically forced him into it. It wasn't his idea.'

Siobhán didn't say that all the best con-men make you think you're deciding something for yourself. She just nodded in acknowledgement of Iona's words.

'Thanks for the coffee.' Iona smiled and Siobhán suddenly saw what might have attracted Frank to her. Her dark eyes were lighter now, and held a hint of mischief. And even though her face was still pale, the smile changed her look completely.

Iona offered her hand and Siobhán shook it.

'I suppose you'll be in touch?' Iona added. 'If there's any news?'

Siobhán nodded. 'Of course. In the meantime, look after yourself,' she said.

'Yeah. I will.' Iona smiled shortly at her and walked out into the street.

Chapter 15

As she walked back towards the car park, Siobhán wondered just how delusional both Sally and Iona were about Frank and his relationship with them. He couldn't love both of them equally. And surely he couldn't be that good in bed with both of them too. Didn't he ever feel too tired? Or call out the wrong name by mistake? How could he possibly switch from one to the other like that?

Was there the faintest chance, though, that by having two women, and apparently loving two women, it was actually making things better for them all? Because both Sally and Iona seemed to have had happy and fulfilling lives with Frank up to now. And, of course, they both agreed he was great in bed.

She sighed deeply. What wouldn't she give for a great-in-bed moment herself right now. Not that she actually wanted to share Eddie with someone to make that happen, but at least the Harper women were confident about that part of their relationship. Whereas she and Eddie . . . She sighed again. Something had gone horribly wrong in the bedroom between them.

She hadn't realised it until the day after he'd come back from Boston. Obviously she'd been hurt that he hadn't wanted to make mad passionate love to her the day he'd arrived home, but she did understand that he was probably exhausted. But the following day she'd expected that they'd pop the champagne and light the candles and get down and dirty. Well, get down to it anyway – they'd never been madly adventurous in bed together but they'd always enjoyed themselves in a relatively staid kind of way. Occasionally Siobhán had taken the initiative and made things just a little more exciting – like when she'd handcuffed Eddie to the bed (but he hadn't really liked being totally under her control so it hadn't been quite as much fun as she'd expected) – but usually they were quite happy to make conventional love in the dark and beneath the sheets.

Only that hadn't happened. Neither on Sunday nor the following day – not at all since he'd come home. She'd tried to kiss him and cuddle him but each time he'd turned away from her and told her that he really just wasn't in the mood. And when, last night, she'd asked him straight out what the hell was going on, he'd responded by saying that they didn't have to be screwing each other senseless every single night and that he was under a huge amount of pressure at work and was there even the faintest chance that she'd let him get some sleep?

Siobhán had been shocked by the tone in his voice. She'd asked him whether there was anything the matter, whether she'd said or done something to upset him. And he'd rolled on to his back and said that the biggest problem any bloke could have with a woman was that she wanted to analyse every single thing in their lives together, and no, she hadn't said or done anything but could she just, for once, stop interrogating him like a suspect in the fucking cells.

She blinked away a tear as she remembered the harshness of his voice and the way that he'd rolled away from her. And she wondered what the hell had happened in Boston, because everything had been fine until he'd left. Had he met someone else there? Was he afraid to tell her? But Eddie had never been afraid to tell her things before. They'd always been upfront and honest in their relationship. They'd shared their likes and dislikes. They got on well together.

So what the hell was going on?

Maybe he'd simply gone off her. She wasn't sure what to do if he'd simply gone off her. She didn't want to lose him. She hadn't realised, until he'd gone away, just how much she really loved him.

Siobhán crossed the road and turned towards the car park. But her attention was caught by the window display of the shop nearby. The store had opened recently, she knew; she remembered there had been a takeaway sandwich store on the site. Now it was a lingerie boutique and the display was of ethereal wisps of pastel chiffon and lace floating on a background of soft white feathers.

Would that make a difference? she wondered. If she wore sultry lingerie for Eddie instead of her slightly greying M&S knickers and sturdy bra, would he want to make love to her again? She didn't always wear sensible underwear, of course, but on work days it was usually her plain white or black cotton Lycra mixes with her equally plain support bra. Siobhán had (as Eddie had told her on one of their early dates) a fine chest which needed decent support. So that was what she gave it. But she never bothered to change when she got home, even though, perhaps, her day-time bras weren't exactly knee-tremblers.

Is it me? she wondered. Have I just become so caught up in the whole work thing that I've forgotten how to be feminine? It isn't, after all, as though I have to wear frumpy underwear to be a good cop. But maybe wearing frumpy underwear is making me a terrible girlfriend.

She hesitated for another moment or two and then pushed open the door of the shop. A bell pinged with a genteel chime and a woman of around Siobhán's own age emerged from the back of the shop. She smiled helpfully at her and Siobhán felt herself flush. 'Just looking,' she said hastily and knocked against a display of thongs, sending them scattering to the floor. She felt her face flame red. 'Sorry.'

'No problem,' said the sales assistant as she began scooping them up again. 'I'm afraid we're a bit tight for space here.' She began to replace the wispy thongs on the rack. 'Are you looking for anything in particular?'

Siobhán stared at the insubstantial piece of lace in the woman's hand. Surely she was looking for more than that, despite wanting something sexy. She needed more than a wisp to cover her generous bum, after all. She cleared her throat.

'I'm not sure,' she said. 'Something . . . well . . . nice, I suppose.'

'We've lots of nice things!' The assistant smiled at her. 'And some naughty things too.'

'How naughty?' Siobhán felt herself flush again even while she told herself that she was a policewoman, for heaven's sake, and nothing could be too naughty for her to think about.

'Well, we have crotchless panties and peephole bras,' said the shop assistant. 'Very tasteful, though. All of our goods are tasteful and of very high quality.'

Would crotchless knickers turn Eddie on? Siobhán's teeth worried her bottom lip.

'Or, of course, we have a superb collection of basques and French knickers too,' continued the saleswoman. 'You'd look great in a basque,' she added. 'You have the chest for it.'

'You mean I'm big and bulky?' suggested Siobhán.

'Not at all!' The assistant looked horrified. 'You're voluptuous. You should enhance that look.'

Siobhán snorted. 'I can't afford to look voluptuous – even if I was – during the day.'

'Everyone can and should look their best at all times,' said the sales assistant firmly. 'But of course, if you're looking for something more in the playwear line . . .'

'No,' said Siobhán hastily. 'I just want something . . . something nice.'

'Have you tried a basque at all?'

Siobhán shook her head.

'I promise you, you'll love it. And you'll look fantastic!' The woman moved across the tiny shop to another rail. 'Look at these. Absolutely exquisite.' She picked up a black and cream lace basque and held it up for Siobhán to inspect. 'Chantilly lace. Very popular and not too expensive at all.'

Siobhán looked at it. Like much of the rest of the stock, it seemed to her almost impossibly delicate.

'Of course, if you want something more . . . more substantial . . .' the sales assistant was watching her closely, 'you could try this one. She picked up a confection in red lace. 'It's La Perla so it's one of our more expensive items but worth every cent. Feel the quality of that! And,' she added, 'it really emphasises the cleavage. Which is perfect for you! You're a 36C, right?'

Siobhán nodded but looked undecidedly at the basque.

'And if you do go down the more playful route . . .' the woman grinned at her and opened a drawer, 'there's always good old Agent Provocateur.'

Siobhán's eyes narrowed as she saw the assistant take out what appeared to be a selection of PVC strings.

'They call it a playsuit,' she told Siobhán as she handed her a brochure. 'And you put these little pasties on your boobs.'

'You've got to be kidding me.' Siobhán looked at the picture of the model wearing nothing but the PVC strings and two tassels hanging from her nipples. 'People buy this stuff? Here? In Bray?'

'Of course they do,' said the assistant. 'After all, everyone can do with adding a bit of spice to their sex lives, don't you think? And what man could resist you in this?'

Eddie, probably, thought Siobhán glumly. She gazed at the selection of goods on the counter in front of her to which the sales assistant added another couple of basques, one of which was straight out of a porn fantasy.

'It depends on the man, of course,' added the assistant helpfully. 'Some of them like the kind of dominatrix approach. But others prefer you to look a bit more helpless.'

And which would Eddie prefer? wondered Siobhán. Did he want to dominate her? Or did he want her to appear in need of rescuing? He hadn't liked the handcuffs, so she supposed he wouldn't be too enamoured of black leather and whips. Yet she couldn't see herself looking sweet and virginal in black and cream lace.

'I also have a lovely Moschino,' the assistant continued. 'Just in. Dark lace with a little silver detail. Fabulous. Matching thong, or, if you prefer, little boxers. Looks less like a *Playboy* centrefold and a bit more assertive.'

Siobhán looked at the Moschino basque. The assistant was right. If any of this frothy stuff could be described as being her, this was the most likely candidate. It was sexy without being submissive; seductive without being trashy.

'How much?' she asked and nearly fainted when the saleswoman told her. But, she thought, it was an investment in her future. If she was to save her relationship, then maybe this was the way forward. She took out her credit card and handed it over before she changed her mind.

'Are you taking the thong or the boxers?' asked the assistant.

She couldn't do the thong, she really couldn't. She wanted to attract Eddie again, not repel him.

'The boxers,' she said.

'You can try on the basque,' said the assistant. 'You might want to be sure that it fits. Though I'm pretty certain it'll be great on you.'

Siobhán shook her head. She didn't want this woman poking her head into the changing room, watching her wobble over the top of the silk and lace garment. She'd try it on at home and hope to hell that she hadn't blown half her salary on a wasted piece of lingerie. Because if it didn't fit, there was no way she'd have the nerve to come back with it.

She watched as the assistant lovingly wrapped her purchases in swathes of tissue paper and then put them in a discreet box.

'We also have toys,' she added, 'if you're interested in anything else for fun.'

Siobhán really wasn't sure how Eddie would feel about sex toys. They were a perfectly normal and acceptable part of people's lives these days, but they'd never been part of hers and Eddie's. So if she brought something home . . . She shook her head. 'Not right now,' she said.

The sales assistant smiled. 'No bother. Enjoy these. It'll all look fabulous on you.'

'I'll do my best,' muttered Siobhán.

She made one more stop on the way back to the car park, and that was in the little home accessories shop, where she bought a selection of scented candles and aromatic oils. Not exactly sex toys, but the ambience might help. Eddie wouldn't know what had hit him, she thought as she handed over her credit card yet again. He'd be overcome by her sensuality, and if that didn't kick-start their sex life again, she simply didn't know what would.

When she got back to the station she took out the Golden Pages and looked up house cleaning agencies. She called the one with the biggest ad and organised for them to come twice a month to clean the apartment, feeling confident that Eddie would approve. After all, she told herself as she replaced the receiver, if she was going to turn into some kind of sex goddess she couldn't be expected to spend hours cleaning and scrubbing. She had to be in the mood. Actually, she was getting quite excited about the thought of turning herself into a sex goddess for Eddie that evening. Maybe she was spending too much time trying to be tough in her job and not half enough time being a bit more feeble at home.

She turned her attention to the folders on her desk and tried to stop thinking sexy thoughts. There were a couple of files from the DPP which she had to look through, as well as a report to write on the money-laundering enquiry. And, of course, she had to finish her work on the Frank Harper case too. The fact that the man was in a coma didn't make him any less of a bastard, thought Siobhán. And those women were really nice. She'd liked both of them, even though her initial reaction had been to think that it was poor Sally who'd been hard done by. She couldn't help remembering the night they'd told Sally about the accident and how shocked she'd been. So her sympathies had somewhat naturally lain with her. But then, having met Iona, she'd found herself feeling sorry for her too. Iona seemed tougher than Sally, but Siobhán wasn't sure that was truly the case. She wondered, quite suddenly, how Iona would have coped with a man who didn't have sex with her. She rather thought that she would just have walked out. After all, she'd simply stopped going to see Frank at the hospital, which proved that she could made tough decisions. She probably wouldn't give Eddie a second chance either.

Siobhán frowned. It wasn't a case of second chances. It was a case of working through something that had become a problem even though she didn't know why.

'Hey, Siobhán!' Larry Masterson, her usual partner, walked into the room and sat down at his desk. 'Looking forward to tomorrow?'

She looked at him in surprise and then groaned. She'd been so caught up with Iona and Sally and her own problems with Eddie that she'd forgotten about her upcoming court appearance. She supposed that the good thing about everything that was going on in her life was that she hadn't had time to be nervous about it. She tapped her pen against her teeth and shook her head in determination. She had work to do to prepare for tomorrow. But tonight she'd deal with Eddie.

She was home ahead of him that evening, which she'd expected, as he was meeting a client for drinks after work. Although she didn't quite turn into a cleaning tornado, she did tidy the apartment a little more, this time concentrating on the bedroom, where she hung up the piles of clothes that she'd left on the armchair in the corner of the room; then she ruthlessly dumped a variety of half-empty and little-used jars of face creams in the bin. She hated throwing things out unless they were finished, but, she muttered, if she hadn't used them for more than a month, she wasn't going to miss them now! She filled the washing machine with laundry from the laundry basket, although she decided not to switch it on. It wouldn't do for their moment of passion to be interrupted by the asthmatic rattle of the machine as it settled into the spin cycle.

She placed the scented candles in small glass bowls which she arranged carefully around both the living room and the bedroom. Then she went into the tiny bathroom and had a shower, lathering herself with the Chanel shower soap which she'd bought in the airport on last year's holiday to Spain but hardly ever used because it had been so bloody expensive. But she knew that she smelled good when she patted herself dry and she asked herself why on earth she didn't use the damn soap regardless of how much it had cost, since it wasn't doing a lot of good simply sitting on the bathroom shelf.

Then she went back into the bedroom and slid her new purchases out of their box.

The sales assistant had been right. The black and silver basque made her look extremely voluptuous. Rather like a Tudor girl, thought Siobhán, as she looked at her pale breasts pushed into two round globes over the cups of the basque. She was glad she'd elected to get the little boxer shorts, though. The thong would have simply made her look like a trussed chicken.

She pulled her hair back into a ponytail and then pinned it to the top of her head. In all the romantic fiction she'd read as an impressionable teenager (well, the two historical romances she'd ploughed through before she'd turned to police procedurals instead), the heroines had allowed the hero to unpin their hair from the top of their heads. It was, apparently, very sensual to have your tresses fall down across your face, and she was going to work her sensuality to its utmost tonight.

She looked at her watch. It was nearly nine and Eddie had said he'd be home before then. She hoped that he wouldn't choose this evening to be late or to drink so much that all her efforts would be in vain. She put on her dressing gown (that would have to be changed too, if sexy nights together became a regular feature – it was positively tatty) and sat on the edge of the bed with a book.

It was nearly half past when she heard the sound of his key in the lock. She pulled off the dressing gown and lay back on the bed, striking a pose which she hoped was provocative, playful yet vulnerable.

The door opened and Eddie walked in. The colour drained from his face as he saw her.

'Jesus Christ, woman,' he said eventually. 'What the hell d'you think you're doing?'

'Waiting for you,' replied Siobhán in what she hoped was a sultry voice. 'I know you've had a long, hard day. But I wanted to give you a long, hard night too.'

'Are you all right?' he asked. 'You haven't been raiding the station's supply of illegal substances, have you?'

'Of course not.' Siobhán abandoned her provocative pose and sat upright. 'I just thought this would be . . . that you'd find it . . . attractive. That's all.'

Eddie stared at her.

'Why on earth would you think that?' he demanded. 'Have I ever expressed an interest in having you dress up like a slut?'

'I am *not* dressed like a slut!' she cried. 'This is perfectly acceptable underwear. Loads of women wear it.'

'Loads of women who aren't you!' retorted Eddie.

'Great.' She swung her legs over the side of the bed. 'That's just great. I suppose it's those loads of women you're interested in. Not me. I don't know what I've become to you, Eddie McIntyre, but a girlfriend isn't one of them. There isn't anything I can do that's right any more, or anything I can give you that you want. Well, fine! Most normal men would love their girlfriends to greet them after a business trip with champagne and sex. You wanted to go to sleep instead. Most normal men would think it was great that their girlfriend was prepared to buy the world's most uncomfortable underwear just to look good for them. You don't. So there's only one conclusion, isn't there? There's someone else. Who is she? Have you met someone else? How about that girl in your office – what's her name, Carol McClelland? The one you told me looked like a waif who needed protecting? Is that it? That what you prefer?'

'For heaven's sake, Siobhán, of course not!'

'Oh really? Why of course not? You're a hotshot business bloke. You probably like them helpless. I bet you if Carol danced around in front of you in a basque and knickers you'd be gagging for it!'

'No I bloody wouldn't!' cried Eddie.

'No? So you're not interested in me and you're not interested in her? What the hell is it then, Eddie? Are you interested in blokes?'

'Don't be so fucking ridiculous.'

'It's not me being ridiculous!' Siobhán's voice rose higher. 'I just want normal, that's all. I want a boyfriend who comes home after five weeks away and makes love to me. I don't think there's anything fucking ridiculous about that.'

'I can't talk about this right now,' said Eddie tightly. 'I just can't.'

'When?' demanded Siobhán. 'Why should we pretend that everything is all right when it so obviously isn't?'

'I don't want to pretend everything is all right. I just . . . I just . . .'

'Just what?'

'I can't talk about it,' repeated Eddie. 'I'll – I've got to go out.' He turned away and strode through the apartment.

'Don't you dare!' cried Siobhán, running after him. 'Don't you dare walk out on me.'

But he'd already opened the apartment door.

'For God's sake, Eddie.' She went out after him. 'If we don't talk about this now, we never will.'

He hesitated, and then hurried along the corridor towards the stairs.

'Eddie!' Siobhán moved after him and then whirled around as the apartment door clunked shut behind her. And she realised that she was standing in the corridor in a basque and knickers. Without a key.

She wasn't going to cry. That was the first thing. If any of her neighbours opened their doors she didn't want them to see her sobbing in her basque. All she had to do was stay calm. She'd been trained in calmness in difficult situations. The police were supposed to be good at that.

Chapter 16

Iona leapt out of the chair when the phone rang. She'd been sitting staring at the TV and drinking wine, not taking in anything of the history programme that was showing. The picture was just a blur in front of her, the narration a meaningless jumble of words. She yanked the receiver off the stand and said, 'Yes,' in a breathless voice.

'Iona, sweetheart, it's me.'

Her heart plummeted. It wasn't that she didn't want to talk to her mother, but she couldn't bear having to explain it all to her. And God knows what Lauren had already said, what slant she'd put on things.

'Darling, are you all right?'

'Of course I'm all right,' she said quickly. 'I'm fine.'

'You can't possibly be fine,' said Flora. 'Who in their right mind could be fine after what you've gone through?'

'Oh, I'm sure there's worse.' Although right then Iona couldn't think of what.

'Someone really close to you is critically ill,' said Flora. 'That's one of the worst things that could happen.'

'No, Mum.' Iona choked on the words. 'What's worse is that he wasn't close to me at all.'

'Of course he was,' said Flora firmly. 'You loved him and he loved you.'

'Don't be stupid,' said Iona. 'He used me, that's all.'

'He loved you – I could see it when you were here,' said Flora.

'But you thought there was something odd about him.'

'No. I thought he was very . . . self-contained,' said Flora. 'Which is understandable now. But I never thought he didn't love you.'

'He wasn't entitled to love me!' cried Iona. 'He was supposed to be in love with Sally.'

Flora said nothing.

'I hope he dies,' said Iona.

'Do you?'

She swallowed the lump in her throat.

'He deserves to die. He doesn't deserve to end up a vegetable.'

'Maybe neither of those things will happen.'

'I dunno.' Iona wiped her eyes.

'Do you want to come here for a few days?' asked Flora. 'Get away from it all?'

'I can't,' said Iona. 'I can't be away if . . . right now, I can't.'

'I understand,' said Flora. 'You know you're welcome to come. You only have to call me.'

'I know.'

'I want to be there with you,' said Flora. 'I want to put my arms around you and hug you and tell you everything will be all right.'

'I don't think everything will be all right,' said Iona. 'But I can pretend that you're hugging me.'

'Will I come over now?' asked Flora. 'Lauren warned me against phoning you too soon and absolutely forbade me to come haring home, but—'

'No,' said Iona. 'I'm better on my own right now. Maybe later.'

'Sure?'

'Certain.'

'OK,' said Flora. 'Look after yourself, honey. Dad sends his love. Take lots of echinacea.'

'I was actually thinking of alcohol,' said Iona as she refilled her glass.

Flora chuckled. 'That's my girl.'

Iona hung up and went back to staring at the TV screen.

Siobhán stood indecisively in her basque and boxers and shivered. Brilliant, she thought. Just bloody brilliant. She thought about running after Eddie and demanding that he at least let her back into the apartment, but she knew that by now he'd be in the communal hall area, and running down there in her underwear really wasn't an option. There were times when she complained that the apartment block was soulless and that you never really met anybody, but she knew that today would, of course, be the day that everyone would suddenly congregate in the damned hall and see her in her basque and boxers.

A door opened and she stood stock still. Then she groaned. Of all of the people she'd choose to walk out of their apartment right now, Carl O'Connor would have been bottom of her list.

'Good grief!' He looked at her in complete astonishment and then his face broke into a wide grin. 'Well if that's the new uniform for the Garda Siochana all I can say is that criminals will be simply queuing up to be arrested.'

'Oh, give it a rest, O'Connor,' she said shortly.

'Well, honey, you've got to admit that it's a new approach from the force,' he said. 'Are you undercover? Though cover isn't exactly the right word, is it?'

Siobhán said nothing. Carl O'Connor was a journalist. Her least favourite kind of journalist too. He wrote a scathing gossipy column in a Sunday tabloid called 'Carl's Corner' and an equally scathing column in an evening paper under the banner 'Carl Cares'. In it he supposedly exposed the injustices perpetrated on the ordinary people of the country – drivers caught for barely exceeding the speed limit, people arrested for drunk and disorderly offences when, according to Carl, they were just being high-spirited – failures on the part of the state and the system where decent law-abiding citizens were concerned. Siobhán didn't disagree that sometimes the system was unfair. But it irritated her that Carl only ever showed things from one point of view.

'So do tell me,' he continued. 'What's the ploy? Is someone in our apartment block running a brothel?'

She looked at him edgily.

'I got locked out of my apartment,' she said. 'My . . . Eddie had to go out in a hurry and . . . and I . . . needed to go after him for something but I missed him and the door closed behind me.'

Carl regarded her thoughtfully with his deep blue eyes and Siobhán felt herself blush.

'You know,' he said, 'if I was living with you and you were gadding about in that little outfit, I wouldn't care who tried to get me out of my home urgently, I'd tell them to sod off. Your boyfriend . . . your fiancé . . . is clearly a man of little taste.'

'Don't be stupid,' said Siobhán wearily.

'But seriously.' This time Carl's eyes twinkled at her. 'I didn't realise you had such hidden depths. Or such charming assets.'

'Look, I'm freezing my butt off out here,' Siobhán told him. 'Is there any chance I could use your phone so that I can ring him and get him to come back?'

'Of course you can,' said Carl. 'I was just about to bring my rubbish to the bin. I'll do that while you phone Mr Plod.'

'Eddie isn't a policeman, as well you know,' said Siobhán.

'True. But he's part of the Plod family, isn't he, thanks to you.' Carl grinned at her. 'I'd have thought you'd be pleased to see a kind of reverse discrimination in play.'

Siobhán made a face at him and then shivered. Suddenly Carl's voice softened.

'Ah, look, I'm sorry for teasing you,' he said. 'Come on in before you do actually freeze to death. And call your fiancé.'

'Thanks,' she said, surprised by the unexpected gentleness in his voice. She walked into his apartment and stood uncertainly in the middle of the room.

'Hang on a second,' said Carl. He disappeared into the bedroom and then emerged with a heavy blue T-shirt in his hand. 'You might want to put this on,' he said. 'It's a warmer option and it'll stop me running after you too!'

She pulled the T-shirt over her head and immediately felt a little better, although she knew that her figure was still stunningly buxom beneath it thanks to the uplifting powers of the basque. Carl handed her his phone and she dialled Eddie's number. She grimaced as she got his message-minder.

'It's me,' she said urgently. 'I'm locked out of the apartment. Can you come home as quickly as possible? I'm at Carl's place.' She ended the call and looked apologetically at her neighbour. 'I'm sure he'll be back soon,' she said.

'Hey, you can stay here as long as you like,' said Carl easily. 'I wasn't doing anything much. As I said, I was only going out to put my rubbish in the bin.'

'What?' Her smile was a little wobbly. 'No lurking among the trash to find out the dirt on the inhabitants of our little community? No trawling the nightclubs for celebrities off their heads with drink?'

'You have a very low opinion of me, don't you?'

She shrugged. 'I just don't think that what you do is very helpful,' she said. 'Who really needs to know that some two-bit singer is having an affair? And what's the point in slagging off the police all the time, saying that we're crap at our jobs, just because the justice system means that we have to pick our way through a damn minefield to get a conviction.'

'Everyone has their rights,' Carl reminded her.

'Oh, please.' She looked at him in disgust. 'You're the one who does the sob story on the victims. And then you do a different sob story on the criminal – you know, my sordid life of crime but it's because my parents wouldn't buy me a PlayStation when I was six.'

He laughed. 'People want to read it,' he said.

'And then . . .' her voice rose in indignation, 'you journalists give them all nicknames like the Safecracker or something so that they think they're some kind of celebrity themselves and they then need to live up to it.'

'You're exaggerating,' he said mildly. 'Anyway, what about corruption in the police force, or gardai failing in basic procedural actions so that the trials collapse?'

'Everyone makes mistakes,' she said. 'We do a million things right but do one tiny thing wrong and some shifty barrister is getting a criminal off on a technicality. Plus there'll always be corruption. It's there in everything. I bet there are corrupt journos too. Except you guys can slag off everyone else and not have to take it yourselves.' She rubbed her forehead and looked at him tiredly. 'Look, I don't want to argue about this with you. I don't want to talk about work or anything. I just want to go home.'

'I'm sure Mr Pl . . . Eddie, isn't it? I'm sure Eddie will come rushing back when he gets your message. In the mean time, let's call a truce on dissing each other's jobs. How about a cup of coffee?'

She nodded. She was dying for a coffee. Although, she thought as she accepted the steaming mug from him a few minutes later, what she really needed was a major blast of alcohol to wipe out the memory of a horrible day.

Sally wouldn't have minded a drink herself. She was fed up with the lukewarm, watery coffee that the hospital vending machine dispensed.

She'd tried all the choices on offer by now – black, white, cappuccino, espresso, tea and hot chocolate – and they all tasted exactly the same to her. She only drank them for something to do. Sitting around the hospital was mind-numbingly boring. It was amazing how quickly she was getting into a routine of driving to Dublin and waiting for Frank to wake up. She knew all the nurses on the floor now and most of the doctors. They all smiled at her when she came in but pretty much left her to her own devices, which meant that she sat beside Frank and talked to him about inconsequential rubbish or read pieces out of the paper. She was doing the kind of thing that she'd read about in books or seen people do in movies, and it seemed totally unreal to her that this was actually happening in real life. She kept expecting Frank to wake up and laugh at her for reading the editorials in the *Irish Times* out loud to him, or to snap to attention when she told him that Jenna and her boyfriend were practically inseparable these days.

Which was why Jenna hadn't come to the hospital this evening. Gerry had asked her to go to the movies with him. Following their earlier conversation about how to deal with hospital visits, Sally had suggested that Jenna come to see Frank every second day, and her daughter had agreed with alacrity. The only worrying factor, as far as Sally could see, was that Jenna was spending more and more time with that boyfriend of hers and Sally wished she knew a little bit more about him. It wasn't that she didn't trust her daughter (at least, she more or less trusted her), but she'd have preferred it if Jenna was hanging out with her girlfriends rather than a new boyfriend right now.

She folded the newspaper and looked at Frank. It seemed to her that he was becoming less and less like the man she knew with every passing day. His face was thinner, his whole body appeared weaker in the bed. Of course she wasn't used to seeing him in bed at all – at least, not lying in bed asleep. He was always first up in the mornings, always full of get up and go. That was the thing that had always attracted her to him. The fact that he crackled with vitality. The fact that he loved life so much. The fact that just seeing him every day made her feel good about herself. The sleeping man in front of her was almost a stranger. They told her to talk to him and tell him things about their daily lives, remind him of things that had happened in the past, but she found it really difficult to do that when nothing got a reaction. So it was easier to read the newspaper editorials or talk about the traffic. It was harder to talk about the things that really mattered. But maybe the fact that she hadn't was part of the problem. She bit her lip as she studied Frank's expressionless face and then took a deep breath.

'We need to talk,' she said.

He didn't move.

'I know that's silly,' she continued. 'I mean, you can't talk, can you? Or maybe you won't talk. I don't know which.'

He still didn't move.

'But the thing is, there's a lot for us to talk about.' She moistened her lips. Should she start by freaking out about Iona? Or by giving him the news about the baby? Which was more likely to get a reaction?

'I didn't tell you this before,' she said quickly, 'because I wanted you to be properly awake when I did. The thing is, I don't know *when* you'll be properly awake again. It could be weeks. And it wouldn't be fair to spring it on you then, not that I actually could, I suppose. So . . . so I have to tell you now.' She swallowed hard. From the moment she'd discovered it herself, she'd wondered how she'd tell him. She hadn't expected it would be like this. She took a deep breath again. 'You're hardly going to believe it, darling, because it's so unexpected – the thing is, we're going to have a baby.'

From the moment she'd discovered it, she'd imagined his reaction. He lay impassively in the bed.

'I suppose it's a shock to you,' she continued. 'It sure was a shock to me after all this time. I hope you're happy about it, though. It's going to be a big change for us all.'

It was amazing, she thought, how still a living person could be. That was what was so difficult to accept. That Frank, who was always on the go, could remain so immobile.

'I haven't told Jen yet,' she said. 'The only people who know are the nurses here. I don't know what they'll say at school when I tell them. I'm going back next week. Well, Frank, I have to. I can't spend all of my time here, can I? I mean, we've got to go on living and . . . I'm not abandoning you, you know. I hope you realise that. But . . .'

She swallowed hard as he continued to lie there, oblivious to everything she said. Somehow she'd expected a reaction to the news of her pregnancy. She didn't know what sort of reaction, but she'd thought that he might move, give some kind of a sign that he'd heard her. She really couldn't believe that nothing was getting through to him. She threaded her fingers through his and squeezed gently.

'You know, it's really hard,' she told him. 'I'm pregnant and you're lying here and I just don't know when you're going to wake up. And when you do . . .' She faltered. 'When you do, there's such a mess to deal with.'

She took a deep breath. He deserved to know everything. She'd been too nice until now, talking to him in her most soothing tone of voice, reading him chunks of the paper, telling him that she loved him. She'd been treating him like a sick person, only he wasn't really sick, just out of it. She was fed up with being nice.

'Look – not that I particularly want to worry you,' she said as she disentangled her fingers, 'especially given the new state of affairs in our family; but there's a policewoman preparing a file about you. You might be prosecuted, you know. For . . . for . . .' She stopped. She hadn't brought up the subject of his second wife before. She'd only talked about herself and Jenna and how worried they were about him. She hadn't even mentioned the fact that Iona had called to the hospital and gone absolutely nuts. 'Well, Frank, for getting married to someone else,' she continued. 'I mean, it was a pretty bizarre sort of thing to do. And I have to tell you that me and Jen were very hurt by it. Not just hurt, furious. I'm furious with you. Jen is devastated. And both of us hate you for what you've done.'

His eyes opened. She stood up abruptly and the plastic chair scraped against the floor.

'Frank?' She reached towards the buzzer to summon the duty nurse. 'Frank?'

He stared straight ahead.

'Can you hear me?' she asked breathlessly as she kept her finger on the buzzer. 'Frank, do you understand what I've just told you?'

Terri Cooper hurried into the room. 'Everything OK?' she asked.

'He opened his eyes.' Sally's own eyes didn't leave Frank's face. 'He must be awake. He opened his eyes.'

'We told you about this, Sally, remember?' said the nurse gently. 'Sometimes this happens. It doesn't mean that the patient is alert. It's a motor function.'

'But I was talking and he just . . . it . . .' Sally was on the verge of tears. 'I said something and I know he heard me. I know he did.'

'Maybe so,' said Terri as she looked at the monitors beside Frank's bed. 'But he's still not conscious, Sally. I'm sorry.'

Sally said nothing, but walked out of the room. Her body was trembling. She'd felt sure that somehow she'd connected with Frank. She'd sensed something in him when she'd spoken about his marriage to Iona, something that hadn't been there for anything else, not even when she told him about the baby. But he'd heard her when she spoke of Iona, she knew he had. It was guilt over the whole thing that had got to him and that was why he'd opened his eyes!

'Here.' Terri stood beside her and handed her a cup of the disgusting coffee. Or tea. 'Drink this.'

'I don't want it.' She shuddered. 'I've been drinking it all evening and it's horrible.'

'I have to agree with you there,' said Terri. She looked at Sally. 'What were you talking to him about when he opened his eyes?' she asked. 'The baby?'

'No,' said Sally. 'The other woman.'

Terri's silence was sympathetic.

'I talked to him about the baby too,' said Sally tightly. 'But it meant nothing to him. It was only when I mentioned her that . . . that . . .'

'I really don't think his eyes opening had anything to do with it,' said Terri.

'But you don't actually know, do you?' demanded Sally.

'No,' said Terri. 'Though like I said to you, Sally, it's a motor function.'

'Yeah, well the motor function happened when I mentioned his damn bit on the side.'

Terri remained diplomatically silent.

'I know. I know. She's not really a bit on the side, is she?'

'I think you're all in a really difficult situation,' said Terri gently.

Sally said nothing, but swallowed hard over and over.

'Maybe you should go home,' suggested Terri. 'Get some rest.'

'Do you think she should be here?' asked Sally. 'Do you think it would help him to hear her voice?'

Terri shrugged.

'Maybe she doesn't even want to be here,' said Sally. 'After all, she didn't put up much of a fight once she realised that her marriage was a sham. She didn't even try.'

'Different people have different ways of reacting to things,' said Terri.

'Do you think I'm wrong?' asked Sally. 'To want to have things the way they were?'

'But what exactly is the way they were?' asked Terri.

'Me and Jen and Frank,' said Sally angrily. 'A family.'

Terri said nothing.

'Do the doctors think it would help if she came back?' asked Sally eventually.

'They haven't said anything to me.'

'If he reacted to her name, maybe hearing her voice would bring him out of it.'

'He did hear her voice on the first night,' Terri reminded her.

'Yes, but it was all a bit mad then, wasn't it?' Sally nibbled at the tip of her finger. 'Maybe it would be different now.'

'Maybe,' said Terri.

Sally stared back in through the window of the room. Frank's eyes were still open and he stared unseeingly in front of him.

'If it helps, maybe she should come in. Although she might not want to. She might be as furious with him as I am.'

'You still love him, though,' said Terri. 'You still want him to get better.'

'And if he does, what then?' Sally frowned. 'There's still the whole crazy situation to deal with.' She closed her eyes and swayed gently on her feet.

Terri took her by the arm and made her sit down.

'You need to look after yourself,' she told her. 'It won't help anyone if you become ill.'

'I know,' said Sally. Her eyes flickered towards Frank's room again. 'Sometimes I wish I was him,' she told the nurse. 'Out of it completely.'

Frank loved Sally. He hadn't expected to fall in love with her, because he'd found getting over Marion really difficult. He still thought of Marion occasionally, off in the States, meeting new men and sharing her gorgeous body with them. Whenever he thought of her he grew angry with himself for not having tried harder to keep her. She would have been a good wife and a good mother and they could have been a good family together. And then he wondered why he would think that when he knew that Marion was actually just good at socialising and great at sex.

Sally was good for him. She was more practical, more down-to-earth than Marion had ever been. She was a steadying influence. She encouraged him but she also pointed out the down side of some of the things he wanted to do. She was the kind of person that any man could love because she was clever and sweet and he couldn't help falling for her. He loved her sparkling eyes and her river of thick copper hair. He loved the way she put her head to one side and stuck the tip of her tongue out of the corner of her mouth when she was thinking hard about something. He loved her intelligence. He told her that she was wasted in teaching, that she should be out there doing something for herself. But then he loved the way she said that she got more out of seeing a young girl understand something that she'd never understood before than anything else. Sally Campion was a good person and Frank Harper wanted her to be part of his life for ever.

But now she was talking to him and he could hear her voice but he couldn't make out her words. And suddenly he knew that she was telling him that she was thinking of moving to England, where there were more jobs and where the salaries were higher.

'Why on earth would you want to go there?' he demanded. 'Sure isn't their education system a mess? Aren't we always reading about overcrowded schools and wayward pupils?'

'Get over yourself, Frank,' she replied in amusement. 'Some schools are crap; some are great. Just like here. Just like anywhere. There's a friend of mine working near London and she says that there are vacancies in her school for teachers of maths and English. The great thing about being a maths teacher is that there are always vacancies! It's a nice school in a good area and the pay is a damn sight better than here.'

'But what's wrong with here?' Frank asked her. 'Why would you want to go away?'

'I have to think about my life and what I want from it,' she told him. 'I feel it's time for a change.'

He stared at her. He couldn't believe that another girlfriend was leaving him to work abroad. He knew that lots of people were leaving Ireland, where the prospects for work were pretty grim, but Sally had a good job and there was no need for her to leave. Marion had had a good job too, of course, but she'd gone all the same. Why did they always have to leave? What was it about women? What was it about him?

'Don't go,' he said abruptly. 'I'll miss you.'

She laughed. 'I'll miss you too. But it's a great opportunity.'

'Marry me,' he said quickly. 'I love you, Sally. I don't want to lose you. Marry me and stay.'

'I don't know, Frank,' she said. 'I don't know whether you're the marrying kind.'

He stared at her. 'I'm absolutely the marrying kind,' he told her. 'And I've met the woman I want to marry. I love you, Sally. I always will. I want us to be together and I want us to have a family together.'

'You do?'

'Yes. Lots of kids. Dozens of them.'

She laughed. 'Then it's definitely not me you want.'

'Don't you want children?' He looked at her. 'I thought you liked kids.'

'Of course I do,' she said. 'And I certainly want more than one. I didn't like being an only child, Frank. I want a family too. But cut me a bit of slack – dozens!'

He grinned at her. 'A round dozen then.'

'Get back in your cave, you Neanderthal!'

'Half a dozen?'

'Frank, I'm not a pea pod. I won't be able to pop them out like that.'

He laughed. 'Three?'

'How about four?' she suggested.

'Four it is.' He put his arms around her and pulled her close to him. 'I love you,' he said again.

'I love you too,' she whispered. 'I always will.'

Terri Cooper changed the drip which was feeding Frank Harper. He was a devastatingly handsome man, she thought, even in his current state, even with his eyes closed and his face expressionless. She wondered what his chances were. And, if he pulled through, which of the two women would look after him.

'There you go, Mr Harper.' Terri always chatted to her patients, even the ones who could talk back. 'That should help to keep you going. Let me know if there's anything else you need.'

Frank said nothing. Terri smiled at him and left him on his own again.

Iona was still curled up on the sofa, her knees drawn up underneath her chin, but now she was listening to the gentle music of her well-being CD as it wafted around her. She was trying to be very chilled out and relaxed because the bottle of wine had made her sleepy and she wanted to stay that way.

She looked around the room. After her marriage to Frank she'd had to rearrange things somewhat to take account of the fact that there were now two of them using the space. Previously, and in accordance with her feng shui book, she'd used bright colours in the room to keep the energy moving. But Frank had brought enough energy for both of them and she'd toned things down a little, replacing some of the primary-coloured cushions with more muted tones. She'd kept her cheerful prints on the wall, though, and her ornaments grouped in pairs so that the energy would remain positive, but she'd still worried that she was slowing it down.

It's all nonsense really, she muttered as she looked at the pictures of Gavin and Charlotte in the children area. Nothing actually slowed Frank down in the end except a damn freak accident, and I'm never going to have a child of my own. She blinked back the tears that threatened to fall as she contemplated the carved wooden bird which she'd bought on the day she'd first moved into the house. The idea of the bird had been to make the energy of the house soar. Right now, her energy levels were somewhere around zero.

That was why she was being so passive about everything, she thought miserably. Letting things happen around her, not doing anything about the situation even though Myles had found out the name of Frank's solicitor and told her to contact him. But she hadn't done that. She hadn't been able to.

The reality was that she'd been so shocked by what Siobhán Farrell had told her that she'd simply walked away from Frank and from her marriage to him. OK, it might not have been a valid marriage, but he'd still loved her enough to want to marry her, hadn't he? And he'd lived with her and talked about having a family with her. Flora had said that he loved her and Iona trusted her mother's judgement when it came to people. She was also grateful that Flora hadn't got at her for being stupid enough not to realise that Frank had a whole other life. It was the feeling of stupidity that really upset her, she thought. Well, that and the feeling of worry and every other damn feeling . . .

She sighed. Maybe there really was nothing left between him and the boring middle-aged woman who'd somehow managed to be the one everyone deferred to. Maybe he'd wanted to leave Sally only he didn't know how. Maybe his plan had been to divorce her anyway. Maybe she should fight to keep her relationship with Frank in everyone's minds instead of simply backing off. She was just as entitled as anyone to have a say in his treatment. Maybe not legally. But surely morally.

The phone rang and she picked it up immediately, her heart thumping again.

'Is that Iona?' The voice at the other end was nervous.

'Yes.'

'This is Sally. Sally Harper.'

Iona felt her grip on the receiver tighten so much she thought she was going to shatter it.

'I think we need to talk,' said Sally. 'I'd like to meet with you. As soon as possible.'

Chapter 17

Each time Carl O'Connor's phone rang Siobhán hoped it was Eddie to say that he was on his way back home. And each time she was disappointed. Actually the journalist's phone never seemed to stop ringing; Carl walked around the apartment with the handset jammed against his ear for most of the evening as he carried on conversations with a wide variety of people, peppering every second sentence with comments like 'You can't be serious!' and 'She did what?' so that Siobhán desperately wanted to know who he was talking about, even though she totally disapproved of his career. But she studiously avoided catching his eye even when his final conversation ended with him asking, 'And how d'you think the duck felt about it?' which had her both gagging for further information and not at all sure that she really wanted to know what was going on.

'You'll never guess who that was about,' said Carl as he finally took the phone away from his ear and grinned at her.

'Probably not,' she said drily.

'Don't you want to know?'

'Not really.'

'Oh, come on, Mizz Plod. You're an investigator. Surely your instincts are all fired up?'

'As you so pointedly tell me often enough, my job is to catch criminals, not listen to salacious gossip,' she told him tartly. 'I think you have a nerve being even the tiniest bit critical of my job when you spend your life fishing in the bottom of life's murky pond.'

He laughed. 'You're priceless,' he told her. 'Do they teach you to talk like that in cop school? Or are you totally strait-laced?'

'I'm only saying what loads of people believe,' she snapped.

'Everyone has to earn a living,' said Eddie mildly. 'OK, I'm hardly going to win Pulitzer prizes, but I'm not actually a criminal myself.'

If only Eddie would come home, thought Siobhán miserably. She didn't want to be here. She felt the tears prickle at the back of her eyes again. How could he do this to her? She'd made such an effort tonight. She really had. How many other men would walk away from a woman dressed as she'd dressed that evening? How many men would feel nothing at the sight of her? Even Carl, horrible journalist though he was, had appreciated her appearance.

'Are you all right?' There was concern in his voice as he sat down in the deep armchair opposite her.

She blinked a couple of times and looked up at him. 'Yes, I'm fine,' she said wearily. 'I'd just rather be at home.'

'I'm sure he'll be back soon,' he said. 'In the meantime, would you like another tea or coffee?'

She shook her head.

'A drink?' he suggested. 'A short? A beer? A glass of wine?'

A drink would be nice, she thought, but she really didn't want to sit here sharing glasses of wine with Carl O'Connor. Anyway, she needed to keep a clear head. She didn't want to drop her guard in front of a journalist. She glanced down at her shapely figure beneath his T-shirt. Maybe it was a bit late to worry about that!

'I'm opening a bottle of Sangre de Toro myself,' he told her. 'Nod if you want some.'

'Some wine would be lovely,' she admitted finally.

Siobhán had always loved the sound of a cork popping from a wine bottle and the comforting glug-glug of the ruby-red liquid into the glass. He handed one to her and she tasted it.

'Very nice,' she said.

'Brought it back from Spain,' he told her. 'A third of the price of here.' His blue eyes twinkled at her. 'I suppose you'll arrest me if I tell you that I brought home loads!'

'That's Customs and Excise,' she told him. 'You can bring home casks of it for all I care.'

'Look, I know you hate and despise me, but you're sitting in my living room wearing my T-shirt,' said Carl. 'I think the least you can do is be nice to me.'

'I don't actually hate and despise you, but – but how can I be nice to you when I know that you're cracking up with amusement at the situation and I'll probably end up as the anonymous prostitute policewoman in one of your articles?' She looked at him miserably.

'That won't happen,' he promised her. 'You know, Mizz P., the people who appear in my columns want to appear in them. It's important to them. The celebs, the party-goers – they measure their lives in column inches.'

'Well all I can say is that they're sad individuals if that's what they think is important in life,' she said.

He shrugged. 'Anyway, I won't be writing about you if that's all that's worrying you.'

She smiled ruefully at him. 'It'd be a good story, though.'

He grinned. 'And I'd love to put you on the front page in that get-up. But I won't.'

She shuddered at the thought. 'Eddie would have a fit.'

'Hmm.' He grinned some more. 'Then we could have a fight over you and—'

'And I could arrest you,' she finished.

Carl looked at her curiously. 'Would you really be able to restrain me and handcuff me and frogmarch me to your car?'

'Of course.'

'I love that in a woman,' he said with mock wistfulness. 'Authority.'

'You probably don't really,' Siobhán told him. She sighed as she thought of how Eddie had also seemed to like the fact that she could throw him over her shoulder in a judo move, but how nowadays he wouldn't let her get near enough to put her arm round his shoulder.

She drained her glass and sat back in the chair. She still wished Eddie would come home. But at least she didn't feel quite so uncomfortable with Carl now. She nodded as he refilled her glass. Sod it, she thought. It didn't matter how many glasses she drank. She still wouldn't let her guard down in front of him.

She'd actually nodded off when there was a firm rap at the door which startled her into wakefulness. Carl was already out of the chair and peering through the peephole.

'It's Mr Plod,' he told her. 'Come to rescue you at last.'

Siobhán blinked a couple of times and yawned widely. 'You said you wouldn't call him that.'

'Sorry,' said Carl as he opened the door.

Eddie strode into the room. His six-foot-two frame towered over Carl and the difference in their physiques was unmistakable. Carl's slightly pudgy stomach looked positively fat beside Eddie's lean, muscular body.

'Jesus Christ,' Eddie said as he took in Siobhán in Carl's blue T-shirt, her boobs still defined by the basque she was wearing underneath. 'What the hell is going on here?'

'I told you,' said Siobhán. 'I came out of the apartment and the door closed behind me.'

'You never said that you came out of the apartment dressed like that!'

'Actually she didn't,' remarked Carl. 'She came out wearing an enticing little lingerie number which, I have to tell you, makes the most of her undeniable charms.'

'What the fuck . . .' Eddie looked from Siobhán to Carl.

'I was wearing my underwear,' said Siobhán.

Eddie stared at her. 'You mean you . . .'

'I told you,' she said. 'I came after you. I was still wearing my underwear.'

'Have you no sense?' he demanded.

'Obviously not,' she said. 'But fortunately Carl was kind enough to let me stay in his apartment. Just as well, because you weren't answering your phone.' She glared at him in a way that told him that she knew he'd decided to ignore her request to come home quickly.

'Well, let's get back now,' said Eddie. 'Carl, thanks for putting up with her.'

'Hey, no question of putting up with her,' said Carl. 'We had fun. Though she refused to throw me over her shoulder and arrest me.'

'I'm so glad to hear that.' Eddie's tone was glacial.

Siobhán smiled tightly at Carl and thanked him for the wine and the company. She told him that she'd wash the T-shirt and return it the next day. Then she followed Eddie back to their apartment. As soon as they were inside, he turned to her.

'What in God's name made you run out of the apartment dressed like a tart?' he demanded angrily. 'I told you I was going out.'

'Yeah, you did. I did my best to do something for you, something for our relationship, and all you can do is storm out!'

'I never asked you to dress up like a whore for our relationship.'

'I did not dress up like a whore,' she yelled as she pulled the

T-shirt over her head and stood in front of him in the basque and boxers again. 'This isn't cheap or nasty stuff. This is silk and lace and it was bloody expensive and I bought it because I thought that by wearing it there might be a rat's chance in hell that you'd look at me as the woman you love and not some stranger who's sharing your house.'

Eddie said nothing.

'I've done my best to figure out what's gone wrong between us,' cried Siobhán. 'I've asked myself over and over what it is that I could do. Whether I haven't been around enough. Or loving enough. Or . . . or . . . anything really! I know I'm not the housewifely type, but I didn't think that was what you wanted. But I cleaned the place today and I've arranged to have someone come once a fortnight to keep it clean . . . I don't know what else I can do. I don't know what you want from me.'

'I don't want anything from you,' said Eddie.

'Brilliant!' Siobhán felt the sting of tears in her eyes. 'You don't want me. But you're prepared to keep living with me instead of having the decency to tell me that you don't love me any more and that it's over between us.'

'It's not like that,' said Eddie. 'I didn't say that I didn't want you. I didn't say our relationship was over. I just said I didn't want anything from you.'

'Don't be so fucking pedantic,' snapped Siobhán. 'People who love each other want things from each other. People who love each other talk to each other. People who love each other make love to each other. You can't want me and not want the rest too.'

Eddie stood in front of her, clenching and unclenching his jaw.

'If it's over, it's over,' said Siobhán. 'You made me feel cheap and awful tonight. You're making me feel cheap and awful now, standing here like this, in these things. I don't know what you want but I can't live like this any more.'

'Siobhán, please.' Eddie swallowed hard. 'Don't . . . don't . . .'

'Don't what?' She looked at him pleadingly. 'What the hell is it, Eddie? What's gone wrong?'

'I know we have to talk about it.' He moistened his lips with the tip of his tongue. 'I guess I've been avoiding it. And I *will* talk about it with you. But not tonight.'

'Why the hell not tonight?' she demanded. 'When will there ever be a better night?'

'Because I just can't talk about it now. I'm stressed out and I'm really tired. And I have an early start in the morning. I'm due in for a breakfast meeting and it's after midnight now and if we start talking—'

'So your job is more important than us?' said Siobhán tartly.

'Look, how many times have we come home from things early because you've had to be in work early?' asked Eddie.

Siobhán said nothing.

'That's your police mode, isn't it?' He snorted. 'Staying quiet in the hope that the suspect says something incriminating.'

'For heaven's sake, Eddie. You're my fiancé! Not a suspect in a crime.'

'Yeah, but you're treating me like one.'

'Because you're acting so out of character!' she cried. 'We're supposed to love each other. But all you've done since you've come home is push me away and I can't take it any more. If it's something I've done, then for God's sake just tell me!'

'It's nothing you've done,' he said tersely.

'What then?' She looked at him in frustration. And then warily. 'Is it something you've done?'

'You just can't leave it alone, can you? Of course it's something I've done.'

'There's nothing you could do that should make you act like this.'

'Oh, don't be naïve.' He looked at her with a mixture of anger and despair. 'I slept with someone else. It was a big mistake. OK? Satisfied?'

She stared at him wordlessly.

'So, yes, this is something we have to discuss,' he said. 'But I can't do it now, Siobhán. I need to get my head together about it. And I do have this big meeting in the morning.'

'Yes, but . . .' Her tone was shocked.

'At the weekend. We'll talk at the weekend.'

'I—'

'Please. I know you're upset now. I'm upset. I don't talk well when I'm upset. Leave it til Saturday and we'll have the big discussion and you can . . . you can . . . well . . . whatever.'

'Oh, Eddie.'

'Don't say anything else.' His voice held more despair than anger now. 'I know I've done something terrible. You're right to be mad at me. But we have to talk about it properly. And we can't do that now.'

They looked at each other in silence for a moment and then Eddie walked into the bathroom and closed the door behind him.

Chapter 18

The city streets were thronged with people lured out of their homes by an unexpectedly warm Saturday morning and now strolling around town chatting happily as they popped in and out of Dublin's boutiques and department stores.

Iona strode along Dame Street, the sun warm on her back as she made her way to the small café where she had arranged to meet Sally Harper. Iona was incapable of walking slowly, even though she'd left the house far too early for her twelve-thirty appointment with the other woman. She snorted as the phrase came into her mind. Sally wasn't the other woman. *She* was the other woman. That was how everyone else would see it, wasn't it? That was how Siobhán Farrell, the kindly detective garda, saw it. That was how Lauren and Myles saw it. That was the reality of her situation.

Iona didn't know why Sally wanted to meet her. She couldn't see what there was to talk about. But Sally had been insistent, and in the end Iona had been too intrigued to turn down the invitation. Besides, she wanted to know what was going on with Frank. How he was. What sort of treatment he was having. What they thought might happen to him.

She bumped into a hand-holding couple as she spun around the corner into Trinity Street. She apologised briefly, but the young girl and her boyfriend didn't even react. They were caught up in each other and barely noticed her. Me and Frank were like that, thought Iona sadly. When we were out together nobody else mattered. And then she wondered how strictly true that was, because it suddenly occurred to her that she and Frank had rarely come into town together and that all of their socialising seemed to have been on the north side of the city, despite the fact that they could stroll into Grafton Street in about fifteen minutes.

Had he been trying to keep her out of sight, afraid that his other friends, the people who knew him and Sally, would spot them together? She realised, too, that she and Frank had rarely socialised with any of his friends. It hadn't really cost her a thought until now, but the truth of the matter was that when they went out in a group, it was always with people she knew, never with friends of his. Frank had always told her that most of his close friends were still in Sligo, where he'd originally come from, and that he wouldn't dream of dragging her along to the occasional business dinner he went to as part of his work. They'd existed for the past few years in a tight-knit bubble of their own making, and Iona couldn't help asking herself how it was that she hadn't really noticed the limitations of their social circle before. But then Frank had always wanted to be alone with her when he came back from his business trips, and she liked being alone with him too. Only it wasn't normal, was it? She couldn't believe that it hadn't bothered her before now.

She continued to walk briskly towards Wicklow Street while her thoughts spun around in her head, making her feel dizzy. She was glad to arrive at the café even if she was ten minutes early. She ordered a skinny latte and took a copy of the *Irish Times* from the stand on the wall. Then she sank gratefully into one of the soft leather sofas beside a low table. She turned to the letters page of the newspaper first and then blinked back the tears which suddenly threatened to fall. Turning to the letters page first was one of Frank's habits which she'd adopted. She squeezed her eyes closed and tried hard not to cry.

It took Sally longer than she'd thought to drive from the hospital into the city centre. And then she'd got lost coming along the quays because she hadn't been able to turn left where she'd anticipated. Of course she hadn't driven around this part of the city in years and so she was completely unfamiliar with the latest one-way system. She wasted nearly twenty minutes looping around the congested streets before managing to find a car park, and then had to drive to the very top of it to find a space. It occurred to her that the city had grown out of all recognition in the few short years that she'd been living in Bray. She'd hated moving away from Dublin at the time, but now she felt overwhelmed by the sheer volume of traffic and numbers of people clogging up the streets.

She manoeuvred the car carefully into what seemed to be the last available space, cautiously checking for unexpected pillars to pop up and scrape it. Parking wasn't Sally's strong point – actually she didn't really like driving very much – but the few days without the car had been a nightmare. Siobhán Farrell had arranged for it to be brought back from Ardallen and at first, Sally had wondered whether Iona would try to claim it for herself. But she hadn't tried to claim ownership of anything. The weird thing about Iona was that after those first terrible hours she'd simply stepped back from the whole situation as though it had nothing to do with her.

Well, thought Sally as she got out of the Honda and locked the doors, she'd soon get a handle on Iona's thought processes about the whole thing. If the girl had waited for her. She looked at her watch and frowned in agitation. She'd intended to be early but she was nearly half an hour late. And she couldn't be sure that Iona was the sort of woman who would hang around for her. In fact she rather thought she'd be the opposite.

She hurried out of the multistorey and along the street, perspiring slightly under her wool cardigan, which had been perfect earlier in the morning but was now too warm for the early May sunshine. She arrived at the café and pushed open the door.

Iona had been thinking of leaving. She'd finished her coffee and the paper and for the last five minutes had been working herself up into a rage over the fact that she hadn't really wanted to meet Sally Harper but she'd come all the same and now the damn woman hadn't shown up. And she'd wondered whether it hadn't been some evil ploy of Sally's to . . . to . . . Well, she hadn't been able to figure out the context of Sally's evil plot, but she felt sure that there was something. But just as she'd folded the paper and was gathering her things together, the door opened and the other woman walked in.

Iona's first thought was that Sally had lost an incredible amount of weight. It wasn't that she'd spent ages sizing her up when they'd met at the hospital, but she'd gained the impression that Sally was a slightly overweight middle-aged woman with a dull dress sense. The woman walking through the café towards her was taller than Iona remembered, and certainly thinner, at least facially. It was hard to tell about the rest of her as she was wearing a loose black skirt and a chunky jade-green wraparound cardigan. The jade green would probably have brought out the colour in her eyes and hair except for the fact that her eyes were lost in the pallor of her face and her hair was pulled back into the same tired-looking plait she'd worn the first time Iona had seen her.

Iona was glad that she'd taken the time that morning to wash and gel her own ink-black hair and that she'd made an effort with her tinted moisturiser, eyeliner and lippy. She'd worn her large silver Celtic-knot earrings and matching chain and had dressed in faded jeans teamed with a shocking-pink top which emphasised her blackberry eyes and lightly tanned skin.

I am the younger woman, she thought, as Sally walked towards her. I'm prettier. I have more sense of style. I'm the fun person in the relationship. She's pathetic.

'Hello,' said Sally as she arrived at the table. 'I'm sorry I'm late. The traffic was terrible and I took a wrong turn. It's ages since I was in town. I was afraid you'd be gone.'

'I was thinking about it,' said Iona.

'I would've called,' Sally told her. 'Only I didn't have a mobile number for you.'

And you're not likely to ever get it, thought Iona darkly. 'Would you like a coffee?' she asked.

'Um, yes. Sure.' Sally looked around the café.

'It's OK,' said Iona. 'You have to order at the counter. I'll get it for you. What do you want?'

'Skinny latte,' said Sally.

'Anything else?' Iona was startled that Sally drank the same coffee as her.

She shook her head. 'I'm not hungry.'

Iona ordered two skinny lattes and a blueberry and apple muffin. She wasn't hungry either but she decided that if Sally wasn't going to eat, she was.

'Thank you,' said Sally as Iona placed the coffee in front of her.

The two women sat on opposite sides of the low table and looked at each other.

'How is he?' asked Iona eventually.

'Still unconscious.'

'Is there any improvement at all?'

Sally sighed. 'I guess not. Sometimes I think he hears me, and then other times . . . nothing.'

Iona peeled the waxy paper from the muffin and said nothing because she didn't trust herself to speak. The image of Frank as she'd last seen him in the hospital had rushed into her mind and it was all she could do to stop herself crying out in pain at the thought of him.

'The longer it goes on, the more worrying it becomes,' said Sally.

Iona was surprised that Sally was talking in such a matter-of-fact kind of way. She'd thought her hopeless and befuddled before, and she still seemed slightly dippy and unfocused, yet she was suddenly dealing with the situation in a very down-to-earth manner.

'There's brain activity,' continued Sally, 'he's not brain-dead or anything, but he just won't wake up. And the problem is that if he doesn't wake up and he loses his higher brain functions then he could be like that for ever. Until he gets some kind of infection and dies from it.' At these words she choked slightly and Iona looked up from the muffin. She could see that Sally's eyes were clouded with tears.

'And have they any suggestions for waking him up?' Iona knew that her own voice was harsh, but it was the only way she could keep from crying herself.

'Not really.' Sally cleared her throat and then took a sip of coffee. 'I've done all the stuff they suggested. I've read him bits of the paper. I've talked to him about work. About Jenna. About the house. But nothing.'

'What bits of the paper?' asked Iona.

'Well, the editorial.' Sally looked surprised at the question. 'And Weather Eye. He loves Weather Eye.'

'What about the letters?' asked Iona. 'Do you read him the letters?'

Sally said nothing. Iona watched her intently.

'Of course I read him the letters,' said Sally eventually. 'He loves the letters.'

'I think he prefers them to Weather Eye,' said Iona.

Sally shook her head. 'Weather Eye first,' she said. 'Then the letters.'

'I don't think so.' Iona frowned. 'Letters first, then Weather Eye.'

The two women looked at each other warily.

'Well, not that it matters,' said Iona eventually. 'You're reading him the papers.'

'And the radio is on beside him,' continued Sally. 'He likes classical music.'

'I know,' said Iona. 'And Enya.'

'And Pavarotti.'

'And Madonna.'

'And Frank Sinatra.'

'He doesn't!' Iona looked surprised. 'Sinatra?'

'Yes.' Sally nodded. 'He has a greatest hits collection.'

'I've never seen it.'

'Maybe he doesn't do Sinatra with you. But at parties he sings "Mack the Knife".'

Iona was shocked. 'He's never sung "Mack the Knife" when he's been with me.'

Sally shrugged.

'You're making that up,' said Iona accusingly.

'Don't be stupid,' said Sally. 'Why would I make it up?'

'What's his favourite colour?' Iona's voice was abrupt.

'He doesn't have one.'

'Wrong. It's red. That's why he does so many shows with red lights. His favourite computer game?'

'He doesn't play computer games,' said Sally. 'He doesn't have time.'

'Wingnuts,' Iona told her defiantly. 'And he's brilliant at it.'

'I've never even heard of Wingnuts,' said Sally sharply.

'He plays it all the time,' Iona said. 'It's loaded on the laptop.'

Sally snorted. 'Computer games are irrelevant,' she said. 'What about his favourite food?'

'Spaghetti carbonara,' Iona responded almost before Sally had finished asking the question.

'Roast pork with apricot and coconut sauce.'

'Oh, come on!' Iona looked at her sceptically. 'Frank hardly ever eats roast dinners.'

'Not with you, obviously,' retorted Sally. 'But I'm a good cook.'

Iona looked at her angrily. 'I can cook. I just don't do traditional meat-and-two-veg things.'

'Nor do I,' said Sally. 'I liven them up with nice sauces. And I make the veg interesting.'

Iona felt the rage simmer within her. She bit into her muffin furiously. 'His favourite book,' she said through a mouthful of crumbs. 'What's his favourite book?'

'*Goldfinger* by Ian Fleming,' said Sally at once. 'I always felt it was a silly choice but he really loves it for some insane reason.'

Iona closed her eyes. She could see the copy of the book on the bookshelf in the bedroom. She'd bought it for him shortly after he'd moved in. They'd been talking about books, and he'd told her he'd read it as a teenager and had got into the whole Bond thing way before he'd ever seen a movie. And that it was a brilliant book but that he hadn't seen it in a bookshop in years. So she'd gone looking for it and found it. He'd laughed with delight when she'd given it to him, telling him he couldn't really have looked very hard. But if it was his favourite book he probably had a copy in his other house too and her gift was meaningless. She took a tissue from her bag and blew her nose.

'Oh, look, I didn't ask to meet with you so that we could score points over him!' cried Sally, seeing Iona's very real distress. 'I – well, I wanted to ask you to visit him.'

'Huh?' Iona looked at her in astonishment.

'Like I said, I've tried everything,' Sally told her despairingly. 'Jenna's tried everything too. We've talked and talked until there's nothing left to talk about. I thought that maybe the reason he's not responding is because . . . because he actually needs to hear your voice.'

Iona replaced the half-eaten muffin on the plate and pushed it to one side.

'He heard my voice,' she said. 'On the first night.'

'Yes, but he was totally traumatised that night,' said Sally. 'I thought that maybe now . . . it'd be different.'

Iona twisted her earring around in her ear while she tried to compose herself again.

'And what then?' she asked. 'What if I talk to him and he wakes up?'

Sally shrugged. 'I don't know. But we have to try, don't we?'

'Do we?'

'You don't have to if you don't want to,' said Sally. 'But it's for his sake.'

'Oh, don't be fucking stupid,' snapped Iona. 'It's killing me not being able to see him, not being able to comfort him. I want to talk to him. I love him.'

Sally flinched. 'But you didn't come back to the hospital.'

'Why the hell would I, with you and your kid getting so possessive about it all?' demanded Iona. 'I didn't know what to do. I was giving it some time. But I'm going crazy.'

'So you'll talk to him now?'

'Of course I will,' she said.

'Thanks,' said Sally. 'Thanks very much.'

They sat in silence. Iona finished her muffin and sipped her coffee, although she noticed that Sally wasn't drinking hers.

'Is it all right?' she asked abruptly.

'What?'

'Your coffee,' said Iona. 'You're not drinking it.'

'I'm not very thirsty.' Sally didn't think it was a good time to tell Iona that the last few coffees she'd drunk, including the one with Siobhán Farrell, had left her feeling queasy. She was sure it was something to do with her pregnancy but she wasn't going to talk to the younger woman about that. And then she remembered the question she had to ask.

'Have you and Frank any children?'

Iona felt as though she'd been kicked in the stomach.

'Why?'

'I just . . . wondered,' said Sally.

'No, we haven't.' Iona tried to sound dismissive, as though it didn't matter to her.

'Probably just as well given the circumstances,' said Sally.

'How the fuck do you know what's good or bad for me?' demanded Iona angrily.

Sally flinched at her words. 'I only meant . . . with him sick and everything . . .' she didn't want to continue the conversation. She wished she hadn't started it. She was afraid that Iona would somehow guess about her own pregnancy and she simply wasn't prepared to talk to her about it.

There was an awkward silence which Iona eventually broke.

'Were you at the hospital today?'

Sally nodded.

'So when do you want me to go?'

'Whenever you like,' said Sally.

'How about tonight?'

Sally swallowed. 'I was going to come in with Jenna tonight. I'm not sure whether . . .'

'Tomorrow then,' said Iona. 'I'll go in tomorrow morning.'

'OK.' Sally looked at her uneasily. 'But I want to be there too.'

'Why?' demanded Iona. 'You asked me to go and see him. Why do you need to be there? What about our privacy?'

'What if he wakes up?' asked Sally simply. 'I want to be there.'

'Why?' This time Iona looked at her wryly. 'You want to rush in and hit me over the head so that he doesn't get to see me?'

'Don't be silly.' Sally rubbed the side of her nose. 'I just – well, if he wakes up I want to be there.'

'And then what?' asked Iona.

'Then . . . then I don't know,' admitted Sally.

'We have to have some kind of plan,' said Iona. 'I mean, what if he wakes up but he's lost his memory? What then?'

'Depends on which bit of it he loses, I suppose.' Sally smiled faintly. 'If he forgets about being married to me then you're in pole position. If he forgets about supposedly marrying you—'

'It wasn't supposedly,' said Iona heatedly. 'It was real.'

Sally shrugged.

'It was fucking real,' said Iona fiercely. 'It might not have been legal but it was real. I have the photos.' Her voice cracked and she was horrified to find her eyes fill with tears.

'Oh God, I'm sorry.' Sally looked at her contritely. 'I didn't mean to upset you.'

'What did you think meeting me would do?' Iona sniffed. 'I was always going to get upset no matter what the hell you wanted.'

'Yes. I should've thought of that.' Sally exhaled slowly. 'I suppose I wasn't thinking about you. Only Frank.'

'Yeah, well, I guess I'm thinking about Frank too,' said Iona. She blew her nose again. 'This is all so weird. It's not what happens to normal people. I feel like I'm in some awful reality TV show, expecting them to jump out any minute and tell me it's some kind of joke.'

'I feel a bit like that myself,' admitted Sally. 'Though joke is probably the wrong word.'

'Well, you know what I mean.'

Sally nodded.

They sat in silence again.

'There is another issue,' said Iona.

'Yes?'

'His business.' She told Sally that Myles had found out the name of Frank's solicitor and accountant and that he'd been in touch with them on her behalf. They'd told him that the directors of the company were Frank Harper and Sally Campion. She said that she'd seen S. Campion on the letter heading before but that Frank had never told her who it was and she'd assumed that it was a business colleague or accountant or someone like that.

'Yes. I'm a director,' agreed Sally.

'So what's happening about the business?'

Sally looked at Iona wryly. 'Richard Moran, the accountant, has contacted Frank's clients and contractors. There are fewer clients than I thought, although they're more profitable than I thought too. He didn't need to be away half as much.'

'That figures.'

'Anyway, Pete Maguire, one of the contractors, is looking through the schedules of maintenance and all that sort of stuff. A lot of it is booked in well in advance and there's no big problem there. So it can run itself with a bit of input from Richard for a couple of months. I don't know what happens after that.'

'Are you telling me that he didn't need to be away at all?' asked Iona.

'No.' Sally shook her head. 'There was a lot of client visiting to do but half of it was just because he liked it. And half the time both of us thought he was with clients . . . well, he wasn't.'

'You know, part of me feels he can stay in a damn coma,' said Iona angrily.

'I know how you feel.'

The two women shared a sudden complicit glance.

'But he needs someone to care for him,' said Sally eventually.

Iona nodded.

'So is it OK if I come tomorrow morning too?' Sally asked.

'Yeah. Sure.' Iona reached for her bag and flinched as Sally caught her by the hand. The other woman looked at her third finger where Iona wore a half-hoop of rubies in place of a traditional wedding ring.

'I don't like diamonds,' she told Sally. 'And I always thought that a gold wedding ring was a bit . . . possessive.'

'I can't believe he did this,' Sally said tightly. 'I really can't.' She swallowed hard as she looked at the glow of the rubies under the café lights. 'It's a lovely ring.'

'Are you thinking that it should have been the electricity bill or something?' asked Iona.

'No.' Sally shook her head. 'I'm thinking that it's really classy.' She extended her own hand and showed Iona the narrow band with three tiny diamonds which was her engagement ring. 'We didn't have a lot of money at the time,' she said. 'He always talked about buying me one to replace it but I didn't want him to.'

'Of course not,' said Iona. 'Why would he think you'd want another one?'

'More expensive. Better. He always told me I deserved it.'

The two women fell silent again. Then Iona stood up.

'I'll see you tomorrow,' she said.

Sally stayed sitting down. She nodded. 'Tomorrow.'

She watched Iona stride out of the café and on to the sun-drenched street outside, then got up from her seat and ordered a tea, which she took back to the table. She sipped it cautiously. It didn't have the same heaving effect on her stomach as the coffee. She'd been afraid that she'd chuck up the coffee in front of Iona, and that would have been a complete disaster. She didn't want to give the younger girl any more ammunition. She could tell that Iona had despised her by the way she'd looked appraisingly at her before she'd sat down. Iona's dark eyes had flickered with a degree of superiority as she'd looked Sally up and down and Sally knew that her judgement had been made. She guessed that it had been unfavourable. She imagined Iona's thoughts – that she, Sally, was old and dowdy. That her clothes had been unsuitable for the warmth of the day. That she was, relative to Iona's dark, exotic looks, plain and middle-aged. But she didn't normally look like that. People generally thought she looked good for her age. Not, perhaps, as stunning as she could be (and there was always the dreaded struggle with her weight), but then she didn't have time to look stunning, did she? She had a job and a family and she was always running around trying to keep all the balls in the air because the smooth operation of the home depended on her. It had to – Frank was away too often for it to depend on him.

Away with Iona!

Despite the fact that she was drinking tea and not coffee, Sally barely managed to stop herself from throwing up at the thought. She got up abruptly and walked out of the café, catching sight of herself in the plate-glass window as she pushed open the door. She frowned and walked slowly down Exchequer Street. When she came to a shop with a mirror in the window she looked at her reflection again.

She looked wretched. Really, really wretched. If she went into the hospital in the morning looking like this, and if Frank came out of his coma and saw her standing there beside Iona – well, the first thing he'd do would be make comparisons. And she'd lose out big-time, because Iona was gorgeous. Sally hadn't realised how attractive she was before, but those smouldering eyes and that dark elfin hair were extremely eye-catching. Maybe, she thought, maybe Frank would see both of them and pretend that he didn't know who Sally was because he'd want to be with Iona.

Only he couldn't really do that. In the whole mess she had to remember that she was actually his wife. Not Iona.

She turned in to Grafton Street. She didn't know why she was walking this way, away from the car park, but she wasn't ready to get into the car and drive home yet. She strolled up the pedestrian street, noticing the mime-artists and the musicians, the hair-braiders and the flower-sellers, all of whom were getting on with their lives not knowing that she, Sally Harper, was going through hell.

She stopped in front of a hairdressing salon. The door opened and a woman walked out, her hair expertly cut and styled. The scent of shampoo and hairspray wafted on to the street. Sally stood indecisively for a moment and then pushed the door open and walked inside.

Chapter 19

At eight o'clock on Saturday morning the phone rang with an urgent call for Siobhán to attend a possible crime scene. An elderly woman had been found dead in her home and the circumstances were described as being suspicious. She could see a mixture of accusation and relief in Eddie's eyes as she spoke on the phone – he was peeved at her for having to go out so early but relieved that he didn't have to talk about his infidelity yet.

'I'll be back as soon as I can,' she told him as she dressed hastily. 'And then we're talking.'

He shrugged and rolled over in the big bed which they had continued to share despite the fact that Siobhán was sleeping on the very edge of it and, since his confession earlier in the week, hadn't made the slightest attempt to come near him.

She tried not to think about Eddie and what was going to happen to their relationship as she drove to the small detached house where the elderly woman had died. A neighbour had called and, not getting any reply, had eventually phoned the police. When they'd entered the house they'd found the woman, Claudia Hill, lying at the bottom of the stairs with an open hardback book nearby. Siobhán could see, from the condition of the body, that she'd been dead for a couple of days.

The first time she'd seen a dead body she'd wanted to throw up. She'd never really got used to it. But she could cope with it.

The local garda on the scene introduced her to the neighbour who'd alerted the police. From her she learned that Claudia was a lovely woman but a bit scatty.

'In what way was she scatty?' asked Siobhán, wondering whether the woman had been absent-minded enough to leave her door unlocked so that someone could have come in and attacked her.

'Ah, you know. She'd forget to eat and things like that. She used to spend all her time reading books. There's millions of them in that house. She'd walk around with her head stuck in a novel and you wouldn't get a word out of her until it was finished.'

Theresa, the neighbour, confirmed that Claudia had been in good health and wouldn't have dreamed of leaving her door unlocked.

Siobhán nodded and left Theresa with another female garda. She wandered around the house, noting the overflowing bookshelves and the general air of untidiness; the sparsely stocked kitchen cupboards, the few generic tablets in the bathroom cabinet and the sterilising lotion for false teeth on the sink. Claudia's bedroom was like an antiques shop with its big bed covered in pillows, maroon satin quilt and assortment of delicate glass bottles in a variety of colours on the dressing table. The room was airless, although a hint of lavender overlaid the slightly musty smell. Siobhán opened the window to allow some fresh air in.

As she contemplated the room around her there was a sudden thud near the window she'd opened. An enormous black cat with jade-green eyes regarded her balefully. He stalked across the room and then jumped on to the bed and began kneading one of the pillows.

I might have guessed, she thought. Elderly woman, lives alone, reads books and has a cat. Dies and nobody notices. She's who we're all afraid of becoming. Maybe she's the reason I didn't just walk out on Eddie straight away. I know I should. He slept with someone else. He doesn't love me, and I don't know if I still love him, but I don't want to just walk away. She exhaled slowly and went down the stairs.

The doctor told her that Claudia had fallen down the stairs, broken her neck and died instantly. He couldn't tell whether she'd been pushed, although, as he said cheerfully, it seemed a bit unlikely. As far as he could see the poor old dear had just tripped and fallen. Though deciding that was Siobhán's job, wasn't it?

Siobhán nodded. She supposed the coroner would come to the same conclusion. Accidental death. But you had to be certain, had to follow the procedures.

Normally she was able to put cases like this out of her mind fairly quickly. But as she drove back to her apartment later, she kept thinking about Claudia Hill. Although the pathologist had said she'd died instantly, Siobhán couldn't help wondering what would have happened if she'd simply broken a leg in the fall. Would she have been able to call for help? Or would she have died anyway simply because nobody visited the house every day?

I don't want to be on my own, she thought, I want to have someone who matters to me in my life.

The low hum of the TV greeted her as she put her key in the door and she realised that she'd been holding her breath, afraid that he'd gone out despite his promise to her when she'd rung to say that she was on the way home.

'Do you want something to eat?' he asked.

She shook her head. 'I'm not hungry.'

'Horrible scene?' His voice was sympathetic but edgy.

'Could've been worse.' She flopped down on to the sofa. 'Old woman falls downstairs and dies. Nobody notices.'

'It wouldn't happen to you,' said Eddie. 'You're too smart to fall down the stairs. And everyone would notice if you weren't around.'

Siobhán laughed shortly. 'Who knows? The future might be . . . well . . . who knows?'

Eddie said nothing and the silence between them began to grow. Siobhán felt more and more uncomfortable.

'So?' she said eventually. 'Tell me about it. Who is she?'

Eddie looked at her in a hunted kind of way. As though he was afraid of her. No need to be, she thought. I can't throw you into the cells for sleeping with another woman.

'Nobody important,' he said.

Siobhán frowned. 'Then why did you sleep with her?'

'Because I could.'

'Great,' she said.

'That's not strictly true,' he told her. 'I'm being flippant, I suppose.'

'Do you love her?'

'Oh, come on, Siobhán. Don't be stupid. Of course I don't love her. If I loved her why the hell would I have come home?'

Loads of reasons, thought Siobhán. She could have dumped you. You could have wanted to have two women on the go. Just like Frank Harper. Except for the great sex.

'How often?'

'Just once.'

'Lambay Rules?' she asked.

He shrugged. She knew that there was a general decree in Eddie's firm – anything goes when you're overseas; you just forget about it once you return home and catch your first sight of Lambay Island as your plane descends into Dublin airport.

'I didn't mean to do it,' he said.

He sounded like a child who'd broken a window. She said nothing.

'It was a big night out,' he continued. 'Peter Murtagh arranged everything. We went to a superb restaurant and a club and then afterwards back to his apartment.'

Siobhán clenched her jaw. Peter Murtagh was a high-rolling businessman who was a client of Eddie's firm. Sometimes the newspapers called him an entrepreneur. Other times a mogul. Other times, in the less flattering pieces, a Svengali. They made a big play about his palatial home in the exclusive Dalkey enclave in Dublin, and of his other homes in Spain, Cape Town and Boston. Of his fleet of expensive cars. Of his jet-set LA lifestyle and his incredible wealth. Whenever he was photographed, it was with a huge cigar in one hand and a glass of whiskey in the other. And there was usually a gorgeous girl draping an arm around him too.

'There were a lot of us,' continued Eddie. 'Mostly blokes. When we got back to Peter's place he made a few phone calls. Next thing I know the place is crawling with stunning girls. Absolutely gorgeous. And they were all over us.'

'You mean he ordered them?' Siobhán frowned and Eddie sighed.

'I knew you'd react like this,' he said. 'You're thinking that they're prostitutes and wondering does he do that sort of thing here so that you can arrest him.'

'No I'm not.'

'Yeah, right.' Eddie didn't believe her.

'Look, I don't care about Peter Murtagh and his girlfriends,' snapped Siobhán. 'Especially his overseas girlfriends. Although I do happen to know that he sails close to the wind age-wise with some of them and that one day it'll all come crashing down for him. All I care about is that you slept with one of them and obviously it was the best night of your life because you haven't slept with me since. So what's the deal, Eddie? Was she so wonderful that you can't get it up for me any more? Is that it? Do you want me to move out only you haven't got the bottle to ask me? Or – despite what you've said – are you actually in love with her?'

'Stop it!' he cried. 'It's not like that at all.'

'Then what *is* it like, Eddie? Tell me. I'm obviously not such a great detective after all, because I sure as hell can't work it out for myself.'

'You're right,' he said. 'They were prostitutes.'

Siobhán crumpled into the seat.

'Look, I know what you're thinking!' cried Eddie. 'You're thinking that I'm a complete bastard who can't keep his dick in his trousers for a few weeks just because I'm out of your sight. You're feeling betrayed and let down and you hate me.'

'Something like that.' Siobhán's voice cracked.

'And you're right,' he told her. 'I was a fool, Siobhán. A complete and utter fool. I can't believe that I got suckered in by the whole thing. But it was – well, it was like a movie set or something. Loads of girls, loads of drink . . .' He hesitated. 'Soft drugs. Coke, you know.'

'Christ, Eddie.'

'It was wild and crazy and . . . and I just felt wild and crazy too. I'm not normally. You know that. I know that. I'm a bit anal and stodgy and I know that you sometimes get frustrated with me because I don't like change and I don't do wild things in bed with you—'

'So you thought you'd do wild things in bed with someone else instead?' Siobhán stared at him. 'And I'm supposed to be happy about that?'

'Of course no,' said Eddie. 'It was . . . I'm just trying to explain what happened. Everyone was there. The buzz was fantastic. And the girls—'

'I'm not sure I want to hear about the girls,' said Siobhán.

'The girls were beautiful,' said Eddie simply.

She closed her eyes and compared herself to beautiful girls. There was no contest, of course. There couldn't be.

'Look, Siobhán, I didn't mean to let you down,' said Eddie. 'But—'

'What I don't understand,' she said quietly as she wiped away the tear that had escaped from the corner of her eye, 'is why you're bothering to tell me all this. Lambay Rules, after all. You could've just pretended it never happened. You could have made love to me the day you came home and I'd never have guessed because I trusted you completely.'

'I know,' he said.

'So why?'

He looked at her pleadingly. She stared back uncomprehending. And then he spoke again.

'I might have contracted a disease,' he told her.

For a moment the words didn't penetrate her mind. Then she understood what he was saying.

'A sexually transmitted disease?' she said, aghast.

'Peter called me afterwards. The girls weren't from his usual supplier. Some of them might not have been . . . entirely—'

'Oh, Jesus, Eddie!' Siobhán felt sick.

'That's why I haven't slept with you,' he said. 'I couldn't take the risk of . . . of . . .'

'What disease?' she asked.

'Well, any of them, I guess,' he replied shakily. 'But I've gone for an HIV test.'

Siobhán had met many people who had been infected by HIV. It wasn't necessarily a death sentence. At least, not in the way it had once been. But she couldn't accept the possibility that Eddie, her Eddie, had contracted it.

'When will you get the results?' she asked.

He shrugged. 'Next week, I hope.'

'What do you want me to say?' Her voice was laden with despair.

'Look, I know it was a terrible, awful, insane thing to do,' cried Eddie. 'Believe me when I tell you that I really and truly wish I hadn't done it.'

'Why?' she asked.

'Why what?'

'Why do you wish you hadn't done it?'

'Because it was a crazy moment,' he told her. 'Because I've put everything in jeopardy. Because I've totally messed up our lives. Because I could die.'

'Not because you're supposed to be in love with me?' asked Siobhán. 'Not because we were supposed to be getting married? Or that by doing this you've betrayed me?'

'Of course I wish I hadn't betrayed you,' said Eddie. 'I hate that damned word, by the way. It condemns without understanding. But I wasn't thinking like that at the time. I wasn't thinking at all. And I know you find that hard to believe with your good-and-evil, black-and-white view of the world, but sometimes normal people do get caught up in things they didn't mean to do.'

'Eddie, what you're describing isn't something that normal people do whether they mean to or not.'

'I suppose for Peter Murtagh that kind of sex, drugs and rock and roll kind of party is perfectly normal,' said Eddie. 'And while I was there it did seem normal. I mean, I know it wasn't really but it seemed like it. Everyone was doing everything.'

'Did you take the drugs too?' she demanded.

'Some coke.'

'Hell, Eddie!'

'Yeah, I know. Garda fiancé in sex and coke drugs bust,' he said grimly.

'That's not what I . . .' She sighed despairingly. 'What I'm thinking is that if you felt it was OK to do drugs and prostitutes – whether it was because you were somehow getting carried away in the moment or not – well, if you felt OK about it all, then you and I . . . I thought we were good together but obviously there's something missing and I . . .' She broke off. She'd cry if she tried to carry on, and she didn't want to cry.

'I promise you that I love you,' said Eddie. 'I know it doesn't seem like it because I know that women and men think differently about things. I know that you think I've been a total and utter shit and that there's no way I should have gone back to Murtagh's apartment in the first place. But it was the opportunity to be a different kind of person for a while. To mix with the kind of people who I don't normally mix with. To live a different sort of life even if it was only for a couple of hours.'

'I'm all for trying out different things, but you've been really stupid,' cried Siobhán. 'And this different life – was it worth it?'

'Of course it wasn't.' He swallowed. 'I've felt terrible ever since. I've been a complete fool and I could be seriously ill and . . . and I know I've been a nightmare to you and that everything I've done is shitty and awful, but I don't want to die.' Eddie started to cry.

Siobhán looked at him in silence. She felt as though she should be comforting him, but right now she wanted someone to comfort her.

'I love you, Siobhán.' He raised his eyes to her. 'I always have. I know that it was an awful thing to do but it was a mistake! It really was. It's hard to stand back from something when everyone else is doing it.'

'You had sex with a woman who isn't me,' said Siobhán. 'You asked me to marry you but you still had sex with someone else. You didn't do it because you loved her or anything. You did it because you felt like it. And you took drugs. Nobody made you do those things.'

'I've said I know it was wrong,' he told her. 'But we can't all live a blameless live, not breaking any rules ever. Even if the gardai would like it, we don't live in a police state yet.'

'So it's my fault?' Siobhán felt herself bubble with anger. 'You sleep with some tramp and it's my fault?'

'No! I didn't mean that. I just mean . . .' He looked at her despairingly. 'I shouldn't have done it. I know that.'

'Does anyone else know about it?' she asked after another silence. 'Your friends? People at work?'

'Are you mad?' he asked. 'Of course not. You're the only person who knows.'

She couldn't think of anything else to say. She stared unseeingly across the room, watching the wisp of voile curtain move gently in the breeze from the open balcony window. She wanted to feel sorry for Eddie, but she was too angry with him for that. She was afraid for him, and for her too. Part of her didn't believe that he could possibly have HIV. Part of her was afraid that he'd been very unlucky and that he did. And most of her was very angry that he'd gone away and behaved like an idiot and betrayed her with a woman who meant nothing to him.

She got up.

'Where are you going?' His voice was anxious.

'Out. I'm going for a run,' she replied.

'Don't leave me.'

'I'm not leaving you,' she said sharply. 'I'm going for a run, that's all. I need to clear my head.'

'I'll do anything to make it up to you,' said Eddie. 'Anything.'

But right then she couldn't actually think of anything she wanted him to do.

She ran out of the apartment block and up Temple Hill, following the road along towards Monkstown. She liked running around here, even though it was a residential area. A sheen of sweat covered her body, and her red ponytail bobbed. Normally she didn't think about anything when she ran. But now she was thinking about the bombshell that Eddie had dropped.

Tears began to spill down Siobhán's cheeks. She couldn't believe that this had happened to her. To them. She'd loved him so much but she'd always felt that he was too good for her, too attractive. That was part of the reason she hadn't married him yet. She'd been afraid that in the end someone else would take him away. She just hadn't imagined it would be like this.

It was over an hour later when she arrived back at the apartment building. She stood in the hallway and pressed the button for the lift. Quite suddenly she didn't have the energy to make it up the stairs.

The doors slid open and Carl O'Connor stepped out.

'Hi, Mizz Plod,' he said. 'How's things?'

'Fine,' she said tightly.

He frowned, suddenly noticing her tear-streaked cheeks.

'Hey – something the matter? You don't seem fine.'

'Nothing's the matter,' she told him shortly. 'I'm tired.'

'Hope everything went OK for you the other night,' he said. 'Hope that outfit you were wearing worked its charms in the end.'

'Oh, fuck off, O'Connor,' she said as she got into the lift and stabbed the button with her finger. 'Go and annoy someone else for a change.'

She leaned her head against the mirrored glass of the lift as it moved slowly upwards and brought her back to her own floor.

Chapter 20

Iona walked along the corridors of the hospital. It was busier than it had been the last time she'd been there, and she had to pick her way through the throngs of chattering visitors to reach Frank's unit. Her mouth was dry and she knew that her voice was unsteady as she told the nurse in charge who she was and who she wanted to see. She tried to sound more commanding as she said that the visit had been cleared by Frank's doctor.

Terri Cooper nodded at her. John Carroll had informed her earlier that morning that Iona would be coming in to see Frank. He'd said that Sally and Iona had reached an agreement about it. Terri was pleased that Sally had felt able to agree to Iona's visit, but she hoped that it wouldn't degenerate into some kind of cat-fight between the two women again. She trusted Sally to be calm and measured but, having seen Iona's behaviour that first night, she wasn't so certain that the younger woman would be able to keep her temperament in check. She hoped that Iona was aware that Sally had already been in the hospital for the best part of an hour, reading the newspapers to an unresponsive Frank.

Iona followed Terri to Frank's room, where Sally looked up from the *Irish Independent*. Iona's eyes widened in surprise at her appearance. Sally's long, thick hair had been cut into a shorter, softer style which framed her face and made her seem at least five years younger. She was wearing make-up too, which brought out the light in her blue-green eyes and defined the shape of her wide mouth. She'd replaced her cardigan with a navy-blue long-sleeved T-shirt worn over a pair of loose-fitting jeans. She was totally transformed from the woman Iona had met for coffee.

Iona smoothed her own ink-black hair and sighed with relief that she'd chosen style over comfort that morning herself. She was wearing a black cotton dress which clung to every contour of her slight frame, emphasising the fact that she didn't have a spare ounce of fat on her body. She'd also elected to wear spiky-heeled sandals which showed off the shape of her smooth legs – although the uncomfortable footwear was already giving her blisters on both feet.

'Good morning,' she said to Sally. 'I like you hair.'

'Thanks.' Sally shrugged. 'It's easier to keep this way.'

Iona nodded. My arse, she thought, as she pulled up a chair and sat beside the bed. You've had it cut because you know that beside me you were a total frump and you were afraid of what would happen when Frank wakes up and sees both of us together.

'I've been reading him the papers.' Sally was unable to keep the hint of despair out of her voice. 'No reaction, though.'

Iona got up from the chair and leaned over Frank's immobile body.

'It's me,' she whispered softly. 'I'm here. I've come to be with you.'

It was unbelievably disconcerting to talk to someone who didn't react at all. Somehow she'd thought that it would be like speaking to him while he was sleeping, but it wasn't like that. He was in a completely different place to the rest of them. She knew that he hadn't heard her.

'He doesn't react,' said Sally brutally. 'At least, not usually. He did once. He opened his eyes. But according to the nurse, that happens sometimes. It didn't mean anything.'

'Was he just, you know, staring into space, or did he look around?'

'Pretty much just staring into space. His eyes were open but he wasn't seeing anything.'

Iona suddenly felt dizzy. She hated sickness, and all at once she felt overwhelmed by the sense of her own mortality, the hum of the monitors and the sight of the drip on its stand. She steadied herself by holding on to the bed.

'Are you all right?' asked Sally.

'Of course.' Iona plopped back on to the chair. 'Are you going to leave us alone now?'

Sally said nothing.

'After all, you've had time alone. I need time alone too.'

'Sure. I understand.' Sally got up. 'I'll come back in a while.'

'I'll let you know if he wakes up,' said Iona. 'Don't worry.'

It was different without Sally. She leaned her head on the counterpane, holding Frank's hand in hers, squeezing it from time to time and hoping that he would squeeze it in return. But he didn't. She whispered things to him – how worried she'd been about him, how she felt about what had happened, how devastated she was at the thought that she wasn't really his wife.

'But I feel as though I'm your real wife,' she said softly. 'You chose me after her. You love me. I know you do. And I know that you want to get better to be with me because you want me to have your baby. Our baby. I know that, Frank, and that's why I know you're going to wake up.'

She lifted her head. It was impossible to believe that he hadn't heard her or felt the depth of her love for him. Even though, she thought suddenly, she should hate him. As she had, on and off, ever since the accident.

She sat in silence for a few minutes and then took the book that she'd brought with her out of her bag. She opened it at the beginning and began to read.

Sally walked out of the hospital and into the crowded grounds. She'd never had much to do with hospitals before – her only stay in one herself had been when she was giving birth to Jenna; and Frank had never darkened the doors of one before now either. She'd had to rush into Casualty once, when Jenna had fallen off the back wall and broken her ankle, but Sally didn't consider broken limbs to be real illnesses. They were accidents that happened but they weren't organic problems. She didn't mind broken bones or cuts and bruises. She didn't faint at the sight of blood. But she hated the idea of something going on inside someone's body that no one understood – the idea of tiny cellular creatures dividing and multiplying and creating havoc for the person whose body they had invaded. Or in Frank's case, what bothered her was the thought that the whole structure of his body had changed, that the cells were doing the wrong things simply because they'd been shaken up by the accident, but because of that Frank might die.

She caught sight of herself suddenly, reflected in a car window. She saw her shorter hair and her specially chosen clothes and she wondered why she had bothered. Jenna had been shocked at the haircut.

'You've never worn it that short before,' she'd told Sally accusingly. 'Why have you done this now?'

Sally had tried to explain that it seemed the right thing to do, that her long hair had always been difficult to keep tidy and that plaiting it every day had been a real chore. But Jenna had chosen to ignore Sally's efforts at explanation.

'Is it because of her?' she'd demanded aggressively. 'Is it because she has short hair?'

Sally had also tried to explain that it wasn't a matter of short hair or long hair, that it was about not letting yourself go. But Jenna was having none of it.

'You've always worn it long,' she said accusingly. 'I don't see why you've cut it now. Besides, you look shit.'

Sally had wondered about that. About whether the new style really suited her. It had looked great in the salon but now, at home, she worried that she'd been conned into something that wasn't really her after all. And yet, as she looked at herself in the mirror, she couldn't help but think that the style was much better than the one she'd had before. That she looked more confident and controlled with shorter hair. And that she needed to look like that.

She sat down on one of the wooden benches in the garden of the hospital and wondered what Iona was talking to Frank about. What could she say that Sally hadn't already said a thousand times? Was there anything she could offer that would be different to what Sally had already tried? Part of her knew there wasn't. Part of her was afraid there was. All of her worried about the outcome.

Because what if Frank did wake up and decide that Iona was the one he wanted for his wife? Where did that leave her? Looking for a divorce, she supposed. Right now she could see that it had its attractions. Frank was a shit and he deserved to be divorced. But it was hard to accept that she should be the one to divorce him.

Time had looped back on itself. Frank could feel it. He was sitting in the attic and rummaging through the big cardboard box with *Tayto* written across the side and he knew that he was fifteen years old. Except . . . except somehow he was sure that he had done this before. It was more than a sense of déjà vu. He couldn't explain it. He was watching himself but he was also participating in the action. It was a weird experience.

Maybe it was because of the beer he'd drunk the previous night at the GAA disco. Far too much beer, he knew. He'd been sick on the way home but was kind of glad that he'd thrown up outside the house rather than inside. His father, Derek, who liked a drink himself, nevertheless strongly disapproved of Frank even touching a drop. But then, thought Frank, as he pulled at the contents of the box, Derek strongly disapproved of everything. Frank had investigated the box because he'd hoped – for all of half a second – that it was a supply of crisps for the coming Christmas, but he soon realised that it was packed with stuff that his father hadn't got around to throwing out. Frank knew that he should've had more sense than to think that Derek Harper gave a toss for Christmas. His dad made Scrooge seem positively benevolent by comparison. When Frank was five years old Derek had sat him down and told him that the whole Santa lark was a complete load of nonsense and that anyone with a bit of wit could see that it was impossible for a fat man to get down all the chimneys of the world in one night.

Frank's lower lip had trembled as he looked at his father. 'What about magic?' he asked.

Derek snorted. 'No such thing,' he said. 'If there was, your mother would be back here.'

Frank took out a manilla folder. It was stuffed with receipts and invoices and newspaper clippings about the building of a new school in the area. Derek had worked as the school gardener ever since it had been built. Frank didn't know what his father had done before that. A blue sheet of paper fluttered out of the folder and he picked it up. The sender's address, in the top right-hand corner, was Mount Street, Dublin, and it was dated 1958.

Dear Derek,

I really don't know what to say. I'm honoured that you would want me to be your wife, but you know how I feel about marriage. It's an outdated institution. I love you too and I'd be happy to live with you here (despite how scandalised everyone would be!) but I won't marry anyone. I beg of you to read Simone de Beauvoir to understand how I feel about being a woman. I don't dislike or despise men as so many feminists seem to, but I don't want to be the chattel of one either. And so I can't marry you but I will live with you.

Love always,
Christine

A small photograph was attached to the letter. Frank stared at it. It was a photograph of his mother. He'd never seen a photograph of his mother before. Derek didn't have a camera and had told him that taking photographs was a waste of time and effort anyway. The only photograph in the house was one of Frank himself as a baby, propped up on a white blanket, staring out at the camera, his eyes big and enquiring.

His mother was stunningly beautiful. She had dark hair, laughing eyes and an upturned nose. Her skin appeared flawless. She wasn't wearing any make-up in the photograph (Frank recalled others of that time where the women all seemed to wear very dark lipstick), but her features were well defined without it. And he could see his own likeness in the shape of her mouth and her high forehead.

Frank dropped down from the attic and walked out into the garden, where Derek was pulling weeds from the flowerbeds. He thrust the letter in front of him. Derek's face darkened as he read it.

'I suppose I'd better tell you,' he said, 'now that you're practically grown. She was crazy, that's what. I thought she was a bit flighty but that in the end she'd be sensible. But she never was.'

'All the same . . .' began Frank.

'You deserve to know the truth,' Derek told him sharply. 'I suppose I protected you when you were younger. Had to really, this town being the gossipy place that it is. But she isn't dead.'

Frank stared at his father. He could almost feel the blood drain from his face.

'No. I had to say that for your sake. Couldn't let you know it. Would have hurt you. But she didn't die. She bolted.'

'You told me . . . you said that she'd been sick . . .' Frank couldn't take his eyes of the set face of his father. 'You lied to me.'

'Not a lie,' said Derek. 'Saving you from the truth.'

'But everyone else knows!' cried Frank. 'I know they know. It makes sense now. The way the old biddies in the shops look at me sometimes. I thought it was because my mother had died. But that's not it at all.'

Derek shrugged.

'For crying out loud, Dad!' Frank looked at him in anger and disbelief. 'All these years. What the hell were you thinking?' He scratched the back of his head. 'Did she look for me? Did she want to know anything about me?'

'No,' said Derek shortly. 'Never once. She didn't care about you and me. I should have done it differently with her. Made her care. Made her get married like she should have done. I should have made her realise how important family is, got her pregnant again, got a brother or a sister for you.'

'You never got married? You and Ma? Never got married?'

'What does it look like, boy? You have her letter. You can see what she says.'

'Yes, but – I thought she changed her mind.'

'That woman! No chance.'

'If she was so different from you, if she didn't want to be married or to have a family, then why did you want to marry her at all?' asked Frank.

'Look at her,' said Derek. 'Lovely girl. And a sensible person when she wasn't going on and on about being oppressed. Women's movement.' He sniffed. 'Feminism. Her bloody Simone de bloody Beauvoir. Complete bollocks.'

Frank stared at his father in utter astonishment. Derek never swore in front of him.

'Oh, she was a part-time feminist all right,' said Derek. 'But it was a passing thing. When I took her back here, she was happy enough to pretend. She was pregnant, you see, and despite everything she couldn't quite bring herself to correct people when they called her Mrs Harper. She sad she was doing it for your sake. I thought she just needed a bit of time and then we could get married properly. Nip over to London and do it, I thought.'

'What went wrong?'

Derek sighed and rested his chin on the handle of the garden spade.

'We disagreed. I wanted more kids. She didn't. I told her that if she was married to me she'd have them, and she said maybe it was just as well she wasn't. She said she was trapped enough the way things were. Strangled, was what she told me. Suffocated. A load of nonsense. She said she never meant to have a baby. I told her that it was what she was put on this earth for when it came down to it. That all her poncey ideas were well and good when she was a single woman but she was a mother now and that changed everything.' Derek snorted. 'She said she was still a single woman. I told her that if she walked out on me she'd be an unmarried mother with a crying kid and that she could sing for her supper then because no man would ever look at her.'

Frank blinked. 'Did you have to be so cruel?'

'It wasn't cruelty,' said Derek. 'It was love. I needed to bring her to her senses.'

'But you didn't,' said Frank. 'Because she left us.'

'Stupid, stupid woman,' said Derek. 'She didn't know when she had it good. She didn't love you. Couldn't have. No woman leaves her child. Not with only a bloke to bring him up. Selfish bitch is what she was. I couldn't believe she left you.'

He took the photograph from Frank and studied it for a moment. Then he tore it into little pieces and threw them on the pile of weeds.

'Well shot of her in the end,' said Derek. 'Well shot of her.'

His father stomped back to the house. Frank waited until he was inside and then retrieved the pieces of the torn photograph. He liked the idea of his mother being an unconventional person, but there was a hollow feeling in the pit of his stomach whenever he thought of her simply abandoning him. She hadn't loved him enough. She'd walked out and it had been easy for her because she hadn't married his dad. And his dad had been horrified at her leaving him behind. If she hadn't done that, Derek might have been able to find someone else. But not with a toddler.

Frank clenched his jaw. Neither of his parents had really wanted him when it came down to it. It'd be different when it was his turn. He'd be a good father to his kids and a good husband to his wife.

Unless, of course, he didn't bother with all that marrying nonsense and just became a spy instead. He blinked a couple of times. He'd never thought about being a spy before.

Iona stopped reading as the door opened. She'd reached the third chapter of *Goldfinger*, the chapter where James Bond first sees Auric Goldfinger. Frank had told her, when the film was on TV and they were watching it together, that the description of Goldfinger was so exact that it was amazing they'd managed to get an actor to fit the role so well. Gert Frobe, he lectured, was fantastic, even if the shorts he wore at the beginning of the movie were somewhat more decent than the 'yellow bikini slip' described in the book.

Sally tensed as she realised what Iona was reading aloud. She was angry with herself for not having thought of the book before now. But her anger disappeared as she realised that it hadn't made any difference. Frank was still immobile in the bed.

'No change?' she said as she walked across the room.

Iona shook her head. 'I suppose I was stupid to think that I'd make a difference,' she told Sally. She closed the book. 'I guess I came here believing that he'd wake up. Because it was me, not you. I was stupid. I'm sorry.'

'No need to be sorry,' said Sally wryly. 'I suppose I was in two minds about the whole thing. I want him to wake up. But I didn't really want you to be the one to wake him.'

Iona nodded in understanding. 'Can I ask you something?'

'Yes?'

'You said that people were looking after his business.'

'Yes.'

'Do you depend on it?' asked Iona. 'The company? For money?'

'We're lucky,' Sally told her. 'The mortgage isn't crippling and we've never been big spenders. I work, of course. I'm a teacher. But I don't know where we go from here with the business. I don't really care, to be honest with you. But I told Richard, that's the accountant, to keep me informed.'

'I accessed his company e-mails last night,' said Iona. 'There are a number of things outstanding. And his calendar is online too. I just forgot about it all.'

'How did you do that when you don't have the computer?' asked Sally.

'We . . . I have one at home. I knew his password.'

'Oh. What?'

'Goldfinger,' she said simply.

The door to Frank's room opened and the two women looked up in surprise.

Siobhán Farrell was equally surprised. She'd more or less expected to see Sally at the hospital but she hadn't expected to see Iona. And even less had she anticipated seeing both of the Harper wives standing side by side at Frank's bed. She frowned slightly as she tried to work out the implications of what she was seeing.

'Hello, Sally. Iona,' she said.

'Siobhán.' Iona was the one who reacted first. 'What are you doing here?'

'I needed to drop in to see him,' said Siobhán. 'So here I am.'

'On a Sunday morning?' Sally looked sceptical. 'You haven't come to. . . ?' She broke off and looked accusingly at Siobhán.

'It was convenient for me today,' said Siobhán. She obviously wasn't going to tell Iona and Sally that she couldn't stay in the apartment with Eddie, that she'd needed to get out and had decided to come and fingerprint Frank Harper instead.

'Iona was reading to him,' said Sally. '*Goldfinger*. His favourite book.'

Siobhán nodded and walked further into the room. She looked at Frank as he lay in the bed, noting the angry bruise over his eye and the dark row of stitches on his partially shaved head. But even with the facial injuries, and even with his expressionless features, she could see that Frank Harper was an attractive man.

'No change then?' she asked.

'No,' said Iona and Sally simultaneously.

'There was some increased brain activity last night,' said Sally. 'But it didn't mean anything in the end.'

'You never told me that.' Iona looked at her accusingly.

'Because it didn't mean anything,' said Sally.

'It might. How do you know?'

'Because that's what the doctor said this morning.'

'That's a load of shit,' said Iona. 'You can't tell me that increased brain activity in a coma patient doesn't mean anything!'

'Well, nothing useful,' suggested Sally. 'I mean, it's hopeful that his brain is still working, I suppose.'

Siobhán looked from one to the other. 'Are you visiting him together from now on?' she asked.

'No,' said Iona. 'But we'll both visit him. I suppose.' She looked at Sally for confirmation.

'We could set up a roster,' said Sally. 'You one day, me the next. It would make it a lot easier.'

Iona nodded slowly. 'Thank you.'

'Do you want to come in tomorrow or will I?' asked Sally.

'We're starting from tomorrow?'

'When d'you want to start?' asked Sally. 'It seems to me if we're doing this we should begin straight away. No?'

'Well, sure, yes,' agreed Iona hastily. 'I'll come tomorrow.'

'The roster will be for the evenings,' said Sally. 'If either of us has time to come in during the day, that's up to us.'

'OK.'

'I'm glad you two have worked that out,' said Siobhán.

'I might have been a bit . . . hysterical . . . the first day,' said Iona. 'But that was shock. I can be reasonable too.'

'When did you arrange today?' asked Siobhán.

'We met for coffee,' said Sally.

'Very civilised,' said Siobhán.

'No point in not being,' said Iona. 'Who knows how long Frank might be like this?'

'Indeed.' Siobhán's eyes flickered over his body.

'I suppose I'd better get going,' said Sally into the silence that had developed between the three women. 'I've been here since early this morning and I've got to get back to Jenna.'

'Doesn't she visit?' asked Siobhán.

'She hates it,' explained Sally. 'She hates the hospital smell and she hates seeing her dad like this.'

Siobhán nodded in understanding.

'I'll go too,' said Iona. 'I've read him loads of the book and I've talked to him and . . . well . . . I guess there's not much more I can do.'

'Did you drive?' asked Sally.

Iona nodded.

'I'll walk with you to the car park.'

'OK.' Iona turned to Siobhán. 'Coming?'

Siobhán shook her head. 'I need to see a nurse or doctor on the ward,' she said. 'Just to get more info on when Frank was admitted.'

'You know that already,' said Iona. 'Walk with us.'

Siobhán glanced from Frank to Iona and Sally and shrugged. 'OK.'

She followed them out of the door. She'd walk to the car park with them, then she'd come back. She had her fingerprint kit in her bag. And, having seen Sally and Iona together, she was beginning to reassess the relationship between the two women. Everything had seemed perfectly straightforward, and she was sure that it still was. But making certain was important too.

Chapter 21

Iona needed to go back to work. She couldn't stay in the house all day, worrying about Frank and frantically trawling her mind for memories which would show her what a fool she had been to believe him when he'd used the words 'forsaking all others' on their wedding day. She needed to be in a place where she couldn't think about it all the time and blame herself for making the issue of being married so important even while telling herself that it wasn't her fault. Frank could have admitted that he was married already when she first broached the subject. He could have dumped her without saying anything at all. Nobody had forced him to lie and cheat and pretend. That had been his own choice. The thoughts whirled around and around in her head like a washing machine on a fast spin cycle, and she knew that the only way she'd get peace of mind was to go back to Rental Remedies and lose herself in something else.

Ruth Dawson smiled at her as she walked into the office and asked her how she was feeling. Although the message she'd left at the office had said that she was off sick, Iona had somehow imagined that her colleague would guess, by some kind of mental osmosis, that the real reason for her absence was entirely different. But Ruth was sitting back in her chair and telling Iona that everyone seemed to be getting crazy virus infections and that echinacea wasn't all that it was cracked up to be, was it, because otherwise Iona wouldn't have succumbed, would she?

'I've got to talk to Garret,' said Iona blankly, ignoring Ruth's puzzled stare as she walked towards their boss's office.

The founder of Rental Remedies smiled at Iona as she sat down in front of him. She was one of his favourite employees, clever and sparky and totally dependable. Her absence through illness had been the first time in two years that she'd taken time off sick from work.

'Feeling better?' he asked casually, and then listened in stunned amazement as Iona told him everything that had happened over the past week. She hadn't been sure what she was going to tell people – had briefly thought about not saying anything about Sally and Jenna at all, just that Frank had been in an accident and she'd been too shocked to tell them about it before – but she simply wasn't able to lie. So she held nothing back, and Garret's jaw dropped lower and lower as she recounted the tale.

'I don't know what to say to you,' he said as she finished. 'I can't believe he would do a thing like that. And the police are involved?'

'They have to be,' explained Iona. 'It's a criminal offence.'

'Jesus wept.' Garret stared at her. 'I'm sorry, Iona. I really am.'

'Yeah, well, so am I.' She gave him a half-hearted smile. 'I'm in a bit of a quandary at the moment. He's still in hospital and we really don't know whether he'll recover or not.'

'Have they given you any kind of time frame?' asked Garret.

'They can't.' Iona shrugged. 'Really, though, from what they say, he needs to come out of it soon.' She swallowed hard. 'The doctor says that there is brain activity but right now he's simply not responding to anything. But that doesn't mean he doesn't know what's going on around him. It's really difficult to tell. Unfortunately, the longer he goes without reacting, the worse it is.'

'I can see that.' Garret nodded. 'You do hear about people coming out of comas, though.'

'Yes, you do. And in the movies they just kind of wake up and everyone clusters around and it's all happy families. But the reality is different. He might be brain-damaged. He might have memory loss. He might not even know who we are. He might be physically impaired. He might have to learn how to do simple things again. Or he might be all right.' She shrugged helplessly. 'We don't know.'

'And this other woman. How are you coping with her?'

Iona sighed. 'We're working things out between us,' she said. 'At the moment it's a kind of one day at a time scenario.'

'I'm sorry,' repeated Garret. 'It must be difficult for you.'

'It was a nightmare.' Iona straightened up in the seat. 'But I'm ready to work again now. I can't sit at home and wait for him to wake up. I need to do things.'

Garret nodded. 'Well, if you need time out, just let me know.'

'Thanks,' said Iona. 'I appreciate that.'

'No problem.'

Garret's eyes followed her as she walked out of his office and then he rubbed his forehead. He never would have imagined that Frank, whom he'd met a couple of times, would have been the sort of guy to have such an involved personal life. Marrying two women! One the one hand Garret couldn't help admiring the fact that he had managed to juggle his life in secret for so long. On the other . . . Well, Garret was married himself. He loved Emily dearly. But one wife was more than enough!

Ruth looked up again as Iona sat down behind her desk. She frowned. But before she had the chance to say anything, Iona launched into a repetition of what she'd told Garret. Ruth was equally shocked and asked exactly the same questions. Iona answered her patiently. Although she hated having to say it all over again, she was finding talking about it to other people a little therapeutic. As though by admitting to what had happened she was lessening the horror of it all.

'He'll come out of it and he'll be fine,' said Ruth finally. 'Frank is such a positive person, he's bound to recover.'

'Yes.' Iona nodded. 'And when he comes out of it, I'll fucking kill him.'

'Iona!' Ruth looked shocked.

'Sorry,' said Iona. 'But I feel a bit like that about it. It's very tiring. I want him to get better and then I want to hit him over the head again.' Her smile wobbled. 'I'm completely schizophrenic about it all, to be perfectly honest with you. However, it's not going to happen in the next couple of hours, so you'd better tell me – anything need doing?'

'Um, sure.' Ruth was still in shock from Iona's news as she looked at her computer. 'We got the final contract to manage that block in Monkstown last week,' she told her. 'Everyone was really pleased about that. Carmela is working on it but there'll be a number of rentals, so I thought you'd probably want to talk to her about it. The tenant in Craighill Manor keeps ringing up with new complaints . . .'

Iona listened as Ruth continued with the list of things that needed her attention. It was nice to have other problems to worry about instead of how Frank was and how things would develop and what the hell she was going to do with her life; but it was hard to concentrate on them. She felt as though she should be doing nothing other than sitting at

Frank's bedside and reading him more chapters of *Goldfinger*. She was sure the novel would eventually reach him. Absolutely certain. And she still wanted to be the person beside him when he woke up.

'. . . you could drop out with them?' Ruth looked at her enquiringly and Iona dragged her attention back to her colleague.

'I'm sorry,' she said. 'What was that?'

'Enrique Martinez,' said Ruth. 'He's signed the contract for Apartment 7 in the Waterside Building, but he's gone back to Spain for the weekend. He sent an e-mail asking if we could get the keys to him today and go through the apartment again with him. D'you want to do that? I could do it but my schedule is a bit crowded.'

'No, it's OK, I will.' Iona nodded. It would be nice, she thought, to get out of the office for a while. She didn't want to see Ruth's sympathetic face all bloody day.

Sally had decided to take another week off work. She simply wasn't able to concentrate on anything long enough to give any kind of coherent lesson to the students, and she knew that her mental state was too fragile to keep a class of thirty adolescent females under control anyway. The previous night she'd phoned Denise to tell her that she simply couldn't come back yet, although, she said, she'd absolutely definitely be back the week after.

'Sally, honey, you'll need more than another week!' exclaimed Denise, who, when she'd eventually heard about Iona, had been apoplectic with rage on her friend's behalf. 'I'll talk to the head about it. She'll understand.'

'I'll ring her myself,' said Sally tiredly. 'I can't let you do it for me.'

'Don't be daft,' retorted Denise firmly. 'I'll do it, you phone her later. Is there anything else I can do for you at the moment?'

Sally had told her that there was nothing anyone could do. Except wait. And worry.

In addition to worrying about Frank, of course, she was equally worried about Jenna, who had retreated into a world of silence about it all. Every time Sally asked her daughter if she was OK, Jenna snapped that she was fine, she wasn't the one who was in a coma and she wasn't the one who was probably going to die. When Sally protested that the fact that Frank was in a coma didn't mean he was going to die, Jenna had responded with a sheaf of information she'd downloaded from the net which gave a variety of prognoses in relation to comas.

'If he doesn't die he could still be a vegetable,' she said shortly. 'He might as well be dead.'

'We have to be positive,' said Sally.

'Yeah.' Jenna tossed back her hair disdainfully. 'If he's a veggie then that other woman can have him!'

'Jenna!'

'Well, why should we have to put up with it?' demanded Jenna. 'I hate him. I wanted to die myself when I saw him in the hospital and I felt so awful for him. And then we find out about her! She's welcome to him.'

'He's your dad,' said Sally gently. 'You don't mean it.'

'I absolutely do.' Jenna got up and stalked out of the room while Sally pressed her fingers to her throbbing temples and wondered how long she could live like this.

She was surprised when Jenna said that she wanted to go to school the next day. She told her that she could stay home if she wanted, but Jenna replied that there was nothing to do at home, and that she wanted to be with her friends. She added that she wasn't going to ruin her life by missing out on her schooling just because of him and that she needed to study. Sally had acquiesced, even though she worried about Jenna's pinched face and tired eyes, and had watched her daughter anxiously as she walked down the road to school, her long uniform skirt flapping in the breeze.

Now, alone in the house, she went up to Jenna's room and switched on her daughter's computer. She opened up the web browser and looked at the history of searches which Jenna had done on comas. There was a great deal of information and lots of different coma stories, but all of it came down to the same thing. Nobody knew. Nobody could be sure. Nobody could predict what might happen.

But Sally had to know. She had to get their lives into some kind of order. It wasn't as though time could stand still while Frank was in the hospital. And it wasn't as though sooner or later Jenna wasn't going to find out about the baby too. If she'd thought it would be difficult to talk to Jenna about the baby before, Sally felt it would be a million times harder now.

'Why?' she muttered as she leaned her head against the screen. 'Why me? Why us? Why now?'

Frank wanted Sally to have a good time. They were in town, in a swanky restaurant on St Stephen's Green where the prices were astronomical and where the wines were the sort you didn't find on the supermarket shelves. But this was a major celebration. They were going to have a baby. Every time he said the word, he looked at Sally as though she was a fragile piece of glass which needed the gentlest of care, even though she looked stronger and fitter than ever.

'I'll look after you,' he said sincerely. And he knew that he would. Because she was giving him everything he'd ever wanted. The family that they'd promised each other. They'd discussed it, of course, after she'd accepted his marriage proposal but before they'd actually got married. She'd been quite specific about it, telling him that they should both know what they wanted from each other, and although he'd been taken aback by her practical way of looking at it, he'd agreed that before they signed up to a lifelong commitment they should set out a few ground rules.

The main rule was that both of them wanted children. And although they'd compromised on four, it didn't really matter in the end whether they had four or fourteen or whether this was their only child. They would be a family. A strong unit, there for each other. And this baby was the start of that.

Frank was looking forward to being a father. He wanted to be a good dad. He wanted his kids to look up to him but not to fear him. He wanted them to think that he knew about lots of things but that he wasn't always right. He wanted them to love him, although he was pretty sure that children never loved their parents as much as parents loved their children. In most cases anyway. His had surely been an exception.

She was sitting back in her chair, looking around the restaurant. He wanted to lean forward and kiss her on the lips but somehow his body couldn't quite manage it. Probably because I'm a bit overwhelmed at being here, he said to himself. Probably because I never thought I'd be sitting in a swanky restaurant. So instead of kissing her, he just smiled.

* * *

Siobhán Farrell was waiting for information on the fingerprints she'd taken from Frank Harper as he lay in his hospital bed. Her sudden suspicion that there was some kind of collusion between the two Harper wives had dissipated and she was inclined to go back to her first thoughts, that the whole thing was simply a case of a a devious, if apparently loving, man deceiving both of them. But she still had a process to go through and she still intended to go through with it. She was also running background checks on Frank both in Ireland and the UK, but so far nothing had come back, which reinforced her belief that this was a domestic disaster.

She could see how it had happened, though. At least, she could see why both of the women had been attracted to Frank Harper, because she'd been attracted to him herself. It was hard to believe that this had been the case when he'd been lying there, motionless in the bed, but even in his comatose state he radiated a certain presence. She could imagine that he was an active man, a man of energy, someone it would be hard not to find attractive. And he was probably good in bed. No, definitely good in bed. Both Iona and Sally had said so.

Had he ever worried about giving either of them a sexually transmitted disease? She supposed not. It shouldn't matter, should it, if the sex was only happening in their little triangle, if Frank wasn't going outside it for additional excitement and gratification. Unlike Eddie. She clenched her teeth as she thought about his terrible betrayal.

Was it fair to feel so angry with him? One mistake, that was all it was. Frank Harper had consistently deceived both women in his life, but Eddie's mistake had been a stupid, drunken one. So the circumstances were utterly different. And Eddie, at least, had had the decency not to sleep with her when he realised he could be exposing her to a disease. Which was a point in his favour, surely? Nonetheless, he could have come clean a lot sooner, instead of simply pushing her away every night and making her feel unwanted and unloved. If he really and truly thought he had AIDS then he'd been right not to come near her. But she couldn't believe that he honestly thought that. Siobhán believed that Eddie had been unable to make love to her out of guilt. She was glad if that was the case. She didn't like to think of him having even a moment of pleasure when he was causing her so much pain. He'd apologised to her over and over again, begging her not to walk out on him, repeating how much he loved her and how he still wanted to marry her and how it had all been a terrible, terrible mistake. The people she arrested usually said that to her too. And they still got convicted in the end.

Iona had arranged to meet Enrique Martinez at the entrance to the apartment block. They both arrived at the same time and she greeted him warmly, amazing herself that she could smile at a client when inside she felt an emotional wreck.

She unlocked the apartment and then handed the keys to Enrique, telling him that it was all his.

'We go around to check everything together first?' he said, and she nodded. She followed him as he identified everything on the inventory, ticking it off with a beautiful silver fountain pen. He was going through the kitchen equipment when her phone rang.

'Hello,' she said.

'Iona!' Flora's voice was crystal clear. 'I called the house and there was no answer. Are you all right?'

Iona groaned inwardly. She didn't want to talk to her mother right now, but Flora was asking whether she was all right and fussing as Iona knew she would, shocked when she heard that Iona was at work and telling her she needed time to grieve.

'For heaven's sake, he's not dead yet,' snapped Iona. She winced as she saw her client glance in her direction. 'Look, Mum, I appreciate your calling, but I'm busy right now. I'll call you later.' She closed her mobile and shoved it back into her bag.

'Problems?' Enrique looked at her sympathetically.

'Not at all,' she said briskly. 'My apologies. Now, is everything in order? Is there anything else that you need?'

It was good to do ordinary things, she thought, as she eventually left the apartment block. Ordinary things made her feel as though she was living an ordinary life after all. And that was all she really wanted to do.

Chapter 22

It was four weeks since the accident.

Sally had insisted that Jenna come to the hospital with her that evening because she felt that it was more important for both of them to be around tonight than ever. In her mind, and especially because of what the doctors had told her, she'd set four weeks as the target for Frank to recover. Until then she was prepared to allow his brain to stay switched off from reality, thinking that maybe he needed time to heal himself. But four weeks was her mental cut-off time, the date for things to return to normal.

She didn't say to Jenna that she had a feeling Frank would wake up tonight. She didn't want to raise her daughter's hopes in the same way as she was raising her own. But he had to come out of it now, he just had to. The doctors said that there was no swelling on his brain, and that he was recovering from his other injuries too. So with all of that more promising physical improvement, surely he could let himself wake up. Sally had likened Frank's current state to the way she felt in the mornings these days – knowing that she had to get up and out of bed but trying desperately (and out of character for her) to snatch a few more minutes of sleep before the reality of how things were washed over her again.

They walked through the hospital corridors to Frank's room. By now they recognised many of the nurses, and most of them knew them too. Despite the fact that they seemed perpetually busy and always hurrying somewhere, the nurses always had time to say hello and ask them how they were doing. Sally appreciated their concern. She no longer felt as though they were laughing at her behind her back or whispering about her at their coffee breaks. And, she thought, as she pushed open the door and went into the now familiar room, so what if they were? Maybe she would find the situation one to whisper about too if other people had been involved.

'Oh!' Jenna grasped at her hand. 'His eyes are open.'

'But he still can't see us,' said Sally. 'This has happened before, Jen.'

'Not when I've been here.'

'No,' admitted Sally. 'And it freaked me out the first time it happened.'

'Did it?' Jenna was still holding her hand. 'I can't imagine you getting freaked out.'

'You'd better believe it.' Sally squeezed her daughter's fingers and then pulled out a chair. 'Hi, Frank. You scare us when you open your eyes like that.'

He closed them. Sally and Jenna looked at each other.

'Frank?' said Sally. 'You want to open those eyes again for us?'

But nothing happened.

'Dad?' said Jenna. 'Please open your eyes.'

They stayed closed.

'Oh well.' Sally tried to keep the bitter disappointment out of her voice. 'Maybe he'll open them again later. Do you want to talk to him first or will I?'

'I will,' said Jenna. 'I'm going to have a girl-to-father conversation, so actually you can butt out if you don't mind.'

Sally smiled. OK,' she said. 'I'll be back in ten minutes.'

'Fine,' said Jenna.

Once Sally had left the room, Jenna pressed play on the portable CD player she'd brought with her so that he could hear the sounds of Westlife singing Frank Sinatra (she felt it would be just too much for her to have to listen to a recording of Sinatra himself). Then she leaned her elbows on her father's bed.

'I hate you,' she said conversationally over 'Mack the Knife'. 'You betrayed us. We loved you and you lied to us. You always said that we were the most important people in the world to you, but you don't believe that, do you? 'Cos if you did you wouldn't have done what you've done.

'But it probably doesn't matter. Mum thinks you're going to get better and – well – I want you to, but it's not looking very promising. She won't read the stuff I downloaded and she only listens to the good stuff the doctors say. They're muttering about psychological reasons why you won't wake up. Well, it's not really so surprising, is it? You lied to me and to Mum and to . . . to her, that woman as well, and if you wake up now – well, I wouldn't want to be in your shoes! So I guess that's why you're staying in bed. Because you can't face us. Because you're such a shit.'

She sat back and looked at him. His expression hadn't changed. His eyes were still closed. 'So what I want to know, Dad, are all men shits? I'm asking you because I have a boyfriend and his name is Gerry and I love him. I'm not just pretending I love him. I really do. He's the nicest bloke you ever knew and he's been really great to me, especially over all this crap. When I'm feeling bad about everything he tells me that it's not my fault and there's nothing I can do and that I have my own life to lead. That's pretty cool, don't you think? So that's why I'm reacting to this by telling you that you're a shit. But I still love you.'

Her voice cracked slightly. 'I mean, Dad, I remember all the stuff we did together and I know that you loved me then. So what did I do to make you not love me? Or what did Mum do? I always thought it was us three; that's what you told me all the time. So how come there had to be someone else? Anyway, I guess it's all changed now. It's us three and her. And Gerry makes another person because, Dad, right now I love Gerry more than you. Well, it's different of course. I love him like a boyfriend.'

She sat back in the chair and observed her father for a moment. It was hard to imagine that the feelings he and her mother had for each other could ever have been like the feelings she now had for Gerry Cullinan. But she supposed they must have been once.

'I've slept with him, Dad.'

She scrutinised his face for any sign that he'd heard her, but there was nothing.

'I've slept with him more than once. We used condoms, so you don't have to worry about being a grandfather just yet. I wasn't crazy about the first time. It was OK but I was too conscious of everything going on around me, which I guess you shouldn't be. But the second time was great. Really great. I loved it. So I couldn't wait to sleep with him again. He makes me . . . fizz.'

She got up and poured herself a drink from the water jug beside the bed. She wondered why on earth there was a water jug there when Frank clearly wasn't able to use it – when he didn't even know it existed.

'I couldn't help wondering if you and the other woman fizz,' she said as she sat down again. 'I mean, I have to tell you that it's disgusting. For you and for her. You're my dad, for heaven's sake. But if there was something about her that made you feel like I feel about Gerry, then I understand. But I can't forgive you for it. You know that, don't you?'

The door opened and Sally walked in again.

'No change,' said Jenna.

'So I see.' Sally pulled out a chair and sat down beside the bed.

'I'm going for some air,' said Jenna, 'It's far too hot in here.'

'Stay a bit longer,' said Sally. 'Let's be with him together for a while. He needs his family around him now.'

Jenna looked longingly at the door. But she didn't get up from the chair.

The office block was relatively new, but squashed between two older, more elegant buildings. Frank liked the newness but he couldn't help feeling that glass and chrome were out of place beside the Edwardian structures either side of it. He walked into the lobby, which was very modern – red leather and chrome chairs and glass coffee tables strewn with copies of a glossy women's magazine – and stood in front of the elderly security guard, who ignored him for a full minute before looking up.

'I'm here to see Christine Harris,' said Frank.

'Fill out a slip.' The security guard had no interest in him.

Frank did as he was told. The man looked at the slip and picked up a phone.

'Got an appointment?' he asked Frank as a voice at the other end spoke to him.

'Not as such,' said Frank.

'Miss Harris is busy,' said the security guard.

'Tell her I need to talk to her,' said Frank. 'Not seeing me isn't an option.'

The security guard raised an eyebrow and spoke into the receiver again.

'She'll be down in ten minutes,' he told Frank. 'You can sit over there.'

Frank lowered his long limbs into one of the red leather chairs, thinking that it was incredibly uncomfortable. He felt as though it were going to tip over at any minute. He picked up a magazine and flicked through it.

In his teens he'd read a lot of women's magazines. Ones like *Woman* and *Woman's Own* and *Woman's Weekly*. His main interest was in the problem pages, where he was astonished to read of so many women who were unhappy, mostly with their husbands or boyfriends or their sex lives. Frank mainly read the magazines for information on the kind of sex they were having. It wasn't a conversation he felt he could have with his father, and most of his mates in Sligo were equally ignorant of the workings of the female body. Frank had kept his collection of magazines with their advice from Anna Raeburn and Irma Kurtz on the top shelf of his wardrobe. He felt sure that if Derek found them his worry would be that Frank was a poofter, wanting to know about make-up and clothes; not that he was a seventeen-year-old virgin wanting to get it right the first time.

The doors to the lift opposite him opened and a woman, wearing a lilac suit with a nipped skirt and short jacket, walked out. She was tall, her height accentuated by the incredibly high-heeled shoes she wore. Her chestnut hair was scooped into a chignon which emphasised her oval face and slender neck. She looked straight at him from her dark eyes as she crossed the lobby and held out her hand.

'Frank,' she said.

'Mam.'

She raised an eyebrow. 'Christine,' she told him.

'Still Mam,' he said.

'Do you want to go for a coffee?' she asked. 'There's a place around the corner. But I have to be back in forty minutes. I have a meeting.'

He followed her out of the building and along the Old Marylebone Road. The sun shafted between the buildings, reflecting shades of russet from her sleek hair and highlighting her flawless skin. She pushed open the door of a small coffee shop where the aroma of roasting beans was all-pervading.

'Turkish,' she told him. 'The best in London.'

They sat down at a small Formica table. The voice of Michael Bolton filtered through from the radio behind the counter. The proprietor came to take their order, which for Frank was a black coffee and a sticky pastry. Christine just ordered coffee. They sat in silence until their drinks arrived, and then she shook a cigarette from the packet she'd taken from her bag, lit it, inhaled sharply and exhaled slowly so that the blue-grey smoke furled in the air between them.

'Why did you leave me?' asked Frank.

'I'm not the maternal type.'

'Why did you have a baby in that case?'

'I didn't mean to.'

'Why did you live with my father?'

'I thought I loved him. I thought he was a different sort of person. I was wrong.'

'Was it me?' asked Frank. 'Would you have stayed with him if it hadn't been for me?'

She took another deep drag from the cigarette. 'I doubt that very much,' she said.

'Why couldn't you have had the life you wanted living with him?' demanded Frank.

'Be realistic,' she said sharply. 'Sligo? In the sixties?'

Frank shrugged. 'You can't change things by running away,' he said.

Her dark eyes hardened. 'I didn't run away.'

'What else d'you call it?'

She ground out the cigarette in the glass ashtray. 'Your father was the wrong person for me. I don't know why I fell for him in the first place. But he seemed different then. When we got back to Sligo it all changed.'

'And you pretended,' Frank said. 'Pretended to be married to him even though you weren't. Selling out a bit, weren't you?'

'I did that for you,' she said. 'I might not have planned you but I didn't want them calling you a bastard. And they would have.'

'They probably knew anyway,' he told her. 'People find things out.'

'I'm sorry if I messed up your life,' she said. 'I never meant to.'

'That's real easy to say, isn't it?' He looked at her. 'People do it all the time. "I didn't mean to do something awful so you should forgive me." Just because you didn't mean it doesn't make it any less crap.'

She said nothing.

'Did you ever love me?' he asked.

'Of course,' she said sharply. 'That's why I left you. Because if I'd stayed I'd have hated you.'

'Easy way out,' he said.

'It's the truth.'

'You never tried to get in touch,' he told her. 'Not when I was younger and not when I was more grown-up. I had to track you down. And that was bloody difficult.'

'I didn't see any point in getting in touch.'

'Don't you give a toss?' His voice rose. 'I'm your son. Your flesh and blood. I'm family. But you're talking to me as though I was a stranger.'

'You are,' she said. 'I don't know you.'

'You're my mother!'

'That's a matter of biology,' she told him. 'Nothing else.'

'You're a hard-hearted cow,' he said.

She pushed the coffee cup away. 'I'm sorry you think that. I'm not. I do think about you from time to time, but the bottom line is that I would have been a shit mother if I'd stayed. I do actually realise that from your point of view I'm a shit mother anyway. I'm sorry about that. I really am. I got out of your life, which was better for you and better for me and that's the end of it. I wish you every success in the future. I hope you get everything you want out of life. But I'm sorry, I can't be the person you want me to be because that's just not how I am.'

'Are you married?' he asked.

She laughed. 'No.'

'Live with anyone?'

'No.'

'Have any other kids?'

'Absolutely not.'

'Are you lonely?'

She smiled. 'Why do people always seem to think that anyone who lives on their own must be lonely? I've achieved a lot of things. I edit a forward-looking magazine. I have lots of friends and a social life which I enjoy. I occasionally sleep with men but I don't want to be tied to any one of them. I'm happy to be on my own and I'm not lonely.' She crossed one elegant leg over the other. 'I'm happy, Frank. I'm doing what I want to do.'

'You're nothing like me, are you?' said Frank.

'Probably not,' she agreed. 'You're more like Derek. Wanting people to love you. Thinking that everything will turn out for the best. Looking for warm and fuzzy when life is cold and hard.'

'It doesn't have to be cold and hard,' he said.

'I like it like that,' she told him.

'I'm married,' he told her. 'I tried to find out about you before the wedding but I couldn't.'

She pursed her lips. 'Why? Did you want to invite me?'

'Would you have come?'

'Would it have made any difference?'

'Don't you have any feelings at all? What's the matter with you?'

'Nothing,' she said. 'I believe in a different way of life. And that whole maternal thing – well, I'm sorry. You were a cute baby. But it did nothing for me.'

'Bloody hell. Thanks a bunch.'

'I'm sorry. You asked.'

He looked at her, real puzzlement in his eyes. 'How can we be so different? We're biologically the same.'

'I was naïve and silly when I met Derek. But I was right about what I believed. The interlude with him was the biggest mistake in my life.'

'And me? You think I'm a mistake?'

'You were my mistake,' she agreed. 'It doesn't mean I don't care about you at all. I do. I want you to be happy with your life. But not the way you want me to.'

'So you don't want to keep in touch or anything? Even cards at Christmas, that sort of thing?'

'I really don't see the point, do you?'

'I think I hate you.'

'I'm sorry,' she said. 'I just don't do family.'

He stood up. 'Well I do. I'm glad I met you. But you don't have to worry. I won't be in touch again.'

'That's fine by me,' she told him. 'I'm glad that you've found some nice girl who loves you and who's letting you live your suburban dream.'

'Don't patronise me,' said Frank.

She nodded. 'That *was* patronising. I didn't mean it to be.'

'Dad was gutted when you left.'

'Derek always knew how I felt,' she told him. 'I warned him and warned him, but he wanted the warm and fuzzy stuff too. I'm not like that. I wanted what I have now.' She sighed. 'I can't keep apologising to you for the sort of person I am. Your father kind of bowled me over and made me think that perhaps I didn't want what I have as much as

I thought. But I sure didn't want what I had with him. It's my fault for not sticking to my principles.'

'I don't think we'll meet again,' said Frank. 'But it was . . . worthwhile.'

'I'm glad,' she told him. 'I want you to be happy.'

'I guess that's all everyone wants in the end,' he said as they walked out of the coffee shop and back on to the street. He'd been going to tell her about the love of his life. About her granddaughter, Jenna. That was why he'd come. To tell her about his wonderful daughter. But she wouldn't have understood. And he didn't see the point any more.

Iona knew that it was the four-week deadline too. Since she'd been visiting the hospital regularly she'd talked to the doctors and nurses, and she'd bought books about coma and recovery as well as psychology, since she too wondered whether Frank was just too damn scared to wake up. Like Sally she'd set a four-week time scale for his return to consciousness. She couldn't let herself believe that he wouldn't wake up at all. Each evening she'd called to the hospital and seen him lying there motionless she'd wanted to shake him and shout at him and tell him to move his butt – just as she did every weekend when he was home with her. But of course she couldn't do any of these things. She just sat and read her way through more James Bond novels instead.

She closed her eyes and thought about him. Maybe calling in to the hospital and sitting beside him wasn't the answer. Maybe what she needed to do was to try and communicate with him on an unconscious level; the same level that he was on now.

But he was too far away to communicate with. She needed to be closer. She needed to be there. She got up from the sofa and grabbed her bag. It wasn't her turn tonight. But that didn't matter. She let herself out of the house and got into her car, gunning it down the road and on to the busy main street, She was thinking about him all the time, thinking of how important it was that he knew that she still loved him.

Frank, she told him. Listen to me. Think about me too. Think about the good stuff. Think about how much we meant to each other.

She parked the car on the upper storey of the car park and clattered down the stairs and towards the main hospital building.

'You've got to get better,' she whispered under her breath. 'You've got to wake up, Frank. It's time. It really is.'

Frank didn't know why he was somewhere hot. Sun holidays really weren't his thing. He liked travelling around Ireland or Scotland, where the grass was green and the sky could be either the clearest of blues or an unrelenting gun-metal grey. He liked the soft colours of peat and heather and gorse, not the garish pinks and purples of bougainvillea. He'd always choose chestnut trees over palms. And he preferred frothy white-topped waves to the gentle turquoise millpond of . . . wherever he was. He couldn't exactly remember where he was. Nor could he remember why he was wearing a suit. It was far too hot to be wearing a suit – he should be in a pair of shorts and a loose-fitting T-shirt.

Frank looked around him. He was standing in a pergola, looking back towards the beach. He realised now that the pergola was on a tiny outcrop, a miniature island off a bigger landmass. He wondered how he'd got here. There were other people with him too. Two men he'd never seen in his life before. One was around the same age as him and his face was scorched red from the sun. The other man was mahogany brown. He too was wearing a suit.

Suddenly Frank heard the rhythmic cough of an outboard motor and saw a small boat chugging out from the nearby jetty. In the back of the boat was the tiny figure of a girl in white. Frank's eyes narrowed. He knew her, of course. And in fact now he remembered that he was marrying her. Here in . . . well, he still couldn't exactly remember where he was, but he did remember that they were getting married.

He struggled to put that thought into context. There was something wrong about this. He remembered getting married before. To . . . to . . . It had gone from him. It had been at the edge of his mind and he'd seen an image of her face, but it had suddenly slid from his memory. Right now it seemed to him that there were lots of things that had suddenly slipped away from him, names and faces and a whole heap of other stuff that was there somewhere but just out of reach. His head hurt with the effort of thinking about it.

The boat drew up at the island outcrop and the girl jumped lithely on to the soft sand. She held the skirt of her white mid-length dress clear of the water, revealing white flip-flops decorated with brightly coloured shells. She looked up to where he was waiting for her and waved. He waved back. She was beaming with happiness and excitement and he suddenly felt excited too. The other faces, the other people that were lurking in his mind didn't matter right now. The important thing was that this was the girl he was going to marry and he knew that she was beautiful and that he loved her and that they were going to be a family together.

She stood beside him and smiled. The pastor began to speak. Frank was finding it difficult to understand his singsong accent. He wished the man would speak more distinctly because then he'd be able to catch the name of the girl he was marrying. It was, he knew, particularly awful to forget the name of your bride-to-be, but right now it was stuck in the corner of his mind and he simply couldn't remember it. But he knew that he was doing the right thing in marrying her. She was understanding, he knew that. She wanted to be with him, he knew that too. She cared about him.

A warm envelope of contentment sealed itself around him. But something else nagged at him and worried at the edges of his thoughts. He didn't know exactly what it was, since it seemed there was nothing in the world that should worry him now that he was in this wonderful place with this wonderful girl.

He'd never seen eyes like hers before. So dark you could lose yourself in them as they drew you to her. And her mouth was wide, with round, kissable lips. The sun had lent a golden sheen to her skin and the white flower tucked behind her ear emphasised the raven blackness of her hair.

They were going to have a great life together, thought Frank contentedly. If only he could just remember exactly who she was.

Iona was almost running along the corridor. She skittered to a stop outside Frank's room and pushed open the door. Both Sally and Jenna turned to look at her.

'You!' cried Jenna. 'What the hell are you doing here?'

'Iona?' Sally stood up and looked at her in puzzlement. 'Why are you here? It's our night tonight.'

'I know.' Now that she was in the room, Iona was feeling guilty. She looked at Frank and then at Sally and Jenna. 'I know. I'm sorry. But I had a feeling. I just had to come.'

'What sort of feeling?' demanded Jenna. 'Why did you come here?'

'I thought – I thought he was trying to communicate with me.'

'Oh, please.' Jenna looked at her in disgust. 'I never heard such crap in all my life. He's not trying to communicate with anyone. We've been here nearly an hour and all that's happened is that he's closed his eyes.'

'Were they open?'

'Yes. But they've been open before.'

'What were you talking to him about?' asked Iona.

'Mind your own damn business.' Jenna flushed.

'Jenna Harper!' Sally looked at her daughter in annoyance. 'There's no need to be rude.'

'Would you listen to yourself!' cried Jenna. 'This is the woman who tried to break up our family and you're telling me not to be rude to her? C'mon, Mum. Get a life.'

At her words they all looked at Frank, who continued to lie unresponsively in the bed.

'Look, I'm sorry. I never come when I'm not supposed to,' said Iona. 'But it's four weeks and I just thought . . .'

'I know,' said Sally flatly. 'So did I.'

'Just thought what?' asked Jenna.

'He needs to wake up now,' said Sally. 'You know that.'

'Yeah, but it's not like clockwork, is it?' said Jenna scathingly. 'I mean, he doesn't know it's four weeks, does he?'

'Of course not,' said Iona. 'Not consciously. But maybe his body knows.'

'You're such a sap,' said Jenna.

'Please,' said Sally again.

'Why am I the one who's being got at here?' demanded Jenna. 'I'm entitled to be here. She isn't.'

'Look, Jen, we've discussed all this before,' said Sally. 'And I'm really not going through it all again. I'm tired and I'm . . .' She broke off.

'You're what?' asked Jenna. 'You're delusional if you ask me. We come here all the time, talking to him and playing music to him and reading to him, and it *isn't making any difference*. And I'll tell you why. Because he doesn't care!'

'He cares.' Sally's face was contorted with pain. 'He cares for all of us.'

'In some sad-fuck menagerie!' said Jenna.

'Jenna!' Sally gritted her teeth. The atmosphere was upsetting her. And making her feel ill.

'It's always me, isn't it!'

'No.'

'Yes. Jenna this, Jenna that. As though I'm a kid. Well I'm not, you know. I'm a lot more mature and responsible than you think. And at least I'm not shacked up with a bigamist!'

'Oh God.' Sally swayed. Iona reacted first. She grasped the other woman's elbow and eased her on to a chair. 'Are you all right?' she asked anxiously. 'You're very pale.'

'I'm OK.'

'Mum, what's the matter?' Jenna felt terrible. She'd been so annoyed with her mother, and with Iona, but now she could see that Sally was really upset.

The door to the room opened and Susan Carpenter walked in.

'What the hell is going on here?' she demanded. She saw Sally's pale face and her voice softened. 'Are you OK, Sally?'

'I just feel a bit sick.'

'You need to relax for a minute,' said Susan. 'Come outside and stretch on the settee.'

'I'll be fine,' said Sally.

'Just for a couple of minutes,' said Susan. 'Clearly whatever's been going on in here hasn't been exactly peaceful, and that certainly isn't good for Frank. As well as which, really and truly, Sally, you need to take care of the baby, if not yourself.'

'Baby?' said Iona and Jenna in unison.

Susan looked at them in puzzlement, and then at Sally.

'I didn't . . .'

'Oh, shit,' said Susan.

'What baby?' asked Iona tautly.

'My baby.' Sally started to cry. 'Mine and Frank's. I'm sorry, Jen. I should've told you before now. I'm pregnant.'

It was as though time stood still. Iona heard Sally's words but they seemed to float in the air towards her, so that although she knew what the other woman was saying, she hadn't really grasped it. Jenna stared at her mother in silent disbelief. Susan Carpenter kept her arm around Sally's shoulders. And Sally didn't move.

In the bed, unseen by anyone, Frank's eyes opened and closed again.

'I don't believe you!' It was Jenna who spoke first, and her tone was horrified.

'It's true,' said Sally. 'I'm pregnant.'

'Since when?'

'I found out the day of the accident,' said Sally.

Iona couldn't speak. She felt numb inside.

'So you and Dad . . . you were . . . A baby!' The horror still hadn't left Jenna's voice. 'After all these years! Mum, that's disgusting. *You're* disgusting.' She looked over at her father in the bed. 'He's disgusting. God, Mum, he was sleeping with you and making you pregnant and pretending to be married to her – I can't believe what sort of family I'm part of. I always thought we were nice and normal and we're not, we're fucking freaks!' She pushed past Iona and rushed out into the corridor. 'Total freaks!' she yelled through the glass window before striding away.

Sally struggled to her feet, but Susan restrained her.

'I've got to—'

'You've got to stay sitting down for a minute,' Susan said firmly. 'Jenna will be fine. She's just upset.'

'I'm going to get a drink of water.' Iona didn't know how she'd managed to speak because her brain didn't seem to be functioning properly. She wasn't even sure whether the words she'd formed in her mind were the words that actually came out of her mouth. She stumbled out of the room and then pushed open the door of the ladies' toilets. She leaned her head against the wall and tried to control the rising waves of nausea building up inside her. But eventually she couldn't help herself and she threw up into the nearest toilet.

'Are you all right?' It was Susan Carpenter again, standing behind her holding a wad of tissues.

'I'm . . . fine.'

'Come on,' said Susan. 'I'll get you some water.'

'I need to sit down.'

'I know. Come with me and you can go somewhere private.'

Iona felt tears blister her eyes. She couldn't cope with someone being nice to her. She followed Susan to a small room where the nurse sat her down on a padded chair and handed her a waxed cup filled with water.

'Sip it,' she said.

Iona swallowed the water cautiously. She felt its coldness as it flowed down her gut.

'I can't believe it,' she whispered. 'She's pregnant.' She looked up at Susan Carpenter and her eyes filled with tears again. 'We were trying for a baby,' she said shakily. 'To make our family complete. I didn't know about this baby. I didn't know about Jenna. I didn't know about Sally. And I'm not pregnant.'

'Don't upset yourself about it now,' said Susan gently.

'It's kind of hard not to be upset.' Iona wanted to appear strong in front of the nurse, but she had a horrible feeling that she was going to dissolve into little pieces. How can it be? she asked herself in anguish. The accident was bad enough. Finding out about Sally and Jenna was worse. But this . . . As far as Iona was concerned, this was the ultimate betrayal. She'd gone to so much trouble to eat properly and set up the home for a baby and do all the right things, and she wasn't pregnant. But Sally was. And to judge by the huge age gap that would exist between Jenna and the new baby, not to mention the way Sally had kept the whole thing secret, well, it seemed to Iona that this hadn't been planned. And how fair was that? Sally, who probably didn't want another baby, was pregnant. Iona, who desperately wanted her first child, wasn't. And who knew what was going to happen to Frank?

Chapter 23

Ten minutes later Iona felt able to walk out of the tiny room where Susan had left her. Her legs were still shaky and she knew that her hands were trembling, but at least she didn't feel as though she was going to faint any more. Some of her despair had been replaced once again by rage at Frank and at the dual life he was leading. Some of it was still there, lining her heart, a mere moment away from bubbling up to the surface again.

She hadn't expected that Sally would still be there, but she was, sitting on one of the chairs outside Frank's room, her face pale and her hair damp around her face. The new short look had grown out a little and needed to be redone to keep the style. Right now, Sally looked wretched again. Iona suddenly thought that she had picked a really terrible time to get pregnant.

Sally glanced up at her, her eyes dull.

'I'm sorry,' said Iona.

'For what?'

'Coming. I shouldn't have. It wasn't my night. And a day wasn't going to make much difference one way or the other.'

'No,' agreed Sally.

'It was just that . . . I was thinking about him, you see. And the month being up. And I couldn't help feeling . . .'

'I know,' said Sally. 'I was so sure about tonight too.'

They sat beside each other in silence for a moment.

'But instead of Frank coming out of the coma, I discover that you and he are having a baby.'

'You would have found out sooner or later.'

Iona clenched and unclenched her fists. 'It's one more shock I didn't need,' she said.

'We didn't plan it.'

'I guess not.'

'We'd wanted more children but unfortunately it didn't work out that way,' said Sally. 'Frank always wanted a bigger family. Family mattered to him so much. This was . . . a bolt out of the blue.'

'How d'you think he'll feel about it?' asked Iona.

'I suppose that depends,' said Sally wryly, 'on whether he wakes up while I'm still pregnant or not.'

Iona couldn't stop the tears spilling down her cheek.

'What's the matter?' asked Sally.

'It's not important.'

'What?' repeated Sally. She stared at Iona for a moment and then gasped. 'Don't tell me you're pregnant too.'

'No,' said Iona. 'I'm not.' She pinched the bridge of her nose. 'But I wanted to be.'

'Oh.' Sally looked at her blankly.

'We'd talked about it,' said Iona rapidly as she wiped the tears away. 'We were . . . Frank wanted children. More than me at first, but then I wanted them too. I – I set up a feng shui corner of the room to help me get pregnant. It didn't work for me. But – well – it looks like it worked for Frank.'

'Oh my God.' Sally gasped. 'You can't believe that had anything to do with it.'

Iona sniffed. 'Not seriously. Not . . . you know. But still. You're pregnant, and I'm not. And Frank was making love to both of us.'

'I can't deal with this,' said Sally. 'I'm sorry. I could hardly deal with the idea of being pregnant anyway.' She pushed her hands through her hair despairingly. 'I won't accept it's because of some crazy hippy-dippy lifestyle thing Frank was doing with you.'

'Feng shui isn't hippy-dippy,' said Iona. 'It's about harmony.'

'Yeah, well, that worked, didn't it?' Sally laughed wryly. 'Things have been very harmonious around us all lately, haven't they?'

Iona's smile was ironic. 'You have a point.'

'How was he going to deal with it?' demanded Sally. 'Two families? Surely it was hard enough for him without having another child with you?'

'He'd have dealt with it the same way he deals with everything,' said Iona. 'Don't worry. Be happy. You know Frank.'

'Yes. I know Frank.'

They shared a look of understanding.

'But do we really know him at all?' asked Iona. 'Was he really happy? With two of us? It surely must have been stressful.'

Sally nodded.

'So why'd he do it?'

'Maybe it was because of the family thing.' Sally sighed. 'Maybe he wanted more than I was giving him.'

'But you *are* a family!' cried Iona. 'You, Frank and Jenna. What more did he want?'

'Honestly . . . kids,' said Sally. 'We had Jen fairly quickly but I didn't have a very good experience at the birth – it ended up being an emergency Caesarean and scared me rigid. I told Frank I didn't want to get pregnant again for a while and he understood that. The only problem was that once I felt able to think about it again I just didn't get pregnant.'

'Did you try anything? IVF?'

'Well . . .' Sally looked uncomfortable. 'The thing was that, yes, I did want a baby. But I wasn't prepared to go through the whole IVF procedure. Which made me think that maybe I just didn't want one enough.'

'Hey, I can understand how you felt! I wonder about it myself, sometimes, all that messing around with your hormones and everything.'

'It has a reasonable success rate,' said Sally, 'but it was just something I wasn't prepared to do. Frank was OK about it all, though. He always said that whatever we did we did as a couple and as a family. I thought he totally understood.'

'Sally, he wasn't with me simply to have another baby, although we'd decided to try for one,' said Iona.

'Just as well you're not pregnant, I guess,' said Sally. 'Bad enough that one of us is.'

'And what does your doctor say about it this time?' asked Iona.

'Oh, that I'm an old mother and that there are certain things I have to be specially careful about because of that. And because of the problems with Jenna. And that I should be eating well and living a healthy lifestyle and have no stress.'

Iona looked sympathetically at her. 'Like that's actually happening.'

'I know.' Sally sighed. 'I should be looking after this baby more, and I'm not because I'm caught up about Jenna and Frank and you—'

'There's no need to be caught up about me,' said Iona. 'I don't matter.'

'Of course you do,' said Sally. 'He damn well married you!'

They sat in silence. Iona couldn't believe she was actually talking to Sally and feeling sorry for her when she'd just delivered such shattering news; yet in a way it was comforting to talk to someone else who knew Frank and cared about him.

'What do you think is really going to happen to him?' she asked eventually.

Sally shrugged wearily.

'Stupid question.' Iona shook her head. 'This whole thing is making me feel more and more stupid by the day.'

Sally nodded, then got up and said that she was going to phone Jenna so that they could go home. Iona stayed where she was, watching the other woman walk down the corridor to make the call. She continued to observe her as she walked back again. How hadn't she realised before now that Sally was pregnant? It was obvious in the way she carried herself. I'm a fool, thought Iona. A complete and utter fool.

'She's not picking up,' said Sally. 'She hates me, of course.'

'Why?'

'She thinks it's my fault that Frank and you . . . well, you know.'

Iona shrugged.

'Do you?' asked Sally. 'Do you think it's because of me?'

'I honestly don't know,' said Iona after a pause in which she struggled not to lash out and say that of course it was Sally's fault, that there was obviously some issue going on about the whole baby thing and that somehow Frank hadn't found what he was looking for in his wife because otherwise why the hell had he started a second relationship? Because the thing was, of course, that Frank might have started a second relationship, but he sure as hell hadn't finished with his first.

'It's got to be him,' she continued. 'Much as I love . . . loved . . . well, it's got to be his fault. After all, he's the bigamist. Not you or me.'

Sally smiled faintly. 'It sounds so – so dramatic. Not like it really is.'

'I know.' Iona nodded. 'How is it that when you're living in a weird situation you don't think it's weird at all; but if you read about someone else's weird situation you think they should all be carted off to the nearest funny farm?'

'I keep thinking that if we were a plot line in *Coronation Street* it'd be written out as being too implausible,' said Sally.

'Well, obviously,' Iona told her. 'They all live within a few hundred yards of each other on that soap. Frank was very careful to keep us a good distance apart.'

The two of them sat in silence again as they contemplated Frank's adept handling of his two wives. Eventually Sally looked at her watch and then checked her phone again.

'I'll go and look for her,' she told Iona. 'She's probably in a snit somewhere having decided to give me the cold shoulder.'

'D'you mind if I stay here a bit longer?' asked Iona.

Sally shook her head. She got up and walked out of the unit. Iona went back in to Frank's room. Jenna's portable CD was on its second run-through of *Allow Us To Be Frank*. She switched it off. She remembered Sally saying that Frank had sung 'Mack the Knife' at parties, but of course she'd never gone to a party with Frank.

How could she not have known? Why hadn't she guessed that there was, at the very least, someone else? Was she impossibly naïve? Or was Frank just a very, very good con-man?

She switched off the CD and took her book out of her bag. She'd moved on to *Moonraker* since finishing *Goldfinger*. Frank had said that he liked all of the Ian Fleming books but she didn't know his main preferences after *Goldfinger*. She'd expected the book to be different from the film (after all, they were written in the 1950s and 60s, so no chance of space-age technology then), but she was surprised to see that there was actually no relationship between novel and movie at all. Other than the title and the name of the main character.

'Hugo Drax,' she said out loud. 'He cheats at cards. And Frank Harper cheats at wives.'

Her gaze flickered to Frank and she stifled a gasp. His eyes were open again.

'Can you hear me?' she demanded. 'Can you understand what I'm saying?' She grasped his hand. 'Squeeze if you can hear me.'

She couldn't feel any response from him. But she was certain that he could hear something. That he knew she was there.

'Oh, come on!' she cried. 'You're with us somewhere, Frank. I know you are.'

She squeezed his hand, but it remained limp within her hold.

'Fuck you!' she yelled, picking up the paperback and hurling it across the room so that it clattered into an empty plastic container and knocked it to the floor. 'Make a fucking effort.'

'Iona?' It was Susan Carpenter again. 'I think maybe you should go home for the evening.'

Iona dropped Frank's hand on to the bedspread and turned towards the nurse.

'I'm sorry,' she said. 'I just thought there was something . . . I'm sorry.'

'No need to be,' said Susan. She picked up the book and handed it back to Iona.

'Do you think he's afraid?' asked Iona.

'Afraid?'

'Of what will happen to him? Everyone is saying that now. Saying that's why he's still in the coma.'

'I don't know,' said Susan. 'The mind is a very fragile thing.'

'So maybe that's it, and maybe he will wake up but he'll be . . . he won't be himself?' Iona's voice was agonised.

'Don't torture yourself about it,' said Susan. 'His physical injuries have definitely improved. There are certainly issues about his relationships. But you can deal with those.'

Iona put *Moonraker* back into her bag. 'Has Sally gone?' she asked.

'I presume so,' Susan told her. 'I haven't seen her in a while.'

Iona nodded. 'Well, OK. See you.'

'See you,' said Susan. 'And don't worry, if there's any change, we'll call you straight away.'

'Thanks,' said Iona as she walked out of the door.

Susan watched her leave and then moved towards her patient. She straightened the bed covers and checked the monitors. No change as far as she could see. She knew how hard it was to believe that those open eyes weren't seeing anything. But, she thought as she closed the door behind her, if she was in his situation, she'd be having a long think about waking up and embroiling herself with two spouses again.

Iona walked towards the car park, past the cluster of people smoking outside the hospital entrance and past the group of taxis waiting to pick up fares. She frowned as she saw the auburn hair of Sally Harper in the queue for taxis. She'd presumed Sally drove herself to the hospital every day. And then she realised that Sally wasn't trying to hail a taxi, she was talking to the cab drivers and looking at the passengers.

'Hey, Sally, everything OK?' she asked.

Sally turned hunted eyes towards her. 'Not really.'

'What's up?'

'I don't know where Jenna is.' There was a note of desperation in her voice. 'I've called her and texted her but she's not responding.'

'Maybe she's just gone home,' suggested Iona.

'Maybe. But it's not easy from here. She'd have to get to the nearest Dart station, and that's quite a distance away. I don't know what the buses are like on this side of town. I thought maybe she'd taken a taxi to the Dart.'

'You're asking them if they picked her up?'

Sally nodded. 'I know it's daft to be worried about her. She's seventeen. She's not a baby. But . . . she's upset about everything and . . .'

Iona nodded too. 'Maybe she got a taxi all the way to Bray?'

'I doubt it,' said Sally. 'She probably wouldn't have enough for the fare.'

'If she got a taxi to the Dart as soon as she left the hospital, would she be home by now?' asked Iona.

'Perhaps. If she was lucky with the timing,' said Sally.

'Why don't you try your landline?' suggested Iona.

'I did, although I don't really think she could be home yet. If she is, she's not answering,' said Sally ruefully. 'To be honest with you, our relationship wasn't great before all this started. Initially Frank's accident drew us together. Finding out about you drove us apart. But we'd started to get a bit of a thing going in coming to the hospital and it was improving. The news about the baby . . . well, that sure hasn't helped.'

Iona nodded. 'I think you're wasting your time hanging round a taxi rank in the hope that you'll either see her or find the bloke who drove her somewhere,' she said. 'You should get home yourself and wait for her.'

'I know.' Sally looked at her ruefully. 'Thing is . . . thing is . . . right now, I don't think I can drive.'

Iona stared at her.

'I'm a crap driver at the best of times,' Sally told her. 'This isn't the best of times.' She sighed. 'I'm still shaking. I feel dizzy. My head is buzzing. Bad enough for Jen to have one parent in hospital, without me smacking the car into a lamp-post or something and ending up here too.'

'I'll drive you,' said Iona abruptly.

'That's stupid,' said Sally. 'My car is here. I'll still have to come back and fetch it later.'

'Let later worry abut itself,' said Iona. 'Come on, I'll drive you home.'

Sally stood indecisively beside her. 'I can get a taxi. You don't need to drive me. It's miles out of your way.'

'I'll drive and you can keep a look out for Jenna,' said Iona. 'I'll go towards the Dart station in case she tried walking that way.'

'OK,' said Sally eventually.

She followed Iona to the car park and waited while the other girl paid for her ticket. They went up to the third floor and Iona pointed to the bright green Beetle.

'Actually, it's not the easiest car in the world to drive,' she told Sally as she got behind the wheel. 'But it's cute and I like it.' She started the engine. 'Frank always said I'd be better off with a sporty little number, but that's just not me somehow.'

She eased her way out of the car park and into the flow of traffic. She stayed silent as Sally anxiously scanned the streets for any sign of her daughter and continued to drive in silence as they went through the city and out towards Bray. She switched on the radio, which was tuned to Lyric FM. The sounds of Pachelbel's Canon in D Major filled the car. By the time they reached Bray, the station had moved on to Holst's Planet Suite and the music had become fierier.

'Turn here,' said Sally as they approached the housing estate where she lived.

Iona indicated and eventually drew up in front of the neat semi-detached house.

'Come in,' said Sally.

Iona shook her head. 'If Jenna is there I really don't think me coming in would help matters.'

'She's not,' said Sally. 'The house is in darkness.'

'Maybe she's sitting in the dark.' Iona looked at her wryly. 'I do that a lot these days.'

'If she's here you can leave right away,' said Sally. 'Please. I don't want to go in on my own.'

Iona nodded and got out of the car. She felt sorry for Sally, but she couldn't help thinking that the other woman was a bit feeble. Why had Frank, such an outgoing man, married such a wishy-washy woman? she wondered. Was that why he'd hooked up with her instead? Was he fed up with Sally's helpless ways? She noticed, as Siobhán Farrell had done, the neatness of the garden and the carefully maintained front of the house. Obviously Sally, in the depths of her despair about Frank and in the throes of her pregnancy, had still found time to cut the grass and clean the windows. Iona grimaced at the thought of her own once pristine house in the Liberties, where feng shui had been replaced by items left in any old place and which hadn't seen a duster or a vacuum cleaner in over a month.

It felt strange to be inside Sally's house, knowing that it was Frank's house too. Her eyes swivelled tentatively around as she took in the more classical decor, the heavier furniture and the richer colours. How could he like this and like her house too? she wondered. Was he truly a split personality? How could the Frank who'd bought the Joan Miró print with her be the same Frank who'd hung that ornate gilt mirror on the wall? The two styles were completely different.

The kitchen was different too; this was warm and homely against her own clinical granite and steel – though, of course, if her kitchen had been the size of Sally's, maybe she would have done it in a warmer style herself. She could see how a kitchen could be the heart of a home when it wasn't a small utilitarian space tacked on as a virtual afterthought and whose main item of equipment was a microwave.

'Tea or coffee?' asked Sally as she filled the bright yellow kettle.

'Tea,' said Iona. 'Preferably camomile if you happen to have it by any chance. Or green. But any tea is fine really.' She shrugged apologetically. 'Sorry. I shouldn't be so picky.'

Sally nodded and took a packet of camomile tea off the shelf. Neither of them spoke as they waited for the kettle to boil. When it did, Sally poured water into the two blue mugs which she'd taken from the cupboard.

She offered one to Iona and then sat at the table beside her.

'She has to be home by ten every evening,' said Sally. 'She hates it but she knows she has to stick by it otherwise she can't stay out later other times.'

'Fair enough,' said Iona.

'She hates me,' said Sally. 'She hated me before all this and she hates me twice as much now.'

'Of course she doesn't,' said Iona.

'She does.' Sally looked idly into her mug. 'She thinks I'm an old bat. I embarrass her.'

'Why?'

Sally explained about being a teacher at Jenna's school, which she knew Jenna didn't really like. She told Iona that when they did good parent, bad parent, she was always the bad parent. She made the rules, she said. Frank got to break them.

'It's always the way, isn't it?' said Iona. 'Mothers come off worst no matter what. But I bet she doesn't really hate you. She's seventeen. It's all a growing-up kind of thing.'

'I know, I know,' said Sally. 'It's just that it's exhausting being seen as the imbecile all the time.'

Iona laughed, and to her own surprise, Sally smiled too.

'I guess it's not that bad,' she admitted. 'I know it's only a phase. But she's such a lovely girl really, and for the past six months it's all been about wearing nothing but black, and that terrible pale make-up which does nothing for her, and sighing every time I open my mouth. And the fact that I've seen loads of girls at school turn into perfectly adequate adults even when they've been sheer horrors makes no difference when it's your own daughter.'

'I suppose not,' agreed Iona. Her eyes flickered around the room. 'You have a lovely house.'

Sally looked at her warily. 'It's OK. We've been here a long time.'

'I'll level with you,' said Iona. 'Part of the reason I offered to drive you was so that I could get to see where you live.'

'Oh.'

'But then when I got here I didn't want to come in. I didn't want to see Frank's other life.'

'You wouldn't get to see much of it in the kitchen anyway,' said Sally. 'He's not really into cooking.'

Iona nibbled her lip.

'Or does he when he's with you?' asked Sally.

'Sometimes,' said Iona. 'We don't have such a great kitchen, of course, and my efforts are usually with the microwave. I cook healthy stuff, I'm just not very good at it.'

'So what does Frank cook?'

Iona shrugged. 'Pasta mainly. He makes good sauces.'

'Of course,' said Sally. 'You thought his favourite food was spaghetti carbonara.'

'It is,' said Iona. 'When he's with me, anyhow.'

'How the hell can he be two such different people?' demanded Sally in a spurt of anger. 'Roast pork with me. Spaghetti carbonara with you. I'm betting your house is completely different to mine too. It's beyond freaky.'

'You're right about my house,' said Iona. 'All of it would fit into your kitchen.'

'Oh.'

They sat in silence again. Eventually Sally looked at the clock. It was just after ten.

'She'll be back soon,' said Iona.

Sally took out her phone and called Jenna's number. Iona could hear the recording of the younger girl's voice telling callers to leave a message.

'She's doing it deliberately,' said Sally.

'Maybe not.'

'She's punishing me,' said Sally. 'For the baby. For being disgusting. You heard her.'

'She didn't mean it.'

'I think she did.' Sally sighed and rubbed her stomach gently. 'Poor baby. Everybody hates it.'

'No.' Iona looked at her in shock.

'Not hates,' amended Sally. 'Just – it's the wrong time. It really is. To tell you the truth, when I realised I was late, I just thought that maybe I was pre-menopausal.'

The clock ticked around to ten thirty.

'She *is* doing it deliberately,' said Sally. 'Look, you go home. I'm OK now.'

'Are you sure you don't want me to wait till she comes in?' Iona had detected a slight note of anxiety in Sally's voice.

'Why? So you can see me box her around the ears and report me for child abuse?'

Iona smiled slightly and Sally shrugged. 'Perhaps you could stay a little longer. If you don't mind?'

'I don't mind.'

'But I don't want to talk any more,' said Sally. 'I can't. Is that all right?'

'Perfectly fine,' said Iona. 'I'll read the paper.'

'OK.'

They both sat at the kitchen table. Iona read her way through the *Irish Times*, while Sally leafed through a teaching magazine. Every so often one or the other of them would glance up at the clock, but neither of them said anything.

At eleven o'clock, Sally phoned Jenna again. Calls were still being diverted to Jenna's mailbox.

At a quarter past eleven Sally dialled another number.

'We're away at the moment.' Iona could hear a woman's voice. 'Leave a message and we'll get back to you.'

Sally disconnected and tried a third number.

'This is Sam,' Iona heard. 'I'm in Barcelona for the weekend with my folks. Text me.'

'Her best friend,' said Sally. 'I was hoping Jenna would be with her. But they're all away.' Worry lines creased her face. 'I'm not sure where else she might be.'

'Does she have a boyfriend?' asked Iona.

Sally nodded. 'Gerry. But I don't know him. He's fairly recent.' She frowned. 'I have the phone numbers of quite a few of her friends, but not his.'

'Perhaps you should call them,' suggested Iona. 'See if any of them has his number.'

Sally nodded again and began dialling.

Chapter 24

By midnight Sally was really concerned about Jenna and Iona was having to try very hard to keep her calm.

'You know that she's doing it to worry you,' she told Sally. 'And she's succeeded. That's what you can tell her.'

'Right.' Sally dialled Jenna's number again and left a message saying that she was demented with anxiety and that she understood how Jenna felt about everything but could she please come home so that they could sort everything out. 'But what if something's happened?' she said to Iona. 'What if she isn't doing this to worry me at all but has grabbed a lift from some stranger and he's taken her somewhere . . .'

'Oh Sally, you're totally overreacting.'

'I know, I know,' wailed Sally. 'But it's past midnight and she simply doesn't stay out this late. She really doesn't.'

Iona recognised the anxiety in Sally. She'd felt it herself the night that Frank hadn't come home. But she was certain that nothing had happened to Jenna, that the teenager had simply decided to stay out as an act of defiance.

'She's had a hard evening,' she told Sally. 'Cut her a little slack.'

'I would if I knew where she was or if she'd answer her phone. I can't take this, Iona. What if something terrible has happened to her? What if—'

'Come on, Sally,' said Iona. 'In your heart you know that she's perfectly fine and she's just staying out late.'

'In my head I know what she's up to. In my heart . . .' Sally's voice trailed off and she looked at the wall clock again.

'Maybe you should call the police,' said Iona eventually. 'I'm sure there's absolutely nothing wrong and she's probably with one of her friends – or most likely the boyfriend. The fact that none of them have his number is irrelevant. Maybe they just won't give it to you. You know what teenage girls are like. But it'd put your mind at rest if you called the cops.'

'They won't react to this straight away,' said Sally. 'They'll want her to be missing for longer.'

'They reacted pretty damn quick to Frank's disappearance,' said Iona.

'Only because there was something weird going on.'

'Sally, are you always this negative?' demanded Iona. 'Because if you are, I can see how you drive her nuts. No matter what I suggest, you have a reason not to do it. I'm trying to be helpful but you don't want to be helped.'

'All right, all right.' Sally picked up the phone. 'I didn't want a big deal made out of it, that's all. I know what they'll say – that she's upset about her dad. And they'll ask if there was a row, which there was, and they won't take me seriously.'

'Why don't you call the detective woman?' suggested Iona. 'She'll take you seriously.'

Sally looked at her contemplatively. 'That's a good idea.'

'That's me,' said Iona. 'Full of good ideas.'

Siobhán had almost finished her shift. She'd just returned to her desk having brought two young men, arrested on suspicion of drug-dealing, down to the cells. She hated going down to the cells, which were the one part of the station which made her feel grubby about her work. Like every prison cell she'd ever seen on TV or in the movies, they were empty, soulless places. But what the TV and movies couldn't bring to the viewer was the smell of the people locked inside them – fear and bodily scents – overlaid with the of the strong disinfectant that was used every day.

She yawned as she picked up the phone. She was tired. It had been a long day. She was looking forward to going home.

'Hello,' she said.

'Is that Siobhán Farrell?'

Siobhán recognised the voice, although she couldn't place it straight away.

'This is Sally Harper.'

Siobhán listened as Sally related the events of the evening and sighed when she heard that Jenna had run off. She hated missing children reports, even if the children were really young adults and even if they'd apparently gone missing of their own accord.

'Tell me about the boyfriend,' she said. 'He sounds the most likely candidate for your daughter to be with.'

Sally felt like a worse than useless mother as she gave what little information she could about Gerry. She wasn't even sure of his surname, although she knew that Jenna had told her.

'Does Jenna have a diary or anything?' asked Siobhán. 'It's very possible that his name would be in it.'

'Oh God.' Sally sighed. 'I never thought of that. I'm hopeless. Totally hopeless.'

'No you're not, Sally,' said Siobhán gently. 'Why don't you go and have a rummage around in Jenna's room, and in the mean time I'll make sure that the guys are alerted to look out for her.'

'Right.'

'Phone me back,' said Siobhán.

'Will do,' said Sally.

'I've got to check her room,' said Sally.

Iona frowned. 'I never thought of that.'

'I should have,' said Sally.

They both went to Jenna's room. Walking inside gave Iona the feeling of suddenly moving backwards in time to her own teens. Her room had been a bomb-site like Jenna's, with posters of INXS plastered all over the walls. Jenna's tastes were surprisingly rap-orientated for someone who was going through a semi-goth phase, though Iona had no idea who the blinged-up star of the enormous poster at the foot of her bed was.

'Don't ask me,' said Sally. 'I can't keep up with them all. I ask her things like why they can't spell their names properly and she goes crazy.'

Iona laughed. 'What did you say you taught?'

'Maths and English.'

'I wish I'd been good at maths,' she said regretfully. 'I never listened. If I didn't understand it straight away I could never be bothered to try to work it out.'

'You're like most of my pupils.' Sally picked up a Filofax from beneath a mound of books and papers on the desk in the corner of the room and began to look through it. 'Nobody can be bothered to put in the time.' She grimaced as she looked at empty pages where she'd have expected to see names and addresses. 'The trouble, of course, is that nobody writes anything on paper any more. Certainly not Jenna's age group. Phone numbers are just stored on the phones.'

'Oh, that's the same for everyone,' said Iona. 'I'm as bad. I don't even know Frank's number off by heart.'

Sally reeled off a number and Iona frowned. 'That doesn't sound – oh yeah, I forgot. Different phones.'

'He was a shit about things, wasn't he?' Sally was looking more intently at the Filofax. The to-do pages were filled with notes in Jenna's spiky handwriting: meet gang; revise French; read poems; go to library; remember I am smart. She swallowed hard at the last note. Of course her daughter was smart. Of course she was.

'I'm kinda getting used to that idea,' said Iona.

'Here it is!' Sally's grip tightened on the Filofax. 'Gerry,' she looked up, 'and then a little heart, so it must be him. And it's a mobile number.'

She dialled it immediately. This time the message – to leave a message – was in a young man's voice.

'If that's Gerry who's a friend of my daughter, Jenna, can you tell her she'd better get home right now,' said Sally sharply. 'Or else she'll be in even more trouble. I'm worried about her and I'm calling the police.'

She hung up and looked at Iona. 'What d'you think?'

'It'd sure as hell scare me,' said Iona. 'Now why don't you ring Siobhán and give her the number? Maybe she can track it down for you.'

The fact that Gerry Cullinan's phone was on his parents' monthly bill made it easy to find out his address. Siobhán offered to go and see if Jenna was there and to bring her home if she was. Sally was uncertain whether it was a good idea but in the end she agreed. For starters, she didn't have her car and she didn't want Iona to have to drive her to the other side of town. Iona said that it was a small town and that she really didn't mind, but that maybe being picked up by Siobhán would jolt Jenna out of her petulance, whereas being picked up by Iona and Sally would only annoy her even more.

'I can't believe that all this stuff is happening to me,' said Sally as they waited for word from Siobhán. 'This is not my life. My life is uncomplicated. I'm just an ordinary person. I'm supposed to be married with a kid and the only trauma is that she's a teenager and therefore can't stand me. My life should be boring! I shouldn't have a hot-line to a detective at the police station!'

'My life is ordinary too,' said Iona. 'I have a reasonably good job and a city-centre house and I shouldn't have hot-lines to police stations either. I feel like I've stepped into someone else's life by mistake.' She sighed. 'Maybe I should go before Siobhán gets back here with Jenna.'

'She said she'll call if Jenna's there,' said Sally. 'Please just wait until we find out if she is.'

'Sure, if that's what you want.'

Sally smiled faintly at her. 'And in my life I didn't think I'd ever be asking my husband's wife to wait until the police called to say that my daughter was safe.'

'In my life I didn't know that my husband had a wife.'

The phone rang and both of them jumped.

'She's here,' Siobhán told Sally. 'I'm bringing her home now.'

'Oh, thank you.' Sally felt relief flood over her and tears spill down her cheeks. 'Thank you, thank you, thank you.'

'I gather she's found her,' said Iona as Sally replaced the receiver.

Sally nodded. Iona handed her a tissue. Sally blew her nose.

'I'll head off,' said Iona. 'But give me a call, let me know how things go.'

Sally nodded again.

'Take care,' said Iona as she let herself out of the house.

'Thank you again,' Sally called after her as Iona walked down the path.

Jenna face was sullen as she got out of the car. Sally was relieved to see that Siobhán hadn't turned up in a marked car with its blue lights and reflective stripes, giving the neighbours still more to gossip over. She knew that there was already plenty of talk about Frank and the fact that all wasn't entirely well with the marriage, though nobody knew the full story yet. Still, there was enough for them to gossip about.

'It's not that late,' said Jenna as she stomped through the front door. 'And I really don't see why you had to freak out and involve the police in all this. I'm sick of the sight of that woman.'

Siobhán said nothing as Jenna pushed past her and ran up the stairs, slamming her bedroom door behind her.

'Thanks,' said Sally.

'They were watching a DVD,' said Siobhán. 'His parents were out but were due back pretty soon.'

'I'm not naïve,' said Sally. 'I know I must seem like the world's stupidest person to you, but actually I'm not. I'm the vice-principal of a girls' school and I know what they're like.'

Siobhán smiled sympathetically at her. 'She's obviously going through a hard time.'

'Oh, look, I know!' cried Sally. 'We all are. And I suppose I've been so caught up with Frank that I haven't had time to really worry about Jen. Even though I do worry about her. But then she's been a worry for the last few months, so . . .' She let her breath out with a sigh. 'I've no idea where my priorities should be right now.'

'Well, I guess Frank is safely tucked up in a hospital bed,' said Siobhán.

Sally laughed shortly. 'I guess so.' She ran her fingers through her hair. 'I need to get to grips with things again. I used to be organised and in control. I'm not any more.'

'What made you cut your hair?' asked Siobhán suddenly.

'My hair?' Sally was surprised at the question. 'I – I'm not sure.'

'It suits you like that.'

'Needs to be cut again,' said Sally. 'I'd forgotten that I kept it long because it grows like wildfire.'

Siobhán yawned involuntarily.

'You should get home,' said Sally. 'Get some sleep. I'm sorry if I caused you hassle.'

'All part of the job,' said Siobhán. She made a wry face. 'And at least this has turned out OK.'

'Yes.' Sally nodded. 'Thanks.'

'Good night,' said Siobhán, and walked back to her car.

Siobhán was exhausted. What she would really have liked to do was go home and soak in a luxurious bath, only lying in a bath would give her more time to think and she didn't want to think right now.

Eddie didn't have AIDS. Not that she'd ever really believed that he'd turn out to be HIV positive, but the last few weeks had been traumatic. His doctor had contacted them to say that there had been some contamination of the blood in Eddie's test and that it would have to be done again. And Siobhán hadn't felt able to walk out on him while he was so tense about everything. She wanted to – but she couldn't. Then yesterday Eddie had received the all-clear and she'd seen the darkness lift from his eyes and the weight suddenly disappear from his shoulders, and he'd put his arms around her and thanked her for standing by him. He'd told her that he truly loved her and that he was inexpressibly sorry for what had happened and that she needn't have another second's doubt in her life about him because there was no way he was ever going to put what they had at risk again. And then, for the second time in their lives, he'd asked her to marry him.

She hadn't known what to say. She'd looked at him wordlessly and then he'd brought his lips down very gently on hers and he'd kissed her. And although she'd desperately wanted not to kiss him back, she wasn't able to prevent herself responding to something she'd been missing for so long. But when he'd tried to undo the buttons on her cream blouse she'd found it impossible to block the image of him and the Peter Murtagh orgy out of her mind. She told herself that orgy probably wasn't the right word for what had gone on, but it captured the essence of it all the same and she couldn't bring herself to make love to a man who hadn't given her a thought while he'd had sex with a woman whose name he'd never even know.

Eddie had accused her of trying to punish him, and she'd said that punishment was far from her mind but that she wasn't ready to make love to him. That she needed time to think about it.

Now she wondered whether she'd ever want to make love to Eddie again. Or to anyone else, for that matter. Somehow she felt entirely unsexual these days and she didn't really care. The thing was, she mused, as she drove along the Dublin road, she understood how it had happened. But understanding it didn't make it any less hurtful or make her feel any better.

She slowed down at the warning triangle placed ahead of the stopped car. She could see that the driver was a woman. She pulled in to the side of the road.

'Need a hand?' she asked.

Iona looked up in surprise at the voice.

'You looked familiar even in the dark,' said Siobhán. 'You're having an eventful night, aren't you?'

'Far too eventful.' Iona used her foot to unsuccessfully try to loosen the nut on the wheel. 'And it's pretty ironic that I've got a bloody puncture, since you guys seem to think that it was a puncture that caused Frank to call into that pub last month and start this whole mess in the first place.'

Siobhán had given both Iona and Sally the information that the emergency spare wheel on the Honda had replaced one of the rear wheels, and that it seemed, based on how little wear there was on the tyre, that Frank had called into the pub almost directly after changing it. Probably to wash his hands, Siobhán had said, because there'd been a couple of oil-stained tissues in the car. So it was just his bad luck to be in the wrong place at the wrong time. When Sally had got the car back, she'd looked at the replacement wheel and then kicked it in impotent rage.

'Can I help?' asked Siobhán again.

Iona nodded. 'I can't seem to turn the damn screw. It's years since I've had to change a tyre and I'm not sure I was much good at it then.'

Siobhán picked up the wrench and pushed hard on it. The screw loosened.

'Impressive,' said Iona.

Siobhán laughed. 'That's us garda girls. Muscles to burn.' She did the same to the other screws and then helped Iona to jack up the car and change the tyre.

'How're Sally and Jenna?' asked Iona as she rolled the spare wheel round from the boot.

'I don't know,' said Siobhán. 'Jenna didn't say much in the car and I basically left them to it.'

'Crap situation for Sally,' said Iona. 'I'm sure that Jenna is a lovely girl, but she's obviously totally ticked off with her mother about the way things are right now. I think she sort of blames Sally for me and Frank, and now she's disgusted about the baby . . .' Iona's voice faltered.

'Baby? What baby?' asked Siobhán.

Iona told her about Sally's pregnancy.

'What a mess.' Siobhán manoeuvred the new tyre into place. 'So that's why Jenna ran off.'

Iona nodded. 'Jenna called her mother disgusting.' She smiled faintly. 'I suppose it's hard for a teenager to think of their parents having sex without feeling disgusted.'

'I suppose,' Siobhán agreed. 'And how do you feel about it?'

Iona sighed heavily. 'I'm gutted,' she admitted. 'We were hoping to have a baby ourselves.' She handed Siobhán one of the silver screws.

'Oh.'

'Why are men so much trouble?' Iona rubbed her nose, streaking it with dirt from the tyre.

'God, I wish I knew.' Siobhán's words were so heartfelt that Iona looked at her in surprise.

'Are you married?' She frowned. 'Did you say you were?'

Siobhán shook her head. 'I'm . . . I was going to . . . I'm living with someone.'

'You don't sound so sure.'

'I guess right now I'm not.'

'Does he hate the fact that you're a cop?' asked Iona curiously. 'I can imagine some guys might.'

'It's not really to do with me,' Siobhán told her. 'Not entirely. It's more to do with him.' She leaned against the car. 'I'm pretty much trying to decide whether to leave him or not. And I don't know what to do.'

'Yeuch.' Iona looked at her sympathetically. 'I guess I thought of you as a kind of invincible person because you're a garda and because you seem to be so in charge of things. I didn't think you'd be in a man trouble kind of place.'

'Yeah, well, I'm completely in a man trouble kind of place and I can't help feeling that being in charge of my own life might be a good thing.'

'Fancy a coffee?' Iona pointed at the twenty-four-hour newsagent which offered coffee to go. 'I need something to wake me up a bit and, well, why don't you sit in the car with me for a while and tell me about it?'

'I don't need to talk about it,' said Siobhán.

'Y'see, that's what I felt about Frank. But when I started talking to you, it helped,' said Iona. 'OK, you don't have to talk about it, but let me grab you a coffee anyway, as thanks for helping with the tyre.'

'Fair enough.' Siobhán thought she could do with a shot of caffeine. 'If they do double espresso, that's the one for me.'

'You scared the living daylights out of me.' Sally looked furiously at Jenna. 'And I don't care whether you were upset or not, you should've answered the phone. At least then I'd have known you were all right.'

'Get off my case, would you?' Jenna rolled over on her bed and ignored her mother.

'Please, Jen. Can't we just talk about this. Like grown-ups?'

'Oh yeah, it's treating me like a grown-up sending the police after me! Have you any idea how humiliating that was? I'll be lucky if Gerry ever speaks to me again. And someone will be bound to tell his parents.'

'How will they even know?' asked Sally. 'It wasn't as though a posse of cops drew up outside with their sirens blazing. It was just Siobhán in an ordinary car.'

'Just Siobhán was bad enough,' said Jenna mutinously. 'And she must think that our whole family is psycho. We're probably under observation right now!'

'Don't be infantile,' said Sally. 'We have rules in this household and you broke them and you worried me and that's what happened as a result.'

'Oh yeah? And Dad breaks them and what happens? We spend our fucking lives in hospital reading to him and playing music to him and he doesn't even know.'

'Jenna!'

'It's true.' She buried her face in the pillow. 'You're being nice to him and you're trying to make me be nice to him, but it's only because he's in a coma. If he wasn't you'd have thrown him out as soon as you found out about Iona.'

'And is that what you want?' asked Sally.

Jenna said nothing.

'I can't and I won't abandon your father. Even Iona doesn't want to abandon him. What happens when he gets better may well be a different story.'

'And if he doesn't?' Jenna turned a tear-streaked face to her mother. 'You're going to have a baby! At your age. With no dad. So what'll happen is that I'll be looking after it 'cos you'll have to be at work and it'll mess up everything and I might have wanted a brother or sister when I was small but not now. And I just *hate* the way everything has happened.'

Sally leaned down and gathered her daughter into her arms.

'No matter what's happened, the important thing is that I love you,' she told her as she stroked her dark hair. 'I love you more than anything. And however we resolve things, you have to remember that you're a very important member of this family. With or without your dad. With or without a new baby.'

'Yeah, right.' Jenna let her head rest on her mother's arm. None of Sally's so-called comfort was really making her feel any better inside. She didn't want to be here. She wanted to be with Gerry, who really understood her.

Chapter 25

Siobhán stood on the balcony of the apartment and looked across the harbour at Dun Laoghaire. The sun skimmed over the gently rolling waves, reflecting golden light from the water and causing her to shade her eyes from the glare. She turned back into the apartment and walked across the polished floor of the living room again and through to the galley kitchen with its spotless tiles and granite worktop. She noticed that the microwave was expensive stainless steel, boasting an integrated grill and convection oven. Everything I could possibly want, she thought wryly, to heat up the ready meals for one from the supermarket up the road.

She looked at the woman who was sitting in one of the comfortable armchairs waiting for her decision.

'It's a short rental?' she asked again.

Iona nodded. 'Three months, four max. The owner is in Chile. Personally I wouldn't bother renting out a place for such a short time, but I suppose he feels it's worth it to have some extra cash in the bank.'

'What if I want it for longer than that?' asked Siobhán.

'Well, I know that he's meant to be back by the end of the summer,' said Iona. 'But we've plenty of apartments on the books so I could get you something else if that's what you decide.' She looked sympathetically at Siobhán. 'Hopefully things will work out and it won't matter.'

Siobhán swallowed the lump in her throat. 'Hopefully,' she said. She shivered in the cool breeze that wafted through the open patio window. 'But I don't know what working out really means.'

That was what she said to Eddie the following evening when she told him of her decision to move out for a while. She needed some time on her own to think things over.

'I don't know what else I can do to make you see how sorry I am,' he said as he looked at her miserably. 'I've gone through hell over all this. I've apologised a million times. I'm clean and I'm healthy. And Siobhán, I love you, which is the most important thing. You can't tell me that it's all over between us.'

'I never said it was over,' Siobhán told him shakily. 'I said that I needed some time and some space to myself and that's what I'm getting.'

'But you expect me to wait for you?' demanded Eddie.

'That's rather up to you,' she said. 'I can't be with you right now. I'm still furious with you. Making me feel that there was something wrong with me because you wouldn't sleep with me. Eddie, it's been a horrible time.'

'It's been a horrible time for me too,' he said.

'You brought it on yourself,' she told him sharply. 'It's not my fault.'

'You just want to punish me,' he said. 'Make me feel bad about it.'

'Moving out isn't about punishing you,' said Siobhán. 'It's about me. I need to think about what I want from our relationship, Eddie, and I can't do that here right now.'

'And how long will this think-fest take?' asked Eddie curtly.

'I don't know,' said Siobhán. 'But if I move out for a couple of months it'll give us both time to think things over.'

'A couple of months!' he exclaimed. 'Do you really expect me to sit around and wait for that long?'

'Are you trying to give me some kind of ultimatum?' she demanded. 'You were the one who broke the trust, Eddie. Not me. Now you seem to be saying that if I take a bit of time out to get over it all, you might not be there for me afterwards. If that's how you want it . . .' Her voice wavered and she turned away so that he couldn't see the tears forming in her eyes.

He got up from the chair and put his arm around her shoulders. 'I don't want to break up with you,' he said. 'I just don't want you to go.'

'I didn't want you to sleep with that . . . woman,' mumbled Siobhán. 'But you did it anyway.'

'Is it always going to be thrown in my face?' he asked.

'That's why I need to be on my own for a while.' She blinked hard and looked up at him. 'So that I don't keep throwing it in your face. So that I can come to terms with it at my own pace.'

He released his hold on her. 'Why don't you believe me when I say it was a one-off mistake?'

'I *do* believe you,' she said sincerely, 'but that's not the point. The point is that I need some time to remember why I loved you and to trust you again.'

'I still don't see why you have to move out,' he said.

'We're just going round and round in circles,' Siobhán told him. 'I thought we had something good going between us. I still love you, Eddie. But I can't just forgive and forget. If I'm on my own for a while it might help.'

'All right,' said Eddie resignedly. 'If that's what it takes.'

She tugged at a stray wisp of her hair. She didn't really want to go at all. But she knew that she had to, even if it was only for a short time. The whole thing had sapped her confidence in herself and she needed to get it back. But she wouldn't if she didn't leave.

'I'll go and pack,' she said.

He looked at her in complete astonishment. 'Now? You're going now?'

She nodded. 'It's better to get it over and done with right away.'

'You mean you've already sorted out a place to go?'

She nodded again.

'Sometimes you can be very hard-hearted,' he said. 'It's no wonder you're good at your job.'

Siobhán knew that she wouldn't have gone through with it so quickly if it hadn't been for Iona. Sitting in the car at the side of the road a couple of nights previously, her hands wrapped around the takeaway cup of coffee that Iona had brought back from the newsagent, she'd given the other woman a diluted version of events, simply saying that Eddie had slept with another woman and that she was having a hard time trusting him. And that she couldn't help thinking that she needed to be away from him for a while. Iona had listened intently and then told her that she knew of a lovely apartment overlooking the harbour in Dun Laoghaire which was available for a short let at a very competitive rate. If Siobhán was interested in it, Iona could set things up so that she could move in straight away.

Siobhán hadn't known what to say. Moving out had been a vague thought, an idea which she'd felt might be a good one but which she hadn't entirely taken seriously. Suddenly having the option to carry it out had flustered her and she'd told Iona that she'd have to think about it, that she wasn't sure exactly what she wanted to do. And Iona had nodded and handed her a business card, telling her to contact her if she wanted to take it any further. Siobhán had suddenly seen Iona as a professional person rather than (as she'd previously always viewed her) the victim of a crime, no matter how unusual that crime was. The following day, hardly believing what she was doing, she'd called Iona's number and made an appointment to see the flat in Dun Laoghaire and had made the decision to take it.

Now, as she wheeled her suitcase out of the apartment, she still couldn't quite believe that her life had taken this unexpected turn.

'Hi, Mizz P. Off for a jaunt at the taxpayer's expense?' Carl O'Connor was walking up the corridor.

'No,' she said shortly.

'Holiday?' he asked.

She said nothing.

'You OK?' He looked at her quizzically.

'Fine,' she said. She stepped into the lift.

'Sure?' He sounded concerned. 'Everything going all right?'

She wished he'd stop being nice to her. The one constant in her changing world was that Carl O'Connor wasn't really supposed to be nice to her. She was glad when the doors slid closed and hid him from view.

She'd arranged to meet Iona at the apartment as she hadn't yet got the keys. The other woman was there ahead of her, sitting in her green VW and listening to a CD, the window open. The music wafted on the air to Siobhán as she walked across the car park.

'Wouldn't have pegged you for a Sinatra fan,' she said as she arrived at the car.

Iona, who hadn't seen her, switched off the CD player in a hurry. 'Not really my kind of stuff,' she said. 'I was just . . . It doesn't matter.' She got out of the car. 'Here are the keys. You have to sign for them. Do you want me to go in with you and check that everything's OK?'

'If you like,' said Siobhán.

'Come on, so.' Iona led the way.

The apartment seemed smaller than before. Siobhán looked around at it again, not quite able to take in the fact that she was actually going to live here away from Eddie. She twisted her engagement ring around on her finger. She'd wondered whether she should take it off and, while she'd been packing, had slid it from her finger. But she'd felt naked without it and had put it on again, telling herself that she was still engaged to Eddie and that she wasn't ready to break it off with him. The weird thing was that she'd wanted to stay then. She'd been telling herself that she was lucky all this had happened before they got married when she could simply leave and it wouldn't matter. But it was hard to walk out when they'd created a shared past. It wasn't easy to be strong.

'Hey, it'll work out,' said Iona as she spotted the anxious look on Siobhán's face. 'You're right, Siobhán. You need to be by yourself for a while.'

'You think?'

'Absolutely,' she said. 'Anyway, I brought this along to help.' She opened the huge duffel bag which was slung over her shoulder and took out a bottle of champagne.

'Champagne is supposed to be a celebratory drink,' she pointed out.

'Yes. We're celebrating the start of you getting your life back on track,' said Iona. 'Hopefully the end result will be exactly what you want and what you deserve – whatever that is.'

Siobhán smiled slightly and took the bottle. What the hell, she thought. I could do with a drink. She began to twist off the foil.

'Don't open it now!' cried Iona.

'If I don't open it now, when will I open it?' demanded Siobhán. 'No point in me sitting here tonight on my own drinking a bottle of champagne. That's pathetic.'

'I guess so,' admitted Iona.

'So, come on, have some.'

Iona looked at her watch. It was nearly five o'clock and she didn't have any more appointments. And although she had some paperwork to do in the office, she reckoned it could wait.

'There are glasses in the cupboard,' she said. 'I'll get some.'

'Excellent,' said Siobhán as she popped the cork. 'Let's celebrate.'

* * *

Sally didn't feel like celebrating anything. She was sitting in front of the TV, her fingers beneath the elasticated waist of her navy loungers, which had suddenly become too tight. They'd always been comfortable before. Now they weren't. Since the morning sickness had abated a little over the last couple of weeks, she had been able to push the thoughts of her pregnancy to the back of her mind. But now she couldn't. She was getting bigger.

She got up and went to her bedroom. There was another pair of loungers in the wardrobe, an ancient green pair that she knew would be more forgiving. She took off the navy ones and put them on the shelf and pulled on the green ones instead. Instantly she felt better. She wandered down into the kitchen and opened the freezer. There was a tub of Ben & Jerry's Cherry Garcia on the middle shelf. Frank was the Ben & Jerry's fan in the house. She didn't eat much ice cream herself, although that was because she was generally on some kind of diet and almost all of them forbade ice cream of any description.

She took the tub out of the freezer and wiped the smear of frost from the lid. She closed the freezer door, took off the lid, then peeled away the plastic. The ice cream was rock hard. Even stabbing it with a spoon wasn't making much difference. If Frank had been here, of course, it would never have lasted this long and become extra-frozen. She put the tub into the microwave and gave it a few seconds on the defrost setting.

When Jenna arrived home from her art class a few minutes later, Sally was scraping the last of the ice cream from the tub. Her daughter looked at her in amazement.

'You ate Dad's ice cream?'

'It's our ice cream,' said Sally.

'You don't even like cherries,' said Jenna.

'I do now.' Sally rubbed the back of her hand across her mouth.

'I don't believe this.'

'What?'

Jenna dumped her bag on the table. 'You've eaten a whole tub of ice cream that you buy for Dad and that you don't like.'

'I'm pregnant,' said Sally. 'I get cravings.'

Jenna stared at her. 'You can't have got a craving for ice cream.'

'I can,' said Sally. 'I did.'

'I don't know what to say to you.' Jenna sat down opposite her.

'You haven't said very much for the last few days,' said Sally. 'No need for you to start talking to me now.'

'I don't want you to be pregnant,' said Jenna.

'I know.'

'You're too old to be pregnant.'

'Well, apparently not,' said Sally mildly.

'You'll be a laughing stock.'

'I don't see why.' Sally pushed the empty tub away from her. 'I'm sure there are other mothers having babies in their forties. It's just that the gap between you and this one will be big. That's what the problem is.'

'That and the fact that its father may not come home ever again.'

'That too,' agreed Sally.

'Why?' asked Jenna. 'Why now?'

'I didn't choose to get pregnant,' said Sally. 'It wasn't as though we were trying.'

'You should have told me,' Jenna said. 'I hated finding out in the hospital like that. It was awful.'

'I know,' said Sally. 'But I was having difficulty coming to terms with it myself.'

'I don't care,' said Jenna. 'You still should have told me.' She got up from the table. 'Have you made anything for dinner?'

Sally shook her head. 'But there's cold meat and cheese in the fridge. And plenty of fresh fruit. Or you could do pasta for yourself if you like. I did the shopping over the internet.'

Jenna stared at her. 'Why didn't you just go to the supermarket?'

'I didn't feel like it,' said Sally.

'I hate this!' cried Jenna. 'Everything's different and I hate it!' She picked up her bag again. 'I'm going to my room.'

'Sardines,' said Sally suddenly.

'What?'

'That's what I got a craving for when I was pregnant with you.'

Jenna looked at her sceptically. 'People don't get cravings for sardines.'

'Why wouldn't they?' asked Sally. 'Anyway, I ate them every day for about six months.'

'You never told me about that before,' said Jenna.

Sally shrugged. 'You never asked.'

'I'm going to my room,' repeated Jenna. 'I've homework to do.'

She stomped out of the kitchen, her bag banging against the table and knocking the empty ice cream tub to the floor.

'Maybe I should get a test done,' said Sally.

Sally! Of course. That was his wife's name. He remembered again now. The other incident, the wedding under the sun, that must have been a dream. Vivid, though. Very real. He dragged his mind back to what she was saying. A test. About . . . Yes! About the babies. They still only had one child. Their lovely daughter.

'The doctors said everything was fine.' He wanted to be reassuring.

'Doctors! What do they know really?' Sally pulled at her long auburn hair. 'They don't know why I had such trouble with Jenna and they don't know why I had the miscarriage and they sure as hell won't have any idea why I haven't got pregnant since. All they'll say – like they said before – is that I'm a normal healthy woman and so I should get pregnant again.'

'Do you want to get pregnant again?' asked Frank.

She stared at him. 'How can you possibly ask that?'

'It was hard for you, with Jenna. All that last-minute emergency stuff. Maybe it's traumatised you. Maybe there's something stopping you.'

'For heaven's sake, Frank – I got pregnant again, didn't I? OK, it didn't work out, but nothing stopped me.'

He said nothing.

'Are you thinking that it's the miscarriage on top of the Caesarean that's the problem?'

'I don't know!' he cried. 'I just wondered.'

'D'you think I'm on birth control unknown to myself?' she demanded. 'That I'm secretly stuffing myself with the pill?'

'Of course not,' he told her. 'But I do know you're agitated about it and that probably doesn't help.'

'We can't all be as laid-back as you,' she retorted.

He caught her by the arm. 'I'm sorry,' he said. 'I didn't mean to imply that . . . that your state of mind had anything to do with it. I really didn't. I was trying to be helpful.'

She looked at him. His dark blue eyes held hers and suddenly she could feel the familiar spark of chemistry between them.

'Tonight we'll just do it for pleasure,' Frank told her. 'You, me and a tub of Ben and Jerry's. No baby talk. Just us, the way it should be.' He slid his hand beneath her filmy top.

'Frank!' she giggled.

'Think about me licking it off you.'

'It'll be cold,' she protested.

'I'll make you so hot that it'll bubble,' he promised.

She kissed him.

He kissed her.

He loved the taste of her, with or without the ice cream.

Chapter 26

The days grew warmer and the nights grew shorter. There was no change in Frank's condition. Sally and Iona continued to take turns visiting the hospital and didn't meet each other there again. Sally went back to work. Iona took on more work herself.

Iona didn't know whether it was because of work or because of Frank that she was having so much trouble sleeping. It seemed to her that she was always thinking of either one or the other, her concerns about tenants and rental agreements alternating with concerns about Frank. Her life had become one long set of worries – about things she could control, which wasn't too bad; about things she couldn't, which was harder. And as she tossed and turned for the fifth night in a row, she wished that she could be transported somewhere where she didn't have to worry about anything ever again.

She pushed the duvet away from her and sat up. The green glow from the alarm clock beside the bed (not that she needed an alarm to get her up these days) showed that it was four in the morning. She got out of bed and peeked through the slatted blinds.

Faint wisps of light were already sneaking over the horizon. It would be another glorious day. Another day where she sat at her desk in Rental Remedies by day and sat at Frank's beside by night. It wasn't fair, she thought angrily, that she had to put her whole life on hold for him. It really wasn't. They'd planned to travel together during the summer this year. Short breaks. Of course, she thought bitterly now, they had to be short breaks. When they'd discussed it she'd thought the idea of lots of city breaks would be great fun. Frank had suggested that if she was pregnant she mightn't want to go away for longer periods. And she'd agreed with him. Fool that she was, she muttered now. He'd manipulated her into thinking that they were a good idea because they were the only holidays he was able to take without Sally getting suspicious. How stupid could she have been!

She walked out of the bedroom and into the office. She hadn't worked from home very much lately, not liking to be there on her own. Which was silly, she thought, given that she'd lived there quite happily by herself before Frank had come into her life. She'd changed everything for him. But it didn't really look as though he'd changed anything for her.

She switched on the computer and waited as it whirred into life. The only thing she'd done on it lately was – like Jenna – look up information on comas. She sat down in front of it and opened her web browser. This time she typed in the word holiday. It was a stupid thing to type in, of course. There were far too many hits for it to be of the slightest use. So she looked up cheap flights instead. And then she followed the link that led her to a Dublin–New York flight leaving that morning for a ridiculously low fare. It got into New York at lunchtime, US time. That would be fun, she thought. A quick hop to NYC for a bit of shopping. She'd never been to New York before. She'd always wanted to go but had never quite got around to it.

Still, she could hardly just up and go, could she? Not when she was supposed to be visiting him every second day, reading to him, talking to him, trying to bring him out of the damn coma.

She leaned her chin in her hands. It would be nice, though. Nice to be away from everything and everybody. Nice not to feel as though she was being held to Frank and Sally and Jenna by some kind of spider's web. Nice to have fun. It seemed like forever since she'd had fun. It was impossible. She couldn't do it.

It was a very cheap flight, though. And she could get a return one almost as cheaply. It wouldn't do any harm to see, if it was actually available. A couple of days in New York. It was a kind of laid-back thing to do. The sort of thing that a young, free and single girl might do. But she wasn't young, free and single. Was she?

Lauren went to the airport that morning to pick up Flora. She hadn't told Iona that their mother was coming for a visit because she knew that her sister would freak out over it. Iona was adamant that she didn't need her mother fussing over her, but Flora was equally adamant that the time had come for her to see Iona for herself and try to talk to her about her future.

Flora knew that it was difficult. She knew that Iona loved Frank. She'd liked him herself when he'd come to visit them in Javea, even though she'd found him difficult to get to know. But he had undoubtedly been charming, and as far as Flora could see, he was utterly besotted with Iona. He'd treated her well, with an almost old-fashioned courtesy, and Flora had been happy for her because Iona wasn't the sort of girl who lost her heart easily.

And now . . . Flora grimaced. Now it was all an unbelievable mess.

She waved as she spotted Lauren's tall frame standing at the meeting point, waiting for her. Lauren smiled in return and hugged her mother. They made their way to the car park.

'I'm going to invite her to dinner tonight,' said Lauren in response to Flora's question about Iona. 'I won't tell her you're here, though. You know how stubborn she can be. If she thinks it's all a plot to check up on her and see how she is, she's just as likely not to come.'

Flora nodded. 'D'you think she's sticking by him out of stubbornness?'

'I'm not sure about that.' Lauren inserted her ticket into the machine and drove out of the car park. 'If she'd found out about Sally and Jenna before now she probably would have put him into a coma herself! But because he's so sick she can't let herself be angry with him.'

Flora sighed.

'And now she's in this situation where she and Sally alternate nights at the hospital,' said Lauren. 'You know how much Io hates hospitals! But she goes in because . . . oh, I don't know! Because she wants him to choose her when he wakes up maybe.'

'It's not right,' said Flora.

'I know,' responded Lauren, 'but I really don't know what we can do about it.'

Iona slept on the plane. She'd never slept on a plane before because she found it far too uncomfortable, but as she settled into her seat and they began to taxi towards the runway, she was lulled by the engines into a trance-like state which ended up with her nodding off and not waking up even when the steward made an announcement about the in-flight service.

She did wake up when they brought around the food. She ate the meal, watched the movie and then fell asleep again so that by the time they arrived at JFK she was, unlike many of her fellow passengers, completely refreshed and even the security checks didn't bother her.

She caught a cab outside the airport and asked the driver to bring her to a decent hotel in Manhattan. He dropped her at Le Parker Meridien on West 57th and she got out, wishing she'd asked for some lower-denomination bills at the airport bureau de change. But what the hell, she thought, as she wheeled her small case behind her through the huge lobby. It's only money. I saved a bundle on the flight and I paid off my Visa bill last month so I've plenty of credit. She still didn't quite believe that she'd gone ahead and booked it so impulsively. But she was glad that she had. The alternative would have been to spend the day in Rental Remedies listening to tenants complaining about broken washing machines or stuck doors or other equally irritating problems.

It suddenly occurred to her that she'd forgotten to call Ruth and say that she wasn't coming in that day. She'd meant to phone from Dublin airport but it had been frantically busy with long queues and in all of the fuss it had gone completely out of her head. Oh well, she thought, Garret had told her to take time off if she needed it. She wasn't going to bother ringing them now.

Her room was high enough up for her to have a view of Central Park. She smiled to herself as she looked over it and laughed at the idea that a few hours ago she'd been feeling bleak and dull in Dublin and now she was in the city that never sleeps. And she wasn't tired!

She peeled off her travelling clothes and then hopped under the shower. Despite her lack of tiredness she knew that a shower would perk her up even more. Afterwards she dressed in a light top and cotton skirt, slid her feet into her most comfortable sandals and walked out on to the street and towards 5th Avenue.

It was like everything she'd ever imagined. The noise, the heat, the crowds, the whole bustling, teeming momentum of it all. Yellow cabs clogged the streets and every so often an impatient driver would lower his window and shout at another driver just like in the movies. Iona giggled as she walked past enormous condos with awnings covering the pavement (sidewalk, she told herself, sidewalk) to the kerb, where liveried doormen opened the doors for women with more money than style as they went out for a day doing whatever it was that rich New York women do.

It was a world away from Rental Remedies and the intensive care unit in Dublin. In fact, right now, she could almost believe that none of it had ever happened, that she'd never met Frank Harper and married him, that she really was young, free and single in the best city in the world.

She went into Saks and emerged some time later with one bag and a bruised credit card. Then she went into Bloomingdale's and came out with half a dozen bags and a credit card that was almost up to its limit. It was true, she told herself as she swung the bags in her hands, shopping helped. It might be shallow and it might be vacuous and the prices you paid for stuff might be totally outrageous (thought not as outrageous here as in Dublin, she added), but it made you feel good and forget things and that was exactly what she wanted to do today.

They were doing makeovers in Macy's. She sat down and allowed the Benefit consultant to colour her cheeks, lips and eyes and turn her from dull into dazzling in twenty minutes. When she looked in the mirror she recognised herself as the Iona of old and she puckered up her tinted lips to blow herself a kiss. The consultant smiled at her – and smiled even more widely when Iona bought every product she'd used – and then told her to have a nice day.

'I sure will,' Iona replied as she walked out on to the street again.

She was getting tired now, though. She needed to sit down and have something to eat. But she wasn't going to waste her gorgeous makeover and her fabulous new clothes on some fast-food outlet. She caught a cab back to the hotel, changed once again but this time into the stunning Donna Ricco rose-print strapless dress and Joey O sandals that she'd picked up in Macy's (it hadn't just been make-up, and she'd had to move on to her second credit card) and walked back out into the New York streets.

She bought a copy of *Vanity Fair* at a kiosk and then strolled towards Central Park again before heading down Broadway. She stopped outside Gabriel's restaurant. She knew, from what she'd heard, that most restaurants in New York required bookings and that famous restaurants had waiting lists. It would probably be impossible to get a table for one in a restaurant which had, she'd discovered, hosted an Oscar-night dinner and where people like Tom Cruise and Cameron Diaz fetched up from time to time. But there was no harm in asking.

Benny Arvizo, the waiter, looked up as the door opened. He saw a petite girl with dark hair, dark eyes and knockout lips, wearing a figure-hugging dress and high heels.

'Can I help you?'

'Table for one?' She looked at him hopefully. 'I'm starving.'

Benny Arvizo couldn't resist her smile. He showed her to a table, brought her a bottle of mineral water as she requested and left her to look at the menu.

So, thought Iona, I'm here in New York, in a great restaurant, about to have a meal on my own. And it's a damn sight better than being in Dublin picking at a green-leaf salad and not even wanting that. So although it sounded gorgeous, she didn't order the salad at Gabriel's but chose grilled mushrooms instead, followed by a tuna steak. She also ordered a bottle of Dolcetto d'Alba, ignoring the flash of surprise in Benny's eyes at the possibility of her drinking an entire bottle of red herself. Americans, she felt, had a very puritan attitude towards alcohol. But she hadn't enjoyed alcohol in ages. The times that she'd drunk red wine at home had been miserable times. This was different.

The restaurant buzzed and bustled with life. Iona was a little disappointed that she hadn't spotted any celebrities, but she supposed that it was unlikely Hollywood's latest heart-throb would be in town just because she was. And it didn't really matter. The place was great just the way it was.

Lauren, Myles and Flora sat in the living room and looked at each other anxiously. Lauren had first phoned Iona's mobile while her plane was halfway across the Atlantic. She'd left a message about dinner and asked Iona to call her back. When her sister hadn't responded a few hours later she'd phoned again. And got her voice-mail again. That hadn't worried her particularly, because during the working day Iona could be out and about with clients and unable to return calls. But when six o'clock passed and she still hadn't received a call from her sister, Lauren became more concerned.

She didn't know exactly what she was concerned about. After all, Iona was a grown woman and didn't have to come hopping just because Lauren wanted it. Plus, Lauren hadn't said anything about Flora's visit, so Iona wouldn't have realised that the dinner invitation really mattered that much. All the same, Lauren would have expected her to call back even if she couldn't come; she knew that it might be Iona's evening at the hospital. But not responding at all, that was unusual.

Eventually Lauren phoned the hospital to see if Iona was there. Susan Carpenter, who was on duty, said that she wasn't but that Sally Harper was. Did Lauren want to talk to Sally?

Not especially, had been Lauren's first reaction, but then she decided to ask the other woman whether she'd spoken to Iona that day.

'No,' said Sally. 'We don't talk that much. Sometimes we leave each other notes when we've visited Frank. You know, to say that there was no change or that he looked a little better . . . Why?'

Lauren explained that they were anxious to get in touch with Iona.

'Maybe she's just gone out for the night,' said Sally. 'After all, she's an attractive girl. Perhaps she wanted to go socialising.' Inside Sally was kind of hoping that that was the case. It put some distance between her and Frank.

'You're probably right.' Lauren sighed. She hated making plans and having them messed up. But it was her own fault. She should've told Iona that Flora was here.

She hung up and phoned Iona again. This time she left the message that Flora had come to see her. And that they wanted her to call them.

In the end Iona didn't drink the entire bottle of red. After two glasses she was feeling pleasantly relaxed. She didn't want to tip her laid-back feeling into a degree of drunkenness which she knew might happen if she kept drinking. She was tired now and, despite the food, she knew that more alcohol would lessen her co-ordination and dull her senses.

She ordered coffee and the bill and sat back in her chair, the magazine open in front of her.

The restaurant was busier now, but not full. There were tables of women laughing and joking with each other, obviously on some kind of celebratory girls' night out. There were tables of men, businessmen, having serious conversations occasionally punctuated by false laughter. There were mixed tables, some business, some social. And there were couples who were out together, looking lovingly over the starched tablecloths at each other, happy to be together.

Would we have come here? she wondered. Would Frank and I have sat at a table together and kissed like that couple in the corner? Or would we have just gone to the burger joint down the road?

Benny came with her coffee and told her that the bill had been taken care of. She frowned and looked at him enquiringly.

'The gentleman over there.' He nodded towards a table where six men and three women were sitting. She'd put them down on her list as a business group. The man indicated by Benny saw her puzzled look and raised his wine glass in her direction. Iona frowned again.

'Why?' she asked Benny.

'I don't know, ma'am,' he said. 'But the gentleman asked me to take care of it.'

Iona continued to look over at the table. The man had been distracted by something one of his companions had said and wasn't looking in her direction any more. She knocked back the coffee and got up, her chair scraping the floor as she pushed it out of the way. Then she walked over to the table.

'Excuse me,' she said, looking directly at the guy who had paid for her dinner. 'Can I have a word?'

'Certainly.' He got up from the table and smiled at her.

He was in his mid-thirties, she reckoned, well groomed, wearing an expensive suit, although his shirt collar was open. Dark hair, grey eyes, smooth-shaven.

'What's with paying for my dinner?' she asked.

'I wanted to.'

'Why?'

'I got a great deal of pleasure out of looking at you this evening,' he told her. 'You're gorgeous.'

'Well, it was very kind of you, but I'm going to go and pay for my own dinner myself.' She turned away.

He caught her by the arm and she froze. He let go of her immediately.

'I'm sorry,' he said. 'I didn't mean to offend you.'

'How else do you expect me to be when someone says they've paid for my dinner because I look gorgeous?'

'Flattered?' he asked hopefully.

'No,' she said. 'Offended.'

'That's what's so hard with women,' the man complained. 'I'd be flattered.'

'Actually,' she told him, 'you wouldn't. You'd feel like a hooker.'

'I don't think you're a hooker!' He looked horrified. 'Hookers don't read *Vanity Fair* in Gabriel's.'

'You have experience with them, then?' she asked.

'No!'

'Maybe if I was a high-class hooker I *would* read *Vanity Fair* in

Gabriel's,' she told him. 'You're making all kinds of assumptions.'

'I'm sorry,' he said again. His eyes flickered back to the table, where his dinner companions were glancing covertly at him.

'What did you expect to get out of it?' she asked.

'To tell you the truth, I'm not sure,' he admitted. 'Maybe drinks together, an evening together . . . I don't know.'

'You're with people already,' she pointed out.

'Business colleagues,' he said. 'We concluded a good deal today. Minor celebration.'

She nodded.

'I didn't realise you were from out of town. I should have, though. You look different. Irish?'

She nodded again.

'Come on, then, Irish,' he said. 'Have a drink with me.'

It could be a dangerous situation, she thought. She still wasn't convinced about the concept of someone she didn't know paying for her dinner and asking her out for a drink. But maybe it would be fun. And fun was what she was here to have.

'All right,' she said abruptly. 'Take me somewhere nice.'

'Should we be worried?'

At midnight and with still no response from Iona, Lauren didn't know what to do.

'It's been a hard time for her lately,' said Myles. 'Maybe she just wants to be on her own. She might have got your message but not wanted to call you.'

'For heaven's sake!' Lauren was suddenly angry. 'She knows what it's like when someone doesn't call. She was hysterical over Frank when he didn't come home and she was right. What if something has happened to her?'

'She's OK,' said Flora gently. 'I'd know if she wasn't.'

'Mum, I don't want to knock your spiritual side, but you wouldn't,' said Lauren.

'Trust me,' said Flora.

'Till the morning,' Lauren said.

* * *

He brought her to a club on Columbus. The lighting was muted and the music eclectic. They sat in blue suede chairs either side of a black marble table and he bought her a Cosmopolitan. His name was Brandon and he worked in property development. He was interesting to talk to and fun to be with and Iona didn't once think about Frank while she laughed and joked with him about movies they'd both seen or fun things to do in New York or Dublin (he'd never been), and in the moments that they were silent she didn't feel awkward but simply relaxed. It might, she conceded, have had something to do with the second Cosmopolitan. (She was allowing herself two cocktails. She knew that they had nudged her into the silliness she hadn't wanted earlier, but she didn't care. After all, she didn't have to get up in the morning.) But she was too tired for a third. And so she asked Brandon to bring her back to the hotel, slipping her new sandals off her feet as they went outside because they were too high and too new to walk in any more.

He kissed her at the junction of West 57th and Columbus. She kissed him back. She could feel the warmth of his hands through her rose-print dress and the strength of his body as he held her close to him.

God, but it was good to be in someone's arms again. Good to be with someone who didn't know anything about her or Frank or Sally. Because she and Brandon hadn't talked about themselves. Not in any detail. She'd just said that she was over for a break and he'd told her about working for the property company and that had been it. She supposed, as he kissed her, that he was simply looking for someone for the night. Obviously nobody in his group of work colleagues did it for him. But she, Iona, in her summer dress and high heels, had. And he was doing it for her too. Strong and healthy and very alpha-male. She liked it. She liked him. She felt good again.

Flora lay awake in the guest room bed. She was thinking about Iona and hoping that she'd been right when she told Lauren that she was all right. She was sure that she'd know if she wasn't. But how could she be certain?

'I'm sorry.' Iona looked at him. 'I can't do this with you.'

Brandon nodded very slowly. 'I understand that. You want to check me out, healthwise. I should do the same with you. But I can tell you that I get tested every year and that my last test was two months ago and that I'm perfectly fine. Also, I insist on using protection.'

'It's nothing to do with that,' said Iona. 'I . . . well, I know it's a cliché, but I'm not in that kind of place right now.'

'I always think that some scriptwriter came up with that line and people have copied it ever since because they think it sounds deep,' said Brandon. 'But it's complete bullshit really.'

Iona smiled at him. 'OK. I can't sleep with you because I'm mentally fucked up and it would be a really bad idea.'

'I'm not sure about that,' said Brandon. 'It seems like a really good idea to me right now.'

'Are you going to make an issue of it?' she asked.

'God, of course not!' He looked horrified. 'I want to sleep with you. I know it'd be great.'

'Maybe,' said Iona. 'But I just can't do it.'

Maybe if he'd made an issue of it she wouldn't have kissed him good night. But he didn't and she did and she really, really didn't want to sleep alone.

The following morning, with still no response from Iona's mobile phone, Lauren rang Rental Remedies. Ruth told her that Iona hadn't been in the previous day, which was very unlike her, but that given the stress she'd been under, none of them were all that surprised. All the same, said Ruth, it was bloody inconvenient. They were very busy.

Lauren and Flora decided to go to Iona's house. With no answer to the bell, Lauren let herself in with her spare key. They called out Iona's name and then went through the house, noticing that the wedding picture of Frank and Iona was now on the locker beside the king-size bed, and noticing too that the bed hadn't been made.

'So,' said Lauren tartly to her mother, 'do you still think she's OK?'

'Yes,' said Flora, but she sounded less convinced than previously.

Lauren walked out of the bedroom and into the office. She saw that Iona's computer was still on, although in sleep mode. She jiggled the mouse to start it up again.

The screensaver was another wedding picture – this time Iona and Frank toasting each other on the pale sands of the Caribbean island.

Lauren looked at the files on the desktop, realising from the names that most of them were to do with Rental Remedies or Frank's company. She felt bad about looking at Iona's computer, as though she was rummaging around in her sister's desk, but she'd hoped that maybe there'd be something there to give her a clue. She opened the web browser and looked at the history details. She shivered as she noted the coma websites, and then focused on the last site that Iona had visited. The session had been timed out, but it was clear to Lauren that Iona had been looking at flights. The only question was to where.

'Maybe to Spain,' said Flora when Lauren told her about it. 'Perhaps she's at the finca. That'd be just typical, wouldn't it!'

'You'd know by now if she was there,' said Lauren. 'Dad would have called. Or she would.'

Flora and Lauren agreed that Iona could have gone anywhere. And that there was no way to find out where.

'Maybe . . .' Lauren's voice trailed off as she gazed at the screen again. 'Maybe there is.'

'How?'

'Well, Io told me that the garda who came asking questions about Frank also had to go looking for his daughter when she disappeared. Perhaps she can help us.'

'The daughter disappeared!' Flora was astonished. 'When? Where did she go?'

'She didn't really disappear,' said Lauren. 'She just stayed out late. But Sally was really worried and the detective managed to find her. Maybe she can do the same for Iona.'

'She's hardly going to go wherever Iona is and bring her home,' said Flora.

'No, but she might be able to find out if she did take a flight somewhere,' said Lauren.

'Possibly, I suppose.'

'I'll ring her,' said Lauren. 'Anyway, she has a kind of obligation towards Iona. Io found her an apartment to rent. So maybe she'll play ball with us.'

'Iona rented her an apartment?' Flora was even more astonished. 'How – oh, never mind. Give her a call and let's see what she says.'

* * *

Iona decided to devote her day to culture. She'd done the shopping and now she wanted to see the landmark sites. Given her limited time, she opted for an all-day tour package which whistle-stopped its way around the city and then dropped her back at Central Park, where she sat down at Strawberry Fields and thought about the random nature of the things that happened to people. Then she went back to her hotel, took a swim in the pool and went to bed.

'She's in New York.' Siobhán Farrell, feeling as though she'd become a private detective for the Harper and Brannock families, reported back to Lauren at around the same time as Iona was swimming in the pool.

'For God's sake! Why didn't she say anything?'

'I've no idea,' said Siobhán. 'I'm wondering if it has anything to do with the marriage. Whether she's found out something else.'

'Oh, no,' said Lauren. 'It couldn't have. She couldn't have.'

'I'm inclined to agree,' said Siobhán. 'Anyway, she's booked to come home tomorrow. Arriving back at midday.'

'We'll be there,' said Lauren grimly. 'She'll have some explaining to do.'

'Maybe.' Siobhán spoke warily. 'But, you know, I think she's had a really hard time of it. Both of them have. I suppose all wives might wonder at some point about their husbands having an affair. I'm not sure that too many of them discover that they've never been married at all.'

'I don't care,' said Lauren. 'She's scared us all rigid.'

'Sure,' said Siobhán. 'Well, I hope you work it out.'

'Thanks,' said Lauren. 'We will.'

Iona found it harder to sleep on the return flight. All of the thoughts about Frank and Sally and Jenna which she'd managed to put completely out of her head for the last forty-eight hours now came tumbling back. She knew that the break had been worth it. But it had only been a break. Real life was still waiting for her when she got back.

* * *

It was Flora who spotted her walking through the arrivals doors, wearing the Donna Karan jeans and top that she'd bought in Bloomingdale's. Flora scanned her daughter from top to toe, instantly taking in the fact that she'd lost weight since she'd last seen her. That bastard Harper, she thought furiously. What has he done to her!

Iona thought she was hallucinating when she saw her sister and her mother. She stopped in her tracks and stared at them unbelievingly.

'What the hell d'you think you were doing?' demanded Flora when Iona asked why they were there. 'We were worried sick about you.'

'Why?' asked Iona.

'I called and called,' said Lauren. 'You didn't return any of my messages.'

'I was in New York,' said Iona. 'My mobile isn't triband. It doesn't work there.'

'You shouldn't have disappeared without a word,' said Flora.

'It was only a couple of days,' protested Iona. 'I often don't speak to either of you for weeks on end. Get a grip, for heaven's sake!'

'We were worried,' repeated Lauren. 'We thought . . . we thought . . .'

'What?' asked Iona.

'Well, I'm not sure,' said Lauren. 'But with all this stuff about Frank and everything and you being so upset . . . we didn't know what to think.'

'Look, I'm sorry if I scared you,' said Iona. 'But I needed to be on my own for a while.'

'And did it help?' asked Flora.

Iona thought about her shopping expedition and her tour of the city and her night on the town. She thought about Brandon, who'd bought her dinner and kissed her, who had made her feel like she was part of the human race again, even if only for a few hours.

'Yes,' she said. 'It did.'

Chapter 27

The following morning Iona apologised to Ruth and Garret for disappearing without notice and promised that she'd work extra hard to make up for it.

'Ah, don't worry about it,' said Ruth. 'You're entitled to a bit of down time, Io.'

'Not really,' Iona told her. 'I don't want people feeling sorry for me. My mother came haring over from Spain to check up on me too and I hate thinking that everyone is watching me and making excuses for me.'

'OK, so.' Ruth grinned. 'No more Mizz Nice Gal from me. Any chance you could show apartment six in Waterside this afternoon? It's on my agenda but I'm up to my neck because you pissed off without saying—'

'All right, all right.' Iona made a face at her. 'I'll show it. Everyone's interested in that block, aren't they?'

'Near to the lovely coastal town of Dun Laoghaire,' intoned Ruth. 'Spectacular views over the bay. Walking distance of the Dart and—'

'I know the marketing spin.' Iona grinned.

'Good,' said Ruth. 'At the same time you can drop the keys to his mailbox in to Mr Martinez.'

'He already has keys to his mailbox,' said Iona. 'He got them when he took the apartment.'

'Yes, and he managed to post them into it by mistake,' said Ruth.

'Dirty eejit. How did he do that?'

Ruth shrugged. 'Dunno.'

'So do you want me to show the other apartment later tonight instead?' asked Iona. 'To be sure he's in?'

'Nope,' replied Ruth. 'He's working from home today so he said that if someone was around they'd be able to get him.'

'OK.' Iona didn't mind the idea of heading out to Dun Laoghaire again that afternoon. She liked the chi-chi town when the sun was shining. And on a day like this she could see why the apartments were renting out so easily too, making her job a lot easier. It was actually good to be back at work, and after her unplanned break, she felt less stressed out by it.

Iona pulled in to the car park and met her clients – a couple who were looking for something within an easy commute of the city. She showed them around the apartment and was pleased when they said they'd take it. When they'd gone she walked back into the lobby of the block with the intention of checking that the keys which Ruth had given her actually opened Mr Martinez's mailbox. It's the little things, she said to herself as she held open the door for another resident, that can go horribly wrong and make you look like a fool. She didn't want for him to try out the keys in front of her and discover that they were the wrong ones and think that everyone one in Rental Remedies was incompetent.

She stood in front of the bank of mailboxes, looking for the one for apartment 7. It was directly beside Siobhán Farrell's, although Enrique Martinez's was a good deal bigger (and a good deal more expensive).

She checked the keys and was relieved to see that they worked. Then her phone beeped with a message and she stood to one side while another resident of the block checked his mail too. Only he wasn't checking his own box. Iona could see that the one he was looking at was, in fact, Siobhán Farrell's, although Siobhán hadn't got around to slipping her name tag on the box yet. He was peering inside, straining to see if there was any mail, while at the same time trying a couple of keys on the lock.

'Excuse me,' she said as she put her phone back in her bag (the message had been from Ruth to remind her about an early-morning meeting the next day). 'Can I help you?' He turned towards her. The first thing she noted about him was that he was very attractive. He had caramel-blond hair and smoke-grey eyes and his face was smooth and chiselled. He wasn't handsome, thought Iona. He was beautiful. Which was different.

'I'm sorry,' he said. 'I seem to have lost my keys.'

'Are you sure you've got the right mailbox?' Even as she spoke the words Iona realised that she was being incredibly stupid in talking to him at all. The beautiful man could be some kind of thief, robbing people's identities or something. Accosting him wasn't a very clever thing to do.

'Right mailbox but wrong keys,' he said easily. 'Don't worry. I must have left them in my office. It's not far away. I can collect them.' He turned away from her and walked out of the building.

Iona could feel her heart thudding in her chest. She'd suddenly felt very vulnerable in the empty lobby with the beautiful man who was lying to her, and she wondered how Siobhán Farrell managed to control her fear when she confronted criminals. But then Siobhán was trained for it. She wasn't.

She pressed the button for the lift and went up to the seventh floor, where she knocked on Mr Martinez's door. Unlike the last time she'd seen him, when he'd been wearing the obligatory suit, he was now dressed casually in a pair of jeans and a loose-fitting T-shirt. His feet were bare and the door to the balcony was open. Working at home obviously meant working to a different rhythm, thought Iona, as she saw the glass of wine on the patio table. For an instant she remembered Brandon Williamson sitting in her room at the Le Parker Meridien, sipping wine, a New York version of Enrique Martinez. A shiver ran along her spine.

'Thank you.' He smiled at her. 'I'm feeling like a complete fool. I don't know what I was thinking.'

'We all do silly things sometimes,' said Iona, pushing the memory of Brandon out of her mind and wondering instead how on earth Enrique Martinez had managed to post his keys into his own mailbox.

'There was a piece of paper sticking out of it.' He read her thoughts. And I had the keys in my hand. I tried to pull out the paper and I dropped the keys into the box.'

She smiled. 'Never mind.'

'Do you want to take the other set?' he said. 'In case I do it again?'

She followed him down the stairs to the lobby, where he opened the mailbox and handed her the pair of silver-coloured keys.

'I am not always a stupid tenant,' he told her. 'I am sure you will find that there will be no more problems from me.'

'That's what we're here for, Señor Martinez,' she said. 'To fix problems.'

She glanced towards the entrance door as it opened and smiled as Siobhán Farrell walked in.

'Ah, my neighbour.' Enrique Martinez smiled too. 'We met already.'

'Hi, Enrique,' said Siobhán. 'Are you a client of Iona's too?'

'Yes.' He nodded. 'It is a reunion for the Rental Remedies here, no?'

'I don't usually have meetings in the lobby,' said Iona. Her eyes narrowed. Lauren had explained that it was Siobhán who'd discovered she was in New York. 'But can I have a quick word with you?' She looked apologetically at Enrique Martinez. 'I'm sorry. Do you mind?'

'Not at all,' he said. 'But if you wish to join me for a glass of wine on the balcony later, you are very welcome. Both of you.'

'Thanks,' said Siobhán. 'It's very nice of you, Enrique. But I'm working this evening so I'd better pass on the wine.'

'As you wish.' He nodded at them and began to walk up the stairs.

'Gosh, Siobhán.' Iona's eyes were wide. 'You're only in the place a couple of weeks and you have the hotshot financier drooling over you.'

'He's nice,' said Siobhán. 'I've bumped into him a few times. The first time he was working on his balcony and a gust of wind blew some papers straight over the divider between us and practically into my lap. I brought them back to him.'

'Quick work,' said Iona. 'Quick work too in finding out that I was in New York and letting everyone know about it.' Her tone was edgy.

'They were worried about you,' said Siobhán gently.

'Yes, but it was my business,' Iona told her. 'You didn't have to give out information to them.'

'Would you rather they worried unnecessarily?'

Iona sighed. 'No. Of course not. It was just . . . I was surprised when they turned up at the airport, that's all. And it jolted me back to reality.'

'You didn't want to come back?'

'Oh, I was happy enough to come home. I was just planning a few more hours to myself.'

'Did it help?' asked Siobhán. 'Running away?'

'I didn't run away,' said Iona sharply. 'It was only a couple of days! I just needed to get away, that's all.'

Siobhán nodded. 'I do understand. And I'm sorry if I messed it up for you.'

'No, you didn't.' Iona smiled wryly. 'Not really. And the truth is that

I appreciate you looking after my family when you don't have to. You're a nice person and I've no right to bitch at you.'

'You're not.' Siobhán grinned. 'It's fine. You're going through a tough time.'

'So are you,' said Iona. 'How are things?'

'Not bad. A bit weird being on my own again, but I like the apartment.'

'And, of course, your attractive neighbour!'

Siobhán laughed. 'I'm not interested in him. He's very much not my type.' She looked more seriously at Iona. 'Any change with Frank?'

Iona shook her head. 'No. Not at all. And of course my mother has flown over from Spain on a mission of mercy to see that I'm not slashing my wrists or anything.' She frowned suddenly. 'Do you need to interview her?' she asked. 'I don't know what she can tell you, but as part of your investigation into Frank's potential multiple marriages, which I know you still somehow suspect—'

'I don't need to interview her,' Siobhán interrupted her. 'I've done a lot of investigating, Iona. There doesn't seem to be anyone else.'

Iona swallowed. 'You know, that's a kind of relief. There was a part of me that thought . . . well, he goes to the UK quite a bit. Went to the UK, I mean. I thought maybe . . .' She shivered. 'I'm glad there isn't anyone else.'

'I'm glad too,' said Siobhán. She looked at her watch. 'I'd better go,' she said. 'I'm on a shift later tonight and I need to have a bite to eat and change first.'

'Sure. But before you go . . .' Iona looked at her hesitantly. 'I don't know whether there's an innocent explanation for this or not, but when I arrived today there was a bloke trying to break into your mailbox.'

'What!' Siobhán looked at her in surprise.

'I thought that maybe he was an informer or something,' said Iona. 'I mean, at first I thought he was just breaking in. And then I thought about you being a detective and everything and that you must have informers and stuff and so I thought maybe that was it. Although obviously that doesn't make sense because why would he be snooping around your mailbox? I asked him if I could help, you see, and he implied it was his flat and he'd just forgotten his key.'

'What did he look like?'

Iona described the beautiful man. Siobhán opened her bag and took out a wallet, from which she removed a photograph. 'This him?' she asked.

Iona nodded. 'Who is it?'

'Eddie,' said Siobhán.

'Oh.'

'He must have found out where I was living – maybe trying to guess which apartment was mine by checking out the mailboxes. Eejit!'

Iona started to giggle. 'Good job I didn't threaten to report him to the police,' she said.

'Pity you didn't,' said Siobhán. 'I can't imagine how he would've felt if one of the uniformed guys had called around to accuse him of petty theft.'

'He's very attractive,' said Iona after a moment or two.

'Yes,' said Siobhán. 'He is.'

'Do you love him?'

'Hell, I got engaged to him.' Siobhán sighed deeply. 'I must do, mustn't I?'

'He must love you too,' said Iona, 'if he's trying to check your mail.'

'He's an idiot,' said Siobhán, 'and sometimes I think I'm still an idiot for caring about him.'

'Makes two of us idiots, so,' said Iona drily. 'Three if you count Sally.'

Sally was sitting at a table in the staff room correcting English homework. She was thankful that the summer holidays would begin soon because she was finding it very hard to concentrate. She'd set the girls an essay on the topic 'A Person I Admire' and was wading through pages of praise for a slew of pop stars, interspersed with the occasional essay on the latest hot supermodel. She knew that most of the girls in the school were intelligent and hardworking, but she rather wished they admired a greater variety of people than stick-thin celebrities who wore scanty clothes. Although maybe that was because, she thought wryly, she herself was currently madly envious of stick-thin celebrities who could wear scanty clothes. She'd never been stick-thin herself and now, as her pregnancy progressed, she was feeling fatter by the minute. She was scared too, although she didn't really have time to be. Her doctor had been both sympathetic and practical and had arranged for her to be seen by a gynaecologist based at the same hospital as Frank, so that at least she didn't have to spend her life shuttling between various medical centres. And then he had given Sally a pep talk about looking after herself, mentally as well as physically and staying positive. It was easy, Sally had thought ruefully, for doctors to talk about staying positive. It was another matter altogether to actually do it.

She'd made an effort, though, by buying herself some new maternity clothes and getting her hair trimmed again before going back to work.

She knew, too, that Jenna had been only partly in favour of her return to the school. Leaving aside the fact that Jenna had never been entirely happy with her position as vice principal anyway, Sally was aware of her daughter's fear that her mother's return would cause people to start taking notice of her again. When Jenna had first returned after the accident, she'd come home tense and irritable because, she told Sally, they were a topic of conversation. The headmistresses, Mrs Lyndon, had said prayers for Frank at morning assembly one morning (although obviously she hadn't mentioned the secret wife!) and everyone kept asking her about the accident.

Sally had told her to be as honest as she wanted, and so Jenna had told the truth, knowing that everyone would find out eventually anyway. The result of that, though, was that girls looked at her curiously, and although her closest friends tried to be understanding, she couldn't help feeling somewhat isolated from them and so didn't hang out with them as much as before. But she agreed with Sally that it was better to be at school and the object of curiosity than to structure all her days around visits to the hospital. Jenna was doing fewer and fewer of these anyway and Sally had no intention of forcing her to visit her father more often. There wasn't any point, especially when she knew that Jenna was still incredibly angry with him. She hoped that her daughter would get over it some day soon, but in the meantime she was prepared to live with it.

As she finished marking an essay her mobile phone rang and she grabbed it from the table in front of her.

'Is it bad news?' She asked the question before the doctor even had time to speak.

'No, Mrs Harper,' he said. 'In some ways it's the contrary. Frank has been displaying some responses to stimulus in a much more positive way than previously. We thought you might like to know that.'

'What kind of responses?' she asked breathlessly. 'Is he talking?'

'Nothing like that yet,' said Dr Carroll. 'But he does seem to be following certain sounds and we're pretty sure that he can understand what people are saying. It's a hopeful sign.'

'Oh.' Sally felt the tears that she'd managed to keep under control all day suddenly spill from her eyes. 'Thank you. Thank you for calling.'

She packed up her things and went out to her car. Jenna rarely came home with her, preferring to hang around with her friends or attend after-hours school activities, but Sally sat in the front seat and phoned her daughter anyway, glad that although the girls weren't allowed to have their phones switched on in class there was no problem in bringing them to school.

'What?' asked Jenna as she answered.

Sally told her of Frank's improvement.

'So what does that mean?' Jenna sounded young and girlish again, instead of abrupt and sullen as she had when she'd answered the phone.

'Well, nothing much at this point, I suppose,' said Sally. 'But it's a good sign and I can't wait to see him tonight.'

'Sure,' said Jenna. 'But you're not supposed to be going to the hospital tonight. It's Iona's turn.'

Sally closed her eyes. 'So it is. I'd forgotten.'

'Maybe if they've rung her too she won't mind if you go.'

'And you?' asked Sally. 'Do you want to come with me?'

Jenna hesitated. Gerry had asked her round to his house that night. His parents, once again, were going to be away. And she hadn't been to bed with him in over a week.

'Tell you what,' said Sally. 'You don't have to come tonight if you've got plans. I'll go and see how things are. You can come tomorrow.'

'No,' said Jenna. 'I'll come.'

'It's great, isn't it?' Sally couldn't keep the hope out of her voice. 'Maybe in a few weeks everything will be back to normal.'

Although, she acknowledged as she started the car and began to drive home, she had no idea what normal was any more.

Iona had suggested that Flora and Lauren could both come with her to the hospital that evening after Dr Carroll phoned to tell her about Frank's improved responses.

'How important is this?' she asked him. 'If you think that part of the whole problem is actually his mental state, how much does any of this matter?'

'Well, Iona, we don't know how much is his mental state and how much is purely physical,' said Dr Carroll. 'So it's good to see a positive improvement.'

'If he wakes up now, will there still be real adjustment problems? Will he have lost his memory? Will he know how to do things? Will—'

'There are always problems after trauma,' said Dr Carroll. 'Any sort of trauma, whether it's a head injury or anything else. There's physical trauma and there's mental trauma, and sometimes it's harder to deal with things that have happened to us than to repair the physical damage.'

'I guess you're right about that,' she said.

'But you're doing well too, Iona,' he said.

She laughed shortly. 'If only you knew,' she said.

When she arrived home, the light on her answering machine was blinking. The message was from Sally, asking her if she'd mind if she came along that night because the doctor had told her that Frank was getting better. Iona thought about ringing Sally back and saying that better was entirely relative as far as Frank's condition was concerned, but she didn't. She phoned the other woman and said that she was perfectly welcome to show up, but warned her that Lauren and Flora were going to be there too.

'You're lucky,' said Sally. 'You've a good support system behind you.'

'Oh, nonsense,' Iona told her. 'I don't really want them supporting me, asking me questions all the time, telling me what I should be doing with my life. I want to be left alone.'

'I can see your point,' agreed Sally, 'but it's still nice to know that there are people looking out for you.'

'I suppose so,' said Iona shortly. 'Sometimes, though, people meddling in your life is more trouble than it's worth.'

'All the same, it must be nice to have an adult to talk to. Jenna – well, you know what she's like at the moment, and I don't really have anyone else to share it with.'

'Don't you have family or friends?' asked Iona curiously.

Sally explained about her only-child status and the fact that both her parents were dead. 'And I do have a friend, but she lives the other side of the city and I can't keep dumping on her over the phone,' said Sally.

'You can dump on me,' said Iona.

Sally laughed. 'Hardly, if I'm complaining that you exist.'

'I suppose not,' Iona agreed. 'Anyway, I'll see you tonight.'

'Thanks for letting me come,' said Sally.

'Don't be crazy,' said Iona. 'You've more right to be there than me, and you know it.'

Lauren drove to the hospital, and Iona was happy to be a passenger so that she could let her thoughts wander. She wished that the situation with Frank and his condition wasn't so vague. She hated the uncertainty of it all. But this improvement did make the possibility of his waking up a million times less remote. And the consequences of his waking up a million times closer.

She led the way through the hospital to Frank's room, Flora and Lauren exchanging glances as they followed behind her. When she got to the ICU, Iona said hello to Terri Cooper and to Susan Carpenter, who were both on duty.

'An improvement,' Susan said cheerfully. 'You must be pleased.'

Iona nodded. 'Is Sally here yet?' she asked.

'No,' said Susan. 'Is she coming today?'

'Of course,' said Iona. 'She needs to see this for herself.'

'Don't get your hopes up too much,' warned Susan. 'It's not like he's sitting up and watching the telly, you know.'

'I know,' said Iona.

'Did you enjoy your break?' asked Terri. 'You missed a day or two, didn't you?'

Iona looked at her uneasily. 'Did you say anything to Sally about it?'

'Of course not,' said Terri.

'I needed a bit of time,' Iona told her.

'We understand that perfectly,' Terri said.

'But Sally might not. So . . .'

'It's fine, don't worry.' Terri nodded.

Iona walked into the room. Flora, following right behind her, was unable to hold back her gasp of shock at the sight of Frank in the bed, his attractive features flattened out by the lack of expression on a face that was much paler and thinner than she remembered.

'He hasn't been outside in weeks,' Iona said as she sat down. 'You've got to remember that. And of course he's just been lying there too. Hi, Frank,' she added conversationally. 'Mum and Lauren are here too, so mind your manners.'

His head moved slightly and Iona held her breath. He'd never moved at the sound of her voice before. Never.

'And Sally's coming later,' she said. 'So you'll be in deep doo-doo if you actually do arse yourself to wake up.'

'Iona!' Flora sounded shocked. 'You can't talk to him like that.'

'Well how d'you expect me to talk to him?' demanded Iona. 'I've done the sorrowful whispering sort of stuff. I've told him I love him. There's not a lot left.'

The door opened and both Sally and Jenna walked in. Jenna glowered at Iona.

'Hello, Jenna,' she said. 'This is my mother. And my sister.'

'I met your sister already.'

'Of course you did. I'd forgotten.' Iona kept her voice steady.

'Hello, Jenna.' Flora got up from her chair. 'I'm really sorry about your dad.'

Jenna swallowed hard.

'It was an awful thing to happen,' said Flora. 'And it's a mess right now. But it will get sorted out, you know.'

'I don't see how,' said Jenna mutinously.

'Things always do work themselves out,' said Flora easily.

'Yeah, right.' Jenna leaned against the wall.

'He moved his head.' Iona looked at Sally. 'Only a little, but he did it.'

'Really?' Sally edged closer to the bed.

'Yeah,' said Iona. 'I told him you were coming and that stopped him in his tracks, though.'

Sally looked surprised and Iona smiled at her. 'Well, if it didn't, it should,' she amended.

Sally smiled faintly too. She leaned over to look at Frank. 'Can you hear me?' she asked.

There was no response from Frank.

'It's me, Sally,' she said. 'Iona told me you moved your head earlier. Can you do it again?'

But there was nothing. Sally's shoulders sagged.

'Hey, I bet it's not like he does it all the time,' said Iona. 'And I wouldn't worry that he's not responding to you right now. After all, his first response was to the doctors, not either of us.'

'That's true,' said Sally.

'So don't feel personally slighted.'

'I wasn't.'

'You were.' Jenna detached herself from her position against the wall and stood beside the bed. 'Hey, Dad, any chance you'd open your eyes for us?'

All of the women watched intently, but Frank remained still. Jenna walked out of the room, saying that she was going to get a drink.

'It's a bit of a battle.' Iona looked up at her mother and sister. 'To see which of us he responds to the most. Thing is, he hasn't actually responded to any of us. For a while I thought there was another woman.'

'Iona!' Lauren looked horrified.

'Well, it was always a possibility,' said Iona. 'Another woman who really matters. The one who'll unlock his mind for us.'

'God, I hope not,' said Flora.

'Actually, the police don't think so,' Sally told them. 'Siobhán Farrell says they've done a lot of investigating and so far nothing has turned up. She even went to Sligo to check out the tenants there.'

Iona froze. Siobhán had said she didn't think there was another woman, but she hadn't told her anything at all about going to Sligo.

'It's fine, there's no problem with them,' said Sally hastily. 'I've actually met them, they're locals building their own house. They've moved back there from Dublin.'

'Trouble is, no matter what Siobhán says, it wouldn't really surprise me if someone else turned up,' said Iona.

'Realistically I don't think so,' Sally said. 'I mean, he just didn't have the time, did he?'

They both looked at Frank.

'Hope not,' said Iona as Jenna walked back into the room with a bottle of flavoured water.

'Pity he didn't manage to do something about the tenancy agreement before the accident.' Sally sighed. 'It was originally for a year while the family renting it build their own place. But they've run into planning permission problems and now they're looking for an extension to the lease while they sort things out.'

'That's straightforward enough,' said Iona. 'Who's looking after it for you?'

'Well, Frank did it all, that's the thing. They hadn't been too worried because they'd heard about the accident, but then when Siobhán turned up they got into a flap about the renewal and they phoned me last night. I haven't a clue what I'm supposed to do about it. I was going to ring Frank's accountant today.'

'I'll look after it if you like,' offered Iona. 'It's the one thing I know about.'

'Will you?' Sally looked at her hopefully. 'That'd be a relief.'

'Mum!' Jenna exclaimed. 'You can't have her looking at stuff.'

'Why not?' asked Sally.

'I don't mind.' Iona shrugged. 'We don't want everything to fall into a complete mess. Do we?' She addressed her last remark to Frank.

They sat around the bed in silence, nobody able to think of anything to say either to each other or to Frank. Eventually Flora got up.

'Jenna, will you show me where the drinks machine is?' she asked.

Jenna shrugged in agreement.

'Think I'll get something too,' said Lauren.

The three of them walked out of the room, leaving Iona and Sally alone.

'I saw Siobhán Farrell,' said Iona eventually. 'She never said anything about going to Sligo.'

'Why did you see her?' Sally looked anxious.

'Nothing to do with this,' said Iona.

'Really?'

'Yes.' Iona hesitated and then laughed shortly. 'I rented her an apartment.'

'What?' Sally was surprised. 'I thought she was engaged and living with her fiancé.'

'She was.' Iona told Sally about Eddie's unfaithfulness.

'And she felt she had to move out?'

'You know, I get the impression that there was slightly more to it,' said Iona. 'Though I'm not sure what exactly. Anyway, she was very upset. I got her an apartment in Dun Laoghaire.'

'Are men always bastards?' Sally looked at Frank as she spoke.

'I don't think so,' said Iona. 'I sure hope not.'

'She's a nice girl,' said Sally.

'He's a right hunk,' Iona added.

'How d'you know that?'

Iona explained about meeting Eddie at the apartment block.

'That's hopeful,' said Sally. 'At least he cares.'

'Oh, Sally, Frank cared too,' said Iona. 'But he still managed to divide his time between both of us.'

Sally winced.

'I was just thinking,' said Iona idly. 'How about you and me and Siobhán get together?'

'What for?'

'A night out,' said Iona. 'Girl talk. You know.'

'Iona, she's a bloody detective. You can't just chat with a detective. Particularly one who's trying to build a case against our husband.'

Iona giggled.

'What?'

'Our husband?'

Sally smiled too, a wobbly smile. 'You know what I mean,' she said.

'Sure. But we deserve a night off,' said Iona. 'You and me, always coming in here to be with him – and today rushing in because there was some hope . . . we need to do normal things.'

'I'm not much fun these days,' said Sally.

'And I'm not either, mostly,' said Iona. 'But I know I can be. And I don't think it's right for us to sit around being mournful. It's not what Frank would want either. You know that, Sally. And I thought – well, given that Siobhán's going through a break-up, maybe she needs some fun too.'

'Well . . . OK,' said Sally slowly. 'Why not?'

'I'll phone Siobhán and sort it,' said Iona.

The door opened and Jenna, Flora and Lauren returned.

'Any change?' asked Lauren.

Both Sally and Iona shook their heads. And Frank's eyes remained closed.

He wondered if he was dead. He wondered this because he kept hearing strange noises and because suddenly he was catapulted into situations which seemed familiar to him only he couldn't remember how. It was very disconcerting, as if he was stepping in and out of a time machine. Maybe that was what happened when you were dead, he thought. Maybe you were sent back over and over again to relive the parts of your life that you'd messed up. Only that would be a complete nonsense, wouldn't it? After all, how would you know you'd messed things up until afterwards? And if you didn't know what was going to happen in the future, how could you stop yourself from doing the same wrong thing once again? He sighed. It was all too complicated for him. He wanted to rest. He wanted to rid himself of the thoughts and people who crowded into his head and then left so abruptly. He wanted to sleep for a month.

But he couldn't. Because he had to deal with the situation he was in now. It was difficult, but he had to do it. He had to tell her that he was sorry, that he'd made a terrible mistake, that he couldn't come to the event with her. Of course he hadn't meant to say yes to her invitation. It had come out of the blue and he'd been surprised by it and he'd just said yes. And now she was looking at him with a mixture of apprehension and pleasure in her eyes.

But why had he agreed to go with her? It wasn't as though he were a free agent. It wasn't as though he could actually start dating the girl. He frowned. What the hell was her name again? She was a pretty little thing, slight and gamine and with a wicked grin. She reminded him a little of Marion, but not at all of Sally.

Sally, he thought suddenly. That was his wife's name. It had been bugging him for a while, but now he remembered again. Sally of the auburn hair and the porcelain skin. Sally wouldn't be very pleased if he started accepting invitations from strange women to go to parties. Sally would be pissed off with him, in fact. Actually, though, wasn't Sally pissed off with him already? Hadn't he heard her say loads of times that she couldn't take much more of this, that she was exhausted, that she needed him to come back and devote time to his family? He wasn't sure exactly what her problem was. Although . . . it was work, wasn't it? He wanted to set up a new company and Sally wasn't happy because he'd suggested selling their house and moving out of the city. She'd wanted him to sell the house in Sligo instead. But he couldn't do that. Sally didn't understand that he couldn't sell the Sligo house because if Christine came back that was where she'd go first. Not that he expected her to come back, or even wanted her to come back, but still . . .

Sally was angry too, because moving house made it more difficult for her to get to work. She'd been incandescent with rage when he'd suggested that maybe it was time for her to give it up for a while, that if she was at home perhaps she'd get pregnant again, which was what they both wanted. She'd said that a big family was what he had wanted – she was happy with one child. And that losing the second baby had been very difficult for her and that she wasn't sure whether she wanted to go through all that again.

It was strange, he thought, how time changed people. How living together changed people. He'd never before understood how Christine could seem like one person to Derek when he knew her first but someone else completely when he'd brought her back to Sligo. Now he was beginning to feel as though the Sally he'd fallen in love with was a different person altogether. And yet, he loved her. He knew he would always love her. She said that she loved him too. But he wanted her to need him.

The thing was, she didn't. She could walk out if she wanted, despite the fact that he'd married her so that she couldn't ever walk out. Only times had changed. It wasn't such a big deal any more. You couldn't force people to stay with you if they didn't want to. And Sally wouldn't walk out by herself, he knew that. Sally wasn't Christine. She'd take Jenna with her and leave him on his own. At the thought of being on his own he began to shiver. He couldn't let that happen. He really couldn't. He still loved her but he was angry with her for making him feel suddenly vulnerable. She told him that she couldn't constantly massage his ego and tell him that things didn't matter when they did. He asked her what sort of things. She talked about his mood swings, his irritation with her, the fact that he didn't take her into account when he was planning things. She thought that maybe he'd outgrown her and outgrown marriage. He hadn't realised she'd felt like that. He told her that she was being silly and that he loved her. But he wasn't entirely sure that she believed him.

He was still feeling bruised and angry when he met . . . the girl. And she was so sweet and so nice that he couldn't help saying yes to her invitation. And so now he was in the ballroom of a hotel in Dublin with a girl he didn't know, listening to a terrible DJ playing songs of the seventies. She was smiling at him, leaning forward so that he could see her pert breasts underneath the filmy silver-grey dress she was wearing. She didn't make him feel bruised or angry. When she looked at him with her blackberry eyes she made him feel wanted and loved. But guilty. Because he shouldn't be here with her. Even though she was grabbing him by the hand and leading him on to the dance floor because the DJ was playing 'Manic Monday' and she said it was one of her favourite songs. And suddenly they were back in her house and the filmy dress was on the floor by the bed and she was smiling at him again and he wanted to be with her and make it good for her because she'd made it good for him. So he pushed the guilty feelings to the back of his mind and he smiled too.

'He's smiling,' said Sally suddenly. She stared at Frank. 'Omigod, he really is.'

The other women stared at him too.

'Hey, Frank!' Iona took him by the hand. 'Can you hear me?'

The smile suddenly left his face and it smoothed into an expressionless mask again. She dropped his hand and it fell on to the covers.

'He was thinking about something,' said Sally.

'Maybe it was you,' suggested Iona. 'Or Jenna.' Her glance flickered towards the teenage girl, who was looking at Frank with a mixture of hope and despair.

'Probably pizza,' said Jenna abruptly as she stared intently at her father. 'Or ice cream. Food always makes him smile.'

Chapter 28

As soon as she received it in the post, Iona updated the tenancy agreement and returned it to Sally. Then she phoned Siobhán Farrell and asked the detective if she'd like to meet up with them for something to eat.

'Why?' asked Siobhán suspiciously. 'What's happened?'

'Nothing.' Iona told her about visiting Frank and her sudden notion that it would be good for them all to get together. 'We can talk about him if you like,' Iona said. 'If you've any other questions you want to ask us. But to be honest, we just want to go out.'

'You and Sally hate each other,' said Siobhán.

'No we don't.' Iona realised that she must sound crazy to Siobhán now. After all, she'd been white-hot with rage over Sally a few weeks earlier. But there was no point in raging any more. 'We've had to accept each other,' she told Siobhán. 'And . . . well, I kind of like her.'

'Really?' Siobhán was sceptical.

'Yes, really,' said Iona. 'Look, in the whole scheme of things it's Frank who's the bad guy. Not Sally or me. Or Jenna.'

'Well . . .' Siobhán was doubtful about it all. But, she told herself as she tapped her pencil on the pad in front of her, meeting the Harper wives in a social situation might not be a bad idea. As far as she was concerned she'd completed her work on the case, but she never knew what else might turn up. 'What had you got in mind?' she asked.

'Meeting somewhere in Dun Laoghaire,' said Iona promptly. 'It's handy enough for us all. You live there, Sally can get the Dart from Bray and I can get one from Connolly. Everything still OK with the apartment?'

'Great,' said Siobhán. 'It's a nice block.'

'Good. And everything OK with you?'

Siobhán hesitated. 'I'm fine,' she said firmly. 'Just fine.'

'So.' Iona sounded definite. 'How does the weekend suit you?'

'I'm off Friday,' said Siobhán.

'Friday it is. I'll let Sally know. Any suggestions?'

Siobhán suggested a recently opened bar and restaurant near the seafront and Iona agreed.

'Around seven,' she said. 'See you then.'

Siobhán ended the call and put her mobile back in her pocket. She gazed unseeingly at the computer screen in front of her. She really wasn't sure why she'd accepted the invitation to meet up with Sally and Iona. She supposed she could justify it because of the case, although she'd done as much work on it as she could without actually being able to interview Frank Harper himself. There probably wasn't any new information that his wives could give her. Going out with the two main witnesses wasn't exactly professional. Siobhán liked both of them, but she had to keep her wits about her no matter how much she thought the case was closed. She really didn't want to go down in station folklore as the detective who was conned in the bigamy case.

But still . . . she'd done everything possible to check out Frank. His prints had come back negative. Nobody had heard of him in the UK. The tenancy in Sligo had turned out to be OK, and in fact she'd quite enjoyed the drive to the north-west and her meeting with Frank's tenants.

'A lovely man,' Sorcha Sheerin had told her. 'Really gentle and kind. My parents knew the family, of course.'

Siobhán had questioned Sorcha and her husband about the Harpers, although the information she received had tied in with everything she'd already found out about Frank and his family. That Christine and Derek Harper had lived in the area, that they hadn't been married, only nobody had known that at the time. That Christine had left Derek with the child. That Derek had died around sixteen years ago.

Interesting, she thought, that Derek hadn't married Christine. It must have been hard to raise a child on his own back in the sixties and seventies, especially because his wife had left him. That just didn't happen in Ireland back then. Wives put up with things. So did husbands. She wondered what sort of a father Derek had been.

The sound of the office phone ringing jolted her out of her reverie.

'Siobhán Farrell,' she said.

'Hello, Siobhán,' said Eddie.

She groaned softly. She didn't want to talk to Eddie right now.

'What?' she asked.

'I was just checking on you,' he said. 'To see how you were.'

'I'm fine,' she told him.

'I'm not,' said Eddie.

'What d'you mean?' Her heart skipped a beat. What if the tests had been wrong? What if Eddie had contracted an STD in Boston after all?

'I miss you, is what I mean,' said Eddie.

Her heart slowed down again.

'C'mon, Siobhán. Forgive and forget.'

'I'm not ready yet.'

'Are you still wearing my ring?' asked Eddie.

She glanced down at her left hand. 'Yes.'

'Do you still love me?'

'I'm not going to have this conversation right now,' she said. 'Oh, Eddie, by the way . . .'

'What?'

'Don't prowl around my mailbox any more.'

'Huh?' But she heard the tone of discomfiture in his voice.

'I'm a detective,' she told him. 'I detect. It's my job to know stuff like that.'

'I was just—'

'I don't care what you were doing,' she said. 'Don't do it again.'

Eddie gritted his teeth. 'OK,' he said.

'Eddie?'

'Yes?'

'I don't not love you.'

'Jeez, Siobhán.' His tone was dry. 'That makes me feel a whole heap better all right.'

She put down the receiver and stared at the computer screen again. Then the phone rang for a second time. I hope it's something nice and ordinary like a murder, she thought as she picked it up, I've had enough of family drama for a while.

* * *

Sally was in the staff room, on the phone to Richard Moran, Frank's accountant. He'd called to say that they were going to have to make new arrangements about the business. Frank was clearly going to be incapacitated for some time. As a director, Sally was empowered to make decisions on its future.

'Don't you need Frank to sign things?' she asked.

'Not the way it's all put together,' said Richard. 'You can do it.'

'Is it worth anything?' asked Sally. 'Are there buyers?'

'Yes and yes,' said Richard. 'Can you come into the office to talk about it?'

'As soon as the school holidays start,' said Sally. 'I can't take time off during the day at the moment.'

'OK,' said Richard. 'We can more or less keep things going as they are in the short term. But there are a number of new installations that Frank was going to work on. If they're to get done you really have to let someone else take over.'

'Can I appoint someone?' Sally wished she had the faintest clue about business.

'You need someone with skills, Sally,' said Richard. 'It's not like just picking a name out of the phone book.'

'I know that.' She was annoyed at how patronising he suddenly sounded. 'I'll give you a call next week and set something up.'

She slid her phone back into her bag and poured herself a cup of tea, then sat down in one of the less than comfortable armchairs. She wondered whether the head had deliberately bought uncomfortable chairs so that the staff wouldn't be tempted to stay in the staff room for too long. She sipped her tea. She had a free period now which she intended to use to mark up the homework of her third-year class. But first she was going to chill out for a few minutes. She was finding that keeping her concentration for a full lesson period was difficult. Sometimes her mind wandered on to Frank's condition, but more and more it was turning to her own. Her pregnancy was now more obvious. And she was beginning to think more about the implications of having the baby while Frank was still in hospital. She hoped it wouldn't come to that. But even though there'd been the so-called breakthrough when he'd seemed to respond to voices, it hadn't meant all that much in the end. And he hadn't responded to her voice anyway. Bastard!

She drained her tea and picked up an exercise book.

'Am I interrupting?' Marsha Tyndall sat down beside her and Sally stifled an irritated sigh. She put down the book and looked at the geography teacher instead.

'What's up, Marsha?' she asked.

'I just wanted a quick word with you,' said Marsha. 'It's about Jenna.'

Sally's eyes darkened. 'What about her?'

'I've got to tell you that she's being really disruptive in class,' said Marsha. 'I've been cutting her some slack because of all this stuff with . . . with her dad, but honestly, Sally, I've had as much as I can take from her.'

'How disruptive?' asked Sally.

'Not listening. Talking. Making comments.' Marsha shrugged. 'I gave her extra homework but she ignored it. She seems to have fallen out with her friend Sam, too. They were at it hammer and tongs in the cloakroom earlier this week. Now Jenna's hanging around with Aline Keogh and that set and you know what they're like! It's all boys and make-up and a complete lack of interest in their work.'

'Shit,' said Sally.

'Sorry to have to break it to you,' said Marsha sympathetically. 'I'm sure she's just going through a bad patch. You know what they're like.'

'Oh, of course I do,' said Sally. 'And she was already going through a bad patch before her dad's accident. Though at least then she had the decency to do her homework.'

Marsha smiled. 'She's a good girl really and I don't want to see her going down the wrong track.'

'Hopefully she won't,' said Sally. 'I'll have a talk with her. I'm not happy about her taking up with Aline.'

'If she'd been a bit disruptive but still pally with Sam I wouldn't have said anything,' Marsha told her. 'But Aline . . . well, if that girl doesn't get into serious trouble before she leaves school, I'll eat my hat.'

Sally rubbed the back of her neck. 'I know. I just hope she won't drag Jenna down with her. Thanks for telling me.' She picked up the exercise book again, even though she knew that just at that moment she wouldn't be able to get her head around geometry.

* * *

It was searingly hot and Frank was very grateful for the air-conditioning in the rented Ford. He glanced at the girl beside him who was gunning it along the motorway towards the costal town of Javea. Her parents lived in Javea and he was going to meet them.

Why, he wondered, why am I going to meet her parents? If this is a business call I don't have my gear with me. And why on earth am I in Spain anyway? He knew that he was in Spain – they'd just passed a road sign pointing them in the direction of Benidorm. He'd gone to Benidorm with a few of his mates one year. It had been a sun, sand and sex holiday, although less sexual adventuring for him than anyone else. He hadn't really liked the concept of the one-night stand and so he'd found one girl and she'd been his holiday romance, even though both of them knew it wasn't going to last.

It wasn't this girl, though. He frowned. He'd married this one. He remembered now. He'd married her very recently on the island. She'd come out to him on a boat. And he hadn't been able to remember her name. He thought it was Sally but he was convinced that Sally was someone else. And yet whenever he said the name in his mind, it seemed right to him. Frank and Sally seemed to go with each other perfectly.

'Nervous?' She glanced towards him, her eyes full of mischief.

'Why would I be nervous?' he asked.

'Meeting the parents,' she said. 'Big deal. Your first time.'

Meeting the parents! Flipping heck, he thought. He didn't want to meet her parents when he couldn't even remember her name. He frowned again. He'd done this already. He knew he had. He'd met her parents before and he was sure that they'd called her Sally too. So maybe, since he was clearly getting something horribly wrong, the best thing to do was just play along with her and say nothing.

'They'll love you,' she told him.

'I hope so.'

'Oh, absolutely. And you'll love the finca. Some day I want to buy it from them and move there myself.' She chuckled. 'Well . . . maybe. Now that we're married you might have different ideas.'

'A finca sounds good.'

'We can grow our own olives. Oranges too.'

He didn't think she was the orange-growing type.

She laughed out loud. 'Oh, Frank, the expression on your face! Don't worry, honey. I'm not about to turn into a dash-for-the-country person.

I'm a city girl. If we ever move to Spain I want to live in an apartment in Madrid or Barcelona.'

'Watch out for that . . . lorry!'

She gestured rudely at the driver as the oil tanker overtook her. Then she pressed her foot on the accelerator to catch him up.

'Don't,' he said.

'Why not?'

'No point,' he told her. 'I do a lot of driving now and the best thing is to stay cool on the road. Don't let anyone aggravate you.'

'Is that your philosophy?' She eased off on the speed.

'Absolutely.'

'All right then.'

They drove in silence. She was a good driver, he thought, but too aggressive. She needed to chill out. He wished he felt a little more chilled out himself. He couldn't help feeling as though something terrible was about to happen. That was why he'd got so jumpy when she'd speeded up.

'Our turn,' she said eventually.

She'd said it was a finca, and so he'd imagined a run-down shack set in the middle of arid land and surrounded by a few straggly olive trees. But this house was beautifully renovated and clearly well maintained. The walls were white but the roof was made of blue tiles, which, the girl told him, was typically Valencian. And on the other side of the short driveway he could see clusters of round fruit on the lush olive trees. Behind the house the mountains scraped the blue sky with purple tips.

'Palmyra,' she said as she hopped out of the car. 'Not very original, but who cares.'

The door of the finca opened and a tall woman walked out. He could see the resemblance right away.

'Iona!' she cried. 'How lovely to see you.'

Iona! He remembered now. How could he have forgotten? And yet . . . if she was Iona and he was married to her . . . then why was he so sure that he was married to someone called Sally?

Chapter 29

Siobhán arrived at the bar first. She wanted to see whether Sally and Iona turned up together or whether they came separately, so she got there fifteen minutes early. She sat down at one of the outside tables because the day had been another glorious one and the evening air was balmy. She ordered a glass of wine and watched as people strolled along the promenade, while in the background a cluster of small boats skimmed across the blue-green water of the Irish Sea.

She'd drunk about a quarter of the glass when Sally arrived, looking slightly breathless, her hair mussed by the evening breeze. Siobhán raised her hand in greeting.

'Hello.' Sally sat down beside her. 'Sorry I'm late.'

'Not really,' said Siobhán. 'Five minutes.'

'I hate that Irish thing about always being late,' said Sally. 'I don't like unpunctuality but I missed the train I meant to take. Jenna and I . . . well, it doesn't matter.' She opened her bag, took out a wide-toothed comb and ran it through her hair. 'I'm sorry. This is rude. I should go to a bathroom to do this.'

'You're fine,' said Siobhán. 'Would you like a drink?'

'Water.' Sally unconsciously touched her swelling stomach. 'But make it sparkling.'

Siobhán ordered a water and glanced at her watch. 'Iona really is late,' she said.

'It was her turn to visit Frank,' said Sally. 'She'll have been to the hospital first.'

'Oh.'

Sally's jaw tightened. 'Maybe something happened. Maybe he woke up. Perhaps I should give her a call.'

'I'm pretty sure she'd call you if he woke up,' said Siobhán.

'You think?'

'You don't?'

Sally put her comb back in her bag. 'Of course she'd call,' she said, though there was a hint of doubt in her mind. 'We promised each other.'

'Well then,' said Siobhán. 'She's probably just been delayed.'

'I know.' Sally took a sip of the water which had just been placed in front of her. She sighed. 'It's awful suspecting her all the time. Feeling as though she might have some kind of edge.'

'I rather think that she believes you have the edge.'

Sally laughed shortly. 'I don't think so.'

'Why not? He's married to you, after all.'

'But he met her afterwards,' said Sally wryly.

'It must be very difficult,' said Siobhán.

'It's impossible,' Sally stated. 'But we still have to get on with it. And . . .' she half smiled, 'obviously nothing has happened because here she is.'

Iona waved as she walked rapidly towards them.

'I'm so sorry,' she said as she arrived and pulled back a chair. 'The phone rang just as I was leaving. My mother. Nagging. Nothing important.'

'Sally thought that maybe something had happened with Frank,' said Siobhán, 'and that that had delayed you at the hospital.'

'I didn't go to the hospital.' Iona looked at them from her dark eyes. 'I had to show an apartment at five and I wouldn't have had time to get home and change and come out.'

'So nobody's been in all day!' Sally looked horrified.

'Sally, much as I hate to say this, he probably hasn't noticed,' said Iona.

'I know. But . . . I would have gone,' said Sally.

'And then *you'd* never have got here. Be reasonable.' Iona shrugged and stopped the passing waitress, ordering a Bacardi and Coke. 'Diet Coke,' she amended. 'I don't like the other stuff.'

'Maybe today would have been the day,' said Sally. 'And now neither of us has been there.'

'Sally, if anything had changed they would have called us,' said Iona. 'And I know you have your mobile on all the time. Nobody called. It made no difference the last time I didn't call in either.'

Sally looked at her shrewdly. 'When you were out of touch?'

'How did you know about that?' asked Iona.

'Your sister rang me asking about you.'

'For heaven's sake!' Iona was angry that Lauren hadn't told her about contacting Sally. She hadn't wanted Sally to know about her being away at all.

'I was going to check whether you'd turned up at the hospital. But I didn't. And then, of course, there was all that commotion about him responding to sounds. So it kind of went out of my head.'

'It's not important.'

'Where were you?' asked Sally.

Iona sighed. 'I needed a break,' she said. 'It was all getting to me.'

'Where did you go?'

Iona explained about the New York trip while Sally listened in amazement.

'That's why I'm so surprised about you and Frank,' she told Iona. 'You're different to me. You do impulsive things. I don't. And Frank wasn't very impulsive himself.'

'Hey, Frank couldn't afford to be impulsive,' said Iona. 'Otherwise he'd have made a mistake and the whole thing would've gone pear-shaped.'

Sally nodded thoughtfully. 'I suppose, when you think about it, it was always going to be a chance thing that got him found out.'

'That's the way of it.' Siobhán added her voice to the conversation. 'In criminal cases it's always a small thing that breaks it.'

Sally and Iona looked at her.

'Frank's not a criminal,' said Sally evenly.

'I – yes, well, not exactly.' Siobhán wished she'd kept her mouth shut.

The three of them sat in silence.

'Oh, look, don't worry about it,' said Iona. 'We didn't come here to rake over issues about Frank. We're just socialising.'

'Perhaps you should have picked other people to socialise with,' remarked Siobhán. 'After all, we only know each other because of Frank.'

'Yes. I know.' Iona's shoulders sagged. 'I guess this was incredibly stupid.'

'No,' said Sally. 'It's not really. It's easier to be together because we all know about Frank. We should just talk about someone . . . something else instead.'

'OK,' said Iona. 'No Frank talk. Let's discuss . . . I don't know . . . world peace?'

The other women chuckled.

'Well then,' said Iona, 'since world peace isn't on the agenda, have you two any other suggestions?'

'Um, no,' said Sally. 'But you must have something, Siobhán. Any juicy scandals?'

'I don't do scandals,' said Siobhán. 'I investigate crime.'

'Yeah, but there must surely be something scandalous going on,' Iona said hopefully. 'Any cabinet ministers involved in dodgy deals?'

Siobhán laughed. 'I don't know.'

'Jeez.' Iona grinned. 'I didn't realise we lived in such a crime-free state. To read the papers you'd think that there's one committed every second. D'you ever read Carl O'Connor in the evening paper? You'd swear the place was falling down around our ears if you believed him.'

'Don't get me started on O'Connor,' said Siobhán.

'Siobhán!' Sally was intrigued by the vehemence in the detective's voice. 'Why? What has he done?'

'Oh, nothing.' Siobhán wished she hadn't said anything about Carl. 'He lives in the same apartment block as Eddie, that's all. I used to see him regularly and he always had a go at me because he has a thing about the police. And me in particular.'

Sally and Iona stared at her.

'What sort of thing?'

'I don't think he's good with women in authority,' she said quickly.

'Why?' Iona asked.

'It's just the way he is,' said Siobhán. 'And then he tries to cover it up by being nice once or twice . . .'

This time Iona and Sally exchanged glances.

'How is he nice sometimes?' asked Sally.

'What's that got to do with anything?'

'Humour us,' suggested Iona. 'Tell us.'

Siobhán closed her eyes as the humiliation of being locked out of her apartment in her basque and boxers washed over her again. Along with the feeling of despair about her relationship with Eddie and where it had suddenly ended up.

'Hey, Siobhán, are you OK?' Iona sounded anxious.

Siobhán squeezed her eyes tighter, then opened them again.

'Fine,' she said.

'Look, sorry if talking about him actually upsets you,' said Iona. 'I didn't think he mattered to you.'

'He doesn't matter, of course he doesn't,' said Siobhán quickly. 'It was just . . .' She broke off. Iona and Sally felt uncomfortable as they watched her struggle to get control of herself. Neither of them had ever seen Siobhán at a loss for words, but she was clearly distressed now.

'Don't worry,' said Sally. 'We'll talk about something else.'

'No.' Siobhán swallowed hard. 'No. Actually this is something I'd quite like to talk about. I haven't . . . There's no one to talk to.'

'No problem talking to us,' said Iona. 'I mean, we're in no position to pick holes in anyone else's life.'

'You know a bit already,' said Siobhán. 'You found me the apartment.'

'Crikey!' Sally looked at Siobhán, her eyes wide. 'Were you having a bit on the side with the journo and your fiancé found out?'

Siobhán giggled weakly. 'No. I guess you both know that my boyfriend had a bit of a fling.' She looked at Iona who blushed slightly.

Siobhán knew about human nature, thought Iona. She'd guessed she wouldn't have been able to keep it to herself.

'Well,' Siobhán continued, 'It wasn't a fling exactly.' She filled in the details of Eddie's night at Peter Murtaugh's. 'I just didn't even think for a second that he'd do something like that,' she said. 'And I don't know whether he was ever going to tell me.'

Sally frowned. 'But what's this got to do with the journalist?' she asked.

'Ah well . . .' Siobhán filled them in. Iona tried to keep a straight face, but as she pictured the other girl standing in the corridor in her underwear she couldn't help but giggle. Suddenly Sally was giggling too and Siobhán, who'd been close to tears telling them, smiled faintly.

'I know it's not funny,' said Iona. 'I do really. But, well, in your bra and knickers in front of a journalist!'

'If only it had just been a simple bra and knickers combo,' said Siobhán ruefully. 'But it was a really raunchy outfit.'

'Why are men such fools?' demanded Sally. 'What is it about them that makes them be so – so – shitty?'

'I dunno.' Iona sighed. 'I didn't think Frank was shitty.'

'Of course you didn't, neither did I,' said Sally hotly. 'But the bottom line is that he was. And so was Siobhán's bloke. And so's the journalist . . .'

'Actually, I suppose he wasn't in the end,' said Siobhán.

'He made fun of you,' protested Sally.

'Yeah, but I was probably a comic figure,' admitted Siobhán wryly. 'And, well, I hate to admit it, but I guess he was kinda nice to me really. He might have made fun of me, but to be honest it wasn't malicious.'

'Even so.' Sally was still indignant.

'Maybe it's in their nature.' Iona sipped the Bacardi which the waitress had placed in front of her a few minutes earlier. 'I mean, maybe they just can't help themselves. If you read magazines and stuff they're always telling us how men are led by their dicks.'

'Iona!'

'Well, it's true,' she said hotly. 'Frank came after me because . . . sorry to say this, Sally . . . but because we were great in bed.'

'Actually, Frank and I had no problems in that department,' said Sally tightly. 'We got along very well together sexually.' Her eyes narrowed. 'He didn't say anything different, did he? He didn't say that I didn't do it for him any more?'

'Sally, I didn't know you existed. He never mentioned you. And I suppose I just assumed . . .'

'Why should you assume that?' demanded Sally. 'I'm damn well pregnant, aren't I?'

'Yes, but that's just sex. It doesn't have to be good sex,' said Iona.

'Frank and I had great sex!' cried Sally.

Siobhán and Iona shot glances at the nearby tables whose occupants had turned towards them at the sound of Sally's raised voice.

'Great sex,' she repeated more quietly. 'Always.'

Iona made a face. 'I thought it was probably because of the sex,' she said unevenly. 'I know you're pregnant, Sally, but . . . well . . . you're older than me, and I suppose . . .'

'Great,' said Sally bitterly. 'You're thinking that he shagged me once in the past year and only out of sympathy for an old hag and unfortunately knocked me up.'

'God, no. Of course not.' Iona was rattled.

'We had a great sex life, and every time he came home he made love to me, which means that he slept with me directly after sleeping with you.'

'And he slept with me directly after sleeping with you,' said Iona flatly. 'Christ. Maybe we should get ourselves checked out medically too.'

'Not on my account,' snapped Sally. 'I was monogamous in my relationship with him.'

'Yeah, well, so was I!'

'I'm glad for you both,' said Siobhán drily. 'I, too, was monogamous but it didn't do me and Eddie any good.'

'Oh, Siobhán, I'm sorry.' Iona looked at her penitently. 'You really do have something to worry about on the health side of things, and we – we're bickering over who was a better lover.'

Siobhán shrugged. 'Actually I don't have anything to worry about,' she said. 'Like I told you, Eddie and I didn't sleep together after he came back. So that's not the issue. What is the issue is whether I should even consider going back to him.'

'Thing is, Siobhán,' said Sally, 'you don't have to forgive and forget. You're only engaged to him, not married to him, so you didn't make any "till death us do part" promises. You can walk away.'

'But I don't want to walk away,' protested Siobhán. 'At least . . . in my head it was "till death us do part" already. And I thought he believed that too. We were planning to get married. It was supposed to be for ever. You can't say that it didn't matter just because we hadn't actually made it up the aisle. And even though I'm angry and feel betrayed and hurt and all that sort of stuff, I can't just forget about it even though most of me says I should.'

'I tried to walk away from the Frank situation,' said Iona. 'I didn't go to the hospital. I sat at home and cried instead.'

Sally looked uneasily at her. 'That wasn't my fault.'

'I know, I know,' said Iona. 'You did your good deed and told me I could come and see Frank after all.'

'If you're going to snipe at me all the time then I don't think there's much point to all of this,' said Sally. 'It was your idea for us to meet up and it was supposed to be a social thing, but all you've done is whinge.'

Iona sighed deeply. 'I know. I'm sorry. It's just – well, you two actually have real relationships. You're married, Sally. Siobhán was – is – engaged. I'm not anything.'

'We're supposed to be talking about other things,' said Sally firmly. 'Rehashing it over and over isn't doing us any good. Siobhán, please come up with something awful and gruesome to cheer us up – like a mad serial killer on the loose in Bray.'

Siobhán smiled faintly. 'There's an ID scam going on at the moment,' she told them. 'A gang is printing up fake driver's licences and using them as ID to get money out of people's accounts. We've had three complaints in the last two weeks.'

'How are they doing it?' asked Sally.

'Looks like they're managing to intercept post, finding out people's account numbers and then withdrawing cash.'

'You'd better watch out, Sally,' said Iona. 'You don't want people robbing your identity.'

'Oh, it's OK, I've had that done.' Sally looked at her ruefully. 'You managed it.'

'I thought you said we were talking about something else?'

'We are. It was a joke.'

'Oh.'

'I think it's the first joke I've made in weeks,' said Sally. 'So even if it was awful, I don't care.'

'Fair enough,' said Iona. 'And moving on to other things completely – that guy walking past our table is a George Clooney lookalike. Oh, and the couple behind him rent a flat in your apartment block too, Siobhán.'

'Do they?' Siobhán squinted. 'I haven't seen them before.'

'Have you seen any more of Enrique?'

'Enrique?' Sally looked bemused.

'Bloke renting the duplex in Siobhán's block. Sexy Spaniard. Invited her for drinks.'

Sally looked at Siobhán and raised an eyebrow.

'I've said hello to him once or twice but he hasn't reissued the invitation,' said Siobhán. 'But, you know, he does talk about you a bit, Iona.'

'Me?' Iona looked incredulous. 'I hardly know him.'

'Well, each time I've said hello he's asked after you.'

'Really?'

'Yes. He said you worked really hard to get him the right place.'

'I work really hard for everyone.' Iona's cheeks were tinged with pink.

'You made an impression on him anyway.' Siobhán grinned at her.

'So, Iona, you're moving on?' Sally's voice was carefully neutral.

'You're not getting away with it that easily,' said Iona, pushing the image of Brandon Williamson to the back of her mind and mentally crossing her fingers, because even if she wasn't lying to Sally, she was being economical with the truth. 'I'm certainly not moving on with Enrique,' she added. 'I suppose it's flattering if he finds me attractive, but that's it.'

'The thing is, you *can* move on,' said Sally. 'I can't.'

'Why?' asked Iona.

'There's the more and more obvious matter of my pregnancy,' said Sally. 'You can't have forgotten.'

Iona said nothing. Of course she hadn't forgotten. But Sally's pregnancy was something she was trying very hard not to think about. In all of this mess it was the fact that Sally was pregnant that upset her the most. But she didn't want Sally to know that.

'At least you have something to look forward to,' said Iona.

'You think I'm looking forward to it!' Sally stared at her in disbelief. 'I'd give anything not to be pregnant, even though before now I wanted and wanted it to happen.'

The air between the women suddenly crackled with tension. Siobhán knew for sure now that there'd been no collusion between them. The edginess of their relationship was proof of that. She watched as Iona gulped back the remainder of her drink.

'I know this is cold comfort to both of you,' she said. 'But Frank did seem to love you both. I've checked out everything to do with him that I could. There's absolutely no evidence of any other women stashed away or anything else out of the ordinary going on.'

'And we're supposed to be relieved about that?' asked Iona.

'I thought you would be, actually,' said Siobhán.

'And I am,' said Sally. 'I kept thinking and thinking that maybe there were more of us. Someone before me.'

Iona looked aghast. 'I never thought about that. I mean, I thought of someone else . . . but not before you, Sally.'

'I did. A lot,' Sally told her. 'In which case I'd have been in the exact same situation as you, only with a rebellious daughter and a baby on the way.'

'Another drink?' Iona drained her glass. 'I need alcohol.'

'Let's go inside and order some food,' suggested Sally. 'You can have more drink if you want.' She looked ruefully at Iona. 'You know, I'd love to get out-of-my-tree drunk just to wipe it all out of my head, but because of the baby I can't.'

'I don't drink much,' said Iona. 'I look after my body. But one night I drank all the wine in the house. And in New York I had Cosmopolitans. It didn't actually help.' She stood up. 'You're right. We should eat.'

They didn't talk about Frank or Eddie over their food. Iona said that she was tired of defining herself by her relationship with Frank. She was a career woman, after all. Admittedly, she felt that she could do more with her career, but she was good at what she did. Enrique had said so after all.

'You did a good job on the tenancy agreement for me,' Sally told her. 'So you are good at what you do. You deserve to think of yourself as a person other than Frank's sort-of wife.' There was no irony in her voice. Anyway, she agreed with Iona. She herself was the vice principal of a girls' school with over four hundred pupils. She was more than just the woman Frank had married.

'I'm good at my job too,' said Siobhán. 'I've broken some important cases and I've put criminals behind bars. It won't wreck my life that Eddie McIntyre behaved like a shit.'

They clinked their glasses and toasted their independent womanhood. Then Siobhán grimaced and ducked out of sight.

'What the hell are you doing?' asked Iona as the other girl kept her head below the level of the table.

'That bloke,' said Siobhán. 'The one who just walked in with the dark-haired girl. Is he within visual range?'

'D'you mean can I see him?' asked Iona. 'They've gone to the back of the restaurant. They're in a booth.'

'Oh good.' Siobhán sat up again and patted at her hair, which had fallen around her face in a cloud of fiery curls.

'Is that Eddie?' asked Sally. 'Is he out with another woman?'

'God, no,' said Siobhán. 'That was Carl O'Connor. And the woman he was with is Joely . . . McGuirk, I think her name is. She's a journo too. She works for one of the regional papers.'

'Why don't you want him to see you?' asked Iona. 'I mean, you told us about the bra and pants episode, but that's no good reason to hide.'

'I think it's a very good reason actually,' said Siobhán. 'I just don't want to talk to him, that's all. He's so fucking inquisitive. He'd start asking me about Eddie and calling me Mizz Plod, and I don't have the strength for it.'

'I'll keep an eye out for you,' said Sally, who was facing towards the back of the restaurant. 'If he comes back you can dive under the table again.'

Siobhán sighed. 'I guess that doesn't really make me seem like a woman in control of her life, does it?'

Sally and Iona exchanged glances.

'No,' they agreed in unison.

Chapter 30

Carl O'Connor liked Joely McGuirk. They'd been to college together and she was fun and feisty. After they graduated she'd headed off to work in the UK while he'd cut his teeth on the Irish papers. They'd lost touch and he'd been surprised when she contacted him after ten years, telling him that she was back in Ireland, living in the sunny south-east and working for one of the regional papers there. She'd married a Wexford man, she told him, and he'd always wanted to move back.

Carl was surprised at how many of the girls he'd gone to college with had got married and adapted their lives to fit in with their husbands. They'd all seemed totally fierce and independent when he'd known them, and yet somehow they'd ended up married after all. And he couldn't understand why someone like Joely, who'd been doing well in London, had decided to chuck it all in for a regional rag back home.

'It's about compromise,' she told him as he got on his hobby horse again. 'And quality of life.'

'Yeah, but you were going to rock the world, JoJo.'

'You know, I guess we all want to do that. But sometimes you realise that rocking the world isn't everything. Besides, my world is Michael and Robbie.'

'I can't believe you haven't divorced Michael yet,' teased Carl. 'A PR man, of all people!'

'Ah, I stay with him because of Robbie.' Joely returned his banter. 'I couldn't leave him with a four-year-old. He'd never cope. Anyway, what about you, O'Connor – anyone in your life?'

'No one special,' he told her. 'Don't have time in my life for that sort of thing. Besides, who'd put up with me?' He grinned. 'I'm still waiting to rock the world with my big story.'

'I like the column,' said Joely. 'Even if you are a bit OTT sometimes. The cops must hate you.'

He shrugged. 'Some do, some don't.'

'It's different down my way,' said Joely. 'You can't help getting on with them. Though they can be right bastards about keeping schtum. I was trying to do a story about that case in Ardallen where the wall of the Ardallen House buried the pub next door, but our local boy, Tim Shanahan, won't play ball. I know there's something going on there.'

'Like what?' asked Carl.

'Two issues,' said Joely. 'One, of course, is the whole incompetence thing as far as the builders are concerned in not securing the site properly. I've done a lot of work on that and the fact that they didn't follow the proper procedures. There are potentially huge claims against them. The owner of the bar next door is going to sue. The second is human interest. Remember the bloke who was pulled from the wreckage?'

'Only vaguely.'

'He wasn't a local, he'd just called in for a drink,' said Joely. 'Anyway, there's some story going around that he was married twice.'

'I hate to break it to you, but lots of people get married twice,' said Carl. 'Divorce has so much to answer for!'

'Clown!' Joely gave him a dig in the ribs. 'I mean, married twice without having got a divorce.'

'Really?' Carl looked more interested.

'Yes,' said Joely. 'Tim tried to palm me off on some detective in Bray who's supposed to be looking after the case, but the bitch won't return my calls.'

'What detective?'

'Siobhán Farrell,' said Joely. She noticed the look of surprise on Carl's face. 'You know her?'

'You could say that,' said Carl. 'I'll talk to her if you like.'

'You steal my story and I'll break your neck,' she threatened. 'I might not want to rock the world, but I'm sure as hell not going to let you rock it instead.'

'Don't worry,' said Carl. 'It's not really my sort of thing. But I'll try to get some info for you.'

'Thanks.'

'No problem.'

* * *

'They're heading this way again,' hissed Sally.

Siobhán swallowed the last piece of her apple pie and ducked under the table for the second time.

'You're OK,' said Iona after a couple of seconds. 'They've gone.'

'This really isn't good for my digestion,' said Siobhán as she sat upright.

'Actually, I think it's a bit of fun,' Iona told her. 'Obviously this is real detective agency stuff!'

Siobhán made a face at her. 'Let's get the bill,' she said. 'I'm in work tomorrow and I really want to get to bed at a reasonable hour.'

'And I have to get home before Jen,' said Sally.

The others nodded. Sally had already told them that Jenna was behaving as truculently as ever and that she was desperately worried about her. She'd told them of her concerns that Jenna was hanging around with a bad crowd, but that every time she tried to lay down the law Jenna simply said that at least she knew everything there was to know about the people she was with and that Sally wasn't in a position to pass judgement on her. She'd told them that Jenna resented being picked up from Gerry Cullinan's house by Siobhán and that she didn't seem to trust her mother any more. And, she'd said, Jenna was still utterly disgusted by the idea of the baby.

Both Iona and Siobhán had assured her that Jenna would get over it while admitting that they had no idea about *how* she'd get over it. And although Iona had been vehement in her insistence that Jenna seemed a sensible girl at heart, she felt herself freeze up almost as soon as she uttered the words. Jenna was Frank's daughter. A part of him. Something precious that she had wanted from Frank and now would never have. She wished fervently that her roller-coaster of emotions would settle down. But she really hadn't a clue when, or if, that would ever happen.

'Oh, by the way, Iona . . .' Sally said as she put her share of the bill on the saucer which the waitress had placed in front of them. 'I meant to say to you that I'm calling in to see Frank's accountant about the business. He says that I have to do something about it. He thinks he has a buyer for it.'

Iona looked at her warily. 'You want to sell it?'

'I don't know,' said Sally. 'But it's not like Frank can deal with it. If I don't do something it'll fold, won't it? So maybe if there's a buyer, better to sell it.'

'I really don't want to appear picky or anything,' said Iona, 'but I did a bit of work for Frank from time to time. Records and stuff like that. It's a good business. It would be a shame to let it go.'

'Without Frank it's definitely going to go,' said Sally.

Iona nodded. 'Well, look – let me know what your guy says,' she suggested. 'I could . . .' She hesitated. 'My brother-in-law is an accountant. I could ask him to give a second opinion.'

Sally looked at her curiously. 'Don't you trust our guy?'

'I . . .' Iona was uneasy.

'What?'

'It's just that Frank talked about getting rid of him,' she said finally. 'So I'd like someone else to run over the figures first.'

'OK,' said Sally. 'Thanks.' She winced suddenly.

'You all right?' asked Siobhán.

She nodded. 'Heartburn. I used to really suffer with it with Jenna. I'd forgotten. I used to swig back bottles of bloody antacid.'

'You should try papaya juice,' Iona told her. 'Much better for you and it really works.'

'Maybe.' Sally stood up and burped. 'Oh God, sorry.'

Iona giggled and Siobhán smiled at her. And then Siobhán's expression changed to one of dismay.

'Hello, Siobhán.' Carl O'Connor's voice was both surprised and cheerful. 'Fancy seeing you here.' He frowned. 'In fact, strange seeing you here, because I was here earlier and didn't spot you at all.'

'Didn't you?'

'Nope.'

'Not quite such an observant journalist after all,' she said.

'Did you spot me?'

'I know it'll break your heart to hear this,' she said, 'but I don't spend my time looking out for you.'

'It does break my heart,' he said. 'But I'll do my best to live with it.' He glanced at Sally and Iona. 'Going to introduce me?'

'I'm off-duty. I'm with friends,' said Siobhán. The last thing she wanted to do was introduce Carl to women whom she was sure he'd regard as a great potential story. It didn't matter that sometimes she thought he wasn't as bad as his profession might make him out to be. She wanted to protect Sally and Iona.

'Are you out for the night or can I give you a lift home?' he said. He frowned suddenly. 'Not that I've seen you there much lately. Social life on fire, is it?'

Siobhán shrugged noncommittally. 'Thanks for the offer, but we're . . . um . . . we're heading off somewhere else now.'

'Have a great evening,' he told her.

They stood looking at each other for a moment.

'Did you come back for anything in particular?' she asked eventually.

'Huh?'

'You said you were here earlier. You've obviously returned.'

'Oh, yes,' he said. 'I left a notebook at my table.'

'Right,' said Siobhán. 'We won't delay you. Nice to have seen you.' And with Sally and Iona in tow she swept out of the restaurant.

Carl O'Connor retrieved his notebook and watched the three women leave. But it was Siobhán Farrell he was thinking about. Until recently he'd never really thought much about her at all, other than the fact that she was a cop and on principle he was suspicious of the motivation of anyone who joined the police force. But now he felt differently. Ever since she'd been locked out of her apartment he'd seen her in a completely different light. (Well, of course, that was only natural, given the outfit she'd been wearing!) But it wasn't just her body that had made an impression on him. It was everything about her. He'd enjoyed talking to her, listening to the passion in her voice when she talked about victims of crime. She wasn't the heartless bitch he'd imagined. She was actually rather nice. It was a pity that she disliked him so much. He couldn't help thinking that if only the circumstances were different . . . but then how could they be? She was engaged, wasn't she? And she was a cop, no matter what.

He shook his head. He was being stupid. He couldn't afford to have feelings for Siobhán. He *didn't* have feelings for Siobhán. Not beyond lust, anyway. Obviously it was perfectly acceptable to have lustful feelings for her when he knew just how gorgeous she really was. He needed to put her out of his mind. He had better things to do than think about Siobhán Farrell. But then he suddenly wondered why he'd seen so little of her lately. Now that he thought about it, he hadn't noticed her in the apartment block in ages. He'd seen that irritating fiancé of hers, of course, self-obsessed tosser! Carl had spoken to Eddie once or twice but had always found him pompous and overbearing. He'd wanted to punch him when he'd knocked at the apartment door to collect Siobhán that evening she'd been locked out of their own place.

And then he remembered that he'd seen her leave the apartment block with a suitcase. He'd thought at the time that she was just going away for a few days, but maybe he'd been wrong. Had she left Eddie? That'd be no great loss.

He couldn't contact her, though. He wasn't interested in having a relationship with a detective. Not that sort of relationship anyway! But there was always the story that Joely wanted checked out. He'd promised Joely that he'd try to get information on it. In which case he was obliged to get in touch with Siobhán. For work reasons only, of course.

The house was in darkness when Sally returned. She'd expected it because Jenna had told her that she was going to a party. Sally had asked whether she was meeting Sam there and Jenna had looked at her witheringly and told her that Sam wasn't going to the party, that her friend (and she'd sniggered as she said the word) was too wet to go. Sally had wanted to know what sort of a party it was that Sam wouldn't go, and Jenna had said that Sam just didn't fit in with the crowd any more, that she was no fun. It was an eighteenth birthday party, Jenna said, to be held in one of the bars in town. And Sally had worried about it but hadn't said that Jenna couldn't go, because she didn't think that would help matters. But she'd reminded Jenna that she was too young to drink in bars and she'd also insisted that her daughter keep her mobile switched on and that she was home, as usual for the weekend, at midnight.

She was partly relieved when Jenna had nodded distantly at her. Since Siobhán Farrell had brought her home from Gerry's, Jenna had actually been extremely dependable as far as coming home on time was concerned. So Sally wasn't as worried as she could have been about letting her go to parties. But she *was* worried, ever since her conversation with Marsha, about the kind of people her daughter was socialising with at those parties.

And yet . . . could they be any worse than Frank?

That was what it came down to in the end, wasn't it? That Sally couldn't make any judgements on Jenna's choices because her own had been so spectacularly bad.

She put the kettle on and made herself a cup of tea. It was eleven o'clock. She hoped that Jenna would continue to be dependable.

Iona's house was in darkness too. When she got in she switched on all the lights because she hated the dark. She looked at the children corner in the living room with its photos of Gavin and Charlotte and she thought of Sally Harper and her heartburn and she felt her stomach knot with envy. She didn't want to be envious of Sally. There was so much of Sally's life that she didn't need to be envious about. But Sally was pregnant. And Sally had Jenna. And Iona knew that she could have put up with the idea of having a troublesome teenage daughter in seventeen years' time if only she was pregnant now.

She sat down on the leather sofa and hit the remote so that the TV flickered into life. She changed the channel until it showed Sky Sports. She had no interest in Sky Sports but Frank had loved watching it. Footie, obviously. But golf too. And athletics. Just about anything really. She stared at the screen, not knowing who was playing in the football match that was being shown or what they were playing for. She wished that Frank was with her again. She wondered why she was wishing this when at the same time she was telling herself that she had to move on with her life, but right now she wanted it back the way it had been. And if that meant sharing Frank with Sally . . . A tear trickled down her cheek. She couldn't share Frank with Sally. Not now. Not knowing her. She couldn't ever have things back the way they were. There was no way of turning back time.

There was a faint glow coming from the bathroom, but that was because Siobhán had accidentally left the light on the bathroom cabinet switched on when she'd done her make-up earlier. She was used to coming home in the dark, either to an empty apartment or to one in which Eddie was already soundly asleep, forcing her to tiptoe around as quietly as possible. Eddie told her that she should be good at tiptoeing around the apartment – what about all those stakeouts she went on when she had to be super-quiet? She'd punch him gently on the arm when he said that and remind him (though he didn't need reminding) that she'd only been on a couple of stakeouts where she'd needed to be quiet and that it wouldn't really matter whether she clattered around the apartment because Eddie, when he was asleep, was always dead to the world.

What was he doing now? she wondered. Was he thinking about her? Was he hoping that she was thinking about him? Was he wondering whether she was going to forgive him and come on home?

She walked out on to the balcony of the apartment and stared across the dark water of the harbour. Maybe he wasn't wondering any such thing, of course. Maybe he was finding comfort with somebody else. She closed her eyes. Was this how it would always be? she asked herself. Wondering. Worrying. Not trusting him.

'Damn you,' she muttered under her breath. 'Damn you, damn you, damn you.'

Chapter 31

The bar was noisy and crowded and Jenna could feel a trickle of perspiration slide down her back as she talked (though shouted was really the word, because the music was blaring from a speaker just above her head) to Jerome Knightly, whose birthday it was. Jenna didn't really know Jerome very well. Neither did Gerry, though they both played rugby for the same club.

'I love your outfit!' Jerome smiled drunkenly at her and she could smell the beer on his breath.

'Thank you,' she said. Her eyes flickered down towards the short black dress which she was wearing with knee-high pink boots. The colour of the boots matched her new underwear, and the lacy pink bra peeked out over the low-cut neckline of the dress. She knew her look was great, but the boots were growing more hot and uncomfortable as the night wore on and she couldn't help thinking that shoes would have been a better, if less fashionable, option.

'Any time you get fed up with Cullinan, give me a shout,' Jerome said as he stumbled in her direction. She put out a hand to steady him and he grinned in thanks. She could see that his eyes were bloodshot and unfocused.

She was feeling a little unfocused herself. Despite her promises to her mother, she'd had a few alcopops and, although she hadn't noticed it at first, she realised that they were making her feel slightly disconnected from everything going on around her. But disconnected in an OK sort of way. Not stupid. Just happy. She could understand why people got drunk. It made you feel as though there was nothing so terrible in the world, she thought fuzzily. It made you feel as though you could cope with things. Even things like your mother being as big as an elephant and your father being a shit.

Jerome Knightly stumbled again and, quite suddenly, puked all over her bright-pink boots.

'Oh, you dickhead!' she screeched. 'My lovely boots.'

Jerome sank to his knees and puked again. There was a flurry around the bar area, and before she knew what was happening, two burly security guards had come over and Jenna, Jerome and a group of party revellers were ejected on to the pavement outside the bar.

'Bastards!' cried Jerome, who had recovered remarkably quickly. 'Fascist bastards!'

Jenna looked around for Gerry, but he hadn't been thrown out of the pub with the rest of them. She couldn't remember exactly where he'd been when Jerome had done his chucking-up act. She wrinkled up her nose at the smell now emanating from her boots.

'You've ruined them, you cretin,' she snapped.

'Ah, come on, love. Don't be like that.' Jerome tried to put his arm around her. 'It'll be OK. You can wash it off.'

'Ugh.' She shuddered.

'Kiss and make up?' he suggested, this time managing to drape his arm across her shoulders.

'You've got to be joking!' she cried. 'Let go of me!'

'Come on,' he said. 'We were having fun earlier. You and me. Birthday boy. Birthday girl.'

'It's not my birthday,' she said hurriedly. 'And you're drunk.'

'It's the weekend. Of course I'm drunk,' he said. 'Everyone's drunk! Hey, y'all, let's go back to Jenna's place.'

'You can't come back to my place,' she said, horrified. 'My mum would have a fit.'

The group laughed.

'Don't think the vice principal would take too kindly to seeing us,' asked Aline Keogh, who'd been thrown out too. 'I get the feeling she doesn't entirely approve of me.'

'You could come back if she wasn't home,' said Jenna hastily. 'But—'

'Teacher's pet,' said Aline.

The group laughed again. Jenna felt her eyes well up with tears.

'Where's your boyfriend?' asked Cindy Ryan, Aline's best friend. 'Dumped you at last, has he?'

Jenna looked around, hoping that Gerry had come out of the bar. But he was nowhere to be seen.

'You think that being Gerry Cullinan's girlfriend gives you a bit of cred?' Cindy asked. 'As if. He's only with you because you're an easy ride.'

Jenna said nothing and the other girls giggled.

'Easy-peasy,' said Aline. 'That's what he said getting into your knickers was.'

Jenna felt her heart sink into her ruined boots. 'Fuck off,' she said.

'It's true,' said Aline. 'I was going out with him before you. But I wouldn't put out for him. That's why he dumped me.'

'That's not true,' said Jenna shakily. 'He loves me.'

The girls cackled with laughter.

'He does.'

'Yeah, right,' said Cindy. 'That's why his hand was up Lorraine Brady's skirt, is it?'

'Shut up, you liar!' cried Jenna.

'Make me.'

'I will.'

'Yeah! Go on then. Teacher's pet!'

Jenna lashed out at the other girl and caught her across the face.

'You cow!' Cindy held her hand to her cheek, which had been grazed by Jenna's birthstone ring. 'You've ruined my face, you bitch!'

'Oh! I thought I'd improved it.'

'Go on, ya' good thing!' The others had crowded around the two girls now and were urging them on.

'Give it to her, Cindy!' called a voice.

Jenna didn't want to hang around. But there was nowhere to go. Cindy lunged at her and grabbed a handful of Jenna's dark hair.

'Let go, you wagon!' Jenna felt the tears sting her eyes.

'Make me.'

'I will fucking make you!' Jenna kicked at her with her vomit-stained boots and, much to her surprise, connected with Cindy just below the knee. The girl gave a howl of pain and sank to the ground.

'You've broken her leg!' cried Aline.

'No I haven't,' retorted Jenna. 'If I'd broken her leg she'd be in a damn sight more pain than she is now.' She was panting slightly and her hair was dishevelled. 'She's a stupid cow and she deserves to have her leg—'

'OK, what's going on here?'

Jenna recognised the authority in the voice and her heart sank again. It sank even further when she looked up and, through her bleary vision, recognised the policeman who'd come to the house with that smug detective the night of her father's accident. Cathal someone-or-other. She groaned. She was getting tired of meeting people from Bray garda station.

'That bitch was trying to kill Cindy,' cried Aline. 'She should be locked up.'

Jenna looked around desperately for a way to escape. Or for Gerry to come and rescue her. Then, horrified, she realised that Gerry was standing watching them, a look of disgust on his face.

'I could take you all down the police station for breaching the peace,' said Cathal. 'It's late and you're creating a nuisance.'

'She's the nuisance,' Cindy snarled. 'And I might charge her for assault. Look what she did to my face!' She pointed to her grazed cheek.

Cathal looked at Cindy and then at Jenna. His eyes narrowed as he recognised her. It had taken him a moment or two to realise who she was, because she looked very different from the girl he'd met before. Tonight, with her face heavily made up, wearing the short dress and the ruined pink boots, she looked at least five years older than the anxious young girl he'd driven to Ardallen a couple of months earlier.

'Does your mother know where you are, young lady?' he asked her.

'Yes,' replied Jenna.

'Does she know what you're up to?'

'I'm not up to anything,' said Jenna sullenly. 'She started it.'

'I did not! I—'

'OK, OK, enough is enough,' said Cathal. 'Let's break this up. It's time you all went home.'

The group began to disperse, Cindy and Aline continuing to mutter about Jenna.

'You live on the other side of town, don't you?' said Cathal.

Jenna nodded.

'Do you want a lift home?'

'Are you joking?' she cried. 'My mother would have a fit if she saw a police car outside the door again.'

'To the end of the road,' said Cathal. 'She doesn't have to see the car.'

'I don't care,' said Jenna. 'I can look after myself. My boyfriend . . .' She turned towards Gerry, who was still watching them silently.

'Jenna – it's not that I don't care for you, because I do,' he said. 'But – you were fighting in the street! I really don't think—'

'Because of what they said!' she cried. 'They said you were only going out with me because I let you sleep with me. And they said that you had your hand up Lorraine's skirt!' She broke off as she saw the expression on Gerry's face. And on the face of Cathal Rothery. 'Oh for God's sake,' she snapped, looking from one to the other. 'You're all the bloody same. He sleeps with me, he has someone else on the side, he's a great guy. I sleep with him and I'm—'

'Jenna, I really think it's better if we don't see each other any more,' said Gerry abruptly. 'If you think for one minute that's the sort of bloke I am, then you don't know me at all. And I don't know you either.'

'Yeah, well, that's a good thing.' But her voice cracked as he turned and walked away.

'Sure you don't want that lift home?' asked Cathal Rothery gently.

Jenna swallowed hard. It was three miles to her house and she didn't want to walk it in the boots. But the garda had heard everything. He probably thought she was nothing more than a tramp.

'Someone was sick on me,' she said tiredly. 'I smell.'

'There've been plenty of people in the car who have been a hell of a lot worse,' said Cathal. 'Come on. Hop in.'

His colleague, who'd been standing in support while Cathal dealt with the disturbance, opened the car door. Jenna got inside.

What's happened to me? she asked herself as the car turned in the direction of her house. I used to be an ordinary person. Now I'm in a car with a cop for the third time this year. How the hell has that happened? She closed her eyes as a tear rolled gently down her face.

Cathal was as good as his word and dropped her at the end of the road.

'You OK?' he asked.

'Fine,' she sniffed.

'Look, I know you don't want to hear it from me,' he said, 'but you're better off out of that crowd. Late-night drinking and brawling . . . I know it's not popular to say that it's cheap and common, but honestly, Jenna, there are better things to do with your life.'

'I know that,' she snapped. 'I don't need a lecture from you.'

'Siobhán told me that you'd been in a bit of bother before,' he said.

'Gossiping bitch,' said Jenna. 'All that happened was that my mother got into a state because I was late home and she rang the police! I'm practically an adult, for heaven's sake, and that's what she does, ring the police! So that interfering detective cow found out where I was and brought me home. Can you imagine how embarrassing that was? It's no wonder Gerry doesn't love me any more.'

'It's been a hard time for you and your mum,' said Cathal. 'She was probably just extra anxious about you.'

'She'd have been better off being anxious about my dad, wouldn't she?'

'No news on him?'

'I used to love him,' said Jenna. 'I thought he loved me too. But it's all bollocks, isn't it? Gerry pretended to love me. Dad pretended to love me.'

'I'm sure your dad does love you,' said Cathal.

'Yeah, right.' Jenna got out of the car. She looked ruefully at Cathal from her mascara-streaked eyes. 'Thanks for the lift.'

'You're welcome,' he said. 'But – I have to tell you this, Jenna – if you're involved in any more bust-ups outside pubs, I won't be just running you home. I'll be taking you down to the station.'

She looked at him warily.

'Public order is a big issue these days,' he said. 'Binge drinking and causing trouble afterwards is something that people are getting fed up with. And we have to deal with it.'

'Yeah, right.'

'Take care of yourself,' he said.

She smiled suddenly, transforming herself from the sullen teenager into someone entirely different. 'I'll do my best.'

'Good night.'

She turned on to her road and walked the few yards to the house. When she got to the front door she unzipped the pink boots and slid them off. The whiff of vomit was disgusting. She knew that no matter how much effort she put into cleaning them, she'd never be able to wear them again. So she dropped them into the dustbin before opening the front door and letting herself into the house.

She tiptoed into the kitchen, walking extra carefully so that she didn't bang into anything that would make a noise and wake up Sally. She filled the kettle with water and switched it on, then took a tea bag from the tin on the worktop and dropped it into the big red mug which had always been her special one. When the kettle boiled she made the tea and leaned against the edge of the kitchen table while she sipped it slowly.

Cathal Rothery might be right about Aline and Cindy and that gang. But until tonight they'd been easier people to be with than Sam and Kelly and her other friends. Aline and Cindy hadn't asked questions about her father or her mother. They didn't care. They knew, of course, that there was some hassle at home, but then Jenna knew that Aline's parents were divorced and that Cindy had a kid of her own. And it wasn't that having divorced parents was any big deal these days, or even that having a kid at seventeen was much of an issue, but at least they had something other than a happily married set of parents in the background. What the hell could Sam or Kelly, both of whom had two loving parents (or at least parents who lived together in the family home!), as well as a selection of siblings, well, what the hell could they know about what she was going through? They were probably gossiping about her at every available opportunity. Laughing that it had all gone so wrong for Jenna Harper, whose mother was the vice principal and who had it all so easy.

And now what was she? Jenna Harper who was in a kind of one-parent family right now and whose mother was going to have a baby even though her dad wasn't around. It was all wrong. It wasn't their lives. It wasn't fair. Jenna wiped another tear away from her eyes and dumped the remainder of her tea in the sink.

Then she climbed the stairs and fell, fully clothed, into bed.

Frank could hear the sound of voices in the distance. At first he thought it was Marion again, but he knew that Marion had gone. And since Marion there'd been Sally, who'd given him the beautiful baby daughter. He could feel his heart constrict with love for his baby daughter who, of course, wasn't a baby any more but a young girl on the threshold of becoming an adult. He enjoyed her company. She was fun to be with and hadn't yet turned coquettish and silly like so many of them did around her age. She would talk to him about cars and motorbikes and blokeish stuff and that made him proud to have her as a daughter. Maybe, then, it was Jenna he could hear? But the voice was more mature than Jenna's. And it was saying something about blood sugar and respiration . . . something that he didn't understand.

He tried to move but he couldn't. He felt as though there was a weight pressing down on his body, holding him in position. He thought about lifting his arm but he couldn't quite make the thoughts and the actions connect. It was a horrible feeling. It frightened him. He could hear rhythmic sounds too. Of monitors. Like in a hospital. Which would make sense, wouldn't it, if someone was talking about respiration? So maybe he was in hospital. That would explain not being able to move. Something had happened and he was in hospital and he couldn't move. Was he paralysed? He felt panicked at the thought. Had he crashed? Fallen? Had he been struck down by a mystery virus?

He tried to think about what he'd been doing before being here. But he couldn't. His mind was like a bowl of porridge, thick and gloopy, and he couldn't seem to fix on anything definite. Well, Sally and Jenna were definite, of course. He remembered saying goodbye to them that morning. Or maybe it had been the previous morning? He couldn't quite remember. Sally had said something about cutting the lawn. He could picture that, all right. The grass suddenly spurting higher because of the spring weather and Sally wanting it to look good.

His head hurt. If something had happened and he was in hospital, then maybe, just for a while, he'd give in to it. Let himself drift. They'd probably given him drugs to make him sleepy, which was why he couldn't remember anything. Maybe if he just let them work he'd feel better when he woke up the next time. He sighed deeply and let himself fall into the darkness again.

Chapter 32

Siobhán sat at her desk and thought about the briefing they'd just been given on the fake ID scam. The feeling was that although the initial withdrawals from people's accounts had happened in Bray, the centre of operations was probably somewhere outside the area. In the last week new complaints had come in from the towns of Killiney and Glenageary, still on the east coast but heading closer to Dublin city itself. She'd interviewed the people concerned in her area, and the banks, and she was confident that even if Bray didn't nab the people responsible they would eventually get caught. It was only a matter of time. But of course that was of little comfort to someone who'd just discovered that a complete stranger had managed to empty his or her current account.

They reckoned there were four people involved, two women and two men. The CCTV in the banks had caught pictures of them, but they'd all been wearing baseball caps pulled low over their eyes so that it was difficult to get a clear view of them. Still, in one case they'd managed to get a glimpse of one of the women, and Siobhán was confident that she'd be sighted again soon enough. This was a case that would break, she knew it.

The phone rang and she reached out to answer it.

'Hello, Mizz Plod.'

She jerked upright in her chair.

'Carl?' She frowned.

'I wanted to ask you something.'

'What?'

'A colleague of mine has been trying to get hold of you, but you've been avoiding her calls.' He chuckled. 'Glad you took mine.'

'I didn't know it was going to be you,' she pointed out. Then her voice mellowed. 'What do you want?'

'Ardallen,' he said. 'Man crushed under falling building. Still in hospital, I believe. Married to two women.'

Siobhán said nothing.

'Is that a no comment?' asked Carl.

'I'm just wondering what you want,' she said.

'It's an interesting story,' said Carl. 'JoJo, my colleague, she'd do a sensitive piece about it.'

'I can't imagine any of your colleagues being sensitive,' said Siobhán drily.

'You have such a low opinion of us.' Carl laughed. 'Come on, Mizz Plod, it's human interest.'

'Not this time, really,' said Siobhán.

Carl was acutely aware of her tone. 'There is something?'

Siobhán chewed the end of her biro.

'C'mon, Mizz P. Why don't you talk to JoJo? She works on one of the local papers around there. There is a lot of talk going on in the town about the whole incident. Maybe the truth is less sensational than anything they might come up with.'

'You know, you're always going on at me about catching real criminals,' she said mildly. 'Why don't you go and get a real story?'

'You're very sensitive about this,' said Carl. 'Is there something more to it? Is he linked to serious crime or something? Was the building collapse not an accident?'

'Crikey, O'Connor, I don't know why you're a journalist and not a fiction writer,' Siobhán told him. 'Your imagination is running at about a thousand per cent there.'

'OK, OK. But if I find something out, or if JoJo does, will you talk then?'

'There's nothing important to find out,' she said. 'I honestly don't think it's a story you want to run with.'

'So, what's new with you?' He knew perfectly well that there was something to the story but that she wasn't going to tell him anything about it, so he changed the subject. 'You were looking well the other night, out with the girls.'

She said nothing.

'Any chance we could meet up and talk about the Ardallen case?'

'You never give up, do you?'

'Nope,' he said cheerfully.

'Well, there's no actual chance,' she said calmly. 'But if there's anything really interesting happening about anything at all, I'll be sure to let you know.'

'Oh really?'

'Yes, really,' she said. 'Now I've got to go and make a few arrests.'

'Have fun,' said Carl and hung up.

Siobhán replaced the receiver and stared into space for a few moments. Then she picked it up and dialled a number.

'This is Eddie McIntyre,' said the voice. 'Leave a message.'

'Call me,' she said, and hung up.

Iona was showing yet another apartment in the Waterside building, this time on the ground floor and without the spectacular views of either Siobhán Farrell's small apartment or Enrique Martinez's much bigger one. But, once again, the prospective tenants liked the complex and told Iona that they were interested in renting there. They were, they said, going to see another apartment first, but unless it was absolutely fantastic they'd be back to her about this one.

She gave them her card and told them to call, reminding them that there was a lot of interest in Waterside and suggesting that the apartment would certainly be gone by the end of the week.

As she unlocked her lime-green Beetle, she saw the last couple who'd rented from her hurrying back into the block. And, following close behind them, Enrique Martinez striding up the pedestrian pathway. He caught sight of her and waved. She waved back.

'Everything going all right?' she asked as he veered from the path and came towards her.

'Fine,' he said. 'I like it here. I like being able to see the sea. I'm used to it. In Barcelona my apartment is near the sea. When I worked in London I always felt trapped by the buildings. This is perfect.'

'Good,' she said.

They stood in silence for a moment. Then Iona's stomach rumbled loudly.

'Oh God, excuse me!' She blushed. 'I skipped lunch today.'

'That's not good,' said Enrique sternly.

'I was busy.'

'Why don't you join me for something to eat?' asked Enrique. 'I was just about to have some food.' He grinned. 'At home I eat late, but here it's different.'

Moving on, she thought, like Sally thinks. And Siobhán thinks this bloke is attracted to me. But I'm not ready. Brandon was different. New York was different. This is back home and it just isn't realistic.

'No, no, it's fine, honestly,' she said.

'I have some really nice Serrano ham in the apartment,' he told her. 'But if you're worried about being alone with me . . .' his eyes twinkled, 'well, let's go to the restaurant on the seafront. It's really good.'

'I know,' said Iona. 'I was there very recently. But—' Her stomach rumbled again.

'I can't take no for an answer!' Enrique's voice was firm. 'You are really hungry.'

'Enrique—'

'Oh, come on.' He grinned. 'For the last few weeks all I've done is eat with boring businessmen. And boring businesswomen. I'd like to eat for fun. Also, I want to thank you for finding the right place for me. I know I was a difficult client.'

She was starving. But she couldn't go to a restaurant with Enrique. It just wouldn't be right. He was looking at her enquiringly.

He was a client, though. It was a business thing after all. She knew that she wasn't interested in him, not in any kind of flirty way. How could she be at the moment, when the man she loved (even if he had messed up her life) was still critically ill in hospital? If Frank had been fine and well she would've just told this guy that she was married and that she wasn't available to go to dinner. And if he implied that it was just a casual dinner to say thanks for finding the apartment, well then, because she really was hungry, she might agree and it would all be perfectly above board. That was the problem, she realised. Having a meal with Enrique while Frank couldn't know anything about it seemed somehow sly and underhand. Cheating on him when he wasn't able to do anything. Although hardly as bad as how he'd cheated on her. The thought sneaked into the back of her mind and then she thought of Brandon again. Cheating on Frank in a different time zone. Or not, as it turned out.

She hadn't slept with him in the end. She knew she would have been doing it for all the wrong reasons. He'd been remarkably understanding, even though she knew that he'd been annoyed too. He'd told her that he hoped she'd manage to deal with her issues and that he'd enjoyed her company. And then he'd gone, and despite everything, she had actually slept alone.

'Just a quick bit to eat,' said Enrique easily. 'I have to do some more work this evening anyway so I can't stay out long.'

Having something to eat when she truly was hungry wasn't wrong, she told herself. She was just making it sound wrong because she was still feeling guilty about Brandon and because it seemed wrong to have fun when Frank was ill. Yet she hadn't felt like this about going out with Siobhán and Sally. It was because Enrique was a good-looking bloke. That didn't matter to her, though. Her heart was well hardened against good-looking blokes.

'OK,' she said eventually. 'I suppose – yes, all right. Thanks.'

'Excellent!'

She fell into step beside him and they walked out of the gardens and down towards the seafront.

Because the school holidays had begun, Sally was able to go to the hospital during the afternoon. Rather to her surprise, Jenna had decided to accompany her and was now sitting on the opposite side of the bed, reading one of the Ian Fleming novels which Iona had left at the hospital. She wasn't reading it aloud but to herself, her dark head bent over the book, engrossed in it.

Sally had read the Letters to the Editor and Weather Eye to Frank and now she was skimming through the rest of the paper, also reading to herself. At the same time she was thinking about her meeting with Frank's accountant and his analysis of the business. Basically Richard was saying that they needed to sell it and take what money they could out of it before all of Frank's clients defected somewhere else. Sally supposed that he had a point, but at the same time felt bad about the idea of selling a business into which Frank had poured so much of his time and effort. However, she could see what Richard meant. Unless someone was co-ordinating the maintenance of the installations on a regular basis (and she couldn't expect Richard himself and Pete Maguire, Frank's contractual engineer, to do it for ever), and unless there was someone actively looking for new business, then it would all go wrong. Whatever Frank would have hoped and dreamed for, the company folding because he was incapacitated would not have been on the agenda. He'd prefer her to sell it. She knew he would.

But she was worried about what Iona had said about Richard too. That Frank had been thinking of getting rid of him. As far as Sally knew, Richard had been Frank's accountant ever since he'd set up the company. She'd never heard her husband say a bad word about him. But then, she admitted ruefully to herself, she'd never really listened when he talked about the company. And that was because she'd been so set against the idea in the first place.

Her teeth worried against her lower lip as she thought about it. She remembered Frank's enthusiasm and her own misgivings. She remembered how angry she'd felt about the notion of selling their house and moving further from the city so that Frank could have capital to invest. She remembered accusing him of pursuing a stupid dream when he'd already been offered such a good position in the recently taken-over company. And she remembered that this had been the time when their marriage had run through its really rocky patch so that, in the end, perhaps it wasn't entirely surprising he'd found someone new to confide in. And cheat on her with. She shook her head fiercely. She wasn't going to go down the road of anger again. There wasn't any point right now.

From what Sally could tell, though, Iona knew a lot more about Frank's company. She was more interested in the outcome too. Maybe it was because she worked in the whole area of developing business and clients, whereas Sally was caught up in developing people. She looked at the folder on the locker beside her. She would give it to Iona, she decided, and let her show it to her brother-in-law and see what they had to say about it all. And she'd trust them to give her the right information. She massaged her temples. It seemed extraordinary to her to think that she now trusted Iona more than a professional accountant. But she did.

Her gaze flickered across the room to Jenna, who had closed the Ian Fleming book and was now staring into space.

'Good?' asked Sally.

'Huh?'

'The book.'

Jenna glanced down at the copy of *Dr No*.

'It's OK,' she said. 'Old-fashioned. Not like I thought it would be at all. But it's interesting.'

Sally smiled. This was the most information Jenna had volunteered to her in ages.

'Maybe you'd like to read him something,' she suggested.

'Iona's already read this one to him,' said Jenna.

'Not James Bond,' said Sally. 'Something else altogether.'

'Not really.' Jenna shrugged. 'You're giving him all the newspaper stuff, she's doing the books . . .'

'You can just talk to him,' said Sally.

'I know,' Jenna said. 'But I don't want to.'

'Why not?'

'I've nothing to say to him.'

'Jenna . . . he may not be perfect, but he's your dad.'

'If I was a really horrible person, would you say it didn't matter, I was your daughter?' she asked.

Sally spoke carefully. 'I can't say that I'd tell you nothing mattered. But I'd still love you. Mothers do, with their children. No matter what.'

'Say if – oh, I dunno – if I had an affair with a married man. What would you say then?'

'All these things depend on circumstances,' Sally told her. 'I doubt that I'd be very happy, but I'd listen to your point of view.'

'And if I got pregnant?'

Sally's heart almost stopped. She could see that Jenna's face was slightly flushed and that there was an anxious look in her eyes. Dear God, she thought. Not Jenna. Please. I really don't think I could cope with that right now.

'I still wouldn't be very happy,' she said as neutrally as she could. 'But I would, of course, still love you.'

'How are you feeling?' asked Jenna.

'Me? I'm fine.'

'Because you're getting quite fat now, aren't you?'

'Big,' amended Sally. 'Not fat.'

'Whatever. Is it horrible?'

'It's kind of weird,' Sally said. 'Your body is doing something that you can't control and it's a little bit freaky. But then you feel the baby move and it's magic.'

'Has . . . has this baby started to move?'

Sally nodded.

'Ugh.'

'It's not so bad,' she told Jenna. 'It's actually quite comforting once you get used to it.'

'Did I move?'

'Of course.'

'What did Dad say when you told him you were pregnant with me?' asked Jenna.

'He was delighted,' said Sally immediately. 'He always wanted lots of children. It didn't work out like that, but that's what he wanted.'

'I know. And now, finally, there's going to be another one. Only he might never know about it.'

'He'll know,' said Sally.

'Do you still love him?' asked Jenna.

Sally considered her answer before she spoke. 'Maybe it's the same as how I feel about you,' she said. 'I get angry with you but I don't stop loving you. I don't agree with some things you do but I don't stop loving you. Sometimes I don't even like you! But I don't stop loving you.'

'So you haven't stopped loving Dad?'

'No.'

'Can I be on my own with him for a while now?'

'Sure you can.' Sally picked up her bag and walked out of the room.

Jenna pulled her chair closer to the bed.

'I told you before that I hated you,' she said. 'And I do. But it's like what Mum says. I hate you but then when I see you I still love you. It's wrecking my head.'

She sighed. 'The bloke I told you about. Gerry. He's broken up with me because I got into a fight with some girls outside a pub.' She giggled. 'It was crazy, we were pulling each other's hair and everything. If you can hear what I'm saying I know you'll be freaked out, but I couldn't help myself. It didn't seem real. Gerry wasn't pleased about it so he dumped me. There and then, Dad. On the pavement. In front of the cops. I forgot to tell you that – they turned up because of the fight. It was totally weird. One of them was the guy who told us about you. He drove me home and made me promise to be a good little girl in future.' She leaned her head against the bedspread. 'Thing is, I don't know that I want to be any more. And that's because of you. Everything's because of you. Sam and Kelly kept trying to be nice to me but I hated it. I didn't want them to look at me as though I needed special treatment because my dad hitched up with a younger model. At least if you'd got divorced we could talk about it. People do get divorced. But what you did was so awful that I just can't. So I made friends with the others. Only they're not really my type of person either. I guess I've realised that I don't really like the pub scene, even though getting pissed was sort of fun. But not when it ends up in fighting and people getting sick over boots that cost a fortune. I used to know what I wanted, Dad. But now . . .'

She stopped and looked at him. Despite the fact that he now occasionally moved his head, he was immobile.

'I do love you, Dad,' she said shakily. 'I hate you and I love you and life is so messy . . . I never thought it would be this messy.' She reached out and took his hand. She squeezed his fingers. And then she sat completely still. Because, although his grasp was very weak, she was sure that he'd squeezed her fingers in return.

There were two of them, Frank remembered now. Sally and Iona. He loved them both. He loved Sally because she was strong and dependable and the mother of his beautiful daughter, Jenna. He loved Iona because she was strong and independent and because she encouraged him in everything he wanted to do. He wanted to care for both of them, to protect both of them. He wasn't sure how he'd manage to do this. He knew that most women wanted to feel protected even if they were strong and independent.

Everything he did was geared towards protecting the women in his life. Sally and Jenna and Iona too – even though he knew that Sally didn't understand his need for his own company and had been upset with him about the changes in their lives. But the new company would make him a lot more money than simply being employed by the old one, and even though she'd hated the change, Sally had accepted it now. She'd realised that what he was saying made sense. So he was protecting them by setting it up and running a good business and making sure that they were always well provided for.

Iona – well, she always said that she didn't need protecting, but he could see how hard she worked and how much she wanted to get on and how little confidence she really had in herself. She was good at what she did but there was nobody there to praise her and tell her that. Her parents lived in Spain, and although she said she got on fine with them, she didn't keep in constant contact. Her sister was married and seemed to think that until Iona got married too there would always be something missing in her life. Her brother was in China. Frank thought that Iona was lonely. He was more sure than ever about that when she kept turning the conversation around to marriage. He couldn't marry her, of course, because of Sally. But he wanted to, to make her happy. Because if she was happy she wouldn't leave him. He didn't want her to leave him. She'd become an important part of his life. It was difficult to be in love with two people at the same time, but that was the way it was.

His head hurt again. It was all too much for him. He'd wanted things to be simple because it hadn't been simple for Derek, what with Christine bolting like that. He hadn't wanted to cause hassle himself. But it seemed that he was. He was certain that he could hear Iona now, telling him that she loved him and hated him, and he didn't know why anyone would hate him, because he always tried to do his best. For her. For Sally. For Jenna. Jenna loved him and hated him too. It was Jenna saying these things to him now, he recognised her voice. There were too many voices in his head lately, crowding in on top of him, making it difficult to think. He clenched his hand.

'I love you.'

He heard that clearly. It didn't matter who was saying it. If she loved him it didn't matter. He unclenched his hand again.

Iona realised that she was ravenous when she walked into the restaurant and the aroma of garlic and spices wafted towards her. She was surprised at how hungry she felt. In the weeks since Frank's accident, and except for the night in Gabriel's, food had barely registered in her consciousness. The night that she'd come here with Siobhán and Sally had been enjoyable, but she couldn't even remember what she'd eaten.

The waiter showed them to a booth and handed them menus. Iona opened hers and looked at it intently. She was going to have fish and chips, she thought. Good, solid comfort food, even if fish and chips in restaurants bore no resemblance to the deep-fried cod and greasy chips laced with vinegar and wrapped in brown paper that Frank would sometimes bring home from the chipper down the road. As she thought of

Frank, all her doubts about the wisdom of being here with Enrique rushed through her head again and she almost cried out.

'Everything OK?' Enrique looked at her curiously.

'I . . . well . . . I shouldn't actually be here,' she said. 'I have – other things to do this evening. I can't really stay.'

Enrique's brown eyes regarded her thoughtfully. 'You are hungry,' he said. 'There is nothing that you can do properly when your stomach tells you that it needs food. Have something to eat and then you can do whatever you need to do afterwards.'

'Yes, but—'

'I work in this cut-throat industry,' he said dismissively, 'where they used to say that lunch was for wimps. Some people still take that view. But me, I think we should all enjoy our food and that our lives would be much better for it. You do not have to spend a lot of time with me, Iona, but you should still have something to eat.'

'You don't understand,' she said. 'I can't be here with you. I just can't.'

'Why?' he asked calmly. 'Am I going to do something terrible?'

'No – it's that – well, I'm sort of – sort of married.'

'Sort of married?' He frowned. 'What exactly is that, sort of married? It is not something I have heard of before.'

'No. I'm not surprised,' she said ruefully.

'But does being sort of married stop you from eating?' he asked.

'Of course not. It's just—'

'Then, sort-of married Iona, do not worry about it and have something to eat.'

What was the harm? she asked herself. The idea of walking out when the aroma of food was so intense was deeply disappointing. But if she stayed, it would mean that she was having dinner with a man who wasn't Frank. She mentally shook her head. Of course she'd often had dinner with men who weren't Frank! She'd gone out with Garret a few times, and occasionally with other people in the rental agency business. Having dinner with a man wasn't some kind of declaration of intent. It just meant that you were . . . well, having dinner.

'OK,' she said eventually, closing the menu and putting it down on the table beside her. 'I'll have something to eat.'

'Good,' said Enrique. 'What have you chosen?'

They gave their orders to the waiter who had materialised at the table as soon as they'd closed the menus. Enrique ordered a glass of wine for himself but Iona told him that she had to drive home and was sticking to water. And no Cosmopolitans either, she told herself.

'Do you live far from here?' he asked as he buttered a slice of walnut bread.

She told him about the Liberties and her house and she told him about her parents and the finca in Javea and he nodded and agreed that it was a beautiful place to live. She liked his accent and his slightly gravelly voice. She liked the way he didn't pry but simply allowed the conversation to ramble in a range of directions. But she didn't like the fact that her marital status didn't seem to bother him in the slightest. Is it me? she wondered. Have I become one of those types of women who only see men as potential bedfellows? She laughed internally at herself. She wasn't thinking of Enrique as someone to sleep with. Not really. It was just that he was attractive and it was hard not to wonder about what an attractive person might be like in bed. She'd done that when she was married to Frank too. It didn't mean anything. And, she reminded herself, when she could have done it with no complications, she still hadn't slept with Brandon.

'I am divorced,' said Enrique casually in response to a question she asked him about family life and working overseas. 'My wife didn't like me being away so much and she was right. But I am sorry that it didn't work out. She is a nice woman. She is marrying again. Me, naturally not.'

'Why naturally not?'

'Because when you lose your wife to your job, you must concentrate on your job,' he said.

She nodded.

'And you? Sort-of-married?'

She'd known eventually that he'd ask her about it. But she really didn't know what to say.

'You wear a ring,' he said. 'Not a wedding ring?'

She looked down at her half-hoop of rubies. 'I thought it was,' she said simply. 'It turned out not.'

'And so there is or is not a husband in your life right now?'

'It's – complicated,' she said.

'Ah, yes.' He smiled slightly as he nodded. 'Modern lives, they are always complicated.'

They sat in silence. I wonder is he going to try to ask me out? Iona thought. And if so, what am I going to say? I don't want to have to talk about Frank. I'll say no but it seems rude when he's been so nice . . . but then if he asks me back to his place (even if it's only eight o'clock in the evening) then he won't be expecting nice, he'll be expecting more. Just like Brandon was expecting more. This is why I shouldn't have let Brandon pay and why I shouldn't have said yes to dinner with Enrique. This is why I'm a stupid, stupid person.

'I have to go.' Enrique signalled for the bill and then smiled at her. 'I have a report to write before tomorrow morning and I must start it now to have any hope of finishing it on time.'

'Oh.'

'It was nice to spend some time with you,' he said.

'You too.'

The waiter brought the bill. Enrique picked it up and looked at it.

'Split it,' said Iona quickly.

'But you know I wanted to thank you for the apartment,' he said. 'So I will pay.'

'I'd prefer if we split it.' She didn't want anyone else paying for her meals.

'If that's what you want.'

He took a bank note out of his wallet and placed it on the saucer with the bill. 'The same from you will cover it.'

'Great,' she said. She placed a note on the saucer too.

It was still warm and sunny outside. Enrique extolled the pleasures of long summer evenings as they strolled back to the apartment building together.

'This is me.' She indicated the lime-green Beetle.

'I like your car.' He grinned at her.

'Thank you. And thank you for dinner.'

'Maybe some time we'll meet and I can pay for your dinner,' he said. 'So this time you are just thanking me for making you eat.'

She laughed. 'OK.'

'So, good night, Iona.'

'Good night,' she said.

She was surprised that he hadn't given her the continental kiss on each cheek. But relieved too.

Chapter 33

Siobhán had just returned to her desk following an interview of a suspected burglar when her mobile rang with a distinctive tone.

'Hi, Eddie,' she said.

'You called?'

'I need to see you.'

'Why?'

'I've been thinking things over. It's time to talk.'

'About time,' he said gruffly. 'Tonight?'

'Fine,' she said.

'Call to the apartment?'

She hesitated. Her plan had been to meet Eddie somewhere for a drink and talk to him then. The apartment was a bit too personal. But she was afraid that if she said no, Eddie would think she had a problem with the idea of being alone with him.

'OK,' she said eventually. 'Around seven.'

'Fine,' said Eddie. 'See you then.'

She replaced the receiver. Then she made two calls, one to Sally and one to Iona to tell them about Carl O'Connor and the fact that journalists were digging around at the story. As she'd suspected, both women were horrified. She promised that she'd do everything she could to keep it private and assured them that she certainly wouldn't be giving O'Connor any information and that she was hoping to divert him into something else altogether. But that, as she'd told them before, he was a complete tosser and she found it hard to trust him.

Then she turned her mind back to burglaries.

* * *

Iona rang Sally after the call from Siobhán.

'Do you want to talk to a journalist?' she asked.

'Are you nuts?'

Iona laughed. 'It's just that Siobhán said the journo bloke, O'Connor, insists that some people like to have their stories in the paper.'

'I most certainly am not one of those people,' said Sally. 'Are you?'

'Now who's nuts?' asked Iona. 'Of course not. But I wanted to be sure we both felt the same way. Because if one of us felt differently, it would impact on the other and—'

'We're in this together,' said Sally firmly. 'Nobody does or says anything unless the other person agrees.'

'Great,' said Iona. 'That's perfect.'

'I won't ever agree to do a story about My Marriage Hell,' said Sally.

Iona giggled. 'No My Husband Was A Cheating Bastard headlines, so?'

'No pictures of The Tragic Women Who Were So Terribly Betrayed.'

'No crappy copies of Our Wedding Photos.'

Sally sighed deeply. 'Can you believe it, really? The idea of someone wanting to put it all in the papers?'

'Hey, Sal, you know what tripe goes into the papers these days,' said Iona. 'I'm not surprised. I'm just glad that neither of us wants to do it.'

'Like I said, anything that happens about Frank and his treatment, about the company – whatever – we both have to agree.'

'All for one,' said Iona.

'Something like that,' said Sally.

'You're a good friend,' Iona told her.

'You too,' Sally replied. 'You too.'

At seven o'clock exactly Siobhán arrived at the apartment to see Eddie.

'You have a key.' Eddie's voice came over the intercom when she hit the buzzer.

'Yes, but I wouldn't use it,' she told him. 'It wouldn't be right.'

'Oh, don't be so silly!' But he buzzed the door open for her.

He was standing at the door of the apartment when she got to the fourth floor. He kissed her on the cheek and ushered her inside.

Siobhán stood in the apartment and looked around her in astonishment.

It was pristine. Every surface gleamed with a polished sheen. There were fresh flowers in all the vases. No magazines or circulars or unpaid bills littered the work surfaces and there was no mound of ironing piled up in the armchair in the corner of the room.

'Gosh,' she said. 'This is like it was before I moved in.'

'The cleaners came,' he said drily. 'You organised it, if you remember.'

She nodded slowly. 'Yes. I did. But I didn't realise they'd do such an amazing job.'

'It looks good, doesn't it?' He smiled at her. 'Why don't you sit down?'

She perched nervously on the edge of the armchair. The apartment didn't feel like home any more. It was too clean, too tidy and far to glamorous for her now. She wished she'd called into her rented place in Dun Laoghaire to freshen up before coming out, but it hadn't even crossed her mind. Which makes me the bad girlfriend again, she thought disconsolately. Every normal woman would do themselves up for a meeting with their fiancé. Even if they were going through a relationship crisis.

Eddie had disappeared into the kitchen. He returned carrying a bottle of champagne and two glasses.

'And it's not the same stuff as you bought to welcome me home,' he told her. 'This is the real deal.'

'The stuff I got was the real deal,' she said indignantly.

'This is a 1990 Dom Perignon,' he said. 'You can't get it in the local off-licence.'

She said nothing as he eased the cork out of the bottle with a gentle pop and without spilling a drop of champagne. He filled both glasses and then raised his to hers.

'Welcome home,' he said.

'I'm not home yet.' She tried to keep her tone light-hearted. 'I mean, I didn't bring stuff or anything. This is just to talk it through.'

'Sweetheart, we've talked already,' said Eddie. 'And you've had your time to think about it. To me the time for talking and thinking is over.' He put his glass on the table and walked over to the chair where she was sitting. 'I love you,' he said. 'Since the day I met you I've loved you, and I know that you love me too. And I also know that you know how deeply sorry I am about what happened. But it truly was one moment of utter madness. It's not as though I'm ever likely to do it again. I was stupid and crazy and I paid a hard price for it. I could have been seriously ill and I could have lost you for ever.'

He reached under the chair and took out a red velvet box, tied with a gold ribbon and handed it to her. She turned it over in her hand.

'Open it,' he said.

'Eddie—'

'Open it,' he repeated.

She pulled at the ribbon and lifted the lid of the box. The thin necklace of diamonds sparkled in the evening sunlight slanting through the window and exploded into a kaleidoscope of rainbow colours.

'Oh my God,' she breathed. 'It's beautiful.'

'And you deserve it,' he told her. 'I don't know what I can do to make it up to you, but I will. This is just a token to show you how I feel.'

She was mesmerised by the light and the beauty of the diamonds. She closed the box gently.

'Aren't you going to put them on?' he asked.

'We need to finish talking first.'

'We don't need to talk,' he told her.

'Eddie, you've got to understand how difficult all this is for me. I understand it was a one-off. I understand how it could happen. But that doesn't make it any more acceptable. And that's what I'm struggling with.'

'Siobhán, sweetie, you've seen people at their absolute worst,' said Eddie. 'You've arrested them. Some of them are victims of circumstances. Some of them regret what they did. You must be able to see how sincere I am.'

She knew that he was sincere. She could hear it in his voice and see it in his face. His sincerity wasn't the question.

He leaned his face towards her and suddenly he was kissing her and she was kissing him back. And then he slid his arms beneath her and carried her into the bedroom.

It was the first time he'd ever carried her anywhere, and she felt him stumble as he laid her down on the bed. I'm not built for being carried around the place, she thought wryly. I could have put his back out! But he didn't seem to be too worried about his back. As she lay on the bed he undid the buttons of her pale blue blouse. She sighed with relief in the knowledge that the bra she was wearing – while not as gorgeous and sexy as the basque – was nevertheless a pretty balcony style in a shade which matched the blouse. She'd half-known, as she'd dressed that morning, that she was going to see him. Obviously her subconscious mind had told her that wearing the tired grey M&S wasn't the way to go.

He was undoing the belt on his trousers now, and suddenly he was on top of her, covering her face with kisses, moving his lips down her face and neck and resting them in the hollow between her breasts.

'I love you,' he whispered. 'I've always loved you.'

He entered her quickly and she squirmed slightly because she wasn't really ready for him. She'd wanted to be, of course, and as he kissed her she'd tried to think passionate thoughts, but the problem was that all she could think of was that he'd done this with a prostitute in Boston. She tried to push the image to the back of her mind and concentrate instead on the rhythm of his movement. But it was too difficult. And the idea of him doing it with the Boston girl wasn't a turn-on.

'I love you,' he said as he increased the pace. 'You're my girl, Siobhán, and you always will be.'

She squeezed her eyes tighter and tried to recapture the feelings that she'd had the first time they made love. The feeling that she'd found the right person for her. The connection between them. The sudden sense of rightness about being with him.

He cried out and then pulled her closer to him.

'That was fantastic,' he breathed into her ear.

She tried to move into a slightly more comfortable position.

'I've missed you so much.'

She'd missed him too. Even though there were times when she'd enjoyed being on her own, not having to worry about letting him know where she was or what she was doing or having him tell her that her job took up far too much of her time and that she wasn't paid nearly enough for it, she'd missed his nagging at her and his concern for her and the simple comfort of having someone else in her home and in her life.

'You know you have the most amazing body.' They were lying facing each other, still joined together. He ran his fingers along her spine, which he knew she loved.

'So have you.'

'We're good for each other,' he said softly.

'What was it like?' she asked.

'Huh?'

'With the . . . woman in Boston.'

'Oh, come on!' He looked angrily at her. 'I thought we were over all that.'

'You might be over it,' she said. 'I'm not.'

'Look, I was off my head in Boston,' he told her. 'I'd taken coke and stuff and so I can't even remember it properly.'

'Was it good, though?' she asked.

'If you must know – yes, it was,' he said. 'But for God's sake, Siobhán, she was a professional woman! She knew exactly what she was doing.'

'Any new tricks?' asked Siobhán.

He raised an eyebrow as he looked at her. 'Would you try them?'

'I just asked if there was something different she did,' said Siobhán.

'The whole thing was different,' he replied. 'But I didn't love her. It was just – sex.'

'I've got to go to the bathroom.' She slid away from him and walked into the bathroom. It too had undergone the ruthless cleaning courtesy of the agency, although the bottles of bath essence and pearl bath drops which she'd bought months earlier were still on the glass shelf. She leaned her head against the mirror over the sink. What did she want from Eddie? What was she going to say to him when she walked back into the bedroom?

She didn't want to let go of the life she'd expected to have with him – getting married, being even closer, being a real couple. She wanted all that. She really did. And she wanted the lovemaking too. Not the way it had just been, of course, which she hadn't enjoyed because she was still too upset with him to love him the way he wanted, but the way it had been before, when she'd given herself to him completely, trusting him, believing that he was the only person in the whole world for her. It had been perfect before. And she couldn't help wondering whether it could ever be perfect again.

In the course of her work she met people who were the victims of crimes, who demanded justice and wanted everything to be back the way it was before. And she had to tell them that it wasn't always possible. That even if they got justice, things could never be the way they were. She had to accept that for her and Eddie it could never be the way it was before either. That didn't mean that it couldn't be just as good. But it had to be different.

She walked back into the bedroom and picked up her balcony bra from the floor. She fastened it around her, then picked up the blue blouse and slid her arms into the sleeves.

'Come back to bed,' said Eddie lazily. 'It's been so long . . . I think I'm ready to go again if you're up for it.'

She shook her head. 'I'm not up for it,' she told him. 'You probably realised that I wasn't really up for it the first time.'

'Hey!' He sat up. 'I didn't force—'

'God, no, of course not,' she said quickly. 'What I meant was . . . well, I wanted to but I wasn't really . . . my body and my mind weren't exactly ready for it.'

His eyes narrowed. 'What are you saying?'

'Eddie, I really and truly loved you. I wanted to be with you. I wanted to marry you. But I can't forgive you. I know that maybe I should. I know that you're sorry. It's just that . . .' Her voice trailed off. 'I'm sorry,' she said again as she removed her delicate engagement ring (she'd insisted on something small and neat so that it didn't get in the way) from her finger.

'Don't do this, Siobhán,' said Eddie. 'You're throwing it all away just because of one mistake.'

'I know,' she said as she continued to get dressed. 'I realise that. But it was the wrong mistake, Eddie.'

'It's all so bloody black and white with you, isn't it?' he demanded angrily. 'Crime and punishment. I've committed the crime and now you're punishing me.'

'It's not like that,' she protested.

'Well, how is it then?'

She couldn't answer.

'In that case,' he said, 'don't let me delay you.'

'Oh, Eddie.'

'Tonight you made me feel worse than the girl in Boston ever did,' he said. 'As though I tricked you into having sex with me just now.'

'You didn't trick me,' said Siobhán. 'I tricked myself.'

She took her bag from the armchair in the corner of the room. 'I'll leave my keys on the table. Goodbye, Eddie.'

But he said nothing in reply.

* * *

She was in the underground car park, opening the driver's door, when a car pulled into the space beside her.

'Hello, Mizz P.,' said Carl O'Connor.

She wiped her eyes as she turned around but he could still see that she was upset.

'What's the matter?' he asked.

She shook her head wordlessly.

'Has that shithead you live with locked you out of the apartment again?'

'Don't be stupid,' she said.

'I was only looking out for you.'

'Yeah, well, I can look out for myself,' she retorted.

Carl laughed. 'You needed me once.'

She said nothing but got into the car. Carl stopped her from closing the door.

'Are you OK?' he asked. 'Do you want to go for a drink or anything?'

'I might be upset but I'm not stupid,' she said with a hint of spirit.

He looked at her shrewdly. 'If not now, another time perhaps?'

'Christ, you're all the same, aren't you!' she said hotly. 'I've just – I told you I'm upset and you're asking me for a date. Can't any of you damn well tell when a girl has had enough?'

'I never said I was asking you for a date,' he told her mildly. 'You're upset. I'm trying to be friendly, that's all.'

Her look was pure scepticism. 'Yeah, like you ever were before.'

'C'mon,' he said gently. 'I may be a member of the hated journo class, but it doesn't make me a monster.'

'You know, if you were a computer-generated ideal man I wouldn't go for a drink with you,' said Siobhán. 'I'm not doing men any more. I don't have the energy for it. Murder is easier.'

Iona was in the office the next morning when Sally phoned her to say that she had the accountant's report and, since she planned to be in town that day, would it suit Iona if she dropped it in to the office. Iona told her that she would be there until lunchtime if that suited, and Sally confirmed that she'd be in before twelve thirty.

It was actually midday when she walked into Rental Remedies with the buff folder under her arm. Because the office was open-plan, she immediately saw Iona sitting at her desk, using the tip of her pencil to scratch her head as she peered at the computer screen, a pair of fashionable reading glasses on the tip of her nose.

Sally cleared her throat loudly and Iona looked around. She smiled in greeting at Sally and beckoned her in past the reception desk.

Ruth Dawson looked up as Sally sat on the edge of Iona's desk.

'Sally – Ruth. Ruth – Sally,' said Iona as she put her glasses on the desk.

'Sally?' Ruth's eyes widened in surprise. 'Sally – as in – Sally?'

'Yes.'

'The Sally?'

'OK, I think we've established that this is Sally,' Iona told her colleague.

'Yes. But. Well. Sally. Hi, Sally,' said Ruth finally. 'Nice to meet you.'

'Have I been a topic of conversation?' asked Sally.

'To some extent,' admitted Iona.

'She never said that you were pregnant.' Ruth was staring at Sally's bump.

'Oh. No. I didn't.' Iona shrugged, while Ruth stared at both of them.

Sally blushed.

'Hey, look, Sally – why don't we grab a quick sandwich next door,' said Iona hurriedly. 'Ruth'll keep an eye for half an hour or so, won't you?' She looked demandingly at the other girl.

'Sure,' said Ruth. 'Nothing going on here now anyway.'

'Great.' Iona took her jacket from the back of her chair. 'Let's go.'

She ushered Sally out on to the street and then looked at her apologetically.

'I'm sorry,' she said. 'It's just that I've got used to knowing you. I guess that . . . well, I haven't talked about it much to Ruth since I came back to work and of course nobody wants to ask anything. So I suppose they thought that we were still at loggerheads.'

'And we're not.' Sally followed Iona into the small café. 'I can see why that would surprise people actually.'

'To be honest it kind of surprises me too. What d'you fancy?' asked Iona as they nabbed a table and chairs.

'Salad would be perfect. And a coffee.' Sally had regained the ability to drink coffee without feeling nauseous.

Iona went up to the counter and ordered an Italian salad for Sally and a ham and cheese sandwich for herself, plus a couple of lattes.

'How are you feeling?' asked Iona as she brought the order back to the table. 'You're looking great.'

'Thanks,' said Sally. 'I feel good.'

The benefits of pregnancy had kicked in for her in the last week or so and she definitely looked a lot healthier than she'd done for a long time. Her skin was flawless and her hair gleamed under the soft lights of the café. The tired expression had gone from her face and her eyes sparkled.

Iona, who'd looked at herself in the mirror that morning and wondered if she could possibly flit back to New York just to get another makeover and feel like a normal person again, felt a stab of envy at Sally's new radiance.

'You haven't been contacted by the mad journo, have you?' she asked.

The sparkle went out of Sally's eyes.

'No, but if anyone comes around asking questions I'll kill them,' she said.

Iona chuckled. 'Another crime for Siobhán.'

Sally shrugged. 'I hope she manages to do as she said and distract them.'

'I hope so too,' agreed Iona. 'But the one thing you can say for her is that at least she's on our side.'

'Yes. She's a good person,' agreed Sally.

'And how's Jenna?'

'A bit weird, to tell you the truth,' said Sally. 'I didn't call you last night because like so many times nothing actually happened in the end, but she thought that Frank squeezed her hand yesterday afternoon.'

Iona's spoon clattered to the floor and she left it there.

'Yesterday afternoon?' she repeated.

'We went into the hospital in the afternoon because, of course, I'm off work now with the holidays. And Jenna asked to spend a bit of time with Frank on his own. She said that while she was talking to him he squeezed her hand.'

'Omigod, Sally.' Iona stared at her. 'This is huge progress.'

'I know. I know,' said Sally. 'Only the thing is, he didn't do it again. We stayed there until nine in the evening and nothing happened.'

'You could have called me,' said Iona sharply. 'Maybe if I'd come in . . .'

'I thought about it,' admitted Sally. 'But I wasn't really sure if Jenna had imagined it. That's partly what I mean about her being weird right now.'

Iona's jaw was clenched.

'If something had happened I would have called,' Sally assured her. 'Honestly.'

Iona said nothing but eventually relaxed her jaw.

'And Jenna – well, she's been acting so strange and worryingly,' said Sally. 'I thought maybe this was a good opportunity for her to feel loved and wanted by Frank. I know that's selfish of me, but that's what was going through my mind.'

'How is she acting strange?'

Sally explained about Jenna's friendship with the wild set of the school and her continued truculence at home.

'But a few days ago she suddenly started being sweetness and light again and talked about getting a summer job. Then yesterday she was back to being sullen. She's so difficult at the moment, she really is.'

'If something like that happens again you've got to call me,' said Iona. 'I mean, you said that nothing happens without us both agreeing . . .'

Sally nodded. 'I know. I told the hospital to let both of us know if there's any change.'

'Thanks,' said Iona. She opened the folder. 'Anything interesting in this?'

'I don't know,' said Sally. 'That's why I'm giving it to you.'

Iona skimmed through the sheets of paper and pursed her lips. 'I'll talk to Myles about it,' she said. 'I'm not sure, Sally, because I didn't do that much work for him, but I thought there were more clients than this.'

'It's hard to tell,' said Sally.

'You didn't bring the laptop, did you?'

'Sorry. I never thought of that.'

'When you go home, could you e-mail his client files to me?'

'All of his stuff is password-protected,' Sally told her. 'I know you gave me the Goldfinger password for the laptop itself but that won't let me access the files, will it?'

'You don't need to access the files themselves to send me the database,' said Iona. She cleared her throat. 'The password for that is Pussy Galore. I think there's an income and expenditure account on there too. And the password is simply 007.'

'Naturally.' Sally made a face. 'I should've guessed them all.'

'You probably would have if you'd kept at it,' said Iona. 'My password is Moneypenny.'

Sally smiled wryly.

'Don't get all upset because I have a password of my own,' Iona told her. 'You weren't as involved in that part of it as me. But you are now. So . . .'

'I'll check it out,' promised Sally. 'What's your e-mail address?'

Iona gave it to her.

'As soon as I get home I'll send them,' said Sally. 'If I've got a problem I'll phone you.'

'Great.' Iona closed the buff file and took a bite of her sandwich. 'Hopefully everything's fine, but if it isn't we'll know soon.'

'I won't let anything bad happen to the company,' said Sally. 'It's part of him.'

'I know,' said Iona. 'I won't let anything bad happen to it either.'

When she got back to the office Ruth was sitting at her desk eating a bagel.

'Am I late?' asked Iona.

'No, I just got hungry and ordered in,' said Ruth. 'How was lunch with the other woman?'

Iona shrugged. 'I don't think of her like that any more,' she said. 'We're kind of in this thing together.'

'Iona, you know that's beyond weird, don't you?'

'Why?'

'She's his first wife. You're . . . well, technically I know you're not, but – but morally you're his second wife. You shouldn't be friends.'

'We're not exactly friends,' said Iona. 'We just . . . well, we've had to get on, I suppose.'

'I couldn't do it,' said Ruth.

'You'd be surprised at what you can do when you put your mind to it,' responded Iona as she tapped the mouse and woke her computer from sleep.

* * *

It was Iona's turn to see Frank that night. She was excited about the fact that he might have squeezed Jenna's hand the day before and hoping that maybe this would be the night that he finally came back to them. If it was, she'd be at the hospital all evening. But if not, she thought it might be a good idea to drop out to Lauren and Myles and see if her brother-in-law would look at the accountant's report and the list of clients that Sally had e-mailed her when she got home. She phoned Lauren, who told her that it would be fine to call by and that Myles would look at the files.

Iona took a lot of time and care over her appearance for this visit. She knew that she was on one of the up moments in her cycle of hope with Frank, feeling that he was coming out of the coma, that he loved her, that everything would work out for the best, even while she knew that there could still be months to go before he regained consciousness, and she had no idea whether he loved her and no idea what working out for the best actually meant any more. At the start of the whole thing it had been that Frank would wake up, disown Sally and come home with her. Now . . . now she simply didn't know.

'The worst thing is,' she murmured to him as she sat beside the bed and listened to the beep of the monitors, 'someone's going to be hurt at the end of it all. I mean, me and Sally are hurt already, of course. So are you, although that's physical, not mental. But at the moment we're kind of going through the motions with you. We're in limbo, Frank. We can get up every day and do things, but it's not really getting on with our lives. When you wake up – then we have to decide what's next. And I don't know what she wants to decide. I don't know what I want to decide. And neither of us know what the hell you'll decide, Frank. So it's really, really hard.'

She picked up the copy of the accountant's report. 'I'm meeting Myles about this tonight,' she said. 'I know you never really got on with him, but you know Frank, he's been great. So has Lauren.' Her glance flickered over the report again. 'I think I looked down on them because they were so suburban and ordinary – same way as I kinda looked down on Sally too. But they've all been fantastic really.' She leaned back in the chair and looked at him speculatively. 'I guess there's something else to tell you,' she said. 'I didn't before now because I felt guilty about it.'

Frank still didn't respond.

'I nearly slept with a bloke in New York.'

Frank's eyes opened. He stared straight ahead of him.

'I wish you wouldn't do that,' she told him. 'Unless you're going to participate in the conversation. Are you?'

He said nothing.

'I went for a break and I nearly slept with him because I was lonely. But I didn't because I still love you, Frank.'

Frank continued to stare impassively in front of him.

'And then last night I went for dinner with a client. It was a casual sort of thing, nothing more. But I felt really guilty about it because I liked him, and even though I don't fancy him or anything I just thought you should know. I don't want to hide things from you.'

His eyes fluttered closed again.

She looked at him intently for a while, then got up from the seat beside the bed and kissed him gently on the forehead. 'I'll be back the day after tomorrow,' she said. 'Maybe you'll be ready to talk then.'

Myles and Lauren were sitting in the conservatory at the back of the house when she arrived half an hour later.

'Gorgeous evening,' Myles said.

'Lovely,' Iona agreed. She thrust the folder at him. 'Can you cast your accountant's eye over this, Myles, and tell me what you think?'

He took the folder from her. She'd lost the slightly hectoring tone she normally used when talking to him and he was suddenly interested in what might be going on with the business.

While he looked through the file, Iona and Lauren sat on wicker recliners and watched Charlotte and Gavin race around the garden like mini tornados. Iona felt her heart constrict. It was this kind of domesticity that she'd wanted from Frank, no matter how afraid of it she also felt, and it was the idea that this could never happen for her now that was so difficult to accept. And yet, she realised, she was accepting it. Regardless of what happened with Frank's health, she was certain now that she would never have a baby with him, and although the thought hurt her, it wasn't as numbing as it had been a couple of months earlier.

'I have to tell you something,' said Lauren eventually.

Iona turned towards her and looked at her enquiringly, while Myles peeped over the top of the folder at them.

'Myles and I are going to have another baby.'

Somehow it didn't surprise Iona. Her sister was good with children.

'Congratulations,' she said as evenly as she could. 'When is it due?'

'I'm only three months gone,' said Lauren. 'There's a bit of time yet.'

'I'm glad for you.' Iona was surprised to realise that she actually meant it. She'd thought, as she'd heard Lauren's words, that she'd be jealous, but she wasn't. She was pleased for her sister.

'I know it's not ideal—'

'It's ideal for you,' said Iona.

'I know. But with all this stuff going on with Frank . . .'

'That's my problem and my life,' Iona told her. 'And just because it didn't work out for me, it doesn't mean you should feel rotten about your brilliant news.'

'Thank you,' said Lauren.

Iona got up from her chair and kissed her sister. Then she walked over to Myles and kissed him too.

'Steady on,' he said. 'You've never done that before.'

'I should've,' she told him. 'I was always a bit snotty with you, Myles, and I'd no right to be.'

'Ah, you're grand.' Myles was embarrassed.

'I'm not just being nice to you because you're looking at stuff for me,' added Iona hastily. 'It's because you're a nice bloke and a good husband and you're great with Lauren and the kids.'

'Take it easy,' warned Myles. 'I'll get notions about myself.'

Iona laughed and Lauren, who'd been extremely worried about telling Iona her news, but who knew that she couldn't keep it from her any longer, smiled with relief.

'I need to spend some more time with this,' said Myles after a period of time. 'But it seems to me that your accountant has undervalued the core business. Also, there's a big contract coming up with a leisure and spa complex which could be extremely profitable. I don't know whether any work has been done on it or not, but it's a long-term deal and it would be very good for the company.'

Iona remembered Frank talking about a big one, a great one, that he'd landed.

'I knew it,' she said. 'I knew that there was something not quite right about that bloke. Frank had his doubts too.'

'Seems like he's trying to take the company from you . . . well, I suppose from Sally really, on the cheap.'

'What'll we do?' asked Iona.

'You need to talk to this contractor guy, Pete, and see what's going on. And then talk to the accountant.'

Iona made a face.

'Do you want me to do it?' he asked.

'Would you?'

'Of course.'

'Myles, you're a star!' She beamed at him.

'But someone needs to contact the new client – Belleza del Serene – and see how things are going there too,' warned Myles. 'The installation isn't due to start for a few weeks, so you have time on your side, but it's still important to meet the person in charge and to talk to Pete to see that everything's in place.' He hesitated. 'Do you want me to do that too?'

'Jeez, Myles, that's asking too much,' said Iona.

'I don't mind,' he said. 'The only problem is that the client might want to meet someone from the company itself. Frank ran things on a very personal basis.'

'I'm surprised they haven't been in touch already,' said Iona.

'Maybe they have. Maybe Richard Moran has contacted everyone,' Myles told her.

'And maybe he's trying to get control of everything before Frank wakes up,' said Iona.

Lauren and Myles looked at her sympathetically.

'There was more progress yesterday.' She told them about Frank squeezing Jenna's hand. 'And when I go in I get the impression more and more that he has some idea of what's going on around him. But it's just taking so long.'

'Have you thought any more about what happens when he does wake up?' asked Lauren cautiously.

'No. Not really.'

'How's Sally?'

'Very well,' answered Iona. 'Her pregnancy suddenly seems to be doing her good.' She looked wryly at Lauren. 'You can meet her and share maternity tips.'

Lauren laughed. 'I don't think so.'

'No, really.' Iona's voice was definite. 'You and her have a lot in common. You're both caring sort of people. I'm just a selfish cow.'

'Ah, Io, you're not,' said Lauren.

'I try not to be,' said Iona. 'But sometimes I am. I practically forced Frank to marry me. Or not, as it turned out.'

'Oh, that's a family trait,' said Myles confidently. 'Sure Lauren did it to me too.'

'I did not!' Lauren looked accusingly at her husband and then started to laugh.

And Iona suddenly found herself laughing with her sister and brother-in-law and feeling light-hearted for the first time in months.

Chapter 34

Siobhán went for a run along the seafront. The late evening was an ideal time for running, not too warm but not cold, and with an almost imperceptible southerly breeze behind her. She emptied her mind as she ran, not thinking about the end of her relationship with Eddie or the piles of work on her desk, but simply allowing herself to be taken over by the here and now of running so that by the time she got back to the apartment she was glowing with a sheen of perspiration and physically tired although mentally refreshed.

She pushed open the door to the block and noticed her neighbours – one of the couples to whom Iona had rented an apartment – at the mailboxes. The woman was short and pretty, with a blonde ponytail peeking out from the back of her navy baseball cap. The guy with her was tall and athletic, wearing a matching baseball cap and navy Bermuda shorts. Siobhán smiled briefly at them as she ran up the stairs to her apartment, but the image of them remained in her mind as she let herself in and opened the patio doors to allow the air to circulate. She hopped under the shower and freshened up. Then she dressed in a pair of dark trousers and a white T-shirt, took the lift to the underground car park and drove to the station.

'What are you doing here?' asked her colleague, Joe O'Riordan. 'It's not your shift.'

'I wanted to look at the pix of the bank account scam people,' said Siobhán as she sat at her desk and booted up her computer.

'New info?'

'I'm not sure.' She opened the video pictures and looked at them pensively. Then she glanced up at Joe, who was observing her.

'I think I know where these people are based,' she said.

'Really?'

She studied the pictures again. 'Almost certainly.'

'Excellent! Where?'

'My apartment block,' she told him drily.

Joe's eyes widened. 'You've got to be kidding me.'

'Nope. I moved there a few weeks ago and they took an apartment around the same time. I remember the girl who rented the place out mentioning that she'd made a number of lettings in the block.'

'Are you sure?'

'Absolutely.'

'Well, this will be brownie points for Bray.' He grinned at her and she smiled back.

'We'll organise surveillance, get a handle on what they're doing, when they're there, how things are panning out. And then, hopefully, nab them and the gear in the apartment.'

'Let's go and talk to the Super,' said Joe.

The chief's office door was open. Siobhán looked inside and asked if they could have a chat. He raised an eyebrow at her, sensing from her tone that there was good news brewing, and waved them to the seat in front of him.

'Well?' he asked.

Siobhán gave him a run-down of what she'd told Joe.

'I can get more information about the tenants from the person who did the rental,' she told him. 'She's the person who rented to me too. She cleared her throat and looked at the Super. 'She's actually one of the wives in the bigamy case.'

'What?' He looked at her in astonishment.

'I know, I know. But renting apartments is her business . . .'

'You've nearly completed the work on that case, haven't you?'

Siobhán nodded. 'Just waiting to see whether the husband wakes up or not,' she said. 'Hardly worth going any further while he's comatose.'

'I hate it when cases overlap,' complained her chief.

'They don't,' she told him. 'Iona Brannock has nothing to do with this other than the rental.'

'Fair enough,' he said. 'OK. Let's work out how we're going to deal with it. And by the way, Siobhán – good work.'

'Thanks,' she said as she tried to hide her smile of satisfaction.

* * *

After the meeting she contacted Iona and told her about the tenants in apartment number 4.

'Oh no!' Iona groaned. 'Not again.'

'What d'you mean, not again?' asked Siobhán, suddenly concerned. 'Has this happened before?'

'Of course not,' Iona told her. 'But a year or so ago one of my tenants was busted for drugs. The damn drug squad did a stakeout of the apartment then. I'm beginning to feel like an extra on *The Bill* or something.'

Siobhán laughed. 'Don't worry. You don't have to do anything other than give me some information.'

'You'll need a warrant,' said Iona. 'I can't let you just burst into the apartment.'

'I'll get everything in order,' promised Siobhán.

'Right.' Iona sighed as she replaced the phone. Garret would be really pissed off to discover that another one of their apartments was about to be raided by the gardai.

Almost as soon as she'd finished speaking to Iona, Siobhán's mobile rang.

'Hi,' said Carl O'Connor. 'Busy?'

'Actually, yes,' she said.

'Anything exciting?'

Siobhán thought about it for a moment. Perhaps if she gave O'Connor a little inside information on the ID scam he'd lose interest in the Ardallen case. She'd promised Iona and Sally that she'd protect them as much as possible, and this might be the best way.

'Maybe,' she said finally.

'How about that drink?' he asked.

'OK.'

'OK?' Carl was surprised. He hadn't expected her to agree so quickly.

'I'll meet you in Blackrock,' she said. 'Not in the town centre, though. The Playwright?'

'Fine.' The bar was big and impersonal despite its thatched roof and traditional theme.

'An hour,' said Siobhán.

'Right,' said Carl.

He was there before her and saw her as she walked through the door, tall and confident, her eyes scanning the crowd for him. He raised his hand in greeting and she sat down on a bar stool beside him.

'Drink?' he asked.

'Sparkling water.'

'I'm having a beer,' he told her. 'Just one. So no need to arrest me on suspicion of drink-driving or anything like that.'

'Fine,' she said. 'I won't.'

'I was only kidding.'

'I know.'

He sighed as the barman poured him a pint of lager and placed a bottle of water in front of Siobhán.

'You're hard work sometimes,' he told her.

'I don't mean to be,' she said.

'Maybe it's the job.'

'I like my job,' she told him. 'But it's not about giving information to crusading journalists.'

'All journalists get information from the cops,' he said.

'I know. I know. But . . .'

'I'm not a heartless bastard, you know,' he told her. 'I do have a sensitive side.'

She smiled suddenly. 'I know,' she said. 'You were actually very sensitive when I was locked out of my apartment. And I didn't thank you properly. So – thanks.'

'You're nice when you're not trying to make me feel like a shit.'

'If I've ever made you feel that way, I'm sorry,' she said.

'You're being very understanding tonight,' said Carl. 'It's scary!'

She took a sip of her water.

'I'm going to be completely honest with you,' she said.

Carl laughed. 'That's usually the signal for the big lie.'

'I'm not going to lie to you. What's the point in that?'

She gave him a brief resumé of the facts about Frank, Sally and Iona while he sipped his beer. He didn't take any notes.

'And so,' she concluded, 'those women are trying to get on with things in very difficult circumstances. You, or your friend, writing a story about them is the very last thing they need.'

'Sometimes people like to have their story told,' said Carl. 'We wouldn't print anything unless they wanted it.'

'Oh, come on.' She grimaced. 'You're always printing stuff that nobody wants printed.'

'Not really,' he said. 'Certainly stuff that the gardai don't want printed. But most of the other stuff – people invite us into their homes and tell us.'

'But it's hardly ever what they imagined in the end,' she said. 'Sally and Iona are private people. This is a private tragedy for them. Maybe at some time in the future either one of them might decide that it's newsworthy and decide to spill their guts to you. But couldn't that be their choice, not yours?'

Carl tapped his fingers lightly on the bar counter. 'And instead of this very interesting story, you want me to write – what ?'

'You know the fake ID scam going around?'

He nodded.

'We've got a good lead and a good break in the case,' she said. 'I'll give you the inside track on it plus let you know when the whole thing is going down.'

'It's not as exciting as the bigamy,' complained Carl.

'Oh come on!' she said. 'I bet you'll get lots of interviews from people who were ripped off. And I'll make sure you have exclusive info.'

'Siobhán—'

'I know it's not the same as rummaging around in people's lives,' she said fiercely. 'But it's the best I can do. These are nice women, Carl. They don't deserve to have things written about them.'

'You really care about them, don't you?'

'Of course I care!' she cried. 'That's the problem with you guys. You think it's all a job to us. Well, yes, it is a job, but you'd have to be made of ice not to care about some of the things that go on. And it's not just the victims we feel sorry for. I know that some of the people who commit crimes are products of circumstances. I feel sorry for them too. We're not all heartless bastards in uniform, you know.'

'You don't wear a uniform at all,' Carl pointed out.

'Don't be so pedantic!'

'I'm sorry,' said Carl. He looked at her thoughtfully. 'You're a nice person, Siobhán Farrell, despite your hard heart.'

'I don't have a hard heart,' she said.

'I'll talk to JoJo,' he said eventually. 'I'll let her know the set-up regarding the bigamy case. It is human interest, Siobhán. She's justified in going after it.'

'I know. But you have to ask yourself – what possible good can come out of it?'

'Might stop other blokes with the same idea,' he said.

'If there was a bigamy epidemic maybe,' said Siobhán. 'But there isn't.'

'All right, all right,' said Carl. 'I'll do what I— hey, I've just thought, two women, one pregnant. Weren't they the women with you that night I bumped into you in Dun Laoghaire?'

Siobhán nodded.

'Are you sure you're not the one getting too involved here?'

'Absolutely positive,' said Siobhán. 'I'm not naïve, Carl. I checked out both women thoroughly. And the husband. It's as straightforward as anything like this can be. He deceived them. I met them because . . . well, I liked them and they wanted to go out.'

'Gosh, you're actually a real softie,' he teased gently.

'I'm not,' she assured him. 'I . . .' Suddenly she thought of Eddie. He used to call her a softie too, whenever she cried at something on the TV or a particular piece of music.

'How's things with the fiancé?' asked Carl casually.

'Ex-fiancé,' she told him.

'Ah.'

'Better ex-fiancé than ex-husband,' she said.

'Indeed.' He smiled shortly at her. 'You were right to dump him. Anyone who didn't appreciate you in that bas—'

'Shut up, O'Connor,' she said quickly. 'I'd like to forget about that, thank you.'

'I can't forget about it,' he told her.

'You'd better,' she said.

He grinned. 'Another drink?' he asked.

She thought about it for a moment and then shook her head. 'I've things to do,' she told him.

'Another time?'

'Maybe,' she said as she gathered her belongings. 'You never know.'

Chapter 35

Myles arranged a meeting between Frank's accountant and Sally and Iona. He came along too and was glad that he'd done so because he realised very quickly that Richard Moran had been trying to pull the wool over Sally's eyes in relation to the value of the company.

'You haven't considered the deal with the spa and therapy centre, Belleza del Serene, as far as I can see,' Myles pointed out.

'Yes, but that deal was arranged by Frank and contingent on him getting a team together to carry it out,' protested Richard.

'And you were just going to let it fall by the wayside?' asked Myles. 'You weren't going to get anyone to talk to this guy . . .' he looked down at his notes, 'Anthony Brady, at all?'

Richard looked uncomfortable. 'Well of course I've had a conversation—'

'In which case you should have been considering this deal,' said Myles firmly. He stood up. 'I don't think you've been acting in Sally's best interests, and it's my belief that the ladies would be better off not dealing with you any more. I'll contact you to make arrangements.'

'Hey, you can't do that!' cried Richard.

'Yes I can,' said Myles, and ushered Sally and Iona out of the office.

They went for a coffee in a nearby hotel where both Iona and Sally looked at Myles in admiration.

'You know, I can totally understand what Lauren sees in you now,' said Iona. 'I never knew you accountants could be so macho.'

Myles laughed. 'Don't be such a dope,' he said. 'Now look, we need to organise a meeting with the contractors, particularly Pete Maguire, and see what they have to say about everything. And then, if you agree,

Sally, we'll make the necessary changes to the company set-up. I can get my solicitor to look through this for you.'

'You're being really kind,' said Sally as she shifted in the seat to make herself more comfortable. 'You didn't have to do all this for us.'

'I'm certainly not going to let someone like Richard Moran give all accountants a bad name,' said Myles cheerfully. 'Besides, Iona already has a bad enough opinion of us.'

'Not now,' she said. 'You truly have been great, Myles.'

'Thanks,' he said. 'This afternoon I'll set up the meeting. You'll be able to come along, Sally?'

She nodded and he looked at his sister-in-law. 'Io?'

'Sally's the director,' she said. 'I don't really have anything to do with the company at all.'

'Oh, but you must come,' Sally insisted. 'It wouldn't be right without you. Besides, we have an agreement.'

'What agreement?' asked Myles.

'That both of us have an equal say in what happens about Frank in hospital and the company,' Iona told him. 'Can you set something up for late afternoon? That way I won't have to juggle my time at work so much.'

'Sure,' he said.

Sally and Iona smiled at each other.

'I like having this to do,' said Sally. 'I mean, I know nothing about business and even less about this business, but . . . well, it's good to be involved.'

'I know,' said Iona. 'And I'll tell you something, Sally, when Frank finally does bother his arse to wake up, he'll be gobsmacked at how wonderfully his company has been run while he was out of it. He certainly won't be able to pretend that it's all really technical and difficult any more.'

The meeting with the contractors went extremely well. Pete Maguire was a hardworking man who was loyal to Frank but who had worked under Richard Moran's instructions. Myles took charge of the meeting and introduced Sally as a co-director and Iona as an interested party.

'I worked with Frank on Belleza del Serene of course,' Pete said. 'I spoke to the other accountant, Richard, about it too. We need to get off our backsides and do something about it.'

'But it can be done?'

'If we start now, of course.'

'Excellent,' said Iona. 'Then let's get going.'

Their next step was meeting Anthony Brady, the managing director of the holding company which operated the spa and therapy complex. Anthony had expressed worries about the contract because he hadn't heard from Frank for so long and had only dealt with Richard Moran, but Sally, Iona and Myles assured him that everything was under control, that the work would be done and certified and that Anthony had absolutely nothing to worry about.

Sally herself was worried that Anthony would dismiss them and say that he wanted to deal with a company whose managing director wasn't lying comatose in a hospital bed, but she knew that Myles added a certain air of gravitas to their meeting, while Iona was incredibly brisk and businesslike (and looked, thought Sally, extremely efficient and composed in her tailored suit and high-heeled shoes).

'A good day's work,' said Myles as they drove back from the complex.

'Fantastic,' agreed Sally. 'Thanks again, Myles.'

'You're welcome,' he said. 'Lauren asked me to ask both of you if you'd like to join us for dinner some evening?'

'I'd love to,' said Sally. 'But I'm trying to be around for Jenna in the evenings. She's in a lot right now and I'm afraid to go out and leave her at home.'

'For heaven's sake, why?' asked Iona. 'I thought everything was OK with her again.'

'Since her dad squeezed her hand she's been up and down,' said Sally. 'And me getting bigger and bigger doesn't seem to be helping either. She appears to have rowed with all of her friends, and the relationship with her boyfriend is over too as far as I can see. She was working for a while in the local Spar but gave that up . . . I'm still not sure where I am with Jenna.'

'Is she going to the hospital with you?' asked Iona.

Sally nodded. 'But of course Frank hasn't squeezed her hand since. It's really disheartening.'

'Why don't you get her to do some work on Frank's files?' asked Myles. 'There's lots of stuff to update based on the info that Richard

Moran and Pete Maguire gave us, and there's a whole timetable to be done up for the spa job. Maybe that would interest her?'

'Gosh, Myles, you're hitting all the buttons today,' she said. 'Jenna likes computers. You're right. This could be just the thing for her.'

'Call me a super-god,' said Myles as he turned into Sally's driveway.

Iona giggled. 'OK, now you've lost it completely,' she said as Sally got out of the car and said goodbye.

Jenna was lying on her bed, the earphones of her MP3 player tucked into her ears and the music loud enough to be an irritating tinny beat to anyone else in the room. Sally picked her way through the discarded clothes, magazines and shoes to sit on the edge of the bed. Jenna opened her eyes and stared at her mother.

God, she thought, but Sally was like an enormous blimp now. Plenty of her friends' mothers had been pregnant at some stage or another when Jenna was growing up, but she was a hundred per cent certain that none of them had been as huge as Sally at this point in their pregnancy. Her mother couldn't even get away with wearing bigger-sized normal clothes. Every stitch in her wardrobe was maternity wear.

'I was with your dad's accountant today,' said Sally as Jenna removed the earphones and asked her what she wanted. 'We've done a lot of work on keeping his company going.'

'We?'

'Iona and me. Helped by Iona's brother-in-law.'

'You know that you're getting madder by the minute, don't you?' said Jenna. 'At first you hated her, then you put up with her, and now you're positively friendly with her. This is insane.'

'She has expertise that I don't,' said Sally. 'And she's a victim too. So. Listen to me.'

Jenna made a face of exaggerated boredom.

'This is important,' said Sally. 'You know that your dad kept all his records on computer?'

'Where else would you expect him to keep them?' demanded Jenna. 'The back of an envelope?'

'Well, we'd love you to go through them and update them based on the information we have from the accountant,' said Sally as though Jenna hadn't spoken. 'We realised that he was trying to rip us off.'

'Not really?' Jenna sat upright on the bed.

'Yes,' said Sally. She explained about the new contract and the valuation that Richard Moran had put on the business, and the fact that she and Iona were going to make sure that the system was installed for the spa.

'But Mum, you know nothing about it!' cried Jenna.

'No, but the contractor guy does. And Myles is completely up to speed with everything,' said Sally. 'So what we really need, to get a good handle on everything about the company, is to have those records updated. Iona doesn't have time, she's working. I'm hopeless at your dad's stuff – you know how complicated he always made it with all those folders and sub-folders and God knows what. I e-mailed some files to Iona but we need to have the whole thing looked at properly. Myles has already done loads for us. So we thought about you.'

Jenna looked thoughtful.

'If you don't want to, that's fine. It's your choice, of course.' Sally tried to keep her voice as dismissive as she could. She didn't want Jenna to know how much she wanted her to be involved.

'No . . . it's OK.' Jenna swung her legs over the side of the bed. 'I'll do it. You're right. You're useless with the computer.'

'Great,' said Sally, unable to keep the relief out of her voice. 'It's all on the laptop. Oh, you need a password for that. It's—'

'Goldfinger. I know,' said Jenna impatiently.

'I didn't realise you already knew that.' Sally looked at her in surprise.

'Don't be so feeble, Mum.' Jenna grinned at her. 'How else could I have played games on Dad's computer if I didn't know his password?'

It took Jenna two days to work her way through Frank's clients and update everything. When she'd finished, she had a neat folder of information about the clients and the company and she also had a few ideas about how they should schedule some of the jobs that needed to be done. She was very, very pleased with herself, especially as she hadn't been distracted by the Wingnuts game on the computer, nor the very addictive tic-tac-toe game that Frank also had.

However, with all her work done, and with Sally asleep in the bedroom next door (she had taken to having afternoon naps between two and four, which Jenna thought was both a blessing and a curse), Jenna devoted her time to blasting planes out of the virtual sky and playing twelve games of tic-tac-toe in a row. Before she shut down the computer she checked all of the files once more to make sure that she hadn't missed anything. There was only one folder that was bothering her. Like everything else it was password-protected, and the password wasn't Goldfinger or James Bond or any of the other Bond-friendly words that she tried. Jenna was worried that there might be information on another project like the spa kept there, and that it could be potential business that might be lost to the company.

She frowned as she looked at the little icon on the desktop. From what she could see, it didn't contain a lot of information, which was both bothering and a relief. All of the other individual folders on the computer were quite large because they held digital photographs of Frank's work, schematics of installations or of products and copies of contracts with individual companies. But this folder contained much less. Frank hadn't named it in the same way as the others either; they had company names and a reference of his own, while this was simply a reference, CH1936, which didn't mean anything to her. It was really bugging her that she hadn't managed to figure it out.

Sam was the person to ask about it. Jenna's former best friend knew everything there was to know about computers, and had been suspended from school once for hacking into student records from her own wireless laptop. But, of course, Jenna and Sam weren't speaking ever since Jenna had started going out with Gerry Cullinan and had hooked up with Aline Keogh and Cindy Ryan. Sam hadn't been bothered that Jenna and Gerry were having sex (although at first, and when they'd still been speaking, she'd lectured Jenna about safe sex and not getting pregnant whatever else she did), but she'd been disgusted when Jenna had dropped her in favour of Aline and Cindy. Jenna didn't blame her. If the shoe had been on the other foot, she would have been pretty pissed off with her friend too. After all, Aline and Cindy were the sort of girls they normally didn't hang around with at all. Disruptive, spending all their time and money on boys and make-up, thinking that it was fun to get wasted every night . . .

Well, they were right and wrong about that. Jenna leaned back in the chair and closed her eyes. Getting wasted had been kind of fun until it had all gone wrong and she'd ended up being driven home in a police car. She felt herself grow hot with embarrassment at the memory. But the thing was, Aline and Cindy weren't judgemental. Sam was. As she herself had been until it was her own family which was being judged.

She hadn't seen Sam since they'd broken up for the school holidays. She knew that her former friend was doing some work experience at a local IT firm in the town centre. Maybe she'd be willing to talk to her.

She sent Sam a text message asking her to call and wondered when, or if, her friend would do as she asked. Two minutes later her mobile chirped.

'Hi, Sam,' she said.

'Hello.' Sam's voice was cautious.

'I'm sorry,' said Jenna.

'For what?'

'Everything. Can you talk?'

'Not now.'

'Would you like to call around tonight? Can you?'

'OK,' said Sam.

'Great.'

And as she ended the call Jenna realised that a weight had been lifted off her shoulders.

He could hear the nurses talking, chatting about something that had happened on the wards that day. He couldn't exactly figure out what they were saying because there was a lot of jargon involved and he wasn't able to concentrate on it. That was the problem. Concentrating. He wasn't sure where he was at any particular moment in time. At first he'd thought that he was in another time and place, as though he'd passed through some strange portal into his past. He'd lived events and yet he'd lived them with the feeling that he'd done it all before. Other times he was with Sally or Iona and it seemed as though those times were just happening. His perception of space and time was all over the place. He wasn't able to pin down exactly what was happening and when.

Yet the constant, the thing that kept coming back to him, was that he was in bed and that there were people around him. He would snap into an experience with people he knew which seemed so vivid and so immediate, and then, quite suddenly, he would be back in this other place where he couldn't seem to move or communicate with anyone and where things seemed to be happening around him but he wasn't able to take part. It was a horrible feeling. The other thing was that he couldn't really remember things properly once he'd snapped back to this reality. And so he seemed always to be trying to fight his way out of a kind of mental soup, only he was never sure about what was real and what wasn't.

He didn't want to think that what was real was that there were two of them. Iona and Sally. Sally and Iona. Both loved by him. Both loving him, he thought. Christ, he'd made such a mess of it all. He'd never intended for it to end up like this. He'd never intended to fall in love with two women. But he had. At different times and for different reasons. And he'd been too weak-willed to let one of them go.

He'd married Iona because he was afraid he'd lose her. And he hadn't divorced Sally because he loved her and didn't want to lose her either. He knew that was ridiculous. But both of them gave him different things in his life. And both of them gave him the sense of family that he craved so much.

After he and Sally had come to the conclusion that there wouldn't be any more children he'd felt cheated. He'd wanted her to consider IVF but she wouldn't, and in the end he'd accepted that. He'd thrown himself into his work instead so that he could provide for the daughter he did have. His lovely, lovely Jenna.

And yet the support came from Iona, whom he'd met so unexpectedly, and not from Sally. Iona, who was so different but so much fun to be with. Who made him feel wanted at a time when Sally wasn't able to make him feel that way.

He'd known it was wrong from the start. There was no excuse. He hated himself for what he'd done. He deserved whatever was happening to him now, whatever punishment was being meted out to him.

He was afraid that he was paralysed. He was sure, now, that when he was walking and talking to people it wasn't really happening no matter how real it seemed at the time. The feeling of not being able to move, of being somehow trapped inside his own body, was a much stronger feeling.

He tried to form words but he seemed to have forgotten how. He thought that there might be lots of things that he'd forgotten only he didn't know what they might be. He felt a wave of panic overwhelm him. He tried to cry out.

* * *

Susan Carpenter looked at her patient. Frank's eyes were closed but she knew that she'd heard him make a sound. And his fists were tightly clenched, grasping the sheet that covered him.

'Can you hear me, Frank?' she asked.

He said nothing. But she was sure that his grip had tightened on the sheet.

Sam called around to Jenna's later that evening. Sally was surprised but delighted to see her daughter's friend again, even though both of them disappeared upstairs to Jenna's room almost immediately. The boyfriend was gone, the new girlfriends seemed to be gone too, and Sam was back. Sally wondered whether things were turning the corner for her daughter at last.

'I'm not sure I can crack this,' said Sam as she looked at the laptop files.

'I bet you can,' said Jenna as she watched her friend's fingers fly over the keyboard. 'You're like wired to computer code.'

'Ha-bloody-ha. But of course you've spent the last few months thinking airhead thoughts and having sex so you know nothing about important things like computer codes.' Sam turned to look at her.

'You're right,' said Jenna.

'And you want something done, you come to me.'

'Is it any use to say I was going through a bit of a rough patch?' asked Jenna.

'What happened with Gerry?'

Jenna told her about his dumping of her.

'Bit shitty,' remarked Sam.

'I don't blame him really,' said Jenna. 'I was in a state that night. Aline and Cindy weren't much better. I hate thinking about it.'

'Yeah, but he'd been sleeping with you.'

'You're going to hold that against me for ever.'

'No I'm not,' said Sam. And then she laughed slightly. 'I guess. He's a good-looking bloke, isn't he? Was it good, the sex?'

Jenna shrugged. 'At first, yes. And then it became a bit like something I had to do. I loved him because he was so great about my dad and everything, but in the end I felt like I was sleeping with him to say thanks for being nice to me. But I enjoyed it.'

'I would have been nice to you.' Sam grinned. 'But I wouldn't have made you sleep with me.'

'Eejit.' Jenna threw a small cushion at her friend.

Sam smiled. 'So we're cool again?' she asked.

'Absolutely,' said Jenna. 'I was a bit of a dipstick.'

'Ah, Jen, you were going through a bit of a trauma.'

'I suppose.'

'Look, I'd freak out if my dad did the same as yours. But it's OK. It's not your fault.'

'Thanks.'

'Really.' Sam scrunched up her nose and peered at the computer screen again. 'Why would your dad protect this file differently?'

'Dunno.' Jenna shrugged. 'He's into that, though. He's the only person I know who has different pin numbers for all his cards and stuff and can remember them all.'

'If he picked a random number for this . . .' Sam sighed. 'I need some kind of clue.'

'Like what?' asked Jenna.

'Is there anything else he's into besides James Bond?'

Sam continued to stare at the screen.

'Not that I know of,' Jenna told her. 'If he's just used a number we are in trouble, aren't we?'

'I have a programme at home that might crack it,' said Sam. 'I could copy the file and run it there.'

'OK,' said Jenna.

'Your mum won't mind?'

'She's the one who wants to know all about the company,' said Jenna. She looked at Sam, a worried expression on her face. 'You don't think he was involved with some weird stuff, do you? And that's why he's given it special protection?'

'I protect all my files really well,' said Sam. 'This could be anything. Don't worry.'

'The thing is,' said Jenna gloomily, 'when it comes to my dad, these days we seem to do nothing but worry.'

Chapter 36

Siobhán contacted Iona again about the residents of apartment 4. She explained that they were going to mount some surveillance on the apartment and that the plan was to arrest the two people, hopefully surrounded by plenty of evidence of the ID scam. She asked Iona whether it would be possible to get the key to the apartment since that way they wouldn't have to break down the door. Iona had gone through this before with the drugs bust, although the idea of having to do it all again made her wonder whether she had become utterly hopeless at picking tenants. Yet the couple to whom she'd leased the apartment had excellent references. Now she supposed that they, too, had been faked. She called the landlord and explained the situation to him and, horrified and shocked, he agreed to co-operate as fully as possible with the police. So she met up with Siobhán and gave her the key.

'And we'd really like it if you didn't trash the place,' she told her hopefully.

Siobhán grinned. 'You'll hardly even know we were there,' she said, pleased that everything was coming together so well.

On the day of the planned raid, Siobhán rang Carl O'Connor.

'Thanks,' he said. 'But you've got to know, Siobhán, that if you guys make a complete hash of it, I'll have to report it like that.'

'What makes you think we'll make a hash of it?'

'Nothing,' he said. 'I just wanted you to know that I wasn't going to do a puff piece on how great the cops are.'

'Wouldn't dream of you doing that,' she said. 'Wouldn't dream of it.'

As they approached the apartment building, though, her heart was hammering in her chest. She, too, hoped that they wouldn't make a hash of things. Sometimes a case could fail on the silliest of errors. But they had their search warrant, which she had ensured was properly executed, they had the keys, they knew the movements of the people concerned, and intelligence they'd gathered in recent days meant they were pretty certain that there was a supply of blank driver's licences and passports in the apartment. But it could still all go wrong. Things did.

'Ready to go?' Her partner, Larry, raised his eyebrows at her as they stood in the hallway of the block, the uniformed gardai in support.

'As I'll ever be,' she said.

They knocked at the apartment door and the blonde woman answered it. Her eyes widened in recognition as she saw Siobhán and then darkened as she realised that her neighbour was accompanied by the gardai.

And then they were in the apartment and the pile of blank licences was in full view, piled on a coffee table, while the athletic man looked around him in despair and Larry started to read him his rights.

'You bitch!' cried the blonde woman. 'You were spying on us. And we were nice to you. I said hello every time we met.'

'You do not have to say anything . . .' Siobhán intoned the words hoping that this was an arrest which would lead to a conviction.

There was a notebook on the table too, filled with names and addresses, and a bag containing over ten thousand euros.

'Aladdin's cave,' said Larry cheerfully, after the man and woman had been brought outside. 'Good one, Siobhán.'

'Luck, really,' she said, although she was bursting with pride that it had worked out so well. 'If I hadn't been living here I wouldn't have spotted them. But the case would've broken sooner or later.'

'False modesty *so* doesn't become you!' He grinned.

'I know.' She laughed, feeling the tension that had been building up in her over the days of surveillance disappear. 'Super-cop, that's me.'

'And any chance I could have a few words with you?' Carl O'Connor, who'd arrived in time for the arrests, looked enquiringly at her.

'I've got to get back to the station now,' she told him. 'There's paperwork to deal with. It's not all bursting into apartments and arresting everyone in sight, you know.'

Larry looked horrified at her casual way of speaking to the reporter, but Carl grinned.

'How about later?' he suggested. 'I could meet you for a coffee? There'll be two pieces for the paper. The story of the arrest and then the story behind it – you know, following the gang and all that sort of stuff.'

'Happy to help,' said Siobhán.

'You want me to come along too?' asked Larry.

'I don't think so,' Carl told him. 'I'm sure Detective Garda Farrell will be more than enough help all by herself.'

Iona was thinking about the arrest of her two tenants and wondering whether they'd get bail and return to the apartment (the idea of which was freaking out her landlord) when the phone rang.

'This is Dr Carroll,' said the voice. 'It's another good news update. Frank is showing a much greater awareness of his surroundings now, and we think it would be good for you to come in.'

'And Sally?' she asked. 'Have you called Sally?'

'My colleague is speaking to her now,' said the doctor. 'Of course it's still not what you'd want, Iona. We're not talking about him suddenly waking up, you know. But it's a substantial improvement.'

'I'll be there right away,' Iona said.

She was at the hospital before Sally. Terri Cooper explained that she'd asked Frank to move his hand that morning and that he'd actually done it. She'd asked him a second time and he'd repeated the action. But he hadn't done it a third time.

'Oh, God,' whispered Iona. 'But that's immense.'

'Every case is different, of course,' said Terri. 'But as you both know, the thing about Frank is that there is brain activity. He just doesn't seem to want to come out of the coma.'

'We're not entirely surprised,' said Iona. 'If I were him I mightn't be in too much of a hurry to wake up either.'

She moved closer to the bed. 'Frank,' she said softly. 'It's me. Iona. Can you move your hand? Make a fist?'

She watched as his left hand moved slowly and his fingers curled towards his palm.

'Oh!' She reached out and took his hand. 'Frank, I know you're in there. I know you are. We're all here rooting for you. Come back to us, please.'

He didn't react any more. She sat beside the bed holding his clenched hand until the door opened and Sally and Jenna walked in. Then she gently released his hand and let it lie on the bed.

'He made a fist.' Iona started to cry. 'He did it, Sally. I asked him to and he did it.'

Sally gulped. 'Hi, Frank,' she said. 'It's Sally. Can you hear me?'

He didn't move.

'Dad.' Jenna's words were clear and distinct. 'You need to wake up. You've been lying there far too long messing with our lives.'

Frank's head slowly moved towards the sound of Jenna's voice.

'Oh, Dad!' This time Jenna's voice was shaky. 'You can hear me. You really can.'

Sally held her breath and glanced at Iona, who was blinking away her tears.

'Can you hear me, Frank?' she said softly.

He didn't move.

'Keep talking, Jenna,' commanded Iona. 'It's your voice he's reacting to.'

Jenna looked at them anxiously and then at her father again.

'We've been doing really well while you've been asleep,' she continued. 'Mum and Iona have been keeping the company going. You'd be so proud of them.' She glanced at Sally, who smiled encouragingly at her. 'Your accountant was a shit but they found out about it. There's a new contract which will do really well. Oh, and there's stuff on your computer we want to access,' she added. 'You know, files and things. So you need to wake up to help us.' She sat back.

Frank's head moved slightly again but his eyes remained closed. His fingers, though, tightened around the blanket.

'Don't worry about anything,' said Iona. 'Just get well. We can sort out the other things afterwards.'

But there was a lot to sort out. She said as much to Sally when they went to the cafeteria a little later. Jenna had gone outside, saying that she wanted to phone Sam on her mobile.

'So what are we going to do?' she asked. 'When he wakes up?'

Sally ladled some sugar into her coffee.

'Do we still love him?' she asked thoughtfully. 'Knowing what he did? Or are we just guilty about him because he was in an accident?'

Iona said nothing.

'Jenna talks about it a lot,' said Sally. 'Whether we should throw him out. She said it'd serve him right if he had to live with you for ever.'

Iona looked startled.

'It was when she hated you,' said Sally. 'She'd downloaded the coma information and decided that he'd need long-term care and that you were the person to give it to him.'

'It's bloody difficult, isn't it?'

'I love him,' said Sally. Her hand rested on the swell of her stomach. 'He's the father of my baby. I've been with him all my life.'

'I love him too,' said Iona slowly. 'That's crazy, isn't it? He betrayed us both but we still love him. Thing is, I don't know if I can forgive him.'

'I have to forgive him,' said Sally.

'No you don't,' Iona told her. 'You can throw him out, just like Jenna says.'

'And where would he go? To you?'

Iona sighed. 'Are we arguing about him?' she asked. 'Who gets him? Is he worth it?'

'He'll need care when he gets out,' said Sally.

'And you'll have a baby to care for too,' Iona pointed out.

'So . . . we let *him* choose?' She looked at Iona despairingly. 'Why should *he* get to choose?'

'He shouldn't get to choose,' agreed Iona. 'We have to decide. We have to do what's best for us.'

'Well, then?' Sally looked at her challengingly.

'Right now?' asked Iona. 'You want to decide right now? Without thinking about it?'

'I bet we've both done nothing but think about it,' Sally told her. 'We know the pros and cons for each of us. For me, he's a father for Jenna and the baby and I've known him longer. But against is the fact that he might need help and we'll have a newborn baby to think about. For you – you're younger and better able to look after him. Against . . .' She shrugged. 'Maybe there're more pros than cons for you.'

Iona shook her head. 'You're a family,' she told Sally. 'We're just a couple.'

'You wanted a baby,' Sally reminded her.

'My head is spinning,' said Iona. 'Please, Sally, please can we talk about this another time?'

'I guess so,' said Sally after a pause. 'I guess we still have plenty of time to decide.'

The following evening, since the gardai had finished with the apartment, Iona went to Dun Laoghaire to check it out. The landlord had told her to get new tenants just as soon as everything was sorted out with the gardai, so she planned to have a chat with Siobhán and ask her what was going to happen next. After she'd looked around the apartment she went upstairs and rapped on the door of Siobhán's place, but the detective didn't answer so Iona assumed that she was busy at the station.

She pressed the button for the lift to take her downstairs. The doors eased open and Enrique Martinez stepped out.

'Hello,' he said. 'How are you?'

'I'm good,' she told him. 'I had to deal with some things here.'

'So you are not here to see me?'

She smiled awkwardly.

'It's OK,' said Enrique. 'You have a complicated life, sort-of-married Iona. I understand.'

'I don't think you do really,' said Iona.

'No matter how complicated things are, they can always be helped by good friends,' said Enrique. 'And good wine. I have an exquisite bottle of Spanish white chilling in the fridge. You are welcome to join me.'

Iona thought about Frank's hand gripping tightly to the sheet on his bed. And her conversation afterwards with Sally and Jenna. It would be a betrayal of him to have a drink with Enrique. His invitation wasn't purely out of friendship.

'Also, I have some really fine olives and manchego cheese,' said Enrique persuasively. 'And strawberries.'

It sounded so appealing. It really did. Something different. And she could leave if he started to get too friendly.

'OK,' she said. 'I'd love to join you.'

'Wonderful,' said Enrique as he walked across the hall and opened the apartment door.

She followed him inside. The apartment was little changed from when she'd first shown it to him, although there was a tottering pile of books on the sideboard and a selection of financial magazines scattered around the room.

'The patio door is open,' he said. 'Make yourself comfortable outside and I will bring you some wine.'

'Thank you.'

The wooden furniture and plump cushions had come with the apartment too. Iona relaxed on to one of the loungers and turned her face towards the evening sun.

'It's very peaceful here,' said Enrique as he handed her a glass of wine. 'I like it very much. It was a good choice.'

'I'm glad you like it.'

'Tell me about your complicated life.' Enrique sat down on one of the wooden chairs.

'Not right now,' she said.

'No problem,' he said.

He said nothing more, and Iona closed her eyes. It was quiet and peaceful on the balcony and the sun was warm but not blistering. She felt the tension in her shoulders ease. Her mind wandered on to the future and Frank's real improvement. What plan would they come up with? she wondered. It really wasn't as though they could share him. She didn't think either she or Sally wanted that. She wondered whether either of them loved him any more. That was a difficult question. Her feelings, and Sally's too, she was certain, were entirely influenced by Frank's condition. She'd already said lots of times that she'd thump him when he woke up, but of course she wouldn't. She'd be ecstatic. But after the ecstasy, then what? Who cared? she thought fuzzily. Things would happen. There was no point in always trying and trying to work them out beforehand. She sighed and her shoulders relaxed a little more.

'Omigod!' She jolted into wakefulness, suddenly realising that she had drifted off to sleep. The sun had slid behind the corner of the building and she was now in the shade.

'Ah,' said Enrique. 'You are with us again.'

She looked at her watch. She'd totally conked out. She'd been asleep for nearly three-quarters of an hour.

'I am so, so sorry,' she said hastily. 'I don't know what happened.'

'You were tired. And I was boring.' Enrique grinned at her.

'No, you weren't boring. You were just . . . It was peaceful. I'm sorry.' She felt terrible. But the sleep had been the most restful she'd had in ages. She hadn't been dreaming, for one thing, as she so often did – of being alone in the city, looking for Frank, plaintively calling his name but never seeing him. Her forty-five minutes had been dreamless and refreshing.

'You are obviously working too hard.'

'No,' she said. 'It's not that. It's just the complicated stuff is very tiring.'

'Ah.'

She looked at him.

'I have had girlfriends with complicated lives. They never last very long.'

'Were you planning on me being a girlfriend?' she asked edgily, knowing the answer already.

Enrique shrugged expressively. 'A friend, and then who knows?'

'I'm sorry.' She smiled awkwardly. 'I really like you. But it's . . . it's . . .'

'Complicated,' he said.

A noise from the balcony next door caught their attention.

'*Hola*, Siobhán!' called Enrique. 'Are you home?'

Her red curls preceded her around the dividing wall.

'Hi, Enrique – goodness, Iona! What are you doing here?' But her blue eyes twinkled.

'Sleeping,' said Iona. 'Much to Enrique's despair, I think.'

'Do you want to join us?' he asked.

'Sure. Hang on a minute.' Her head disappeared and a few seconds later Enrique let her in to the apartment.

'Hi,' she said to Iona as she walked out on to the balcony. 'How are you?'

'I came to check out the den of thieves,' Iona told her, 'and bumped into Enrique, who let me sleep on his balcony.'

Siobhán laughed. 'We're very hopeful of putting them away,' she said. 'It was a good arrest.'

'Arrest?' Enrique looked at them questioningly and Siobhán, once again, told the story of the ID scam. 'And hopefully Carl O'Connor will write a piece in his paper that reflects the fact that most of the time we do know what we're doing,' she said.

'O'Connor?'

'He's playing ball,' said Siobhán. 'Quid pro quo on this story as against . . . others.'

'Will they get bail?' Iona looked at her gratefully. 'My landlord is going demented.'

'They're being remanded in custody till tomorrow,' said Siobhán happily, 'but after that – well, I dunno, Iona. It all depends.' She leaned back in one of the loungers and wriggled her toes in the last sliver of sunshine. 'Oh, I do like a day like today.'

Iona laughed. 'I'm glad it went well for you. We had an interesting day too.'

'Oh?'

It was only after she'd spoken that she realised she didn't really want to talk about Frank in front of Enrique. She looked uncomfortably at him and then turned to Siobhán.

'Frank is responding to sounds,' she said. 'He turned his head today. He was listening to Jenna when she talked.'

'Really?' A soft gleam came into Siobhán's eyes.

'They're hopeful that he'll wake up soon,' said Iona. Enrique glanced from one to the other but said nothing.

'I need to know when he does,' said Siobhán.

'Why?'

'You know why,' said Siobhán. 'I have to talk to him.'

'Oh, come on!' Iona looked at her unhappily. 'I thought we'd agreed that there wasn't any point.'

'I can't agree that,' said Siobhán firmly. 'I'm really sorry, Iona. Once he's fit to be questioned, I do need to talk to him.'

'But we've figured it all out!' cried Iona.

'Figured all what out?' asked Siobhán.

'Not what you're obviously thinking,' said Iona sharply. 'Not that there was some malevolent motive behind it. Just that he loved us both and wasn't able to choose between us. For heaven's sake, you yourself did a whole heap of digging and didn't come up with anything.'

'I know,' said Siobhán. 'All I'm saying is that I need to talk to him. That's all.'

'I don't want my life to be a damn criminal case that lights your fire!' Iona got up from the lounger and picked up her jacket. 'Just because I helped you out on the ID people doesn't mean that you can go poking around in my life now. Or Sally's. Or Jenna's. You know how that poor kid has been over the last few months! You can't mess with us now, Siobhán. You can't.'

'Iona, calm down.' Siobhán spoke gently. 'I'm not—'

'Thanks for the drink, Enrique, but I have to go.' Iona blinked away the tears that had suddenly rushed to her eyes and grabbed her bag. 'You were very nice. But now you know how complicated my life is, so there's no need to be nice any more.'

'Iona . . .' Siobhán called after her, but the other girl had already stridden through the apartment and out of the door.

Chapter 37

Every time she thought about Siobhán Farrell wanting to interview Frank, Iona felt herself get into a rage. She'd considered Siobhán to be a friend, and now it seemed the other woman was perfectly prepared to put friendship to one side to secure a conviction that could see him in jail for a couple of years at least. Siobhán had told them that the maximum term for bigamy was seven years but that she couldn't really imagine a judge sentencing Frank to seven years after all he'd been through. And, of course, he'd probably only serve about a third of whatever sentence he might get. Iona couldn't quite believe that Siobhán might arrest Frank at all as he lay in bed, but equally she couldn't see what choice the detective might have. After all, in her eyes Frank had committed a crime. She probably had a quota of arrests she was supposed to make every month, and Frank would help her meet her target.

Iona felt uneasily that she was being unfair on Siobhán, but she couldn't help herself. What on earth would they do if Frank was arrested? What would happen if he went to jail? Would they simply switch one visiting routine for another? And how would they cope with it this time? It was one thing being mature and adult and co-operative when Frank was helpless; it might be something completely different when he was awake again. Maybe it would be better if he stayed in the coma after all.

I can't want that to be the case, Iona told herself, as she drove to the hospital. If he stayed in a coma for ever I'd resent it, because I resent it now. The resentful feelings were with her because Ruth and some of the other girls from Rental Remedies were going out for dinner to a trendy new restaurant that night and she'd really wanted to go. But because of the continuing improvement in Frank's condition she didn't feel as though she could let a day go by without visiting him to help speed up his recovery.

She'd thought of asking Sally if she wanted to go to the hospital that evening instead, but she knew that the trek into the city from Bray was beginning to become a strain for Sally as her pregnancy progressed. Sally's doctor had advised her to relax and put her feet up a bit more, which, she had told Iona, was easier said than done. So because she knew that Sally was anxious about her pregnancy (even though Frank's illness had distracted her from her concerns), Iona didn't want her to feel as though she had to come to the hospital whenever there was a moment Frank might be alone. So she'd turned down the invitation to dinner. But she hadn't wanted to.

Now she strode through the familiar corridors of the hospital as she made her way to Frank's room. Perhaps today, she thought. Perhaps this will be the day when he comes back to us.

She pushed open the door. The evening sun filtered through the window and cast slatted light across the bed. Frank looked as though he were simply asleep. She pulled out the chair and sat down beside him. Then she started to talk.

The enormity of what had happened was giving him a headache. He could hear Iona's voice telling him that she was really confused about her feelings and about her life and he wanted to tell her that she didn't have to be confused, that he'd never meant to hurt anyone and that he knew he'd messed up big-time. He knew that Iona was his second wife, the one he'd chosen after Sally. He knew that he should never have married her, that it had been wrong and illegal and that – now that everyone knew about it – he'd caused nothing but trouble. He knew that to explain he'd done it because he so desperately wanted to keep her close, to have an extra family, because he was always seeking the perfect family, would make no sense to rational people. It didn't make sense to him either, when he thought about it. But it had seemed perfectly reasonable at the time.

He could hear the despair in her voice and it was like a dagger through his heart. How was it, he wondered, that when all he'd wanted was to make women happy, he'd ended up making them miserable instead?

He knew, too, that it wasn't just Iona. Sally's voice hid a tone of despair when she talked to him too. And he thought it was amazing that Sally, who hated illness so much, had spent so much time visiting him. It proved to him how much she loved him. Yet he didn't really deserve her love at all.

He had no idea how long he'd been in the hospital, but he knew it must be a long time now. The smells and the sounds were very familiar to him. The cheery voices of the nurses, the constant beeping of the monitors, the slightly antiseptic smell . . . all of those things were comforting and ordinary. There was a part of him that was happy to stay like this, surrounded by people who cared for him and not having to face the music.

'She loves you, Frank, but she's got the baby to consider,' said Iona. 'So maybe it would be better if you were with me. But you and her and Jenna and the baby – that's the most important thing. And in the end . . . I love you, but I suppose I'll get over you.'

He hated to hear her so miserable. He knew that she wasn't a miserable sort of person.

'And the detective, Frank. I think she wants to arrest you! She's been really nice to me and Sally but she's said over and over again that you've committed a crime. I mean, I know it's not like you robbed a bank or something, but Jesus Christ, Frank – maybe it would've been easier on everyone if you had!'

It was all his fault. He'd never intended for the two parts of his life to collide like this. But they had. Funny, though, he really struggled to remember how that had happened.

And then it came back to him. The pub. The sudden rumbling noise and the darkness that had enveloped him as everything had collapsed on top of him. He remembered gasping for breath and trying to open his eyes and the horrible, horrible feeling of being suffocated by the rubble pressing down on him, of struggling to get free and then of more subsidence around him and something hitting him on the head. He wanted to break free. But he couldn't.

Iona opened the door and called anxiously to Terri Cooper, who was in the corridor outside.

'He's getting really agitated,' she said worriedly. 'I've never seen him like this before.'

They both watched as Frank clenched and unclenched his fists and moved his head on the pillow.

'I'll contact Dr Carroll,' said Terri calmly. 'Reacting is good, but . . .'

'I'll sit with him,' said Iona. She went into the room again. Frank had quietened down but she was still concerned. She waited for a moment and then went outside to phone Sally.

Sally was sitting on the sofa, her legs propped up in front of her. She'd had cramps all day and a vague feeling of nausea that wouldn't go away. Six months into her pregnancy she resented feeling nauseous. She also had a slight headache which she knew was caused by knots in the muscles of her neck. But she was feeling a little better now in the silence of the house. Jenna had gone to Sam's to try to unlock the secret file on Frank's computer. Sally was pleased that she had taken such an interest in the computer and had done such a good job on the client accounts. She'd e-mailed them to Myles and now Iona's brother-in-law had a database of all Frank's contracts. He'd been in touch with the clients and Sally felt much better about things.

She wasn't as concerned as Jenna about the password-protected folder. She knew that Frank loved passwords and code-keys – it was all part of his James Bond obsession. She had, briefly, wondered if the file had anything to do with another secret wife, but she was confident now that it hadn't. At least Siobhán Farrell's investigations had set her mind at rest about that, even if she was concerned about how the detective would proceed when Frank recovered. Iona had phoned her in a fury at Siobhán's reaction to the fact that he might be waking up at last. According to Iona, Siobhán was going to betray them just to have another arrest credited to her. But Sally couldn't bring herself to blame Siobhán. The girl had to do her job. She was just hoping that it wouldn't come to anything in the end.

She sighed as the phone rang and reached out for the receiver. It was Iona, telling her about Frank's agitated condition and sounding very agitated herself. Her anxiety worried Sally, who (despite the other girl's hysteria the first time they met) thought her a very level-headed person.

'Do you want me to come in?'

She hoped Iona would say no. The idea of driving into the city was very unappealing.

'Oh, Sally, I know that I'm probably getting my knickers in a twist over nothing. But he's acting really weird. Part of me thinks it's positive because he's like someone having a bad dream. But it's frightening me too.'

Sally said nothing.

'Shit, Sal, I'm sorry. I don't mean to worry you.'

'Isn't any sort of reaction good?' asked Sally.

'Yes. I think so. But . . .'

'I'll come,' said Sally.

'Thanks,' said Iona. 'I'll be here.'

Sally hung up the phone and frowned. Then she dialled Jenna's number.

'Oh, but we're really, really close to cracking this!' wailed Jenna. 'I'm not sure that I want to leave it now.'

'I'd like you to come,' said Sally. 'Sam can keep working on it.'

Jenna heard a tone of authority in Sally's voice that she never flouted. She frowned. 'OK,' she said eventually. 'I'll be there in five minutes.'

He'd messed up everything. That was the bottom line of it. He'd messed it up and caused needless anxiety and he couldn't blame them for hating him. He remembered them saying that. Both of them. That they hated him. That they'd be better off without him. But they'd said that they loved him too. He could hear Iona's voice again, soothing and soft, telling him that everything was all right and that she loved him.

Iona smiled in relief when she saw Sally walk in the door.

'I'm so sorry for dragging you out,' she said. 'But I thought you needed to be here.'

'What's happened?'

'He's quiet now,' said Iona. 'But he was totally agitated earlier. The doctor came in and they looked at the monitors and gave him some meds, I think. He's been calmer since. But . . .' she glanced at Jenna, who was standing near the top of the bed, 'I don't know why I suddenly felt so worried. Now that you're here, I feel better.'

'Good.' Sally pulled up a chair and sat down.

'Are you OK?' asked Iona. 'You're very pale.'

'The baby was acting up today.' Sally rubbed her stomach.

'Oh God, Sally, I really shouldn't have phoned!'

'I'm glad you did,' said Sally.

'Yes,' said Frank hoarsely. 'It's a good thing.'

Iona, Sally and Jenna looked at each other in silence. Then they stared at the man in the bed. Frank's eyes were open and he was looking at them.

'I'm really sorry,' he said, and closed his eyes again.

'Frank!' cried Iona. 'Frank, wake up!'

'Dad!' Jenna shook him by the arm. 'Dad, it's me.'

'I know it's you.' His eyes opened.

Terri Cooper walked into the room. She saw Frank and the women looking at each other. And she paged Dr Carroll.

'I never meant to hurt you,' said Frank croakily after Iona had given him a sip of water from the glass beside the bed. 'I never meant for any of this to happen.'

'Jesus, Frank, what did you think was going to happen?' demanded Sally, oblivious to the look of surprise from Jenna at the tone of her voice. 'You betrayed me with Iona and you ignored our marriage vows and you lied to us both every single day.'

'You should have told me,' Iona said fiercely. 'You should have told me you were married. I would've been mad at you but I could have got over it.'

'I couldn't,' said Frank. 'I – you were great. I—'

'You're a shit, Frank!' cried Sally. 'You weren't available to meet women, even great women like Iona. She has every right to be furious with you. Like I have.'

'I know. I know.' Frank coughed and Iona gave him some more water. 'But we were going through a bad patch, weren't we? And I was afraid you'd leave me.'

'Why on earth would I leave you?' demanded Sally. 'We were married. Yes, it was a bad patch, but we would've worked it through.'

'My mother left,' said Frank simply. 'And they didn't even go through a bad patch.'

Sally and Iona stared at him.

'You married me because you were afraid Sally would leave you?' said Iona incredulously. 'You didn't want to be on your own, so I was a kind of insurance policy?'

'I didn't see it like that,' protested Frank. 'I fell in love with you. I wanted to keep you. Sally too.'

'You're seriously weird, Dad.' Jenna's voice was shaky. 'You need to see a shrink.'

'Maybe,' said Frank. 'Maybe I should've done it before.'

'I can't believe it's all that woman's fault,' said Sally harshly. 'Bloody Christine! She was never there for him as a kid and you heard what he said. She's turned him into a complete fuck-up.'

'You can't blame her because he decided to marry two people,' protested Iona. 'Maybe she wasn't exactly a great mother, but Frank is responsible for his own actions.'

'I know,' he said faintly. 'I had a wonderful marriage. Two wonderful marriages. I was so lucky. I love you, Sally. I love you too, Jenna. You'll always be . . . my responsibility.' He closed his eyes for a moment and then opened them again. 'But Iona's going to have a baby. I could hear you talking about it when I was asleep. I have responsibilities towards that baby too.'

'You idiot!' said Iona. It's Sally who's having the baby. Not me.'

Frank looked at his wife in astonishment. 'But . . . but I thought you couldn't have any more babies,' he said.

'You thought wrong then,' said Sally shortly.

'My head hurts,' he said, and closed his eyes again.

'So does mine.' Sally rubbed her forehead. 'In fact . . . I don't feel very well.'

Jenna and Iona looked at her. She was as white as a sheet.

'Oh hell,' said Iona, as Sally slid from the chair and Dr Carroll walked into the room.

They put Sally on a trolley and hurried her to the maternity ward. As she was pushed through the corridors she couldn't help feeling as though she personally knew every nurse and doctor in the place by now. Her heart was racing as waves of pain hit her. She was frightened. It was far too early for the baby to come, and yet she was having an almost uncontrollable urge to push. She whimpered softly.

'Don't you worry, pet,' said the orderly who was pushing the trolley. 'We'll have you sorted out in no time.'

'My baby,' said Sally. 'Make sure my baby is all right.'

'Of course we will.'

Sally closed her eyes. Was this what it had been like for Frank, she wondered, as he'd been rushed to hospital? Frightened, worried, wondering what was going to happen to him? But he'd been unconscious, hadn't he? It couldn't have been the same. Pain stabbed her again and she cried out.

'OK, Sally, nearly there.' The voice was comforting, in the same way that the voices that spoke to Frank were comforting. Maybe they think I'm going to die, she thought. That would be just great. Frank would have to get better really quickly to look after Jenna and the baby.

'Right, Sally.' She opened her eyes. Her gynaecologist was standing beside her. 'Let's get you sorted out now. We're just going to hook you up to some equipment and insert a drip. It won't be painful.'

Why did they always say things like that? wondered Sally. Of course it was going to be painful. Everything was painful.

Iona and Jenna sat outside Frank's room. His eyes were closed again and he was perfectly still, but the doctor was in with him, monitoring him again and talking to Terri Cooper about his lucid waking moment. Jenna was chewing furiously at her bottom lip and Iona was racking her brain to think of the right thing to say to her.

'Will my mum be OK?' asked Jenna eventually.

'I'm sure she will,' replied Iona. 'I shouldn't have phoned her, Jen. If she wasn't feeling too good then she shouldn't have driven up. I'm sorry about that.'

'She would've gone mad if she wasn't there when Dad woke up.' Jenna rubbed the corners of her eyes. 'What are you going to do about him, Iona?'

'I think that if you and your mum want him home, then that's what should happen,' she said.

'He's my dad.' Jenna sniffed. 'I'm really angry with him, but . . .'

'I understand,' said Iona.

'I blamed him,' said Jenna. 'For everything. Even for the stuff that I did. But you're right, Iona. You can't blame other people when you make a mess of things yourself.'

Iona put her arm around Jenna's shoulders. 'What did you make a mess of?' she asked.

Jenna poured out the story of sleeping with Gerry and ignoring her friends in favour of Aline and Cindy and their crowd. And she confessed that Cathal Rothery had brought her home the night of the brawl outside the bar.

'Gosh,' said Iona. 'Does your mum know about that?'

Jenna shook her head. 'She doesn't know I slept with Gerry either. So please, please don't tell her.' Her face was anxious. 'We were sensible. We took precautions. I didn't get pregnant or anything. But you know, after the fight I had with Aline and Cindy he was so horrible to me. He implied that I was a cheap alley-cat kind of person.' She sighed. 'I think he was right.'

'Don't talk nonsense,' said Iona. 'You're a great person, Jenna. He was lucky to be going out with you, and Sally and Frank are very, very lucky to have you as a daughter.' Suddenly her own eyes swam with tears. 'I'd have been proud to have you as a daughter myself.'

Jenna looked at her in surprise. 'Thank you. I thought you hated me.'

Iona wiped her eyes. 'Not at all. I envy your mum and dad. I wish I had a daughter like you.'

'Crikey, I wouldn't think so!' Jenna's eyes opened wide. 'I am, apparently, nothing but trouble.'

'Oh, rubbish.' Iona smiled. 'You're seventeen. You're supposed to be trouble.'

'Did you and Dad want a kid?' asked Jenna.

Iona nodded. 'Only that won't happen now.'

'I guess not.' Jenna's gaze flickered towards her father's room.

Frank opened his eyes and stared back at them. Iona and Jenna looked at him in silence.

'I'm sorry.' They could make out the words through the window. 'I love you.'

And then the machines went crazy.

Sally was drifting in and out of consciousness but she knew that she felt better. She knew, too, that she could still feel the baby inside her and that everything was under control again. She felt extremely grateful for the fact that she'd been in the hospital when she'd been taken ill and that they'd been so fantastic about looking after her.

'Hi,' said Frank.

She knew that she was imagining him, but it seemed as though he was standing in front of her, looking fit and handsome as he had been before the accident.

'What are you doing here?' she asked.

'Just saying sorry,' he said. 'I messed up.'

'You more than messed up,' she told him.

'I want to blame loads of people but it's only myself,' he told her.

'It doesn't matter,' she said. 'We'll sort it out somehow.'

'Are you feeling all right?'

'Now I am,' she said. 'I was really worried for a while but they keep telling me everything's OK and I believe them.'

'I can't believe that you're having a baby. After all this time.'

'Neither can I,' said Sally.

'I'm sorry if I pressurised you about it before.'

'I pressurised myself.'

'Most of all I'm sorry about Iona.'

'You love her?'

'I love you too.'

'Oh, Frank. You really dug yourself a hole and jumped right in, didn't you?'

He smiled wryly.

'But I like her,' said Sally. 'She's been someone to lean on. I can see why you love her. In the end, you know, it would've been harder without her.'

'It's still not ideal,' said Frank.

'Oh, hell.' Sally smiled at him. 'When is life ever ideal?'

'Take care of yourself.' The image of him faded and Sally fell asleep.

The doctors and nurses were clustered around Frank's bed. Iona and Jenna were outside the room, arms around each other. When the alarms had gone off on the machines Dr Carroll had come out and told them that there was a problem but that they were dealing with it. Now, Ashley Dalton, a student nurse, was sitting beside them. She'd given them cups of sweetened tea. Iona wondered how often nurses gave out cups of sweetened tea in the hospital.

* * *

Three hours later Dr Carroll stood in front of them, and although he was trying to keep his face impassive, Iona could see that he was shocked as he continued speaking.

'We were monitoring him very closely, as you know. But an aneurysm developed really quickly. We did everything we could.' He glanced at Jenna. 'I can't tell you how sorry I am.'

'You're telling us he's dead?' Jenna was shaking. 'He can't be dead. He woke up.'

They'd watched the team of professionals rush Frank back to the operating theatre and they'd drunk more sweetened tea and they'd worried about what was going on, but they hadn't believed that he could possibly die. After all, he'd spoken to them for the very first time that day. He was supposed to be getting better.

Jenna started to cry. Iona folded her into her arms and looked over the top of her head at the doctor.

'I know this is hard to accept,' said Dr Carroll. 'I know that waking up was a major event. He must have been in pain then, though.'

Iona remembered the anguished expression on Frank's face as he'd talked to them. But she'd thought that was because he realised how much trouble he was in. She tightened her hold around Jenna. 'He talked to us and we talked to him.' Her voice caught in her throat. 'Oh God, what are we going to tell Sally? She can't afford a shock like this now.'

'Sally's asleep at the moment.' Terri Cooper's voice was soft and gentle. 'We won't wake her yet.'

'He can't be dead.' Jenna was angry. 'You can't have let him die like that. Not after all this time!'

'There's a chaplain in the hospital,' said Terri. 'Would you like him to come to you?'

'No,' said Iona. 'Not just now. I want to be on my own.'

'Don't leave me!' cried Jenna. 'I can't be on my own.'

'I won't. I won't.' Iona hugged her again. 'Don't worry. I won't leave you.' She looked up at Terri. 'Can we see him?' she asked.

'Shortly,' said Terri. 'We're just doing some things for him and then you can see him.'

Jenna shivered. 'I don't want to,' she said.

'You don't have to,' said Iona quickly. 'But I do, sweetheart.'

'Will you tell my mum?'

'Yes,' said Iona. 'I'll tell your mum.'

* * *

It was after midnight when she went to the private room where Sally had been relocated. Jenna walked beside her, holding her hand tightly. Iona had gone in to see Frank. He didn't look all that different from when he'd been in the coma. Her tears had dripped on to his face and she'd wiped them away, realising already that he felt different. Lifeless. Gone from them for ever.

'I loved you, Frank.' She kissed him on the cheek. 'I know that some people will say that this was for the best, but I never, ever wanted you to die.'

She looked at him, waiting – as she'd waited so often over the last weeks for a response – but she knew this time there would be nothing. So she kissed him again and left the room.

Jenna had been waiting outside with Terri Cooper and had grabbed Iona's hand as soon as she'd come out. Now Iona could feel the younger girl shivering beside her as they walked.

They went into the room and Sally opened her eyes.

'Hi,' she said.

'Hi,' said Iona.

They looked at each other and then Sally's face crumpled.

'Oh, no.'

'I'm sorry,' said Iona. 'It was an aneurysm. There was nothing they could do.'

'Oh, Mum.' Jenna finally released Iona's hand and leaned across her mother. The two of them hugged each other tightly.

Iona slipped quietly out of the room. She walked through the corridors until she could use her phone and then she called Lauren.

'I'll come,' said her sister.

'Don't,' Iona told her. 'There's no need. I just wanted you to know.'

'Io, you can't be there on your own. Sally can't help if she's hospitalised too.'

'I'm fine,' said Iona. 'I really am. Please don't worry about me. I'll call you tomorrow.'

'Iona—'

'I'll be really annoyed if you come,' said Iona. 'Besides, I might be gone by then. I don't know what I'm doing yet. There's some stuff I need to sort out.'

'OK,' said Lauren, although she didn't sound convinced. 'Call me.'

'I will.'

Iona went back up to Sally's room. Jenna was sitting on the chair beside her mother's bed, but when Iona walked in she got up and took her hand again.

'I knew,' said Sally.

'How?'

'He came to me.'

Iona said nothing.

'I know it sounds nonesense, but he did,' Sally told her. 'He said he was sorry and that he loved me.'

'Dammit, I thought everything was going to be OK.' Iona swallowed hard.

'Maybe everything can't always be OK,' said Sally. 'There isn't always a happy ending. Not that there ever would have been, given the situation we were in.'

'We would have worked something out,' said Iona. 'All of us. We've been working things out for the past few months, haven't we?'

'I know.' Sally's eyes fluttered closed.

Iona looked at Jenna, who was still white-faced and trembling. 'You need some rest too,' she told her.

'Perhaps they can give me somewhere . . .'

'You can't stay here,' said Iona. 'There's hardly enough room for patients, let alone anyone else.'

'I have to go home,' said Jenna. 'But I don't want to be there by myself.'

'You can stay with me,' said Iona. 'If Sally thinks that's all right.'

'Of course it is,' said Sally sleepily. 'It's the best place for her.'

Jenna sat beside her mother while Iona made a final trip to Frank's unit and spoke briefly to Terri Cooper, who hugged her and told her that she was a strong person and that they'd grown to love both her and Sally. Iona was grateful for the other woman's sympathy and understanding. She was just about to return for Jenna when Myles strode into the corridor.

'What are you doing here?' she gasped in surprise.

'Lauren told me that you were dealing with it all yourself. She wanted to come but I didn't want her to. Maybe a few months ago you mightn't have wanted me here, Iona, but you need someone and I thought—'

'Oh, Myles!' She looked at her brother-in-law as the tears flooded into her eyes. 'Thank you. Thank you for coming. I couldn't let Lauren come, she has to look after herself.'

'I know. I know.' He put his arms around her and patted her back. 'Is there anything I can do tonight?'

'Not really,' said Iona. 'I've spoken to everyone.'

'I'm going to take you back to our house,' said Myles.

'You can't.' Iona raised her head from his shoulder. 'I said I'd look after Jenna.'

'Jenna?' Myles frowned.

'Sally's daughter.'

'I know who she is,' said Myles. 'She sent me the computer files, for heaven's sake. I just didn't realise she was here too.'

Iona nodded. 'She's with Sally right now. But I said she could come home with me.'

'You can both come with me,' said Myles firmly. 'You'll have to share the spare room, but there's two beds.'

Suddenly Iona was too tired to argue. 'OK.'

They walked through the hospital to the maternity wing. Jenna was still sitting where Iona had left her, holding Sally's hand.

'I thought you weren't coming back,' she said anxiously. 'You were gone for ages.'

'Sorry,' said Iona. She introduced Myles and told Jenna that they'd been offered a bed at her sister's house. 'If that's OK with you,' she added.

Jenna nodded. 'It doesn't really matter where I sleep, does it?'

'No,' said Iona gently, 'it doesn't.'

Jenna kissed Sally good night and grasped Iona by the hand again. Then they walked out of the hospital together.

Chapter 38

It was the sound of children's laughter that woke Jenna the following morning. It had taken her a long time to fall asleep, and when she had, her dreams were complicated and unsettling. But then, at about six, when the early-morning light was poking through a chink in the heavy curtains, she'd suddenly entered a deeper state of sleep from which she hadn't wakened even when Iona got up.

Jenna blinked a couple of times as the memories of the previous night flooded back to her and hot tears scorched her eyes. It isn't fair, she muttered as she swung her legs over the side of the bed. If her dad had died straight away it would have been easier. There wouldn't have been all these weeks of coming into the hospital, trying to bring him back to consciousness. She wouldn't have spent so long feeling angry with him and her mother and Iona. It would've been over and done with. It would have hurt, but not as much as the last months had hurt. She'd begun to believe that everything could be all right, and now it wasn't and that made her feel much worse.

Someone had left a fresh fluffy towel at the end of her bed. She picked it up and walked into the en suite bathroom, where she stood under the shower and allowed the water to massage her shoulders. It felt disrespectful to be wishing that she had her favourite extra-moisturising shower soap and a change of underwear. And it was weird to be doing a normal thing like having a shower when she'd spent the night in the house of a woman she didn't know, in the same room as the woman who'd tried to steal her father from her mother. That surely wasn't normal. She breathed out slowly through her mouth as she allowed the water to cascade over her face. All she wanted was to be ordinary. To have an ordinary life with an ordinary family and an ordinary boyfriend. She hadn't managed any of that.

She turned off the water and got out of the shower. She looked around her uncertainly and then used some of the moisturising cream from the Boots jar on the shelf before cleaning her teeth using her finger and some toothpaste. After that she got dressed, brushed her hair and made her way downstairs.

Lauren and Iona were sitting at the kitchen table, empty coffee cups in front of them.

'Hi, Jenna.' Lauren got up and hugged her, and tears welled up in Jenna's eyes again. It was hard when people were nice, it really was. 'I'm glad you finally got some sleep. Would you like some coffee? or tea?'

'Coffee, please.' Jenna sat gingerly on one of the kitchen stools. She glanced out of the window. Gavin and Charlotte were racing around the sunny garden, shrieking with enjoyment.

'Did they wake you?' Iona had noticed her look. 'They're complete terrors.'

'I heard them,' admitted Jenna. 'I didn't know where the noise was coming from.'

'They're not the worst.' Lauren placed a mug of coffee in front of her. 'Iona doesn't have the patience, that's all.'

Jenna couldn't understand why they were talking about such mundane things.

'I phoned your mum earlier,' Iona said. 'She's much better.'

'I suppose it's good that one of my parents is all right.' Jenna's voice was shaky.

'Your mum is fine,' said Iona firmly. 'Anyone who's pregnant can have a bit of a scare, and that's all it was. They're going to keep her in for a couple of days, but she's perfectly OK.'

'What about Dad?' asked Jenna anxiously. 'What's going to happen to him.'

It took Iona a moment to compose herself. 'I spoke to Sally about him too,' she said. 'She wants to have the funeral as soon as she's able to leave the hospital.'

'He wants to be cremated,' said Jenna. 'He told me that before.'

Iona nodded. 'He told me the same.'

'But Mum never wanted that,' she said, her voice anxious. 'Mum always said it was undignified. What if she won't agree?'

Lauren glanced between Iona and Jenna.

'You need to sit down with your mum,' she said, realising that Iona was struggling to speak. 'Talk it through with her.'

'He *told* me,' insisted Jenna.

'We'll call in to see Sally shortly,' Iona promised. 'Get things sorted.'

'I need to go home and change,' said Jenna. 'These are yesterday's clothes.'

'I understand,' said Iona. 'But I have to get my car from the hospital car park first.' She grimaced. 'We keep on leaving cars there! So my suggestion is that we call a cab, go in and see your mum, then go to my house so that I can change too, and then I'll drive you home.'

Sally was sitting up when they walked into her room. Her face was pale and she had shadows under her eyes, but she smiled when she saw them. Jenna rushed over to the bed and put her arms around her and Sally held her tightly while Iona stood at the foot of the bed.

'I saw him this morning,' said Sally after Jenna had disentangled herself. 'They brought me up in a wheelchair. He looked . . . peaceful.'

Iona nodded.

'He wants to be cremated,' said Jenna quickly. 'He told me before. He's afraid of being buried alive.'

'I know,' said Sally. 'Though there's no chance of that, is there?' Her lip trembled.

'Well, you have to do what he said,' Jenna told her.

'I—'

'He told Iona too,' she added.

Sally looked up at Iona. 'Did he?'

Iona wasn't sure how to reply. She felt like the intruder again, the person who had no say in the lives of the Harper family. The person who wasn't really Frank's wife and who had no right to be there. So she nodded imperceptibly.

'Is that what you want?' asked Sally.

'I . . . it doesn't matter,' said Iona abruptly. 'Whatever you think is right.' She couldn't stay in the room any longer. She turned around and walked out of the door, leaving Sally and Jenna staring after her.

There was an empty bench seat in the corridor. She sat down and buried her head in her hands. Over the past few weeks she'd been part of everything, but now she was no one. Sally and Jenna would organise the funeral, and it would be their friends and family and neighbours who'd be there. And she'd be a nobody. Because they wouldn't want her to be a focus of attention. They'd want to keep up the façade of Frank being a family man. She supposed that Sally's friends knew something of his secret life now, but his funeral wasn't going to be the place to make it all public. And she wasn't going to fight about it. What was the point now? Frank was gone and none of it really mattered any more.

'Iona?' Jenna's voice was nervous. 'Are you all right?'

She wiped her eyes as she looked up. 'Yes, sure,' she said quickly. 'I'm fine.'

'Mum said that maybe you were worried about the funeral.'

'No.'

'She thought you might think we'd want to shut you out.'

'I—'

'She wants to talk to you about it,' said Jenna.

'OK,' said Iona, and went back to Sally's room.

Somehow it was easier to deal with plans for Frank's funeral than it had been to deal with the hospital visits and everything to do with his coma. They agreed on the type of service and the music, and Iona said that she would meet with a priest from their parish in Bray to discuss it all since Sally would be in hospital for another day or two.

'Though I'm not sure how they'll react to it,' she said. 'I mean, he broke a whole heap of the Ten Commandments!'

Sally laughed. The three of them looked guiltily at each other, because it seemed wrong to laugh, but both Jenna and Iona then smiled too.

'Hopefully they'll consider that they're saving him from eternal damnation,' said Sally wryly. 'Iona, I really appreciate everything you've done.'

'It's OK,' said Iona. 'I'll talk to him about the readings and everything and bring all the stuff in for you to look at.'

'Thanks.'

'And the funeral will be at the weekend. You're sure you'll be out by then?'

Sally nodded.

'What about me?' asked Jenna. 'What am I going to do?'

'A reading?' suggested Sally.

'Not at the funeral,' said Jenna. 'Now. I have to go home and change but I don't want to stay there on my own.'

'Well, you can stay with me, like I said last night,' Iona told her.

'But for a few days? I can't do that,' said Jenna. 'My stuff is at home. I don't want to leave everything.'

'You can't stay there on your own,' said Sally. 'Not . . . you can't, Jen.'

'You'd be fine in my place,' Iona told her. 'Really.'

Jenna looked uncertain.

'Perhaps Iona could stay in our house,' said Sally. 'If she doesn't mind.'

'Oh, gosh, Sally – I don't know.' Iona was shocked at the suggestion.

'Please?' begged Jenna. 'I really want to be at home and I need someone with me.'

'Um . . . I suppose . . .'

'Thank you.' Jenna hugged her. 'Thank you very much.'

In the rush to the hospital the previous evening, Jenna had left her mobile phone at home. As she opened the door she could hear it beeping to signal an incoming message. She hurried through to the kitchen and picked it up, seeing that she had missed half a dozen calls and had a variety of text messages. They were all from Sam. The gist of it was that she had managed to crack open Frank's secret folder and that Jenna should get in touch with her right away.

'Where the hell were you?' demanded Sam as she took Jenna's call. 'I thought maybe you were with Aline and Cindy and that you'd frozen me out again.'

'God, no,' said Jenna quickly. She swallowed hard and told Sam about her father.

'Oh, Jen, I'm so, so sorry.' Sam was shocked. She too had got the impression that Jenna's dad was recovering. 'I'm at work today. I'll try to get off early and come around.'

'Thanks,' said Jenna. 'See you later.'

She turned to Iona, who had followed her into the kitchen and was standing in the doorway, clutching a small holdall which she'd picked up from her house before driving to Bray.

'I guess you need to see your room,' said Jenna. She made her way towards the stairs. 'I'm at the top on the right and the spare room is on the left.'

It was beautifully decorated, with luxurious pile carpet in pale pink, matching curtains and a double bed with a plump duvet with a pink and white cover. Iona wondered again how Frank could reconcile the slightly fussy decor of his house in Bray with the minimalist look of their home in the Liberties.

'There's no en suite bathroom,' Jenna told her. 'But there's one at the end of the landing.'

Iona nodded.

'Are you all right?'

She nodded again.

'Is it weird for you being here?'

'I was here before,' Iona admitted, 'though not upstairs.'

Jenna looked at her edgily. 'When?'

Iona told her about driving Sally home the night that Jenna had gone missing.

'She never said.' Jenna's tone was accusing.

'I don't think you and she were getting on very well at the time,' Iona reminded her. 'And you would have blown a gasket if you'd come home and found me here.'

'I guess.' Jenna sat on the bed. 'Is it all completely bonkers? You and her and Dad and me and . . . well, the way it's all turned out?'

'Slightly bonkers,' agreed Iona. 'But, well, we've got to support each other, haven't we?'

'You've been great,' said Jenna warmly. 'I hated you, of course. But . . . I can see why Dad loved you. I couldn't before. I can now.'

'Thanks.'

'Would you like more coffee?' Jenna got up from the bed. 'I have a feeling that people will start calling round soon. I guess we should be prepared.'

The news of Frank's death spread quickly around the estate. Neighbours called to the house and were surprised when Jenna answered the door and thanked them for calling and told them that Sally was in hospital. And then she invited them in and introduced them to Iona, who, she said, was a close friend of her father's – and, she added, her mother's too. Iona knew that everyone who called around was in a frenzy of curiosity about exactly what was going on, but nobody wanted to cause any kind of scene in front of Jenna. They all asked about Sally, and Iona told them that she was fine and that she'd be coming home in a day or two and that she was staying with Jenna until then and that the funeral would be at the weekend. By the time most people had left (and she knew that they'd all be gossiping amongst themselves at least until Sally returned) she was exhausted.

And then Sam arrived. The two teenagers hugged each other and Sam told Jenna how sorry she was, then Jenna introduced her to Iona. Sam looked at Iona with undisguised interest and said that she was really pleased to meet her. Iona said that she was pleased to meet Sam too. And then Sam reminded Jenna about the password-protected folder.

'It wasn't that hard to crack it in the end,' she said. 'The thing is, Jen . . .'

'What?' Jenna looked at her anxiously. 'Don't tell me that there's something – someone else. Please don't. It would kill my mother.' She shot a look at Iona. 'I mean, I know we're cool about Iona now, but someone else . . .'

'No. Nothing like that,' said Sam hastily. 'I suppose I'd better show it to you.' She powered up the laptop and put it on the table in front of them. 'Here you go,' she said.

Jenna and Sam looked at the screen. The file contained scanned documents. An old photograph which had obviously been torn and put back together. A birth certificate. A death certificate. And copies of letters. Jenna's eyes narrowed as she looked at them. She zoomed in on one of them.

Dear Derek,

I really don't know what to say. I'm honoured that you would want me to be your wife, but you know how I feel about marriage. It's an outdated institution . . .

Christine

She looked at the next:

Dear Frank,

I thought I made it abundantly clear at our meeting that I had no wish to meet with you again. I do not see why the birth of your daughter should change this in any way. I am returning the photograph.

Sincerely,

Christine

And the last, dated a couple of days before Frank's accident:

Dear Mr Harper,

I am writing on behalf of my client, Christine Harris. While she is aware that in the past she informed you that she had no interest in having any familial contact with you, she has asked me to let you know that she would be interested in meeting you sometime in the near future. If you are agreeable to such a meeting I would be obliged if you could contact me at this office at your earliest convenience.

Yours sincerely,

James Carlisle

'Bloody hell,' said Jenna. 'This is Dad's mum.' Her eyes darkened. 'No wonder he blames her for stuff. How could she send back my photo like that? That was horrible.'

Iona hugged her.

'I mean, everyone says I was a cute baby!' But Jenna's lip trembled.

'Well, she might not have wanted to know you as a baby, but obviously she's changed her mind.'

'Too late.' Jenna looked at Iona starkly. 'It's too late.'

Iona nodded. How awful, she thought, for it to be too late. How awful not to have spoken to someone, for whatever reason, and then to make the effort only to realise that you should have acted sooner. She wondered how Christine would deal with the news that her son had died before she had the chance to speak to him again.

'We'll talk to your mum,' said Iona. 'She can decide what to do about Christine.'

The doorbell rang again and Jenna sighed. 'Another nosy neighbour,' she muttered as she got up to answer it.

Iona hurriedly powered down the laptop as Jenna opened the living room door.

'It's Gerry,' she said, her cheeks tinged with pink. 'He heard about Dad and came to pay his respects.'

'Hello . . .' Gerry looked at Iona awkwardly.

'Iona,' she supplied.

'Hello, Iona,' he said. 'I'm sorry about what's happened.'

'So am I,' she said.

Sam looked edgily at Gerry and Jenna. 'I'd better go,' she said.

'Not yet,' said Jenna. 'I was going to make some coffee. Stay, please, Sam.'

'I'm sure you and Gerry have things to talk about,' she said. 'You won't want me around.'

'Not right now we haven't,' said Jenna. 'Maybe later.'

'Actually . . .' Gerry looked embarrassed. 'I wanted to say to Jen that I was sorry. I know that she's a good person. I bet she was provoked by those girls. And Jen, I never, ever did anything with anyone else when I was with you.'

'Oh.' Jenna blushed.

'And I won't hang around if you've got people here,' he told her. 'I just had to call and say I was sorry. I'll see you at the funeral.'

'Stay for coffee,' she said. 'You can go after that.'

So the four of them sat in the kitchen and drank yet more coffee. And every time Jenna smiled (which suddenly she was doing quite a lot), Iona could see Frank's smile. And when Jenna looked intently at Gerry or at Sam, Iona could see Frank's eyes. And she felt as though her heart was going to break.

Chapter 39

The doctor told Sally that she could go home the following day. She was sitting in the foyer of the hospital, waiting for Iona, who had promised to come and collect her, when she noticed the tall woman walking through the main doors and looking around her uncertainly.

'Siobhán.' She called out and lifted her hand and the detective turned towards her.

'Hi, Sally.' Siobhán sat on the bench beside her. 'How are you doing?' She could see dark circles under Sally's eyes, but her cheeks were tinged with pink and she looked somehow less stressed than other times when Siobhán had seen her.

'I'm OK,' she replied.

'I'm really sorry about Frank,' said Siobhán.

'How did you know?' asked Sally.

Siobhán looked uncomfortable. 'They told me,' she said.

'Who? Iona and Jenna?'

'No.' She shook her head. 'The hospital. They called to let me know.'

'Why would they let you know?' asked Sally.

'Because I'd asked them to tell me of any changes in Frank's condition,' said Siobhán.

'Oh.' Sally suddenly remembered what Iona had told her. 'You wanted to question him?'

Siobhán nodded.

'Guess this has messed it all up for you.' There was a trace of bitterness in Sally's voice.

'For sure that's what Iona thinks,' said Siobhán wryly. 'When I told her I'd have to interview Frank when he got better she wasn't happy. So she's bound to think that . . . that Frank's death is a bad career move for me.'

'She doesn't really,' said Sally. 'But she thinks . . . well, I suppose she thinks that you were really quick to remember your job and forget that we were friends for a while.'

'You're right to be sceptical about me,' Siobhán told her. 'The first thing I thought about when she told me about Frank's progress wasn't that it was good or bad for you guys, but what I had to do about it. I'm sorry. I shouldn't have thought that way. Not, to be honest with you, that I ever wanted to have to arrest Frank, but I have to follow the procedure. It doesn't matter that I like you and Iona. That's not the point.'

'I understand,' said Sally.

'But you don't like it. You don't like me for it.'

'It's not that . . .'

'Sooner or later everyone gets furious with the police,' said Siobhán resignedly. 'It's never good for anyone to have to deal with us. Doesn't matter what it's about. If your life is going well you don't need us. If it's not – well, we never do what you want. If a crime's been committed against you and we don't catch whoever did it, you think we're a shower of useless incompetents; if we do but they get off, most people will blame us. If you're the criminal you obviously hate us.'

'Gosh, Siobhán, that sounds a bit bleak.'

'Oh, don't mind me, I'll get over it,' said Siobhán. 'I didn't join the gardai to be liked.'

'Why did you?' asked Sally curiously.

'I have loads of brothers,' said Siobhán. 'It gave me the opportunity to boss them around.'

Sally laughed.

'Seriously,' said Siobhán.

They were silent for a moment, then Sally asked why Siobhán had come to the hospital.

'To see you, of course,' said Siobhán. 'I rang last night. They told me you'd be leaving this afternoon. Glad I didn't miss you.' She smiled at Sally. 'You're actually looking quite well . . . you know, despite everything.'

'I'm fine,' said Sally. 'Junior's OK too. And once the funeral is over . . . well, I guess I can get back to my life again. I know I have to rebuild it without Frank, but I can do that. I've had time to think about it.'

Siobhán nodded.

'What about you?' asked Sally. 'How's your life going?'

Siobhán smiled again. It seemed wrong to be pleased with her life when things were so awful for Sally and Iona, but a lot of good things had been said about her in the aftermath of the ID scam arrests and there was talk of a promotion. Also, she'd received a tip-off about a potential armed robbery on the north side of the city and, acting on the information she'd received, the robbery had been foiled and three men arrested. On the career side of things, everything was going really well.

There was, of course, the personal complication, even if it was quite a satisfying complication. She'd gone out with Carl O'Connor the previous night. A date. A real boy-meets-girl date. They'd met in town and gone to a cheap and cheerful restaurant in Temple Bar where Carl had related anecdotes about interviews from hell and stories that had gone wrong until she'd had to wipe tears of laughter from her eyes. Afterwards he'd brought her back to her apartment building and she'd thought about asking him in for coffee, but at the last moment she'd remembered that the breakfast dishes were still piled in the sink and that she hadn't tidied up in days. And she'd told herself that, much as she didn't agree with the idea of being a perfect girlfriend with a perfect apartment, she was going to have to learn to be just a bit tidier so that she could bring attractive men home and not worry about the state of the place. That meant, she'd realised, that she was thinking of Carl O'Connor as an attractive man she'd rather like to have around the place a bit more. But, hell, she'd thought – a garda and a journalist. A terrible combination! Worse than a garda and a financier. Definitely.

'Can I guess by that self-satisfied smirk on your face that things are looking up?' asked Sally in amusement.

Siobhán blushed. She hadn't realised how easily her emotions had played across her face.

'Who?' asked Sally. 'The old boyfriend or the new one?'

Siobhán was going to ask Sally who she actually meant by the new one when both of them saw Iona and Jenna walk into the hospital.

'Mum!' Jenna hurried over to her.

'Hi, Sal,' said Iona. She looked at Siobhán. 'Hello.'

'Iona, you can't be nasty to Siobhán,' said Sally easily. 'She came here today to see me and say that she was sorry about Frank's death.'

'Sorry because she can't make an arrest,' snapped Iona.

'You know that's not true,' said Sally softly. 'Siobhán is a good person, Iona. She's done her best for us always.'

'Look – it doesn't matter what you think,' said Siobhán. 'None of it matters now anyway. I'm sure you'll be delighted to have me out of your hair from now on. So I'll head off. It was nice to see you again, Sally. I hope everything works out for you. You too, Iona.'

She turned and strode towards the exit.

Sally, Iona and Jenna looked at each other.

'Is she upset?' asked Jenna.

'Just a little, I think.' Iona looked uncomfortable. She raised her voice. 'Siobhán!'

The detective turned around and Iona walked towards her.

'I'm sorry,' she said. 'I was bothered by everything. I didn't mean to lash out at you.'

'And I was insensitive,' said Siobhán. 'I am truly sorry for how things turned out.'

'You were great to us,' Iona told her.

'Part of the job.'

'We'll keep in touch?'

Siobhán nodded. 'That'd be good.'

'Maybe I can help you organise a new apartment?'

This time Siobhán grinned. 'You never know. Different spec next time. Different circumstances. Maybe.'

'Siobhán!'

'Early days,' said Siobhán. She glanced at her watch. 'I'd better go.'

'See you,' said Iona. She watched as the other girl walked out of the building, and then returned to Sally and Jenna.

'It's cool,' she said. 'We're sorted.'

'I'm glad,' said Sally. 'I like her. She's a decent kind of girl.'

'I know,' said Iona.

'Meantime, we have other stuff to talk about, don't we?' said Jenna. 'I'll tell you on the way home, Mum. It's . . . you're not going to believe it.'

'Oh?' said Sally as she got up and followed them to the car park.

Because it was her day off, Siobhán drove back to Dun Laoghaire. She was glad that she'd bumped into Iona at the hospital. She liked her and hadn't wanted to think that there was any sort of edginess between them. She hoped that Iona and Sally would be OK in the future. She rather thought they would be. They were strong, resilient women. She smiled inwardly. Just like herself.

She parked the car and was walking up the pathway to the apartment block when a man stepped out in front of her, startling her.

'Hi,' he said.

'Carl! You scared the living daylights out of me.'

'Really? I thought you were a crack detective who brings down illegal forging cartels with a single move.'

'Get a life!' She shoved him gently. 'What are you doing here?'

'I called to say hello,' he told her.

She regarded him sceptically.

'No, really.' He shrugged. 'I was in the neighbourhood and I thought I'd drop by. I did say, last night, didn't I, that I'd keep in touch? Anyway, you told me that you had a day off today.'

'Yes, I do,' she said. 'And I have plans for it.'

'Like what?' asked Carl.

'I'm going to tidy my apartment,' she said primly.

He roared with laughter. 'Oh, Farrell, that's a good one. I can just see you in your uniform and yellow rubber gloves, squirting Fairy Liquid all around the place.'

'Crikey, crusading journo, you don't know much about cleaning,' she retorted. 'Fairy Liquid is for washing-up.'

'Also available for cleaning floors,' he told her.

They looked at each other for a moment and then she giggled. 'Possibly. I don't know.'

'Here's the thing,' he said. 'I don't know whether your super-powers of detection have made you notice this, but it's a crackingly gorgeous day. And nobody in their right mind would spend it tidying their apartment. So my plan is that we hop on the Dart to Bray and have a stroll along the seafront, and then maybe grab something to eat. And afterwards . . . we'll see how it goes.'

She could be spotted in Bray, thought Siobhán. Someone from the station could see her with Carl O'Connor and get totally the wrong impression. They'd think that she had a personal relationship with him. And maybe that would compromise her in their eyes. And then she admitted to herself that she *did* have a personal relationship with Carl. And maybe she was already compromised.

'You know, for a cop you're really not that good at disguising your feelings,' said Carl gently.

'What d'you mean?'

'Bray. Being seen with me. People asking questions . . .'

'Oh, sod off!' But she smiled a little.

'Siobhán, I won't try to find things out from you. I didn't, did I, about that bigamy thing?'

'No,' she admitted.

'I talked to JoJo and she's agreed to let it lie. I'm not trying to worm deep, dark secrets about the police force from you. I got a story and it was a good one. But that's not why I want to spend time with you.'

'Why then?' she asked.

He grinned at her. 'Oh, come on! I've seen you once in a basque. I'm hoping to see it again.'

She shoved him a little less gently this time.

'I like you,' he told her. 'I have fun with you. Is that so terrible?'

'I guess not.'

'Jeez, Farrell, it's no wonder you didn't make it with your previous boyfriend. You're bloody impossible.'

'I am not,' she said defensively.

'Actually, no.' He grinned again. 'You're nothing but a softie really.'

'I don't think so!'

'No?' He put his arm around her and kissed her. And suddenly Siobhán thought that she was indeed a very big softie. And that if Carl didn't mind the fact that her apartment was a disaster area she'd be very happy to forget about it being a glorious day outside and having a wonderful time with him in Bray, but instead might just drag him to her bedroom and make love to him. Because for the first time in weeks, she wanted to make love to someone again. And he was that someone.

Sally, Jenna and Iona sat at the kitchen table and looked at the open file on the laptop computer.

'I don't believe it,' said Sally as she read the letter from the solicitor again. 'I remember Frank telling me that he'd gone to see her and that she was totally dismissive of him. And then after you were born, Jen, he sent that photo. I remember that too. When she didn't contact him then he was really angry and upset. Not for himself, but he thought she might at least want to know about you.'

'Obviously not,' said Jenna. 'Cold-hearted cow. I don't know why he kept all this stuff.'

'You know your dad,' said Sally. 'He's a . . . he was a hoarder. It wouldn't matter if he never saw her again, he'd want to keep stuff.'

'Why did he scan everything into the computer?' asked Iona. 'Surely he has the actual copies?'

'Oh, Iona, he was forever putting things on the computer. He loved it. More of the James Bond approach, I guess. He had a safe in the attic where he kept insurance policies and things like that. The originals are probably there. Maybe he left them there so that I wouldn't see them and start asking questions about Christine. Not that I ever did, really. At the start, a bit. But he was always defensive about it whenever I tried, so I gave up.'

'He never talked to me much about her either,' said Iona. 'He told me that she could be dead as far as he knew. I didn't think he was all that upset about it, to be honest.'

'I don't think he was,' said Sally. 'At least, I suppose he always felt hurt about it, but he'd got over it.' She sighed. 'Now we have to find her and tell her.'

Iona frowned. 'D'you think she'll want to come to the funeral?'

'I hope not!' Sally looked aghast. 'I couldn't possibly face her.'

'We should contact her anyway,' said Jenna. 'Give her the choice.'

'That's providing she can get here by the day after tomorrow,' said Iona.

'Honestly,' said Sally crossly. 'He was trouble when he was alive, and he's trouble dead too.'

'Mum!' Jenna sounded shocked.

Sally bit her lip. 'I don't really mean that,' she said. 'I miss him very much.'

Jenna put her arms around Sally. The two of them remained locked together for a moment, united in their sorrow. Iona said nothing as she stared away from them, out of the window, at the apple tree in the garden.

She was glad to get back to her own house and be on her own for a while. When she got in she dumped her bag on the sofa and ran upstairs. She opened the wardrobe doors and looked at Frank's suits hanging up in a neat row, his shoes placed in the shoe tidy on the back of the door. It was hard to believe he wasn't coming back. For so many nights she'd imagined what it would be like if he did come back, if she was looking after him as a disabled person, or even just helping him to come to terms with having spent weeks in a coma, but she'd never allowed herself to think of what it would be like if he didn't come back at all.

She opened the drawer of the tall dresser where Frank kept his shirts and T-shirts. She unfolded a long white tee and slipped it over her head. She wished that it had some scent of Frank, but it didn't. It smelled of fabric conditioner.

She closed her eyes. Everyone would be telling her to rebuild her life and to move on. And she knew that one day she would have to do that. But right now she wanted to cry for Frank and the life they'd never had together.

Sally called Christine's solicitor in the UK and told him about Frank's death. James Carlisle was shocked but sympathetic. He said that Christine had assumed when Frank hadn't got back to them that he wasn't interested in knowing her any more. And she'd told him that she'd half expected that from her son and had been perfectly prepared to accept it. James wasn't sure how she would react to the news of his accident and death. But she was a strong woman, he told Sally. She'd cope.

Sally gave him the details of the funeral arrangements but said that she wasn't expecting to see Christine there. It was short notice and Christine really didn't have any connection with her son or her son's family. Besides, said Sally, there was an added complication.

'Oh?' James Carlisle didn't sound as though any complication would be too much for a solicitor to deal with.

When Sally told him about Iona, however, James Carlisle was stunned into silence.

'D'you think she'll come?' asked Jenna as Sally replaced the receiver.

'No,' said Sally. 'Maybe she'll send us a card.'

'I'm glad you're not like her.' Jenna shivered suddenly despite the warmth of the evening. 'I'm glad you never walked out on me. Even if sometimes I might have made you feel that way.'

Sally smiled at her. 'No you didn't,' she assured her daughter. 'You drive me mad sometimes, but that's par for the course. I love you.'

'I love you too,' said Jenna, and hugged her for about the hundredth time that day.

Chapter 40

The day of Frank's funeral was the hottest day of the year. More suited to a wedding than a funeral, Iona thought wryly, although she supposed that just as many people had to be buried on brilliant summer days as on days when the sky was cloudy and grey and chill winds blew from the north. But that day no wind was blowing at all and the air was still and warm, even in the early morning.

Iona got up and showered and then had a cup of coffee and a croissant, sitting in the morning sun on the tiny patio behind the house. In previous summers she and Frank had enjoyed many breakfasts there. She wished all memories of him weren't tainted by the fact that he shouldn't have been with her at all, but should have been in Bray with Sally and Jenna. She wanted to hate him but she couldn't. And, of course, she couldn't hate them either. Somehow Frank had brought them all close to each other and Iona felt that this wasn't exactly a bad thing. It just shouldn't have been something that had ever happened in the first place.

She'd just finished dressing when Lauren, Myles and her mother turned up. Flora and David had arrived the night before and had come back with her to the Liberties house after Frank's remains had been brought to the church for a private ceremony, attended only by Sally, Jenna, Iona and her parents and Lauren and Myles. The funeral, however, was unlikely to be as private, since they were sure that other people would be bound to show up.

Now Iona opened the door and smiled at her family. Her father wasn't coming to the church but was staying at home with Charlotte and Gavin, which was a big treat for them and, Flora had added when she told Iona, a let-off for him because he hated funerals.

Lauren kissed Iona on the cheek and then looked at her critically.

'Amazing,' she said. 'Not what I would have expected.'

Iona had elected to wear a sleeveless white linen dress which buttoned down the front and a pair of dark purple high-heeled sandals with multicoloured glass beading across the straps. Her dark hair was lightly gelled and she'd applied gloss to her rosebud lips. She looked young and pretty and as though she were about to go to a garden party rather than a funeral.

'He liked the summer,' she said. 'I didn't want to do black. And besides, I really wouldn't have felt right in it. But I wanted to look nice for him. Does that make me seem really stupid and shallow?'

'Not at all. And you look lovely.' Flora hugged her.

'Are you ready?' asked Myles.

Iona nodded.

'Let's go,' he said, and they all piled into the car.

Sally and Jenna were waiting for the car to arrive for them. Sally had been concerned that they were getting a car from the funeral directors while Iona was coming with Myles and Lauren, but Iona had told her not to be silly, that it didn't really matter and that she was happy to come with her sister and brother-in-law. Sally hoped that Iona really did think like that. She didn't want the other woman to feel sidelined in any way. Which is a weird way to think, she murmured under her breath as she looked out of the window and saw the big Daimler turn down the road. I wish I didn't like Iona. I wish that this was a private goodbye between Frank and me. And yet, she thought, it's good to know that there's someone else who cares too. Without Iona and her family there would have been very few people close to Frank to mourn him. She looked over her shoulder to where Jenna was sitting and nodded at her.

She was surprised by the large group of people standing outside the church. Sally recognised most of her immediate neighbours, as well as teachers from her school and some of Jenna's friends – including, she noticed, Gerry Cullinan. Pete Maguire, Frank's main contractor and the man she and Iona had been dealing with in relation to the Belleza del Serene contract, was there too, along with a few other men whom Sally supposed worked with him. She also recognised the girl from Iona's office who'd been so surprised to see her a few weeks earlier. And

Siobhán Farrell was there too, looking more formal than she'd ever seen her before, in a neat charcoal trouser suit, her wiry hair pulled back from her face, the young garda, Cathal Rothery, beside her.

As the car eased to a halt, the groups of people moved into the church. Sally looked around for Iona but couldn't see her. She looked at her watch. The mass was meant to start in ten minutes. She hoped that Iona would arrive in time. And that she hadn't changed her mind about coming.

Sally was very aware that Iona felt uncomfortable about the situation now. It was one thing for them to have become friendly with each other when looking after Frank, but this was completely different. This was a statement of how things were. Of who was Frank's wife. Of who was Frank's family.

'She's late,' murmured Jenna.

'I – oh, here they are.' Sally was relieved to see Myles's car pull up beside them.

'Sorry,' he said as he got out. 'I think it's the weather. Everyone was heading in this direction. They're probably all off to the beach!'

Sally smiled at him and then Iona got out of the car. The two women looked at each other for a moment and then Iona laughed. Sally, too, was wearing a white summer dress, trimmed with a navy collar. Her shoes were low navy and white slingbacks which matched her bag.

'Black maternity clothes are strictly evening wear,' she told Iona. 'And besides, it didn't seem appropriate somehow.'

'Even for me,' said Jenna. 'And most of my clothes are black.' She was dressed in a silver-grey jacket and baggy trousers.

Flora kissed Sally on both cheeks. 'You look wonderful,' she said. 'And I'm sorry about Frank.'

'Thank you,' said Sally simply. 'I'm sorry too. For everything.'

'Are you ready?' asked Myles.

The women nodded.

'Let's go,' he said.

The church was cool and peaceful and both Sally and Iona allowed their thoughts to drift during the ceremony. At the end, Myles got up and said a few words of thanks on behalf of the family. He told the congregation that they wanted the cremation to be a private family event but that they were all grateful for everyone's support. And Iona felt tears sting her eyes when Sally reached for her and took her hand.

'We are family,' she whispered to Iona. 'He made us family even if we never intended to be.'

The drive to the crematorium took half an hour. They sat in the mortuary chapel while prayers were said for Frank and then emerged into the bright sunlight. As they left, a woman at the back of the chapel, whom neither of them had seen arrive, got up and followed them outside.

Both Sally and Iona turned to her and stared.

'She came,' breathed Sally.

Iona blinked. Then blinked again.

The woman was an older version of Frank. She had his eyes and his mouth and she was very, very beautiful. She was wearing a dark suit and a wide-brimmed hat which shaded her eyes from the relentless sun. Sally and Iona stared wordlessly at her.

'I'm Christine,' she said. 'Frank's mother. I only arrived this morning. That's why I didn't come to the church. I would've got in touch earlier but I realise that the family situation here is complicated.'

'We didn't see you on the way in to the chapel,' said Sally.

'I – I wasn't sure I'd be welcome.'

'Granny?' said Jenna doubtfully.

Christine pursed her lips. 'I've never been called that before.'

'I guess not,' said Sally sharply. 'I guess you've never been called Mum either.'

'Look,' said Christine, 'I know you're upset about Frank. I understand how you feel . . .'

'No,' said Iona. 'You don't. You don't understand a single thing. You left him. He was a little boy and he loved you and you left him. And I totally understand that you felt trapped and all that sort of stuff, but the least you could've done was once, just once, sent him a card or thought about him or made him feel that you gave the teeniest, tiniest shit about what happened in his life.'

'I really don't think—'

'No! You don't.' Iona couldn't contain herself. 'At least not about other people. You obviously thought about yourself and your career and what you wanted, but never once did it occur to you that Frank actually, stupidly still loved you, you callous bitch.'

'Iona.' Sally put her hand on the other girl's arm.

'Oh, for heaven's sake!' cried Iona. 'She messed up his life and she thinks it's OK to come and mess up his death too. She returned Jenna's photograph! How could she!'

'I'm sorry.' Christine's voice was tight. 'I see I'm not welcome.'

'You're welcome to be here and mourn your son,' said Sally quietly. 'But it would have been so much better if you'd bothered to come when he was alive.'

'I wrote,' said Christine. 'I sent a letter—'

'Your solicitor sent a letter,' Sally interrupted her.

'And it was too late,' added Jenna.

'Why did you bother?' asked Iona. 'After all this time?'

Christine sighed. 'I'm retired,' she said. 'I had a great life and a great career in magazine publishing and even after I retired from that I took a non-executive seat on the board. But then one day I realised that I'd given it all of my life. And that there was nothing else. I'm not saying that I regretted anything, because I didn't. I don't. But I did wonder about Frank and you, Sally. And Jenna. And I suppose I felt a tug of – of kinship.'

'You're a selfish old bat,' said Iona. 'You did what you want and now you've decided that you wanted the other stuff too. Only you can't have it because Frank is gone.'

'Iona!' Flora, who'd been listening, cautioned her daughter.

'She's right,' said Sally. 'Christine wanted everything on her own terms. But you don't always get things on your own terms, do you?'

'I don't expect you to approve of me,' said Christine. 'I didn't even expect Frank to get in touch. I suppose I just suddenly needed to know him.' She swallowed hard. 'And yes, it was all too late.'

Iona had been expecting to feel a little out of place back at Sally's after the cremation. It was traditional that mourners gathered after a funeral and had something to eat and drink, but this was a different situation altogether and she'd already suggested to Sally that maybe she and Jenna would like to be alone. But Sally had been adamant, insisting that Iona was part of the family, and so she'd agreed. Now there was someone else who was part of Frank's family, and this time she was a real flesh-and-blood relative. Sally (who was always so damn dignified and polite, thought Iona) had asked Christine if she wanted to come back for a cup of tea, but Christine had, unsurprisingly, declined, much to everyone's relief. Iona wasn't sure whether her own fury at Christine was because she'd abandoned Frank or because she'd finally shown up.

As they drove back towards Bray, Iona wished they were on their way home. She wanted to go to bed and not get up for weeks.

She was tired. It had come over her suddenly as they stood outside the mortuary chapel talking to Christine. The strain of the last few months had suddenly seemed to overwhelm her so that she wavered on her feet and it was only Flora's discreet grip on her arm that had stopped her from stumbling. She'd glanced at her mother, who'd returned her look with complete understanding, and suddenly Iona had been very grateful for Flora and Lauren and Myles and glad that she'd always had a family to support her no matter what.

'Stupid woman,' said Lauren as they turned on to the main road.

'Who?' asked Flora.

'Christine.'

'Sad woman,' said Flora. 'Abandoning Frank was a sad thing to do.'

'You surely don't feel sorry for her!' Iona was aghast.

'A little,' said Flora. 'I've had such great joy out of my children. She missed all that.'

'She got joy out of her magazine,' muttered Iona.

'And you know that it's a poor, poor second,' said Flora, as she put her arm around her daughter and hugged her close.

Siobhán was sitting at her desk. She and Cathal had returned to the station directly after the Harper funeral mass and now she was going through the notes of an interview she'd done with another one of the ID fraud gang. Following on from the arrests in her apartment block, they'd found links to other people involved and the whole thing had turned into a much bigger case than she'd ever anticipated. Combined with the armed robbery tip-off, her promotion prospects were improving by the second. Not that she was expecting anything immediately, but she knew that her record was now looking very good. And, of course, she'd been able to close the Harper file too, even though that was because the perpetrator had died. She knew that neither Iona nor Sally could possibly feel the same way, but she was secretly glad that Frank hadn't lived. Siobhán knew that neither of the women could have gone through the whole palaver of seeing Frank questioned and possibly arrested. They both loved him too much for that.

It's a strange thing, love, she thought as she closed the file in front of her. It turns your head to jelly and totally messes up your reasoning. And maybe that's how you know you're really in love. It's when the other person becomes more important to you than you ever thought possible.

She wondered whether she'd ever feel that way about someone. She'd thought she'd felt it about Eddie. She'd been devastated by his betrayal of her. And yet she didn't ache inside for him any more. In fact she'd hardly thought of him at all in the last couple of weeks. She thought he might be away somewhere because she hadn't even seen him when she'd called to Carl's flat. And she didn't want to see him. She was astonished at how little she cared any more. Which actually might have had something to do with the fizzy, bubbly, wonderful feeling that enveloped her whenever she thought about Carl O'Connor. A man she never thought she could possibly love.

I don't love him, she told herself sternly as she put the file away. But I'm glad I'm seeing him again tonight.

They were sitting in the garden of Sally's house. It was a pretty garden, surrounded by high-growing bushes and flowers and alive with bees which were working hard in the summer sunshine to gather pollen for the hive.

'Would you like more tea?' asked Jenna, who had taken it upon herself to hand around the sandwiches they'd ordered in the previous evening.

'No thanks, sweetheart,' said Sally. 'You've been great. You don't have to hang around if you don't want to.'

'Are you sure?' asked Jenna. 'I was thinking of calling round to Sam's for a while.'

'That's fine,' Sally assured her. 'Though what about the boyfriend?'

Jenna blushed. 'Perhaps I'll see him this evening.'

'Let me know,' said Sally.

'OK.' Jenna got up and kissed her mother on the cheek. 'See you later.' She kissed Iona on the cheek too. 'And see you too, Iona. Thanks for everything.'

'You're welcome.' Iona kissed her in return.

Sally got up and went into the house, returning with a bottle of champagne.

'It's been in the fridge for ages,' she explained. 'Frank brought it home after a deal he'd done and we just never got around to opening it. I know I can't have any myself, but . . . I'd like to make a toast to him.'

They nodded and held out their glasses.

'To Frank,' said Sally, raising her glass of sparkling water. 'He was more messed up than I ever knew. But he wasn't a bad person.'

'And to Sally and Iona,' said Flora. 'Strong women.'

'Oh, gosh, Flora – I don't think so,' said Sally.

'Of course we are.' Iona grinned at her. 'And we'll continue to be.'

'Can I ask a question?' Myles looked enquiringly at them when they'd finished drinking.

'What?' asked Iona.

'What are you intending to do with DynaLite?'

The two women exchanged glances.

'I don't know yet,' said Sally.

'Because it seems to me,' said Myles, 'there's a really good company there with lots of potential.'

'Yes, but what can we do about it?' asked Sally. 'It's not like we know anything about lighting systems.'

'No-oo,' said Myles slowly, 'but you've both done a great job of keeping things going with the Belleza contract. Pete was asking me whether the company would be sold or wound up or what. He thinks that it should keep going. With you and Iona in charge.' Myles grinned. 'He was very impressed by both of you.'

'You're joking!' Sally laughed. 'I'm hardly a model of a business-woman, am I?'

'You're a perfectly good businesswoman,' said Iona.

'I . . . I've been putting a few bits and pieces together,' said Myles. 'You need a sales manager who understands the business. I spoke to Pete about that. There are some good guys out there. Then you need someone to run the office.'

'Frank did it all on his own,' objected Iona.

'Um, yes. But he was struggling,' said Myles. 'Not financially,' he added hastily, seeing the stricken looks on their faces. 'Just struggling to keep up with things.'

'Yeah, well, he had other things to worry about too, I guess,' said Iona ruefully.

'I know I can get the bank to put a finance package together,' Myles told her.

'So we keep the company and employ people?' Sally looked nervous. 'I'm a teacher, Myles. I've no experience.'

'Iona has,' he told her. 'You've worked on your own before, Io. You're good at office management.'

'You think I should be involved day-to-day?' She looked at him incredulously.

'Why not?'

Iona and Sally exchanged glances.

'Give us a couple of days to think it over,' said Iona.

'Sure,' said Myles easily. 'There's no rush. But Pete was telling me there's a new hotel opening in Drogheda and that lighting for their nightclub is being put out to tender.'

'Let's talk again tomorrow,' said Iona.

'Well, no,' said Sally. 'Iona, if you think this is a good idea and you're willing to be involved, then I think we should go for it. I'm already a director. We can make you a director too.'

'Oh, but Sally—'

'In fact, if you're not a director I won't employ you.'

They looked at each other. Then Iona laughed.

'OK,' she said. 'Why the hell not?'

Chapter 41

Iona was sitting at her desk in the DynaLite office when the phone rang. She liked the phone, which was slim and neat and very stylish. She liked the office too – although it was only a single room, it overlooked the sea and, because it had windows on two sides, was always drenched with warm sunlight. Iona had started work in the office a month after Frank's funeral and after the bank had come up with more money than they'd expected. This had allowed Iona and Sally to choose an office and employ a lighting expert, who was now out and about meeting existing customers and looking for new ones. He was also in negotiation with the Drogheda hotel about the lighting contract and was very hopeful of being successful. And because the spa deal had worked out so well and the building had won an award, they'd also had referrals from Anthony Brady and the order book was filling up nicely. Frank would have been pleased at that, Iona thought. He'd always been proud of his company and it was good to think that it hadn't passed into someone else's hands.

Their joint involvement in DynaLite meant that Iona and Sally continued to keep in contact with each other. It seemed to Iona now that it was almost impossible to remember a time when she didn't know Sally and Jenna. They had become part of her life and she was part of theirs. And, as a consequence, she had become more tolerant, while Sally had become – well, a good deal more adventurous, thought Iona. Because Sally, having had no apparent interest in the business at all while Frank was alive, had suddenly been the one to come up with all sorts of creative marketing plans. Not only that, but she was becoming an expert on lighting too. It was, she'd told Iona, because she had nothing else to do. The baby was due shortly and she was on maternity leave from school, and so she had plenty of time to think about LED lights and halogen lights and a hundred other different lighting options.

Iona reached out and picked up the phone.

'DynaLite,' she said. 'How can I help you.'

'Hi, Iona.' Jenna's voice was breathless. 'It's Mum. She's gone into hospital. She's having the baby.'

Iona felt her stomach tumble. Of all the things that she'd had to come to terms with over the last few months, Sally's pregnancy was still the most difficult. And she was very unsure about how she would feel when she saw Frank's child in Sally's arms. She swallowed hard.

'Is everything OK?' she asked.

'Oh, sure,' said Jenna. 'I'm here with her. But I know she'd like you to come too. And . . .' Jenna hesitated. 'And, Iona, I'd really like you to be here. It's kind of weird being back in the hospital, and I'm OK about it and everything, but . . .'

'I'll be there right away,' said Iona.

She replaced the receiver and switched on the answering machine. Then she took her bag and quilted jacket from the stand beside the door, let herself out, locked the office and hurried to her car.

It was definitely a strange experience to park in the hospital car park and walk through the entrance doors again, knowing that this time she wasn't coming to see Frank. The memories of his time there flooded back to her even as she turned towards the maternity wing and not the intensive care unit where Frank had been.

'Mrs Harper?' she asked a nurse. 'Sally? And Jenna?'

'Oh, yes.' The nurse smiled at her. 'She's just out of theatre.'

'Already?' Iona looked at her in surprise.

'Baby Harper was in a big hurry to enter the world,' said the nurse. 'Room 14. Go on in.'

Iona hurried down the corridor. The door to Room 14 was closed. She took a deep breath, tapped on it once and then opened it gently.

Sally was lying in the bed, a bundle wrapped in white in her arms. Jenna was sitting beside her. They both looked up as she walked in.

'Hi, Iona!' This time Jenna's voice was cheerful. 'Come and join the family.'

Iona walked slowly over to the bed.

'Is everything OK?' she asked Sally.

'Well, I'm knackered of course,' said Sally. 'But – it's totally worth it. Take her, Iona.'

Iona swallowed hard as she peered through the nest of wraps at the tiny baby. Her face was red and wizened and she had a tuft of jet-black hair in the centre of her head. Her eyes were scrunched closed and she held her hands in tight little fists.

'Oh my God.' Iona felt the tears well up in her eyes. 'She's gorgeous.'

'Go on then,' said Sally. 'Take her.'

'Are you sure?' asked Iona doubtfully. 'I've never seen a baby so young before. Lauren's were a day old before I got to them and they'd started to look half normal. She's so . . . so tiny.'

'You'll be fine,' said Sally reassuringly. She held the bundle towards Iona, who took her in her arms and looked at her through her tear-filled eyes.

'I don't think she looks like anyone,' said Jenna. 'But Mum thinks she has Dad's nose.'

Iona blinked the tears away and sniffed. 'It's hard to say at this point,' she said. 'But maybe.'

'And she has your hair,' added Jenna. 'All black and spiky.'

'Yes, but . . .' Iona looked up at her and saw that both Jenna and Sally were laughing. 'Well, maybe I kind of influenced her in the womb,' she said. 'Crikey, she's tiny, isn't she?'

'Well, she's a bit early,' said Sally. 'But she weighed in at seven pounds, so she's not that tiny.'

'Seven pounds.' Iona giggled. 'I remember desperately trying to lose seven pounds so that I could fit into a party dress.'

'I'm going to go on a really strict diet,' Sally said. 'So that I can regain what was left of my figure.'

The baby opened her almost black eyes and looked into Iona's face. They weren't Frank's eyes, of course they weren't, but Iona couldn't help feeling as though she was seeing a part of him again. And then the baby scrunched them closed and she was her own person once more.

'Why don't you sit down, Iona?' Jenna got up from the chair. 'I'm going to phone Sam and give her the good news. She asked me to let her know as soon as the baby was born.'

'OK, thanks.'

Iona settled into the chair. The baby nestled against her. One day, she thought. One day I'll meet someone and I'll have a baby. But even if I don't, I'll always know this baby. And I'll always love her.

She kissed the top of her head. She wasn't supposed to love her, of course. This was Frank and Sally's baby. Not hers. But she couldn't help loving her all the same.

Sally watched her as she gazed at the tiny infant. She knew what Iona was thinking. These days she nearly always knew what Iona was thinking. In fact, she realised, both of them were very good at guessing each other's thoughts. Iona looked up at her and smiled.

'She's truly lovely,' she told Sally. 'And of course I'm a little bit jealous of you, but that'll pass. I'm glad for you too.'

'I didn't want her at the start,' Sally told her. 'I was freaked out at the idea of being a mother again at my age. But I'll cope.'

'Course you will,' said Iona. 'You coped with everything else.'

'Only because you were there to help,' said Sally.

'I was part of what you had to cope with!'

'True. But you know, Iona – all of the time that Frank was in the coma and you were there . . . even when it was niggly between us and everything . . . well, it was support. And I needed it. I needed you.'

'You're getting soppy and sentimental because of your hormones,' Iona told her.

'Probably.' Sally grinned. 'But I'll milk it for all I can. Jenna's being so good and helpful right now, you wouldn't believe! I'm hoping she'll still be the same when the baby comes home and starts screaming in the middle of the night.'

'If you ever need a break, just give me a call,' said Iona. 'You know, if you want to go out for a couple of hours or something. I don't mind.'

'Bloody sure I'll be giving you a call,' Sally said robustly. 'You'll be her godmother, after all. At least, I hope you will.'

'Sally . . . really?'

'Nobody I'd rather have,' said Sally. 'Nobody better, in fact.'

'Thank you,' said Iona. 'I'm glad you feel that way.'

'I absolutely do.' Sally smiled. 'And for your first godmotherly duty, you can help me pick a name for her. Jenna's suggestions have been firmly rooted in gangsta rap so far. I'm looking for something a little less dramatic.'

Iona laughed. 'I haven't even thought about it,' she said. 'But I'll try.'

She dropped Jenna back home later that evening. Sam was coming to stay with her and she'd already stocked up with popcorn and ice cream for the movie they planned to watch.

'What about Gerry?' asked Iona.

'We're not seeing each other any more,' Jenna told her. 'I liked him a lot, Iona. And he was really nice after Dad died. But . . . I've kind of moved on from Gerry.'

'Oh? Anyone else?'

'No. Not that at all. Just that – I don't need someone right now. He was right for me then. He took my mind off what was going on with Dad and everything. But now that I don't need my mind being taken off stuff . . .'

'Fair enough,' said Iona. 'I liked him, though.'

Jenna smiled. 'So did I.' She looked at Iona, an anxious flicker in her eyes. 'You didn't tell Mum, did you? About me sleeping with him?'

'Of course not.' Iona shook her head. 'That's between you and me.'

'Thanks,' said Jenna. 'I mean, she'll have to get used to the fact that I will sleep with guys. Or maybe only one guy. Who knows. But I don't think she needs to know about Gerry right now.'

'Like I said, she won't hear it from me.'

'You're the best.' Jenna hugged her.

'And so are you.'

'So you won't love the baby more than me?'

'Listen, that baby is the most adorable creature in the world.' Iona grinned. 'But I won't love her more. Only differently.'

'That's the thing, isn't it?' said Jenna. 'With you and Dad, and Mum and Dad. He loved you both, only differently.'

'Hmm.' Iona made a face at her. 'It's not an arrangement I'd recommend.'

'No, of course not,' said Jenna. 'But – he wasn't a shit, was he?'

'No,' said Iona firmly. 'He wasn't.'

She wasn't going to go back to the office – after all, she could collect the phone messages and check e-mails from home – but she decided to call in anyway. There were half a dozen messages, all of them confirming contracts, which made her whoop with delight, and an e-mail from Anthony saying that a magazine wanted to do a big feature on the spa and its design and that the people doing it had specifically asked about the lighting.

Iona felt as though she was walking on air as she left the office again.

She was too excited about everything that had gone on that day to simply go home, so she went for a walk along the seafront instead. It was much colder now, and the wind whipped across the bay, so that she burrowed into the warmth of her jacket and thrust her hands deep into its pockets.

'Iona!'

The call came from behind her and she turned around. Siobhán Farrell, dressed in her jogging gear, was running towards her. She stopped and waited for her to catch up.

'I got your text message,' said Siobhán. 'I'm so glad about Sally and the baby. Have you been to see her? How is she?'

Iona nodded. 'Great,' she said.

'I might drop by tomorrow,' said Siobhán.

'She'd love to see you,' said Iona.

'And you?' asked Siobhán. 'How are you?'

'I'm fine.' Iona smiled at her. 'In fact, Siobhán, today I feel better than ever. It's like a weight has been lifted from my shoulders. I was so scared that I'd hate Sally when the baby was born, and hate the baby too. But I don't.'

'I'm very glad,' said Siobhán. 'How's the new business going?'

'Brilliantly.' Iona told her about the potential magazine article.

Siobhán grinned. 'I'm delighted for you. Though it's a shame you're out of the property business. I'm thinking of buying somewhere myself.'

'Really?'

Siobhán nodded. 'Joint purchase.'

'Are you serious!'

'We haven't totally decided yet,' said Siobhán. 'And I'm not rushing into getting engaged again or anything, but . . .'

'I'm so thrilled for you,' Iona told her. 'I know that on the only occasion I saw him you spent half the time under the table, but he actually seemed quite nice to me. Plus you hated him so much! It was a dead giveaway.'

'Sod off.' Siobhán shoved her amiably.

'Where is he tonight?' asked Iona.

'Interviewing someone,' replied Siobhán. 'We both spend our lives interviewing people!'

'I'm glad neither of you really got around to interviewing Frank,' said Iona.

'How about you? Anyone new in your life?' asked Siobhán.

'Give me a break,' said Iona. 'I haven't had the time. And I'm still coming to terms with the whole thing.'

'There's always Enrique.' Siobhán's eyes twinkled.

'Oh, come on. I hardly even know the man,' said Iona. 'And I haven't seen him since that day I walked out of his apartment.'

'He still asks about you,' said Siobhán. 'I don't see him that often these days but every time I do he asks about you.'

'Does he?' Iona felt her cheeks go pink.

'Absolutely. You should get in touch with him.'

'Maybe.'

'Let me know when,' said Siobhán. 'I'll sort it out for you!'

'Why is it that people with new men in their lives are always trying to sort out everyone else?' demanded Iona. 'I'm perfectly fine.'

'Yeah, right!' Siobhán chuckled. 'Anyway, I'd better get going. See you again soon.'

'See you!' Iona waved at her and walked back towards her car.

Chapter 42

The steeple was covered in a deep layer of snow and, in the gardens surrounding the church, glimpses of green from the fir trees was the only colour peeking through the covering of white. As they walked up the short driveway, their breaths hung before them in misty clouds and stray flakes settled briefly on their coats before melting.

'It's very picturesque,' said Jenna through chattering teeth. 'But couldn't we have picked a warmer day to have her christened?'

'It's your father's birthday today,' Sally reminded her. 'That's why.' She peeped in at the baby, who was completely wrapped up in warm blankets. 'Lucky thing, she can't feel the cold.'

'Well I can, and I'm bloody freezing.'

'Ah, quit moaning,' said Iona cheerfully. 'You've got to admit that this was a great idea.'

'I don't think so!' Jenna's smile was sceptical. 'I'm a city girl at heart. This is *so* the back of beyond.'

'It's where your dad was born,' said Sally.

'Yeah, well, he always did say he came from the arsehole of nowhere.'

'Jenna Harper! You're in church grounds. For heaven's sake mind your language.'

'You think God is going to send down a thunderbolt?' Jenna giggled.

'No, but I might clatter you if you're not careful,' warned her mother.

'Or I'll arrest you.' Siobhán Farrell grinned at her and Jenna grinned back. Siobhán had been pleased when both Sally and Iona had insisted on her coming to the christening with them. She'd gone out with them to celebrate a few weeks after Sally had come out of hospital and felt able to leave the baby for a few hours, and she knew that she'd always stay friends with Sally and Iona.

She shivered suddenly and Sally smiled. 'Let's get into the church,' she said. 'Jen's right. It's freezing out here.'

Theirs was the only baptism that day, and the young priest welcomed them warmly as they shuffled into the pews.

'Great to see you,' he said. 'And this is the little one? Isn't she lovely? Are you ready to start? Who's who?' He smiled at Iona. 'You're the godmother, yes?'

'And I'm the godfather,' said Myles.

'Right,' said the priest. 'Off we go. Let's welcome her into the community.'

Frank had been baptised here. Sally knew that because he'd shown her the church on one of their visits to Sligo and told her that it wasn't really surprising that Christine had left; it truly was the back of beyond. Sally thought for a moment of Christine, who had sent her a letter after the funeral telling her that she regretted how things had turned out and that she was sorry she hadn't done things differently. Perhaps, she wrote, it had been wrong to cut Frank and his family out of her life completely, even though at the time it had seemed the right thing to do. She'd asked Sally to get in touch if there was anything she needed in the future, if she could be of any help. And wished her well with her pregnancy. Too late, thought Sally again. It had always been too late for Christine. Too late to realise that she was in the wrong relationship, too late to want to meet her son. She'd send her a photograph of Jenna and the new baby. It wasn't much, but it was the best she felt able to do.

She exchanged glances with Iona, who smiled at her and gave her a thumbs-up signal as she held the baby.

'Francesca Ann,' said the priest, 'I baptise you in the name of the Father and of the Son and of the Holy Spirit.'

Francesca roared as the cool water trickled over her forehead. The priest dabbed at it with a white cloth and Iona murmured words of comfort to her. The baby stopped crying and looked at her from her navy-blue eyes.

'Sorry,' whispered Iona.

Francesca's expression was accusing.

'Ah, get over yourself,' murmured Sally to her, and the baby looked affronted. She closed her eyes and snuggled into her blankets again.

* * *

It was still snowing outside. They got into the cars and drove the three miles from the church to the bay. The beach curved away from them and the green water of the sea churned at the shore. The wind was bitterly cold. Iona, Sally and Jenna got out of the cars.

'It's bleak,' said Iona.

'Yes. He didn't want to live here, but he did love the openness of it,' said Sally.

'I can understand that.' Iona looked inland. At the edge of her sight she could see the gable wall of the Harper family house. They had put it up for sale the previous week and already had an interested buyer. They had agreed to invest half of the proceeds in the business and divide the other half between them. They were, thought Iona, turning into hard-headed businesswomen after all.

'Let's make sure we get the wind behind us when we do this,' said Sally.

Jenna looked aghast. 'Mum!'

'Well, we're all wearing new clothes,' said Sally defensively as Iona chuckled.

'Are we ready?' asked Sally. Her voice shook a little.

'Ready,' said Iona.

Siobhán, Lauren and Myles watched them as Sally took the urn out of its box, lifted the lid and shook the contents into the air.

Frank's ashes were taken by the wind and carried away from them, drifting over the damp, springy grass as they blew out towards the sea.

'Goodbye, Dad,' said Jenna.

'Be happy, Frank.' Iona lifted her hand in a half-wave.

'Goodbye,' whispered Sally.

Then Frank's family turned around and walked, arm in arm, back to the warmth of the cars.